AN UNOFFICIAL GRAPHIC NOVEL FOR MINECRAFTERS

REDSTONE JUNIOR HIGH

CREEPERS CRASHED MY PARTY

BOOK 2

CARA J. STEVENS

ART BY WALKER MELBY

SKY PONY PRESS
NEW YORK

Copyright © 2018 by Hollan Publishing, Inc.

Minecraft® is a registered trademark of Notch Development AB.

The Minecraft game is copyright © Mojang AB.

Sky Pony Press books may be purchased in bulk at special discounts for sales promotion, corporate gifts, fund-raising, or educational purposes. Special editions can also be created to specifications. For details, contact the Special Sales Department, Sky Pony Press, 307 West 36th Street, 11th Floor, New York, NY 10018 or info@ skyhorsepublishing.com.

Sky Pony® is a registered trademark of Skyhorse Publishing, Inc.®, a Delaware corporation.

Minecraft® is a registered trademark of Notch Development AB.
The Minecraft game is copyright © Mojang AB.

Visit our website at www.skyponypress.com.

10 9 8 7 6 5 4 3 2 1

Library of Congress Cataloging-in- Publication Data is available on file.

Cover design by Brian Peterson
Cover and interior art by Walker Melby
Story by Brandon Stevens

Print ISBN: 978-1-5107-3262-9
Ebook ISBN: 978-1-5107-3264-3

Printed in China

Designer and Production Manager: Joshua Barnaby

REDSTONE JUNIOR HIGH

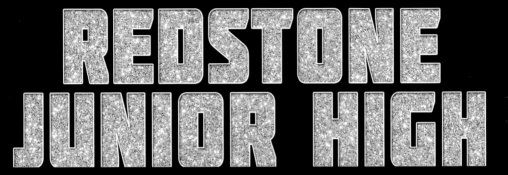

MEET THE

PIXEL: A girl with an unusual way with animals and other creatures

SKY: A redstone expert who is also one of Pixel's best friends at school.

UMA: A fellow student at Redstone Junior High who can sense how people and mobs are feeling.

CHARACTERS

MR. Z: A teacher with a dark past.

TINA AND THE VIOLETS: Pixel's sassy downstairs neighbor and her sidekicks, who are more than they appear to be.

PRINCIPAL REDSTONE: The head of Redstone Junior High

SPRINKLES: A puppy who is fiercely loyal to Pixel, Sky, and Uma.

INTRODUCTION

If you have played Minecraft, then you know all about Minecraft worlds. They're made of blocks you can mine, creatures you can interact with, and lands you can visit. Deep in the heart of one of these worlds is an extraordinary school with students who have been handpicked from across the landscape for their unique abilities.

The school is Redstone Junior High. When we last left off in our story, Pixel and her friends, Uma and Sky, have defeated the evil Saturday, agent of the SAMD, an organization which seeks to enslave and destroy hostile mobs while claiming to protect them. The school has survived a zombie invasion, creeper explosions, swarms of hostile mobs and even a visit from the Ender Dragon, but these invasions remain a secret from the outside world.

As our story begins, things are just starting to get back to normal at school. Classes are in session and the students are eager to put their past adventures behind them and learn all about the mysteries of redstone contraptions and advanced building skills.

While Pixel and her friends want to make friends with the mobs, the memory of the zombie and creeper invasion is still fresh in many people's minds. We can feel the tension mounting between two groups of students, but there is another tension mounting outside the gates, too. One that could destroy the school and mob-miner relations across the world.

CHAPTER 1

A FRESH
START

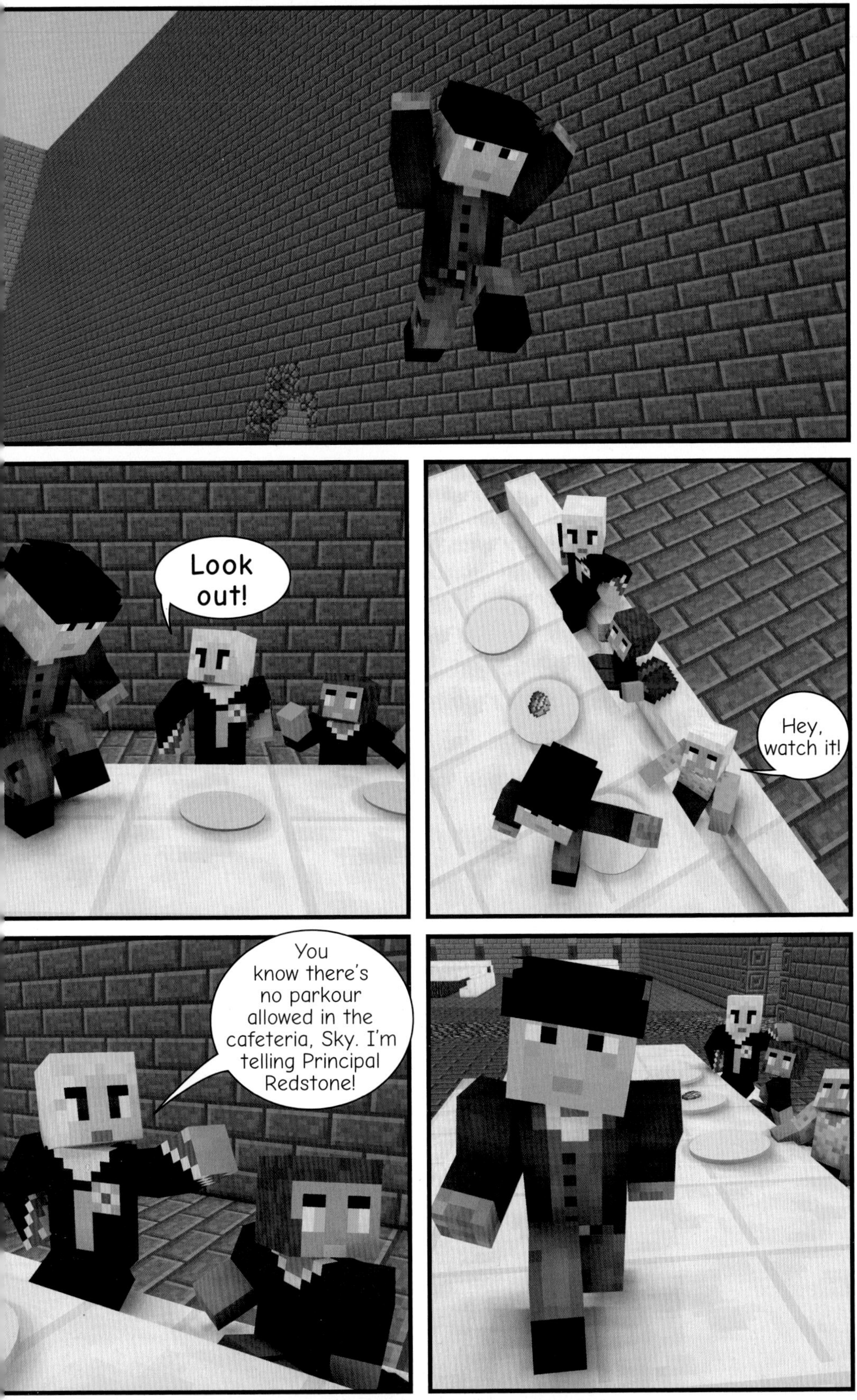
Look out!
Hey, watch it!
You know there's no parkour allowed in the cafeteria, Sky. I'm telling Principal Redstone!

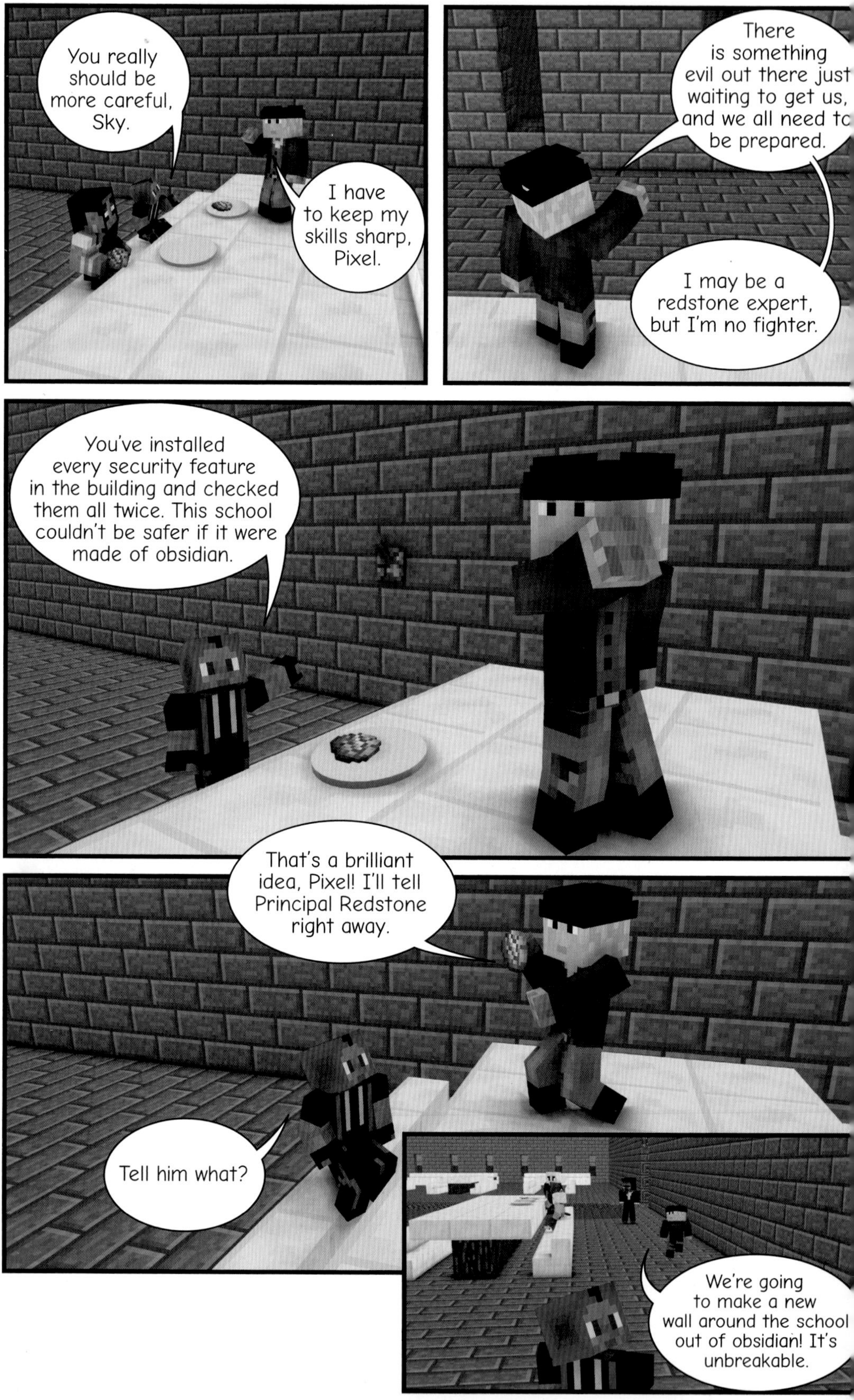
You really should be more careful, Sky.
I have to keep my skills sharp, Pixel.
There is something evil out there just waiting to get us, and we all need to be prepared.
I may be a redstone expert, but I'm no fighter.
You've installed every security feature in the building and checked them all twice. This school couldn't be safer if it were made of obsidian.
That's a brilliant idea, Pixel! I'll tell Principal Redstone right away.
Tell him what?
We're going to make a new wall around the school out of obsidian! It's unbreakable.

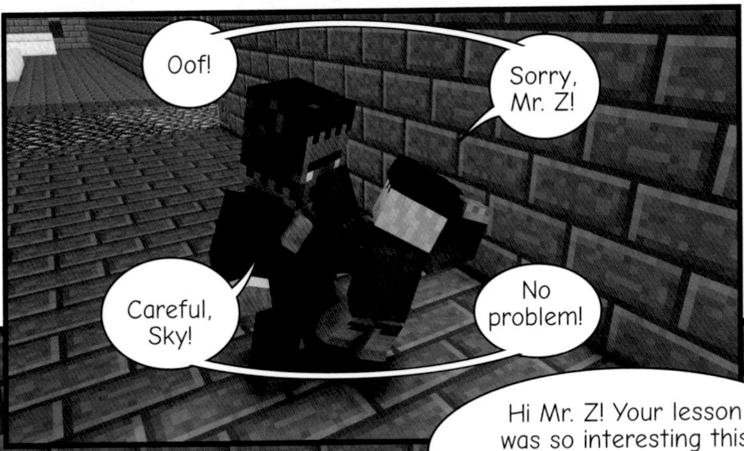
Oof!
Sorry, Mr. Z!
Careful, Sky!
No problem!

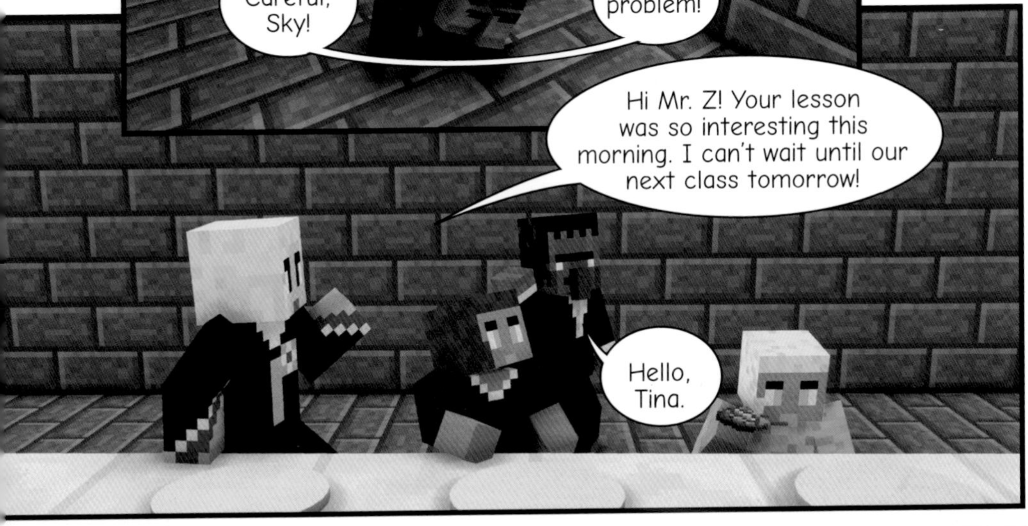
Hi Mr. Z! Your lesson was so interesting this morning. I can't wait until our next class tomorrow!
Hello, Tina.

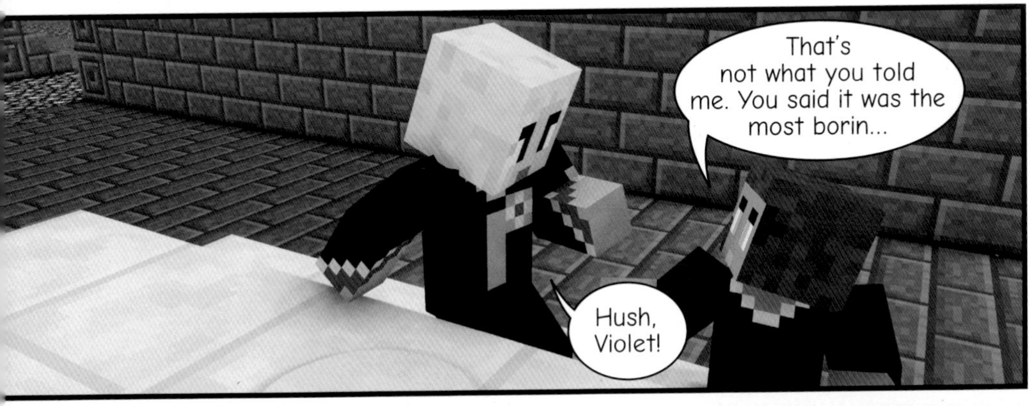
That's not what you told me. You said it was the most borin...
Hush, Violet!

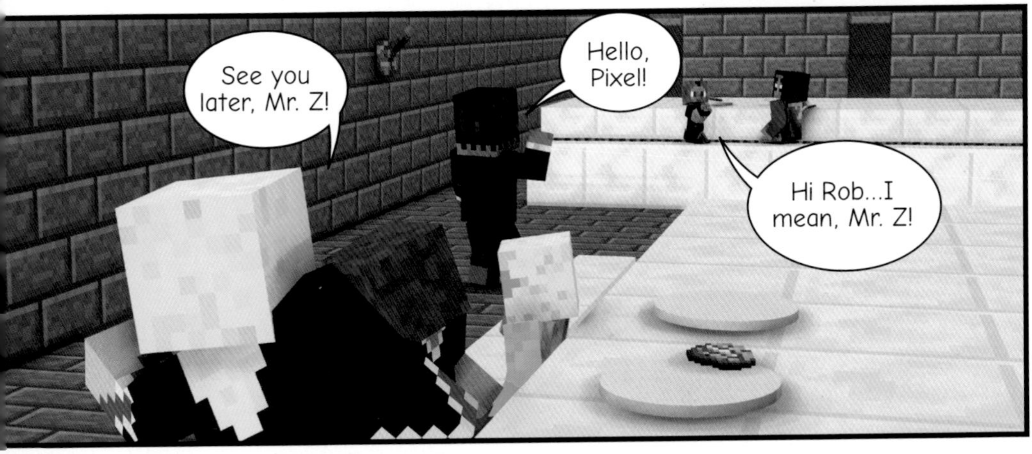
See you later, Mr. Z!
Hello, Pixel!
Hi Rob...I mean, Mr. Z!

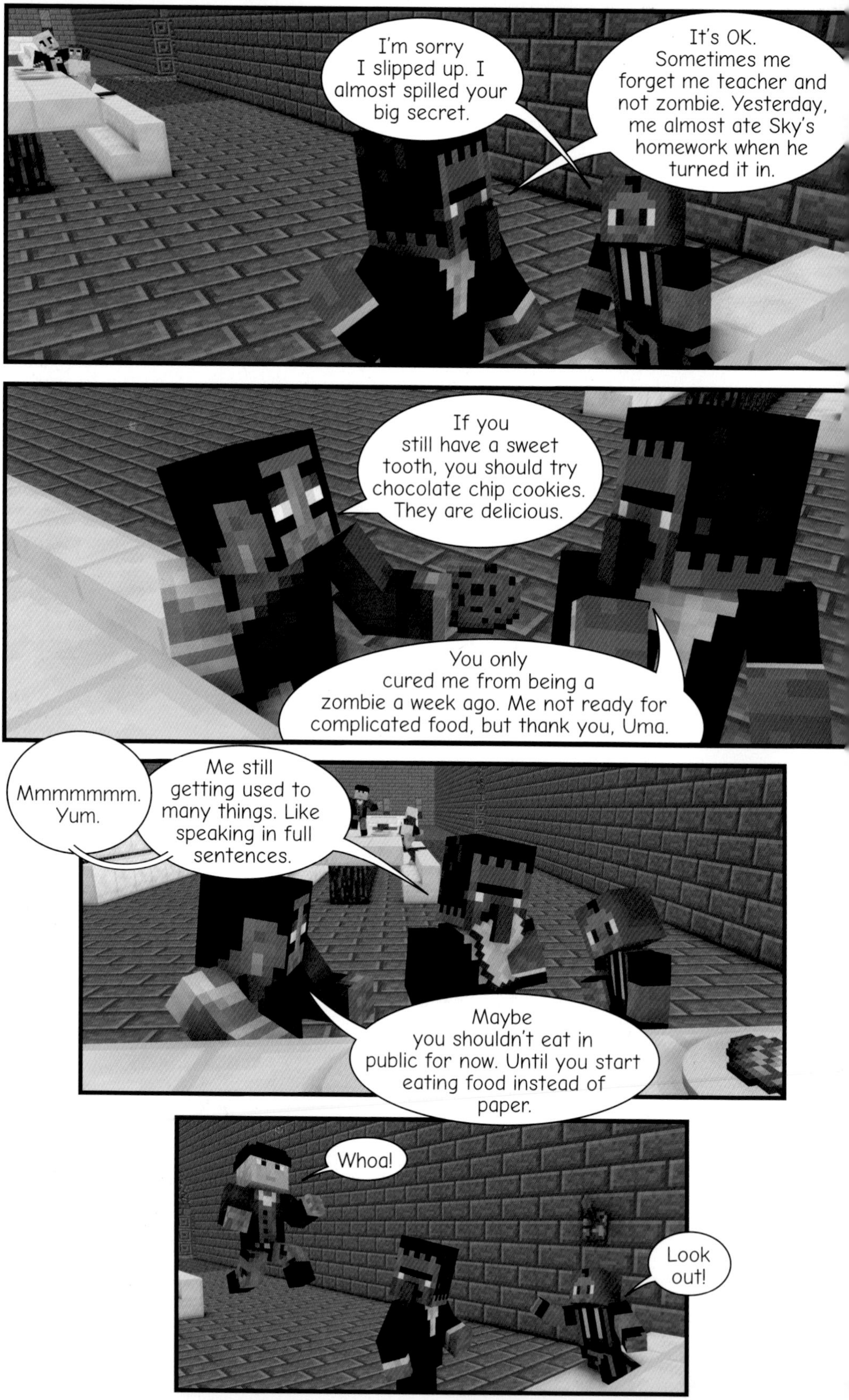
I'm sorry I slipped up. I almost spilled your big secret.
It's OK. Sometimes me forget me teacher and not zombie. Yesterday, me almost ate Sky's homework when he turned it in.
If you still have a sweet tooth, you should try chocolate chip cookies. They are delicious.
You only cured me from being a zombie a week ago. Me not ready for complicated food, but thank you, Uma.
Mmmmmmm. Yum.
Me still getting used to many things. Like speaking in full sentences.
Maybe you shouldn't eat in public for now. Until you start eating food instead of paper.
Whoa!
Look out!

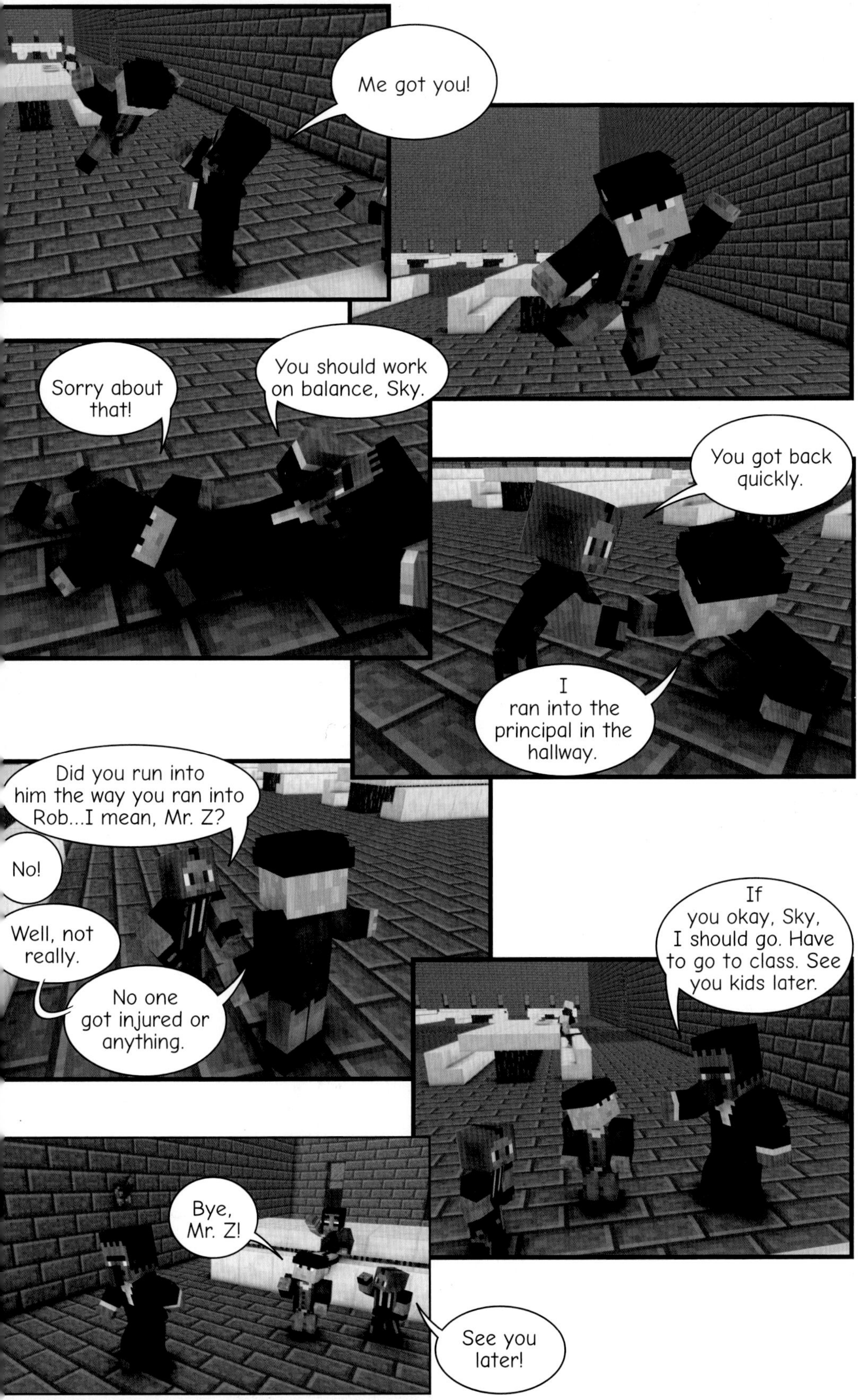

Me got you!
Sorry about that!
You should work on balance, Sky.
You got back quickly.
I ran into the principal in the hallway.
Did you run into him the way you ran into Rob...I mean, Mr. Z?
No!
Well, not really.
No one got injured or anything.
If you okay, Sky, I should go. Have to go to class. See you kids later.
Bye, Mr. Z!
See you later!

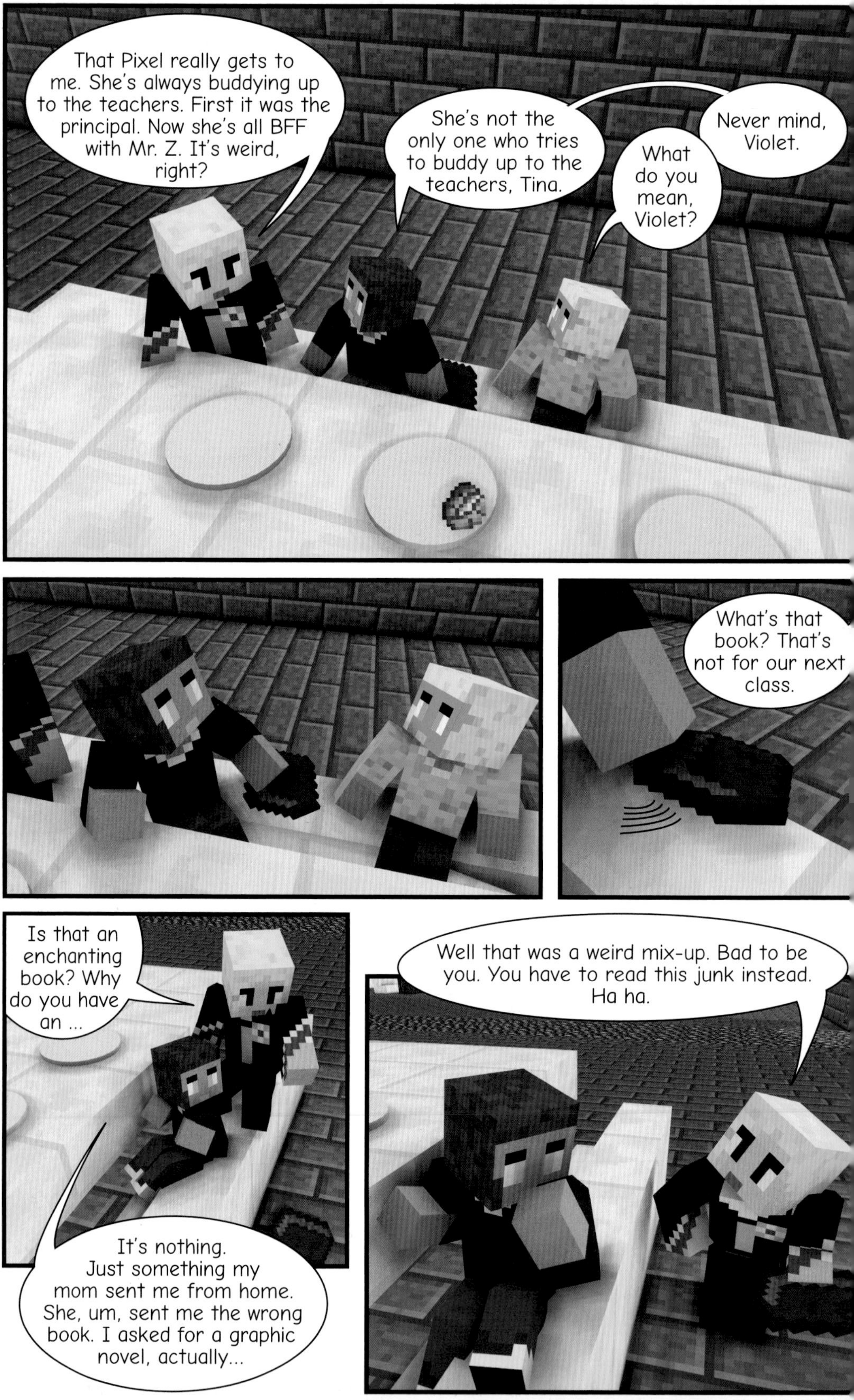
That Pixel really gets to me. She's always buddying up to the teachers. First it was the principal. Now she's all BFF with Mr. Z. It's weird, right?
She's not the only one who tries to buddy up to the teachers, Tina.
What do you mean, Violet?
Never mind, Violet.
What's that book? That's not for our next class.
Is that an enchanting book? Why do you have an ...
It's nothing. Just something my mom sent me from home. She, um, sent me the wrong book. I asked for a graphic novel, actually...
Well that was a weird mix-up. Bad to be you. You have to read this junk instead. Ha ha.

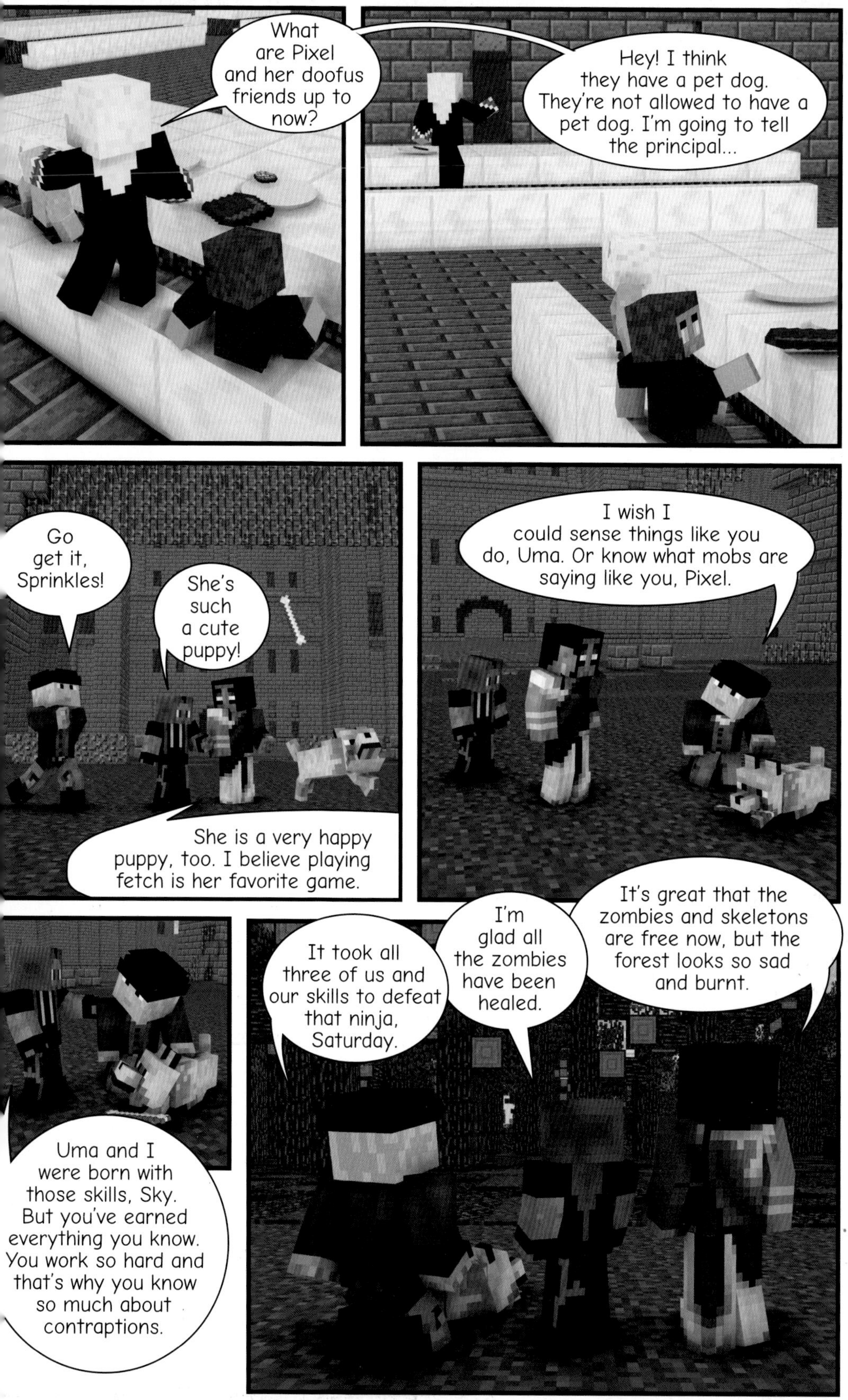
What are Pixel and her doofus friends up to now?
Hey! I think they have a pet dog. They're not allowed to have a pet dog. I'm going to tell the principal...
Go get it, Sprinkles!
She's such a cute puppy!
She is a very happy puppy, too. I believe playing fetch is her favorite game.
I wish I could sense things like you do, Uma. Or know what mobs are saying like you, Pixel.
Uma and I were born with those skills, Sky. But you've earned everything you know. You work so hard and that's why you know so much about contraptions.
It took all three of us and our skills to defeat that ninja, Saturday.
I'm glad all the zombies have been healed.
It's great that the zombies and skeletons are free now, but the forest looks so sad and burnt.

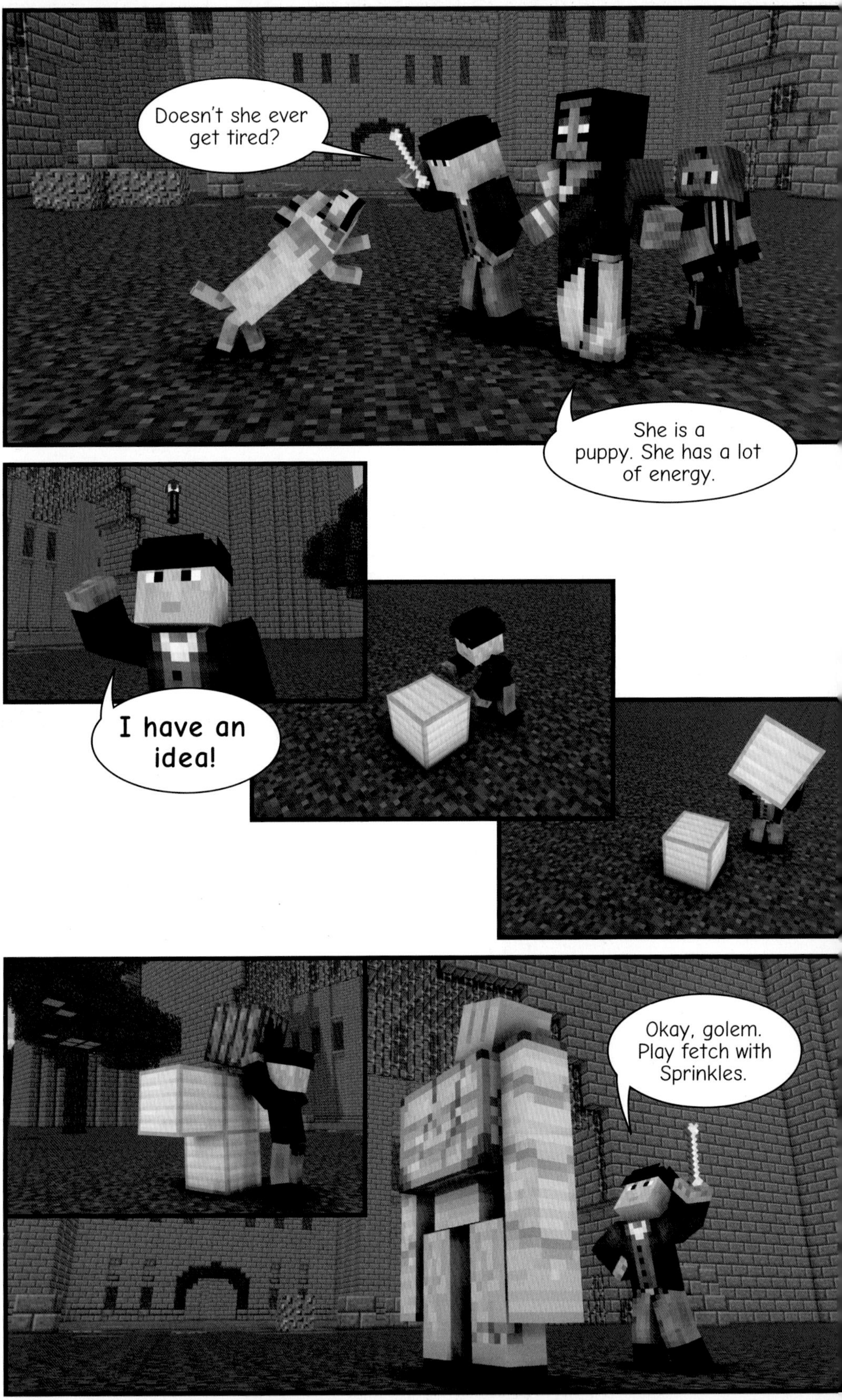
Doesn't she ever get tired?
She is a puppy. She has a lot of energy.
I have an idea!
Okay, golem. Play fetch with Sprinkles.

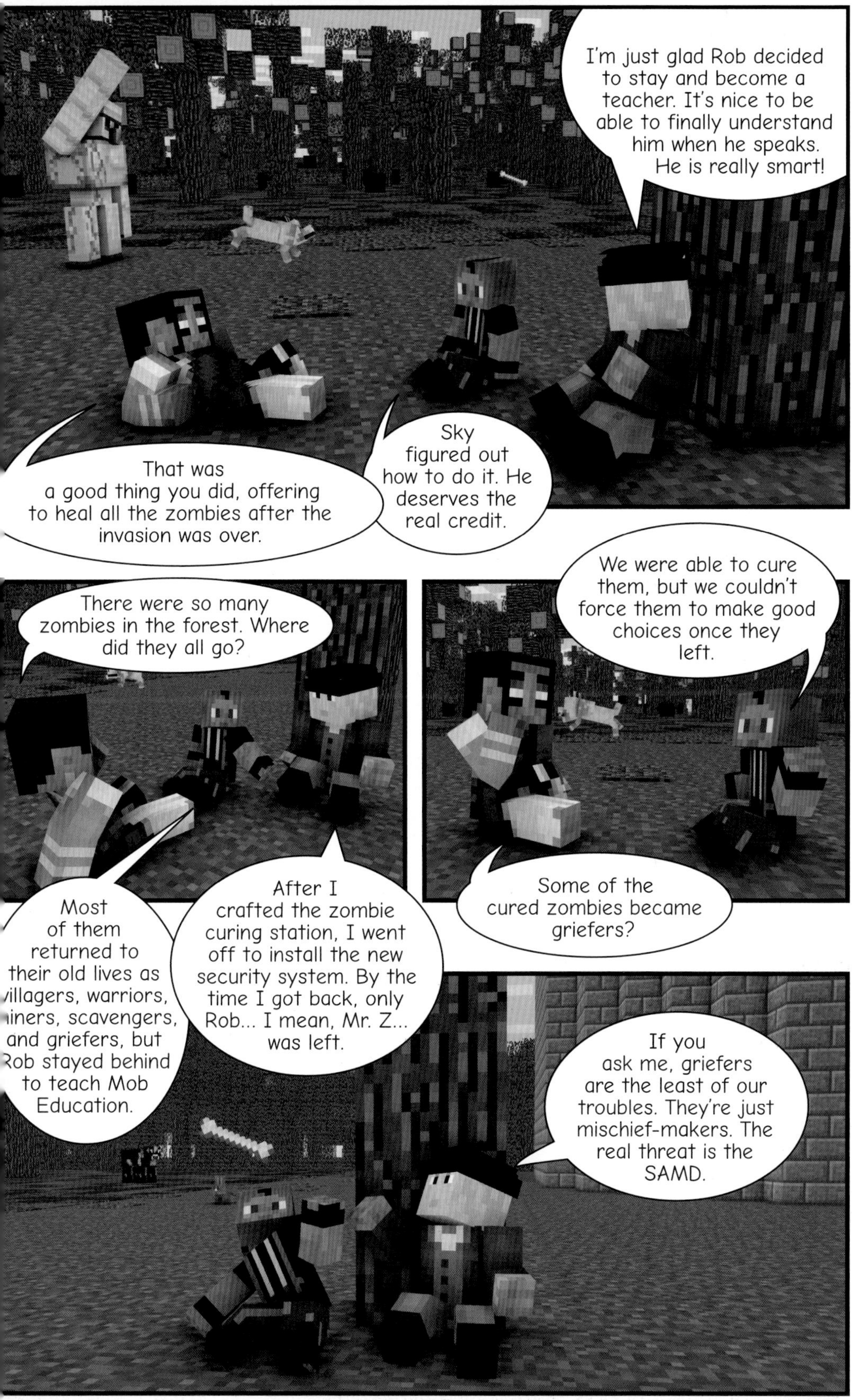
I'm just glad Rob decided to stay and become a teacher. It's nice to be able to finally understand him when he speaks. He is really smart!
That was a good thing you did, offering to heal all the zombies after the invasion was over.
Sky figured out how to do it. He deserves the real credit.
There were so many zombies in the forest. Where did they all go?
Most of them returned to their old lives as illagers, warriors, iners, scavengers, and griefers, but ob stayed behind to teach Mob Education.
After I crafted the zombie curing station, I went off to install the new security system. By the time I got back, only Rob... I mean, Mr. Z... was left.
We were able to cure them, but we couldn't force them to make good choices once they left.
Some of the cured zombies became griefers?
If you ask me, griefers are the least of our troubles. They're just mischief-makers. The real threat is the SAMD.

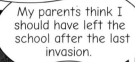

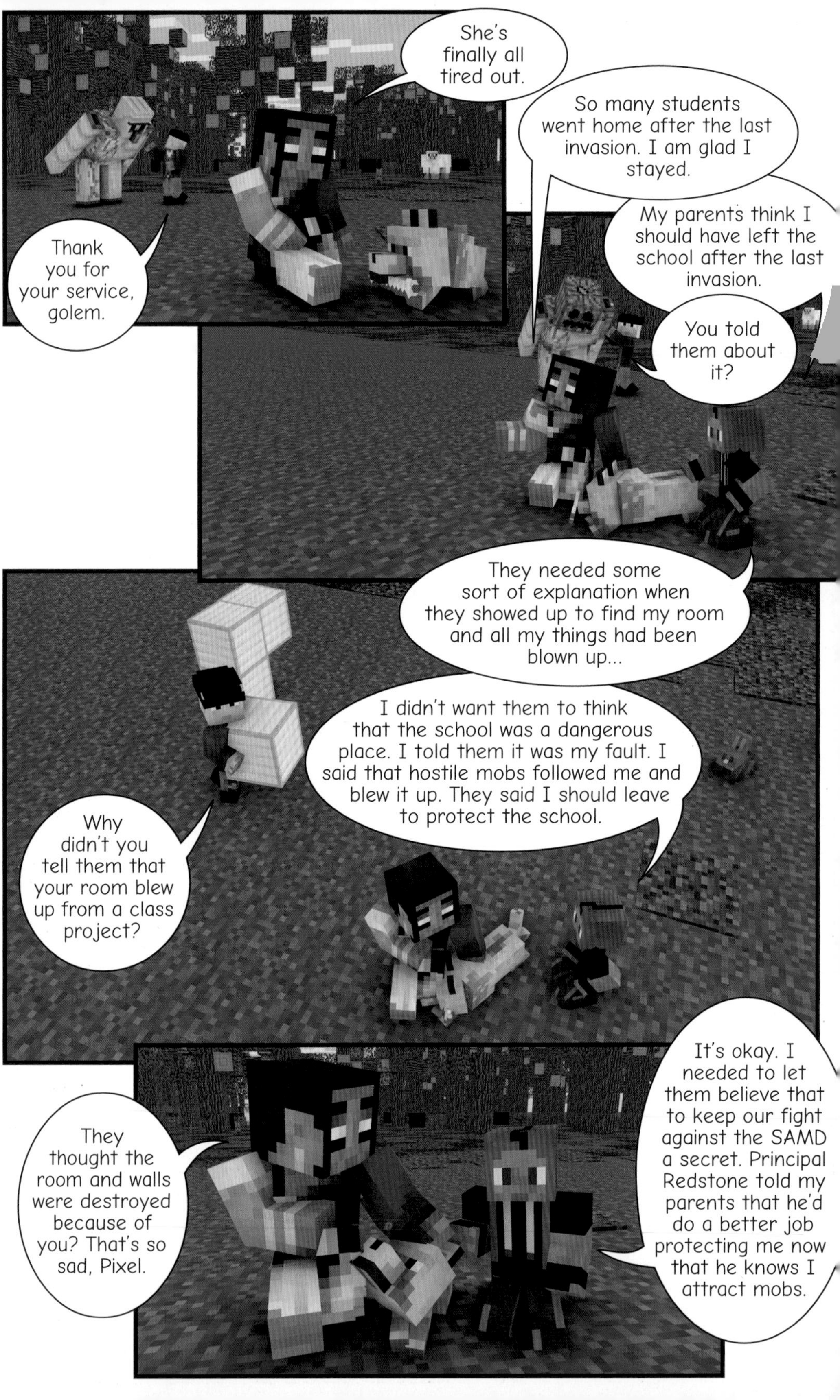

She's finally all tired out.

So many students went home after the last invasion. I am glad I stayed.

My parents think I should have left the school after the last invasion.

Thank you for your service, golem.

You told them about it?

They needed some sort of explanation when they showed up to find my room and all my things had been blown up...

I didn't want them to think that the school was a dangerous place. I told them it was my fault. I said that hostile mobs followed me and blew it up. They said I should leave to protect the school.

Why didn't you tell them that your room blew up from a class project?

They thought the room and walls were destroyed because of you? That's so sad, Pixel.

It's okay. I needed to let them believe that to keep our fight against the SAMD a secret. Principal Redstone told my parents that he'd do a better job protecting me now that he knows I attract mobs.

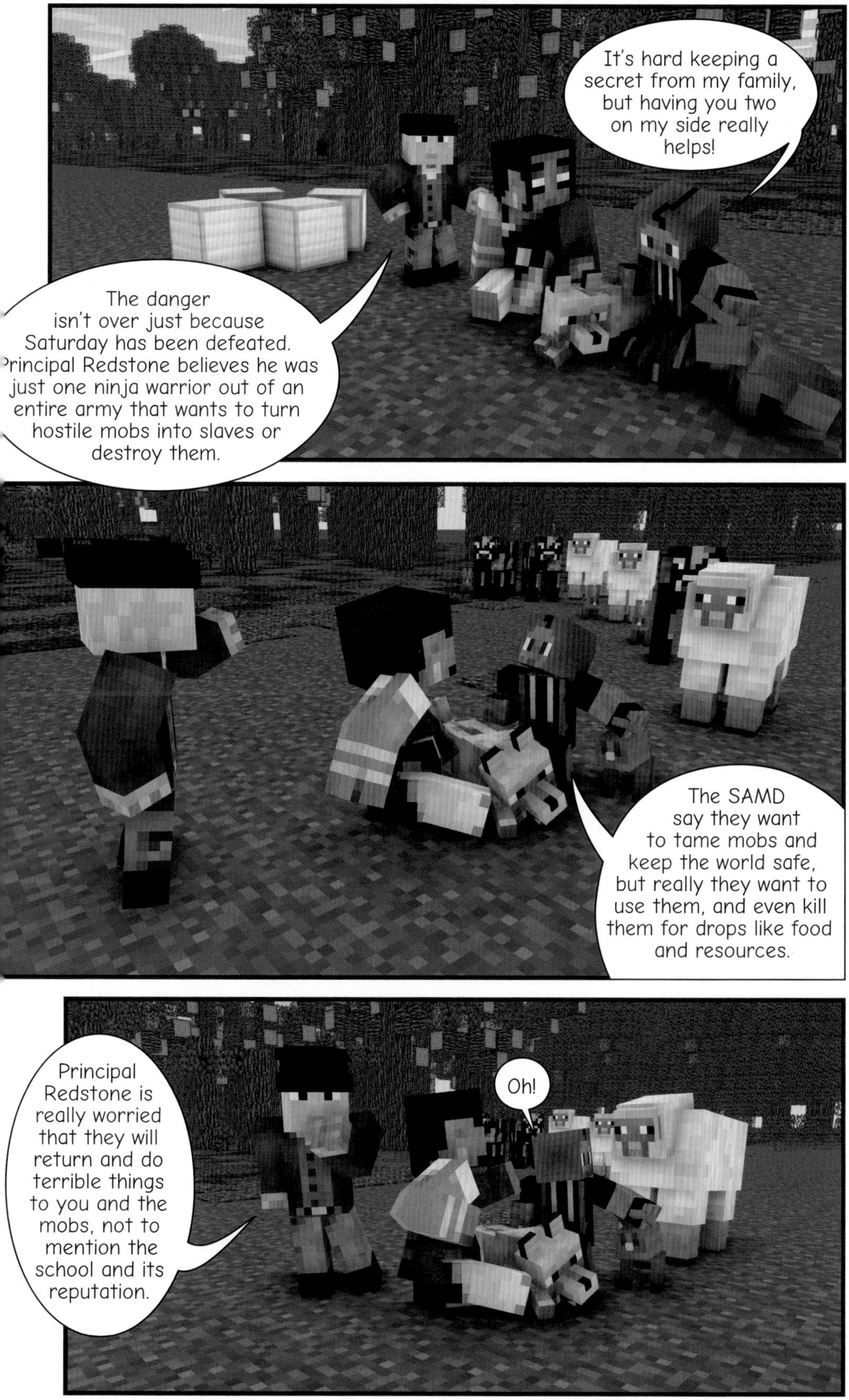
It's hard keeping a secret from my family, but having you two on my side really helps!
The danger isn't over just because Saturday has been defeated. Principal Redstone believes he was just one ninja warrior out of an entire army that wants to turn hostile mobs into slaves or destroy them.
The SAMD say they want to tame mobs and keep the world safe, but really they want to use them, and even kill them for drops like food and resources.
Principal Redstone is really worried that they will return and do terrible things to you and the mobs, not to mention the school and its reputation.
Oh!

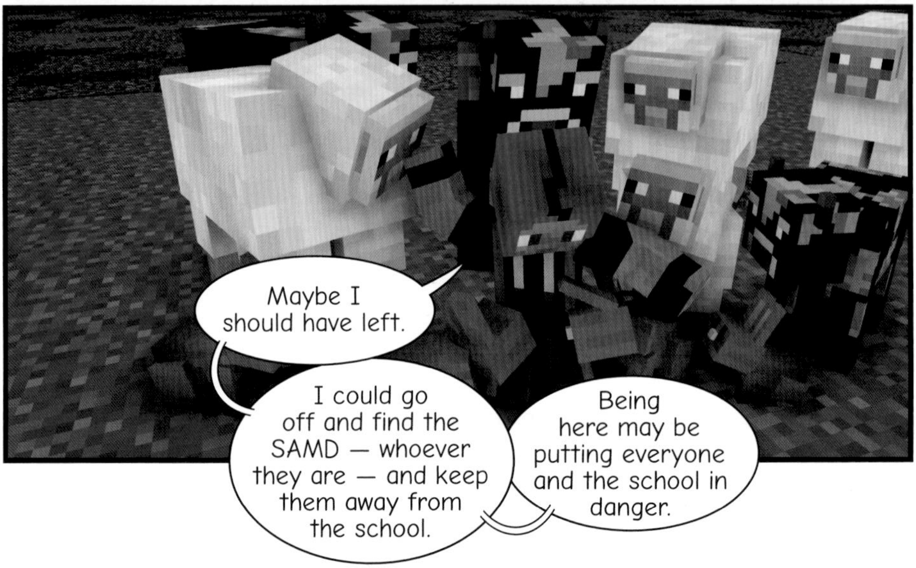
Maybe I should have left.
I could go off and find the SAMD — whoever they are — and keep them away from the school.
Being here may be putting everyone and the school in danger.

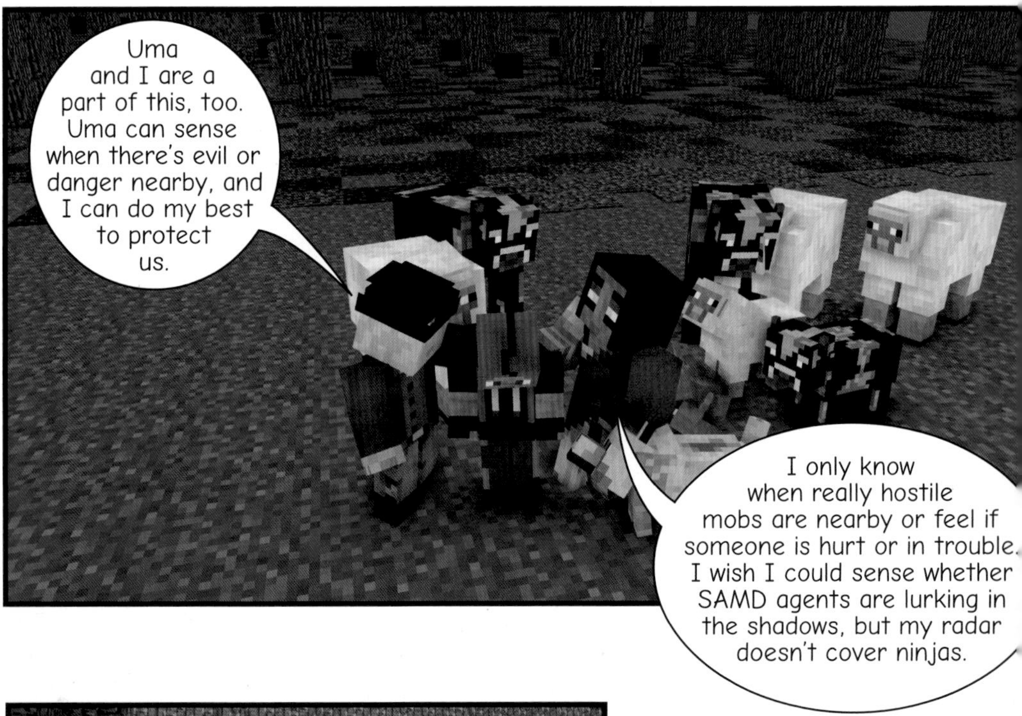
Uma and I are a part of this, too. Uma can sense when there's evil or danger nearby, and I can do my best to protect us.
I only know when really hostile mobs are nearby or feel if someone is hurt or in trouble. I wish I could sense whether SAMD agents are lurking in the shadows, but my radar doesn't cover ninjas.

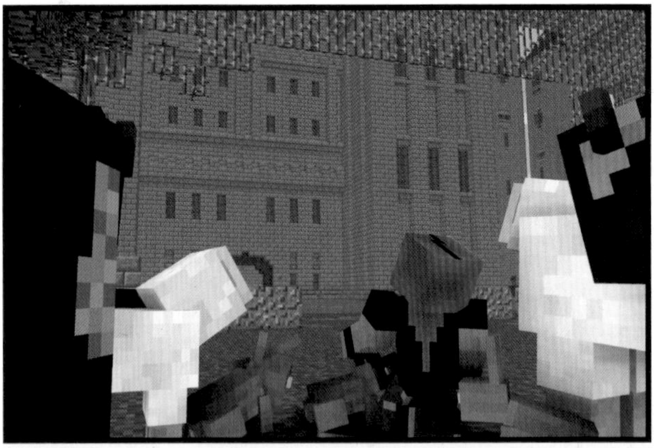

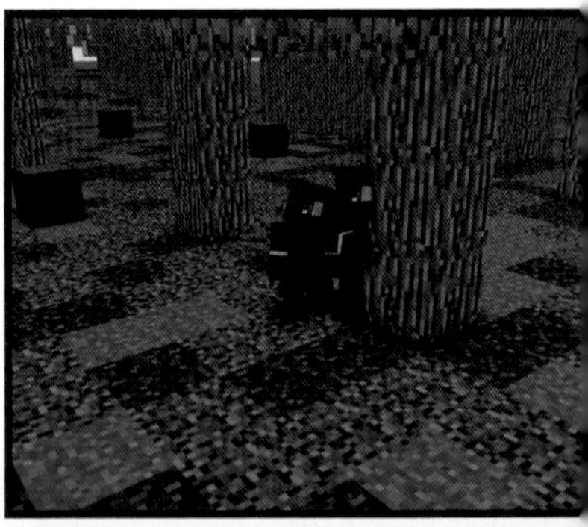

CHAPTER 2

ONCE UPON A TIME

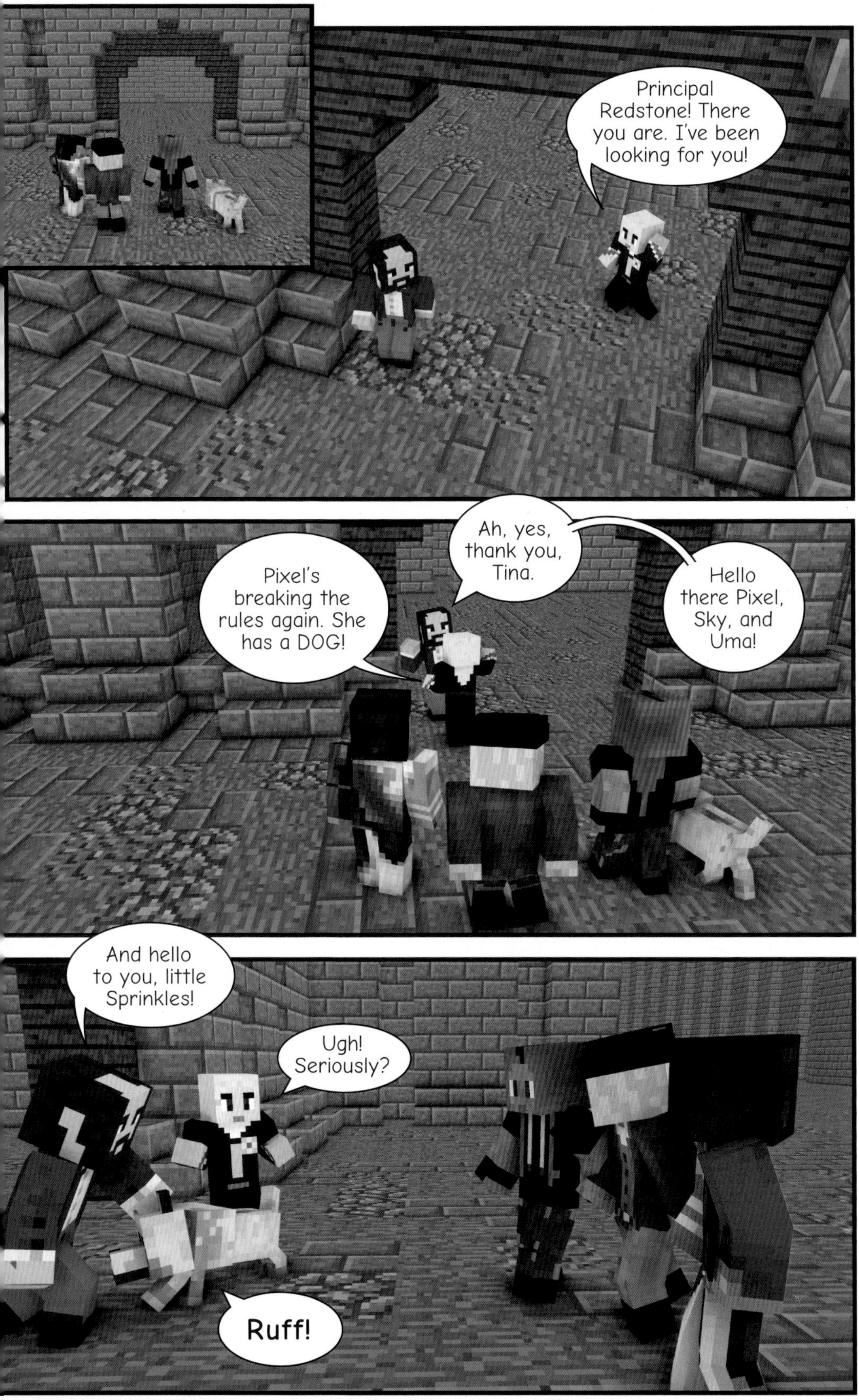
Principal Redstone! There you are. I've been looking for you!
Pixel's breaking the rules again. She has a DOG!
Ah, yes, thank you, Tina.
Hello there Pixel, Sky, and Uma!
And hello to you, little Sprinkles!
Ugh! Seriously?
Ruff!

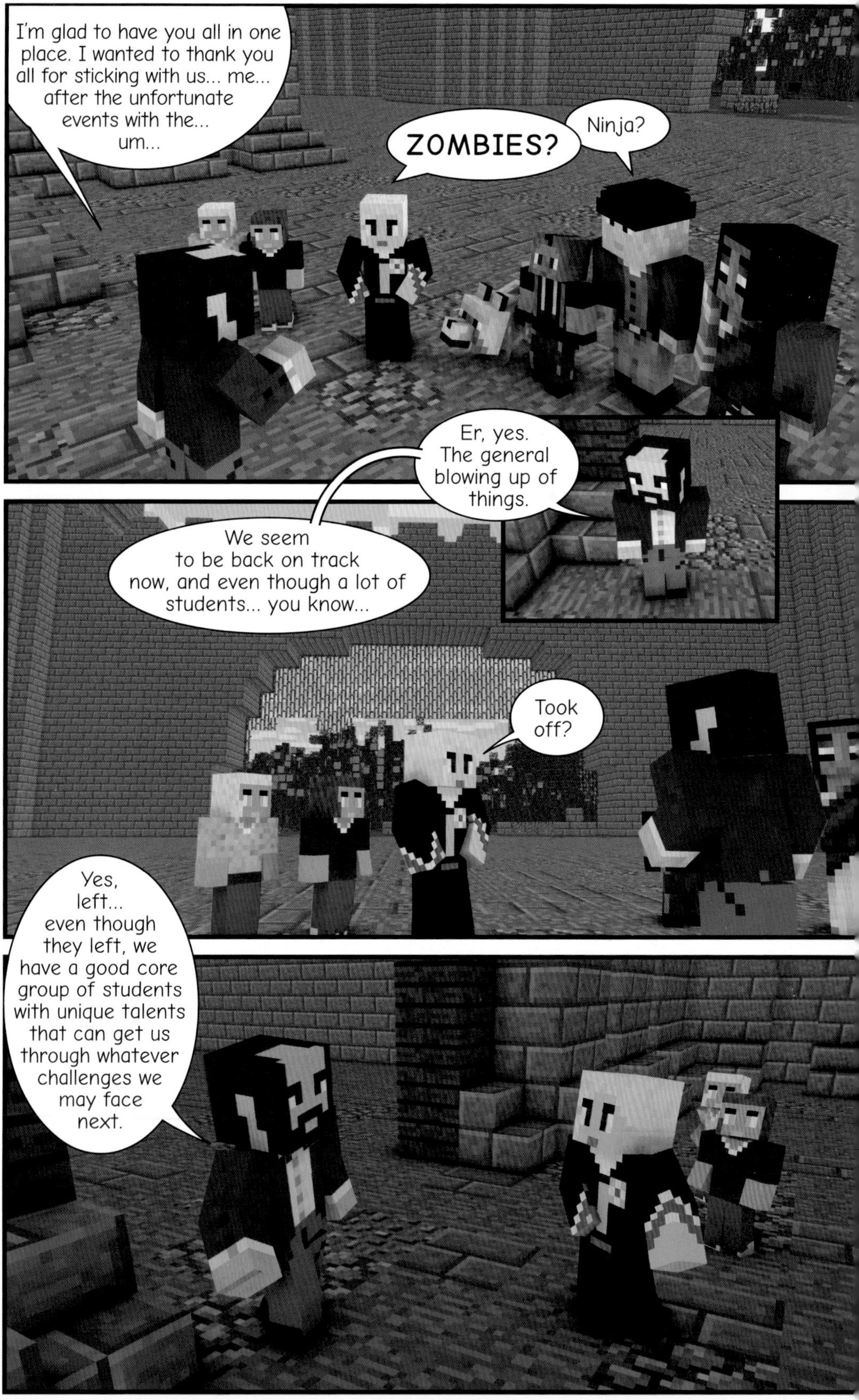
I'm glad to have you all in one place. I wanted to thank you all for sticking with us... me... after the unfortunate events with the... um...
ZOMBIES?
Ninja?
Er, yes. The general blowing up of things.
We seem to be back on track now, and even though a lot of students... you know...
Took off?
Yes, left... even though they left, we have a good core group of students with unique talents that can get us through whatever challenges we may face next.

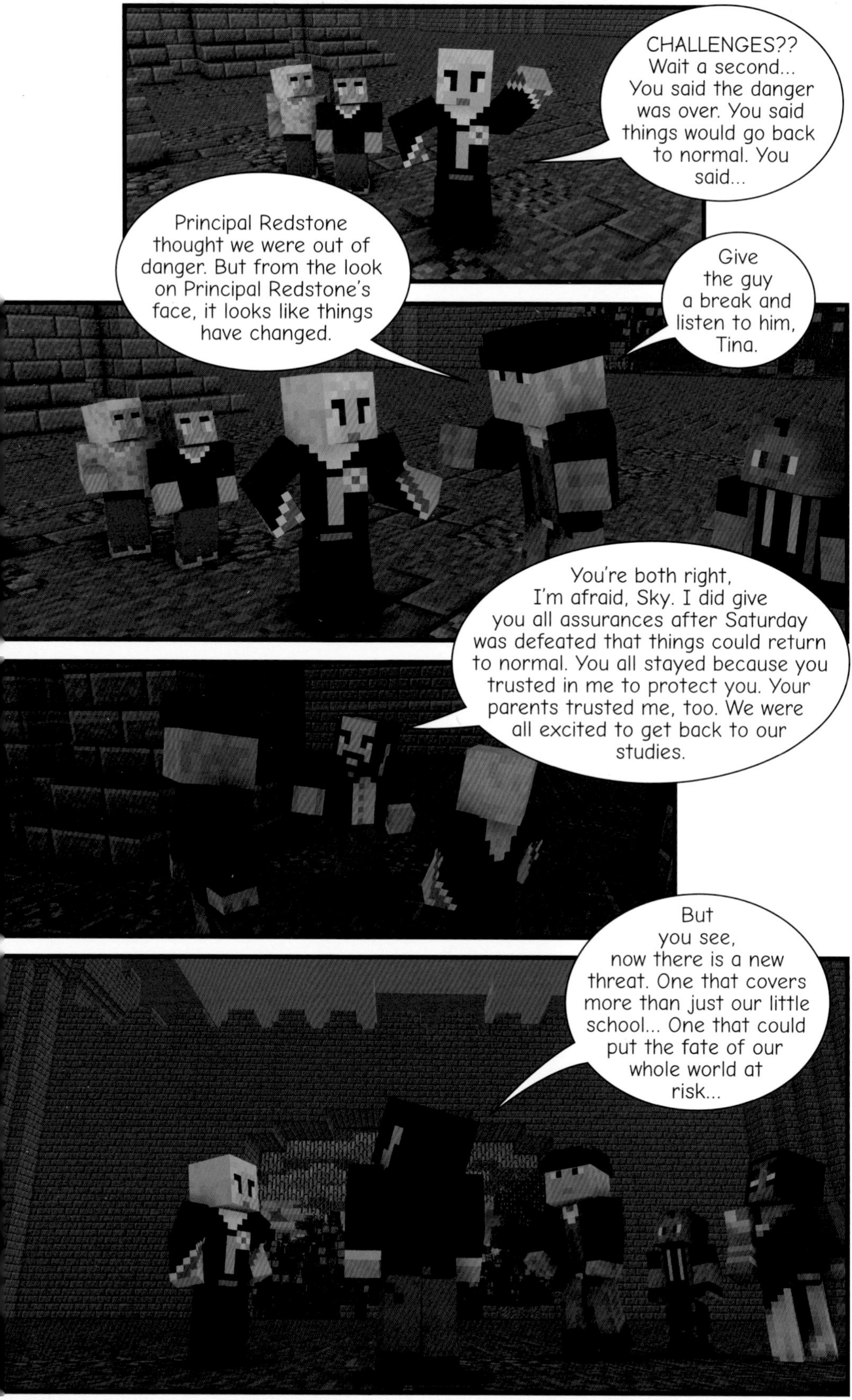
CHALLENGES?? Wait a second... You said the danger was over. You said things would go back to normal. You said...
Principal Redstone thought we were out of danger. But from the look on Principal Redstone's face, it looks like things have changed.
Give the guy a break and listen to him, Tina.
You're both right, I'm afraid, Sky. I did give you all assurances after Saturday was defeated that things could return to normal. You all stayed because you trusted in me to protect you. Your parents trusted me, too. We were all excited to get back to our studies.
But you see, now there is a new threat. One that covers more than just our little school... One that could put the fate of our whole world at risk...

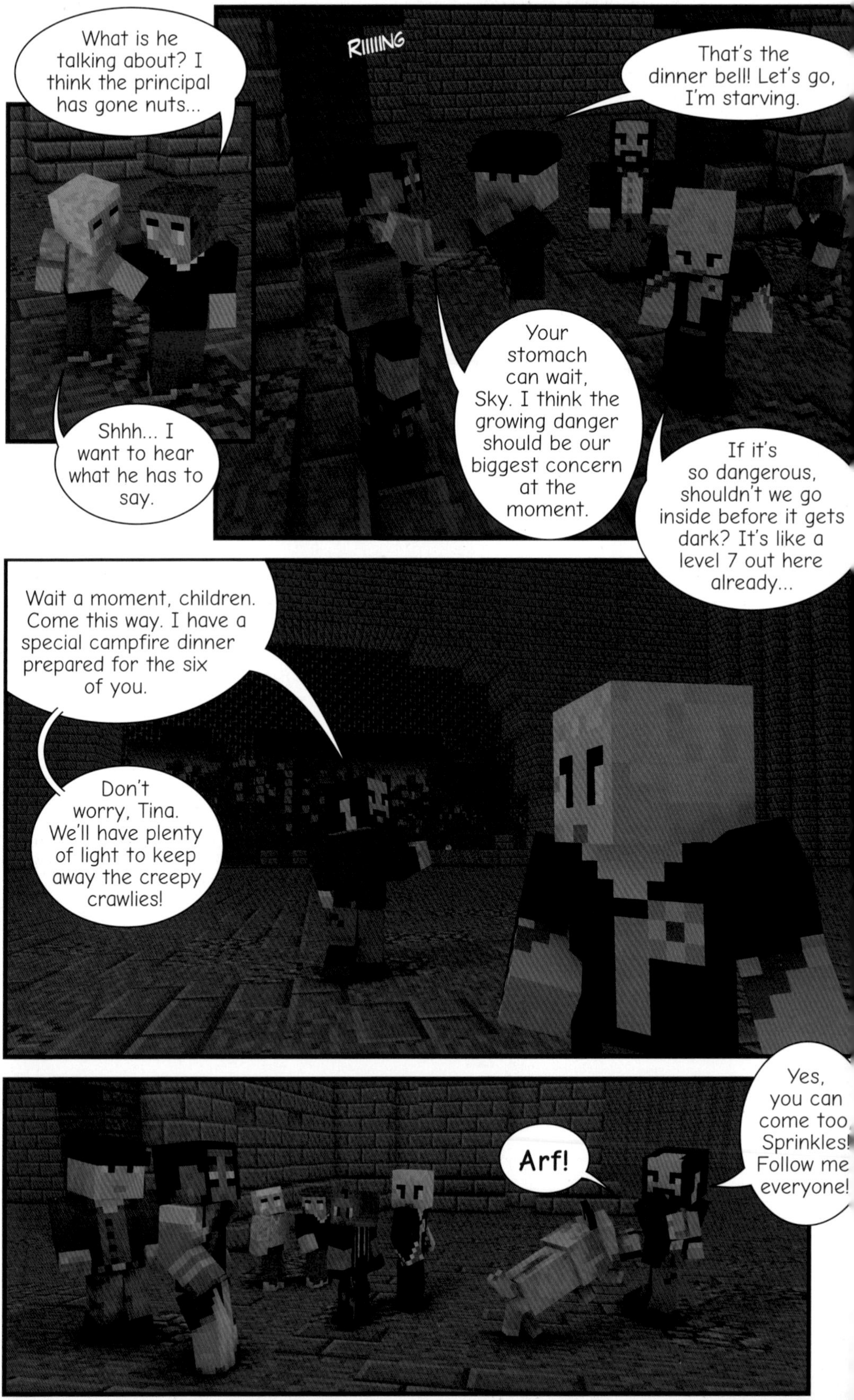

What is he talking about? I think the principal has gone nuts...
RIIIING
That's the dinner bell! Let's go, I'm starving.
Shhh... I want to hear what he has to say.
Your stomach can wait, Sky. I think the growing danger should be our biggest concern at the moment.
If it's so dangerous, shouldn't we go inside before it gets dark? It's like a level 7 out here already...
Wait a moment, children. Come this way. I have a special campfire dinner prepared for the six of you.
Don't worry, Tina. We'll have plenty of light to keep away the creepy crawlies!
Arf!
Yes, you can come too Sprinkles! Follow me everyone!

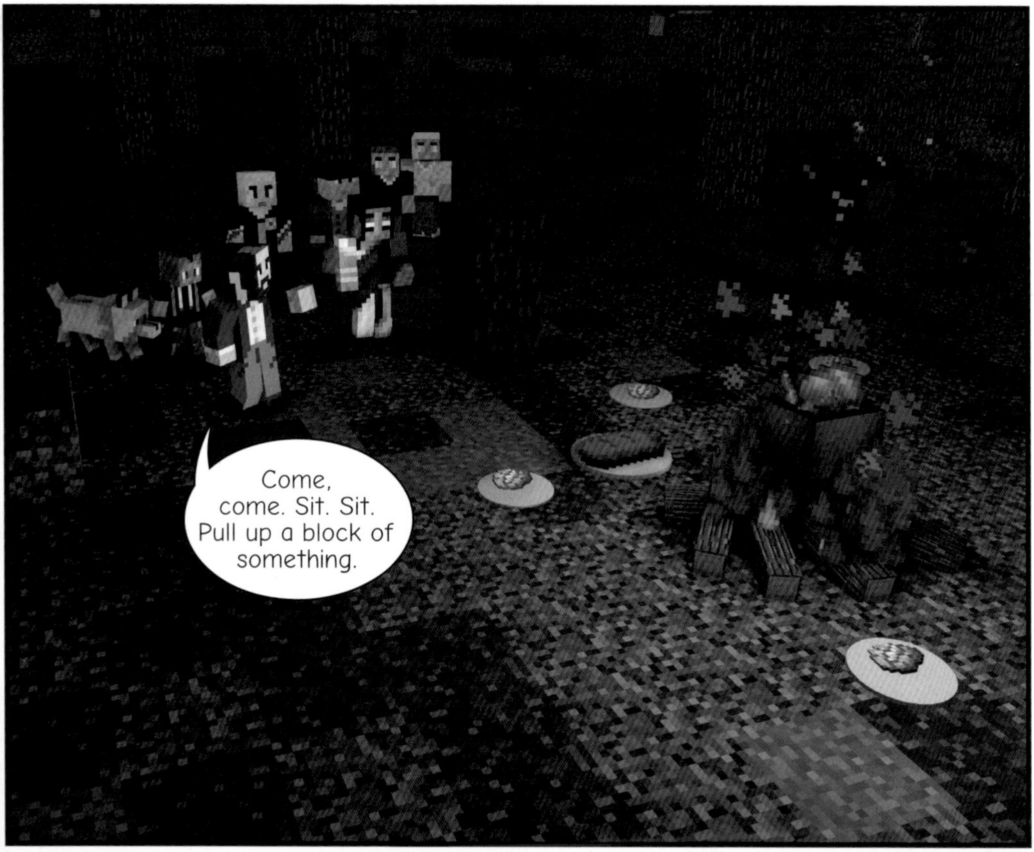
Come, come. Sit. Sit. Pull up a block of something.

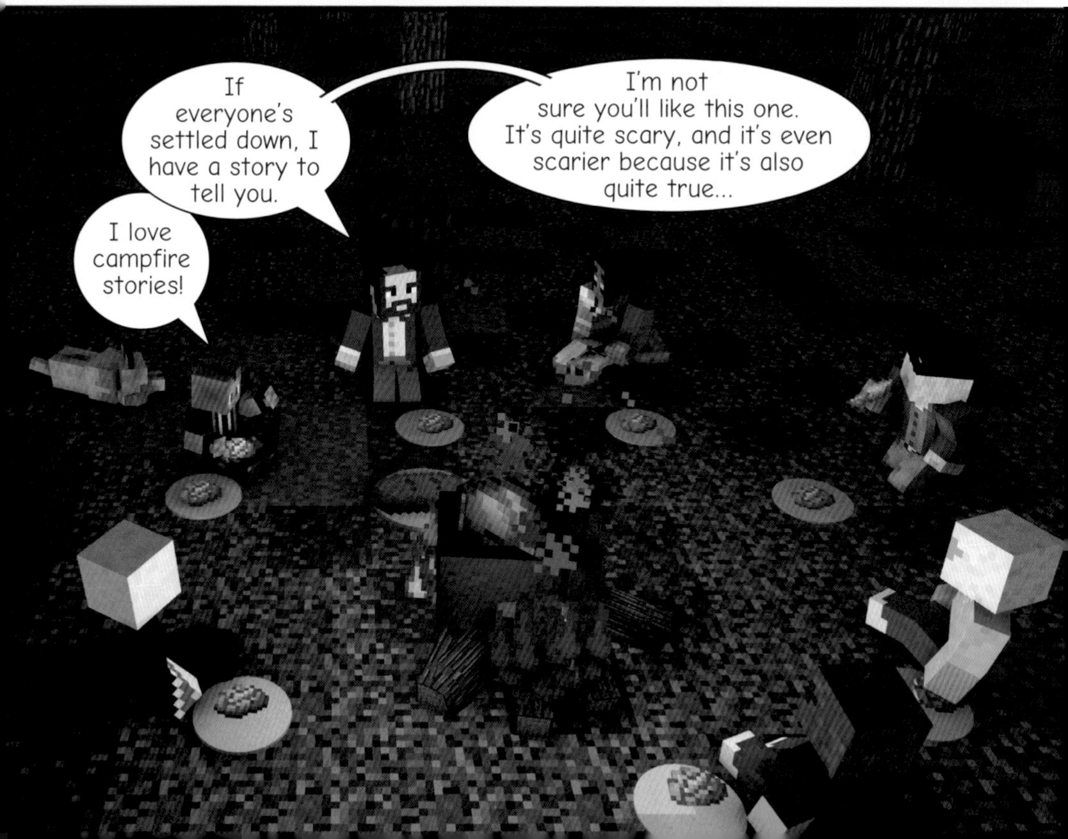
If everyone's settled down, I have a story to tell you.
I'm not sure you'll like this one. It's quite scary, and it's even scarier because it's also quite true...
I love campfire stories!

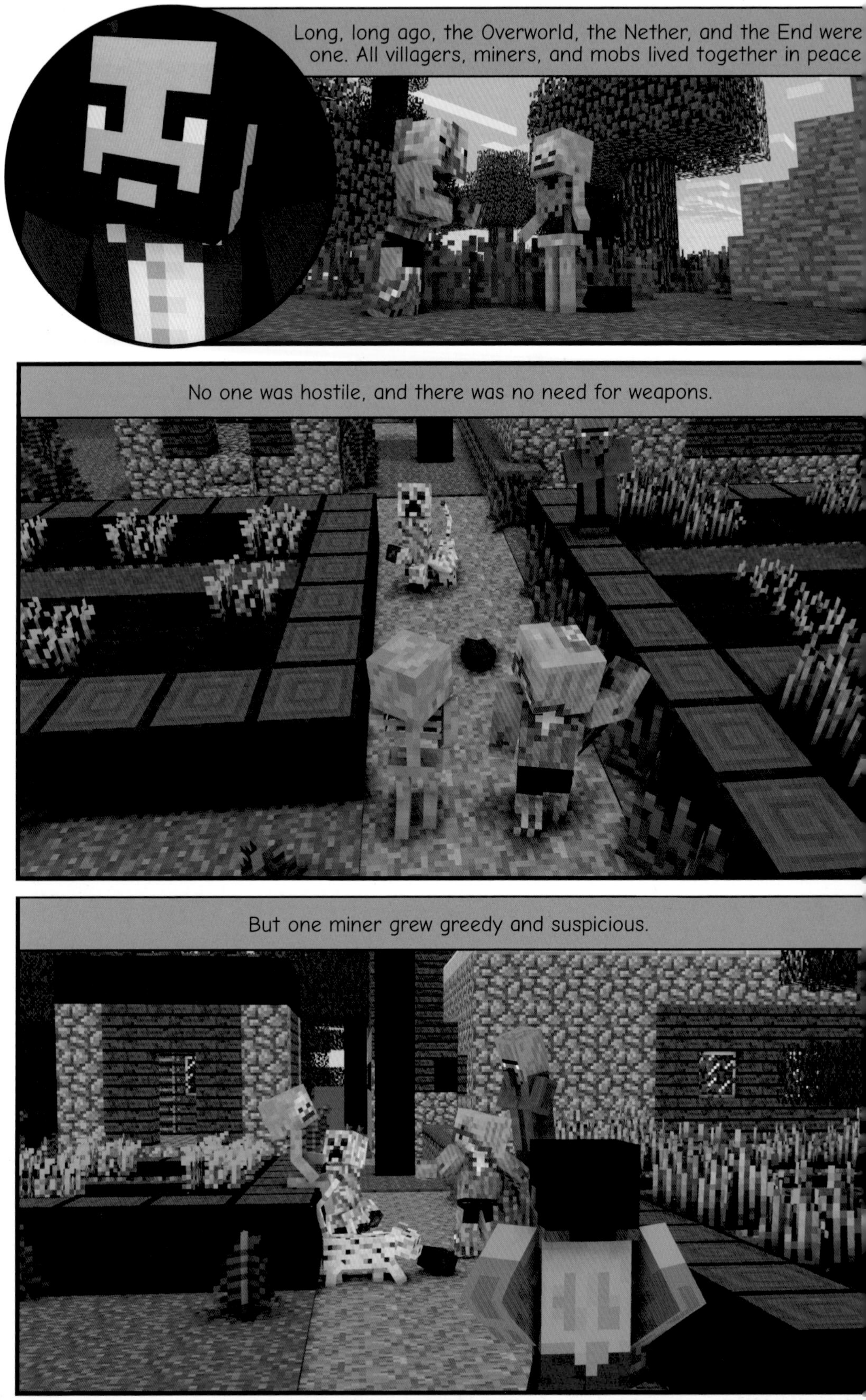
Long, long ago, the Overworld, the Nether, and the End were one. All villagers, miners, and mobs lived together in peace
No one was hostile, and there was no need for weapons.
But one miner grew greedy and suspicious.

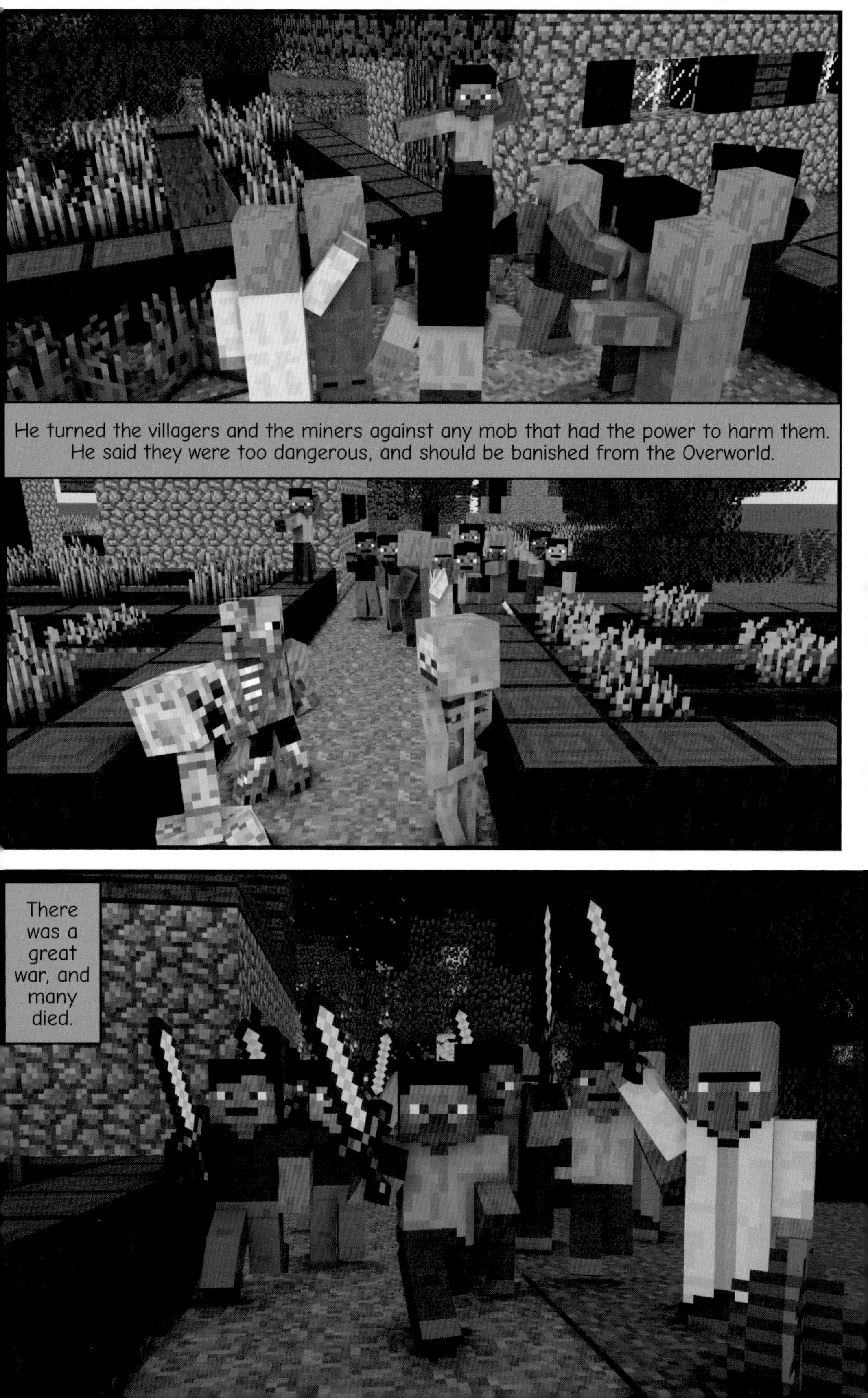
He turned the villagers and the miners against any mob that had the power to harm them. He said they were too dangerous, and should be banished from the Overworld.
There was a great war, and many died.

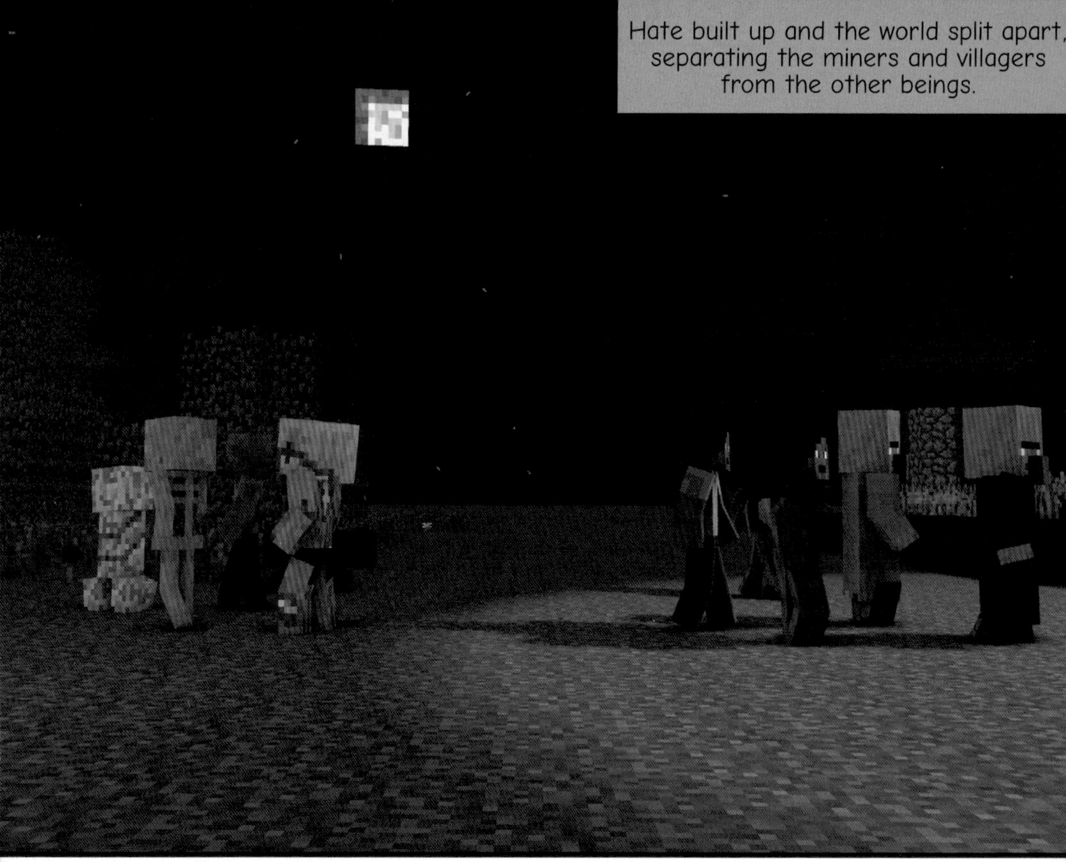
Hate built up and the world split apart, separating the miners and villagers from the other beings.

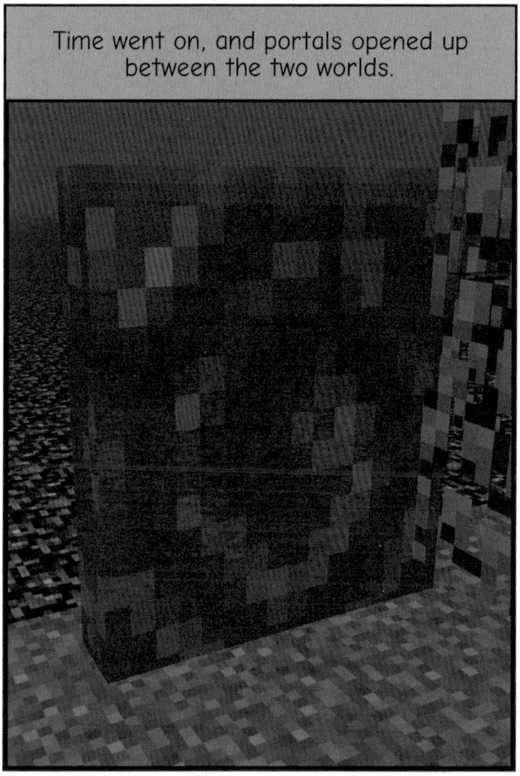
Time went on, and portals opened up between the two worlds.

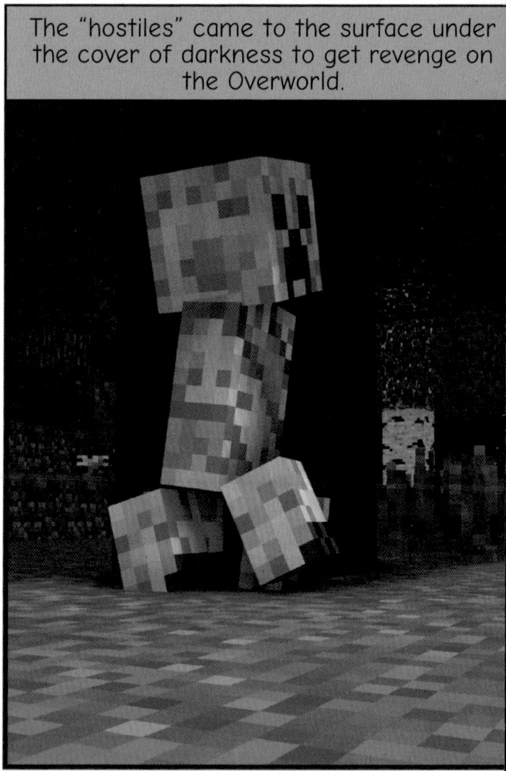
The "hostiles" came to the surface under the cover of darkness to get revenge on the Overworld.

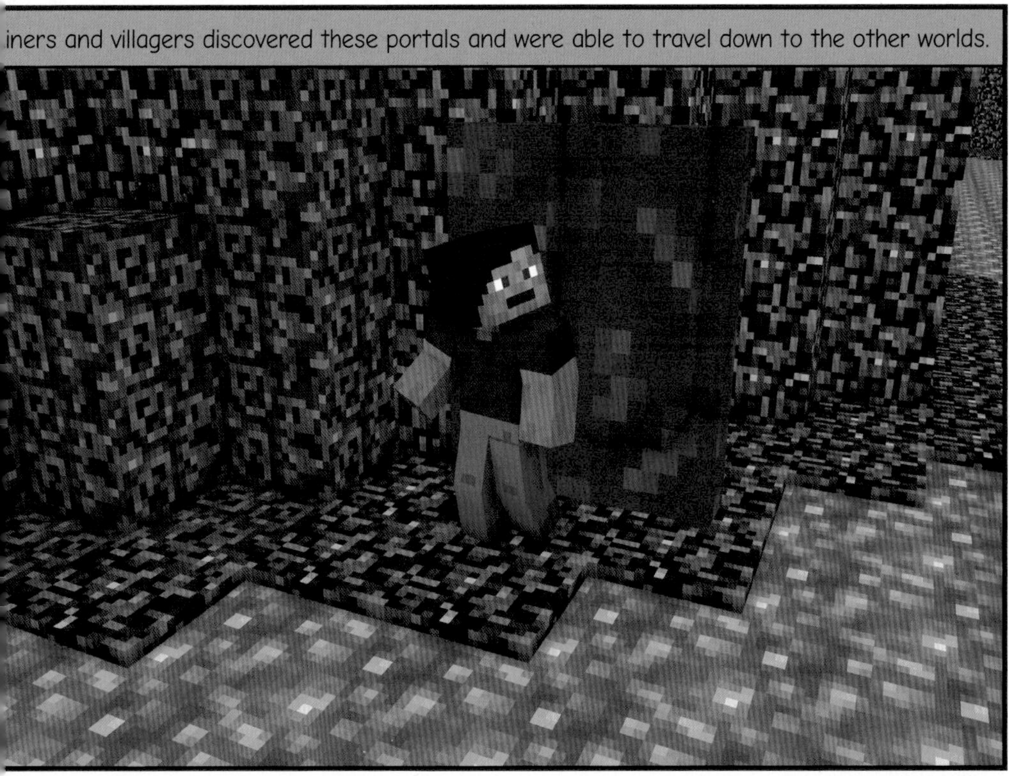
iners and villagers discovered these portals and were able to travel down to the other worlds.

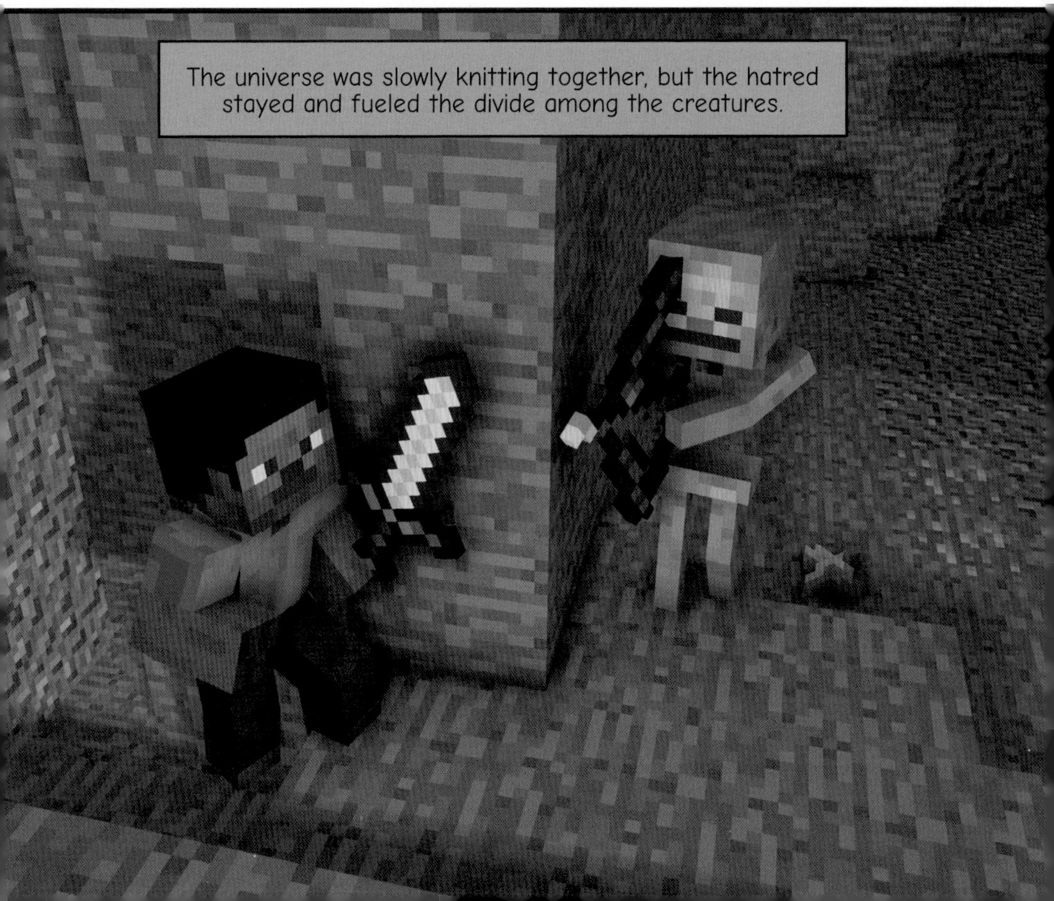
The universe was slowly knitting together, but the hatred stayed and fueled the divide among the creatures.

Some became purely hostile, like most zombies, guardians, and skeletons.

Others, like zombie pigmen, spiders, and Enderman all stayed neutral unless their space was invaded.

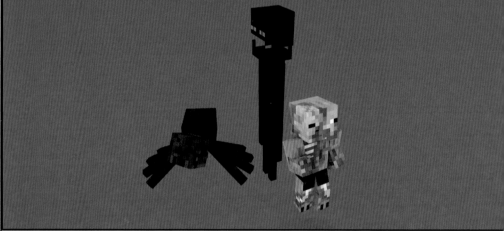

The situation proved to be too much for the sensitive creepers, who shook and exploded at the mere sight of miners.

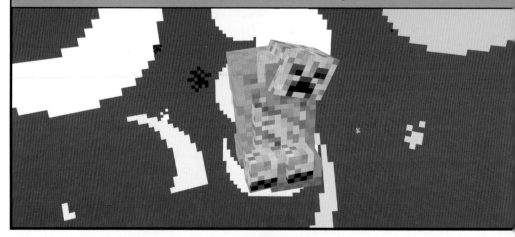

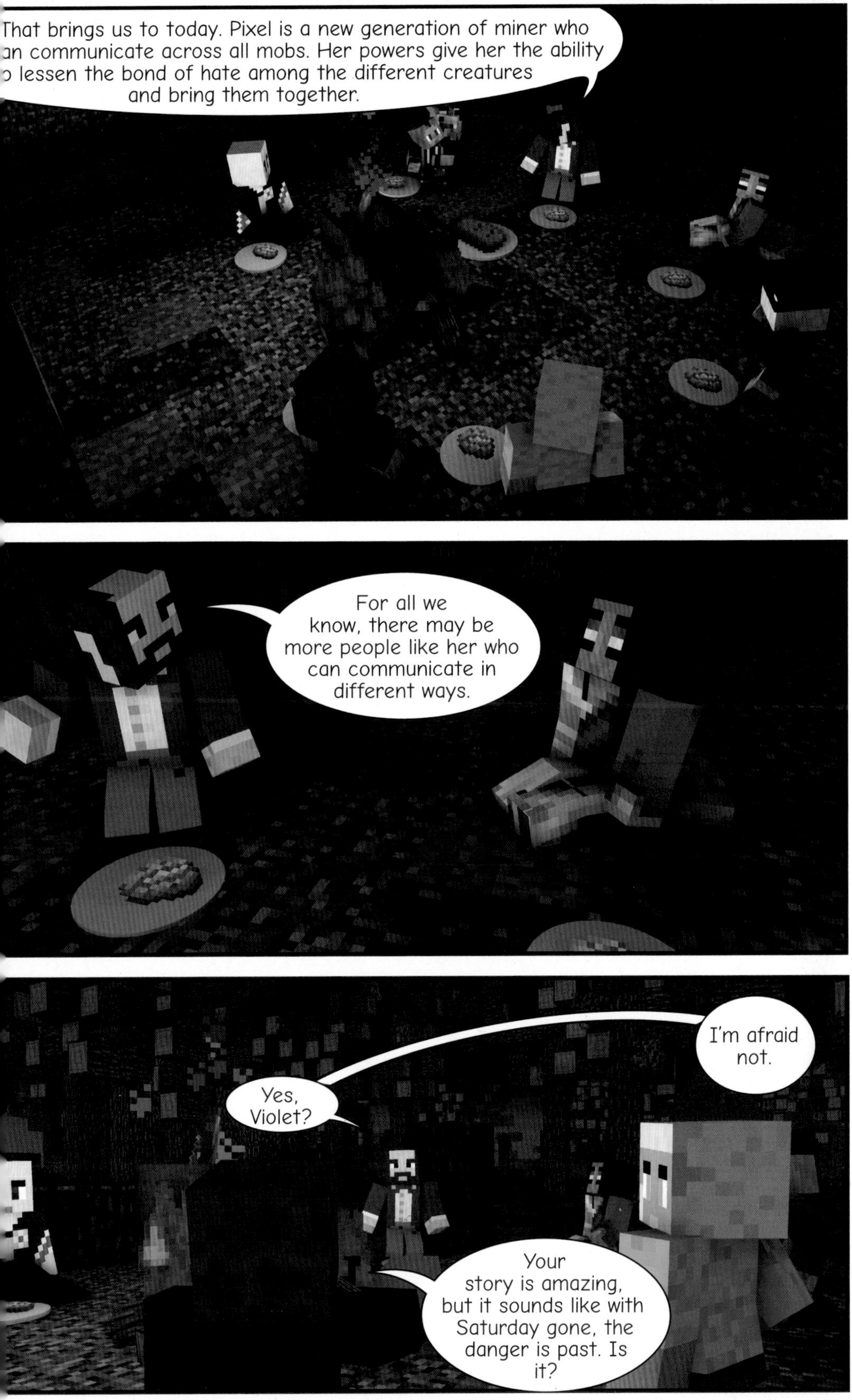

That brings us to today. Pixel is a new generation of miner who an communicate across all mobs. Her powers give her the ability o lessen the bond of hate among the different creatures and bring them together.
For all we know, there may be more people like her who can communicate in different ways.
Yes, Violet?
Your story is amazing, but it sounds like with Saturday gone, the danger is past. Is it?
I'm afraid not.

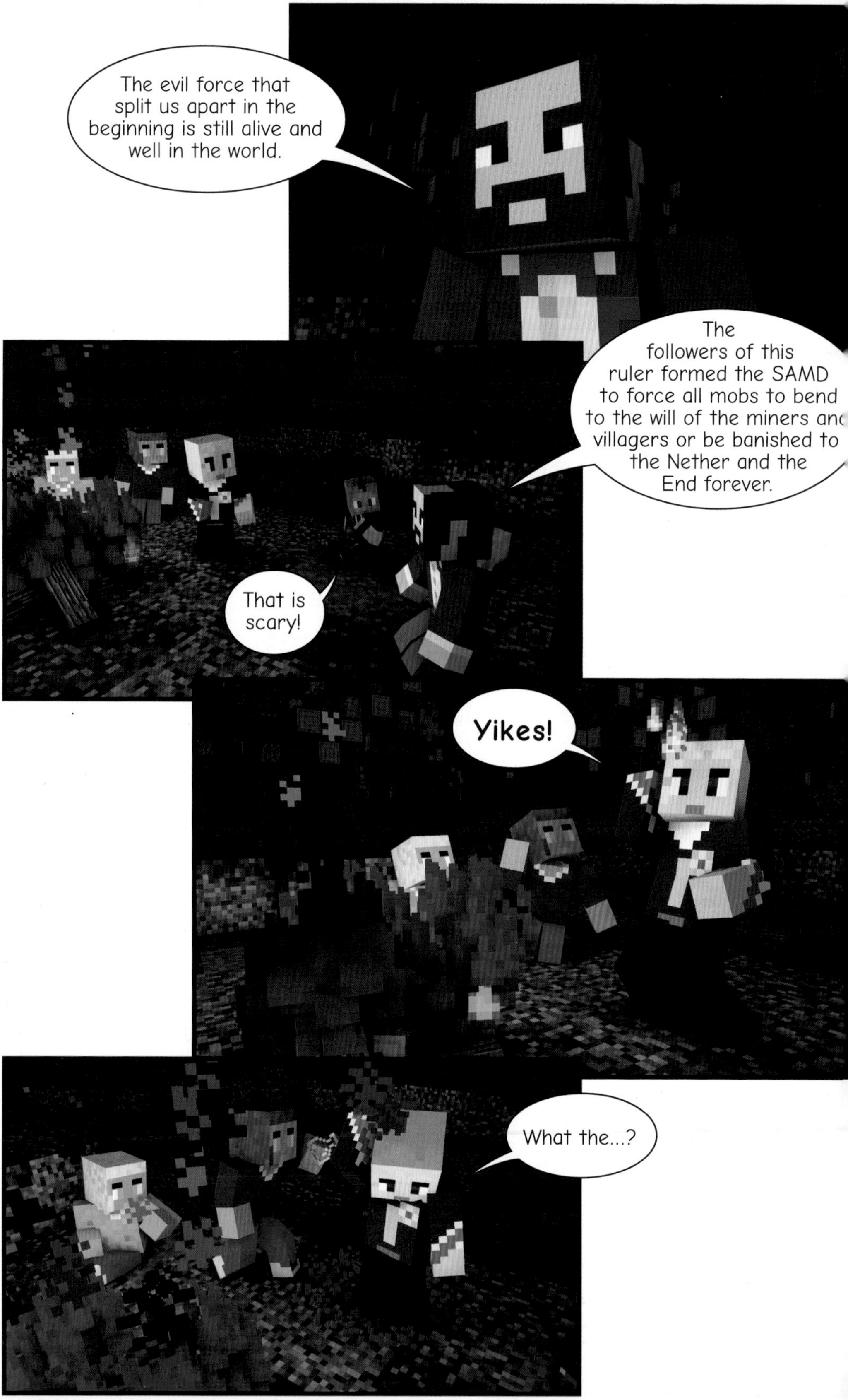
The evil force that split us apart in the beginning is still alive and well in the world.
The followers of this ruler formed the SAMD to force all mobs to bend to the will of the miners an villagers or be banished to the Nether and the End forever.
That is scary!
Yikes!
What the...?

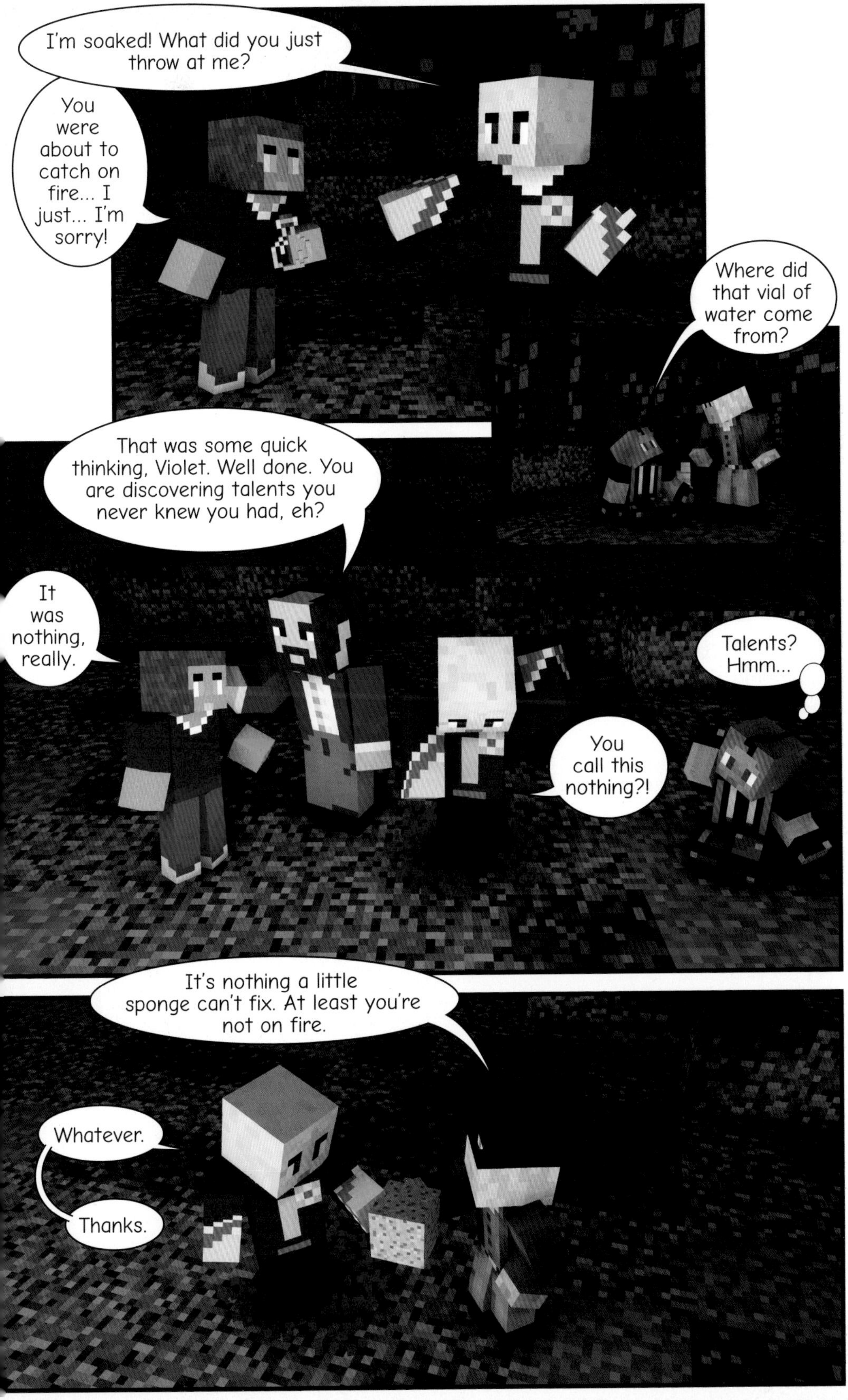
I'm soaked! What did you just throw at me?
You were about to catch on fire... I just... I'm sorry!
Where did that vial of water come from?
That was some quick thinking, Violet. Well done. You are discovering talents you never knew you had, eh?
It was nothing, really.
Talents? Hmm...
You call this nothing?!
It's nothing a little sponge can't fix. At least you're not on fire.
Whatever.
Thanks.

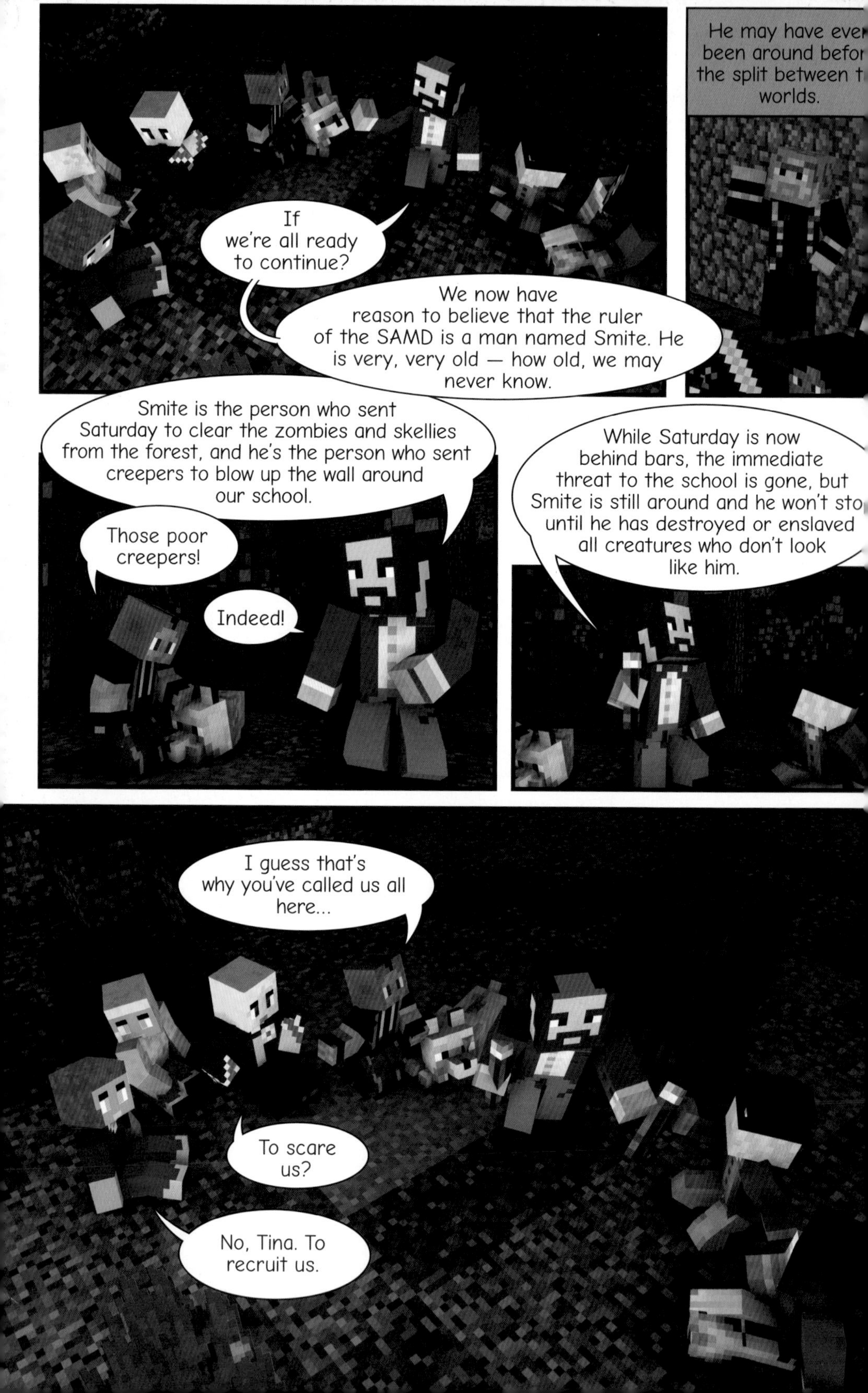
If we're all ready to continue?
We now have reason to believe that the ruler of the SAMD is a man named Smite. He is very, very old — how old, we may never know.
He may have eve
been around befor
the split between t
worlds.
Smite is the person who sent Saturday to clear the zombies and skellies from the forest, and he's the person who sent creepers to blow up the wall around our school.
Those poor creepers!
Indeed!
While Saturday is now behind bars, the immediate threat to the school is gone, but Smite is still around and he won't sto
until he has destroyed or enslaved all creatures who don't look like him.
I guess that's why you've called us all here...
To scare us?
No, Tina. To recruit us.

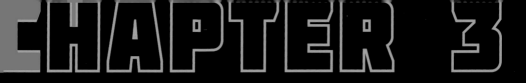

CHAPTER 3

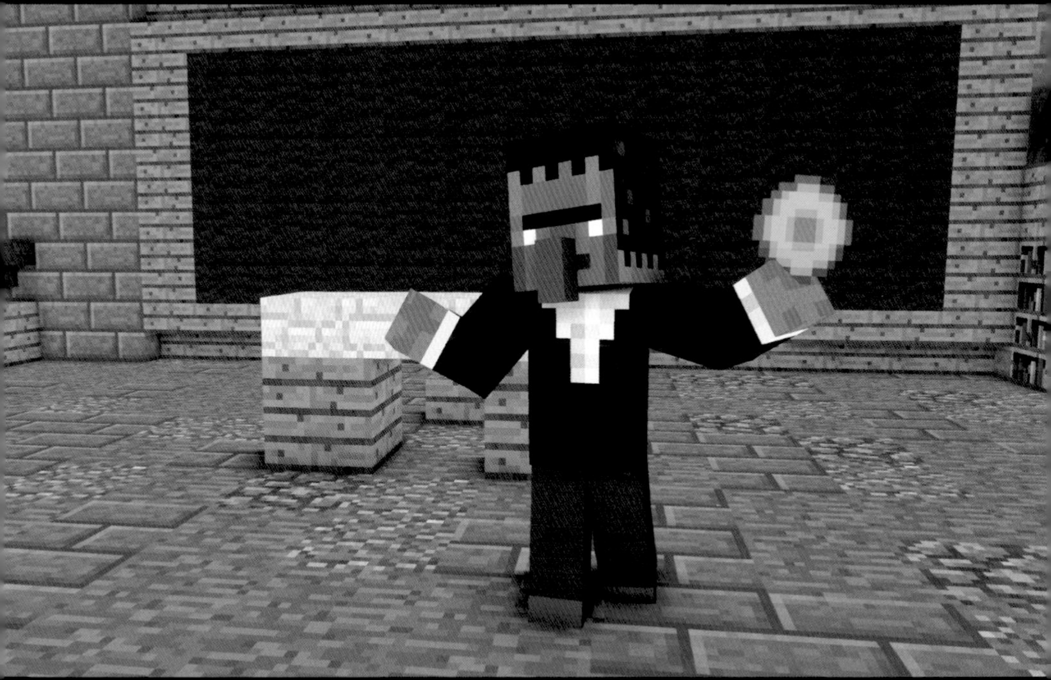

A CHALLENGE

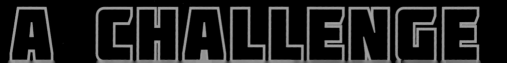

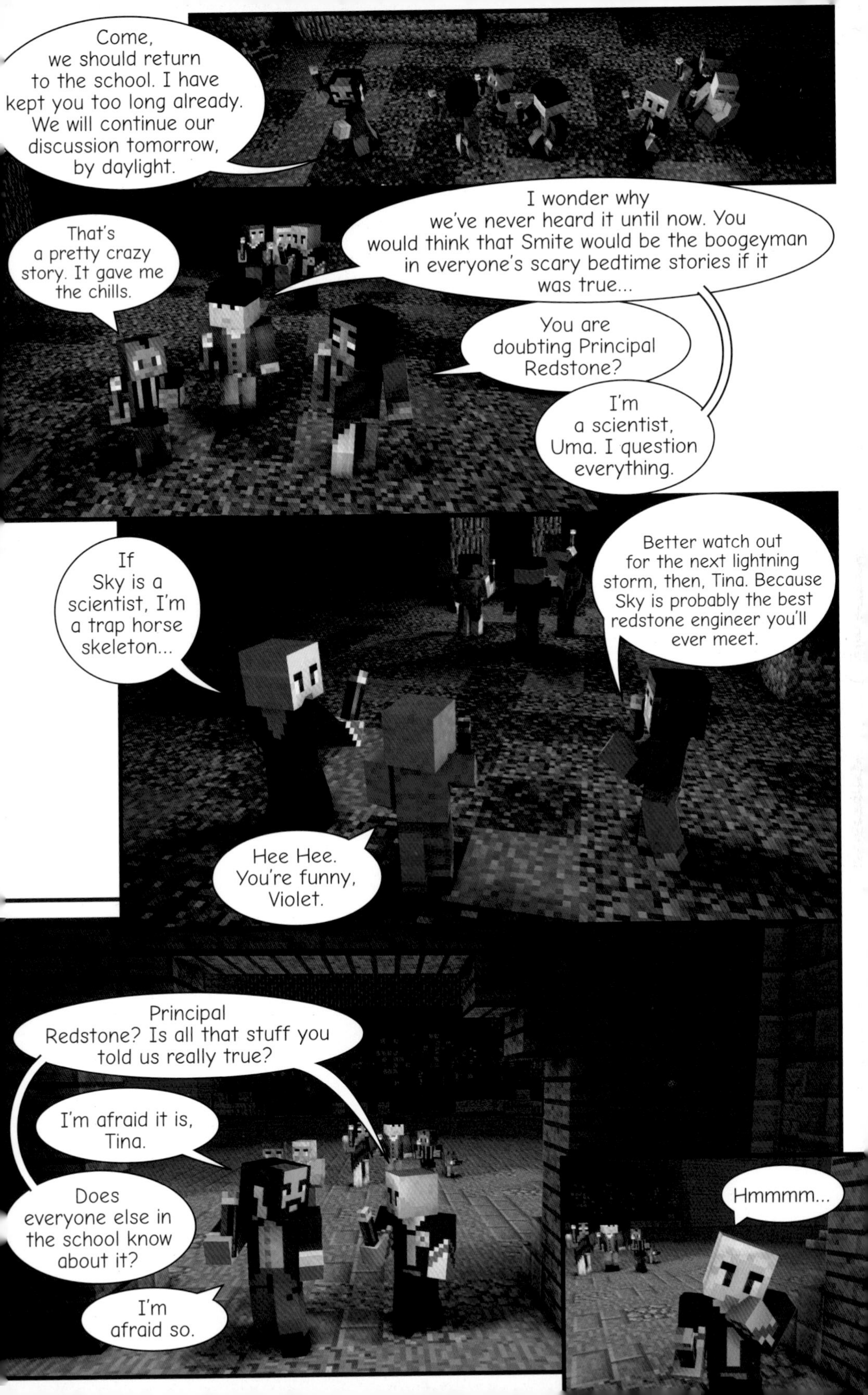
Come, we should return to the school. I have kept you too long already. We will continue our discussion tomorrow, by daylight.
That's a pretty crazy story. It gave me the chills.
I wonder why we've never heard it until now. You would think that Smite would be the boogeyman in everyone's scary bedtime stories if it was true...
You are doubting Principal Redstone?
I'm a scientist, Uma. I question everything.
If Sky is a scientist, I'm a trap horse skeleton...
Better watch out for the next lightning storm, then, Tina. Because Sky is probably the best redstone engineer you'll ever meet.
Hee Hee. You're funny, Violet.
Principal Redstone? Is all that stuff you told us really true?
I'm afraid it is, Tina.
Does everyone else in the school know about it?
I'm afraid so.
Hmmmm...

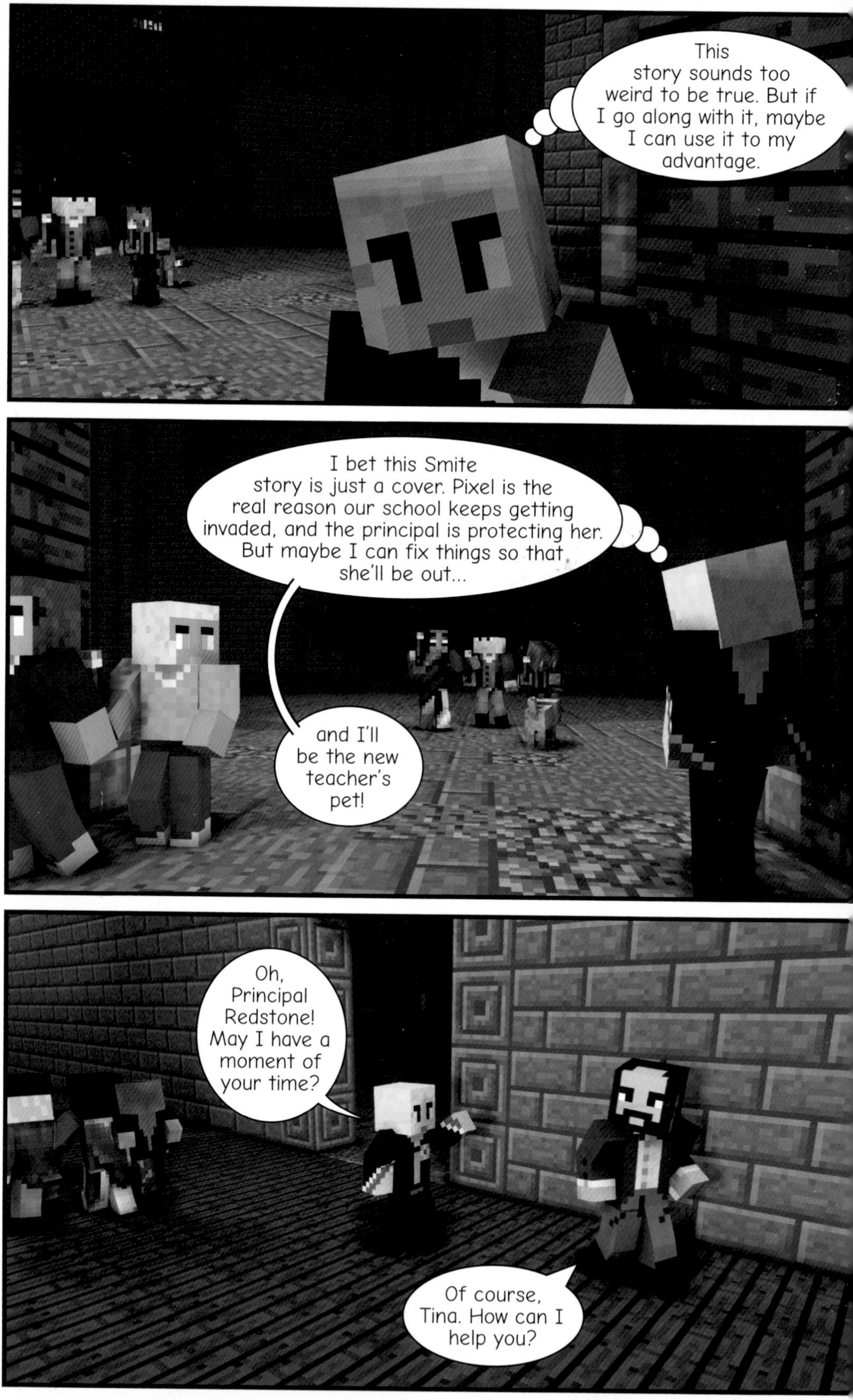
This story sounds too weird to be true. But if I go along with it, maybe I can use it to my advantage.
I bet this Smite story is just a cover. Pixel is the real reason our school keeps getting invaded, and the principal is protecting her. But maybe I can fix things so that she'll be out...
and I'll be the new teacher's pet!
Oh, Principal Redstone! May I have a moment of your time?
Of course, Tina. How can I help you?

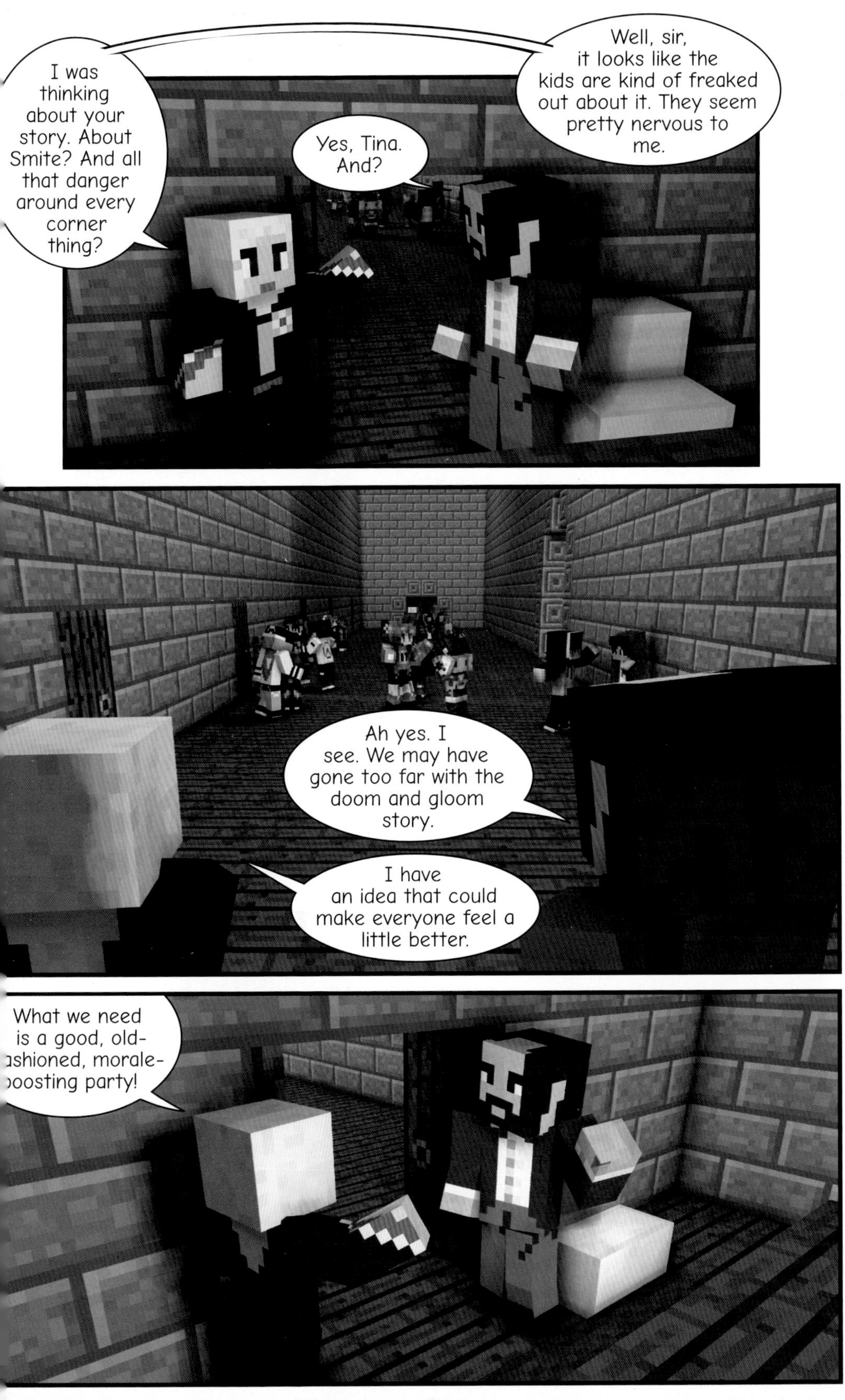
I was thinking about your story. About Smite? And all that danger around every corner thing?
Yes, Tina. And?
Well, sir, it looks like the kids are kind of freaked out about it. They seem pretty nervous to me.
Ah yes. I see. We may have gone too far with the doom and gloom story.
I have an idea that could make everyone feel a little better.
What we need is a good, old-
ashioned, morale-
oosting party!

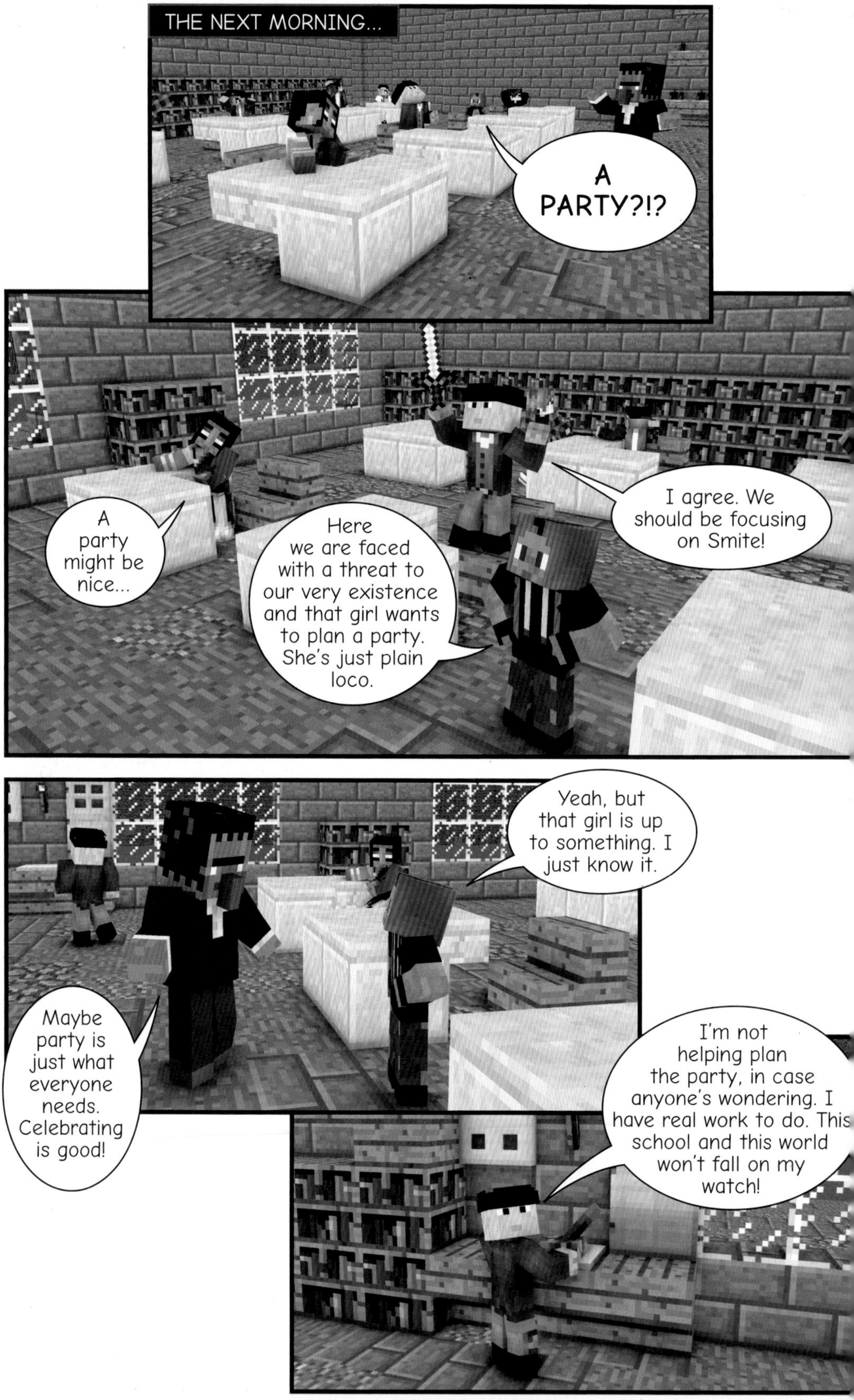

THE NEXT MORNING...
A PARTY?!?
A party might be nice...
Here we are faced with a threat to our very existence and that girl wants to plan a party. She's just plain loco.
I agree. We should be focusing on Smite!
Yeah, but that girl is up to something. I just know it.
Maybe party is just what everyone needs. Celebrating is good!
I'm not helping plan the party, in case anyone's wondering. I have real work to do. This school and this world won't fall on my watch!

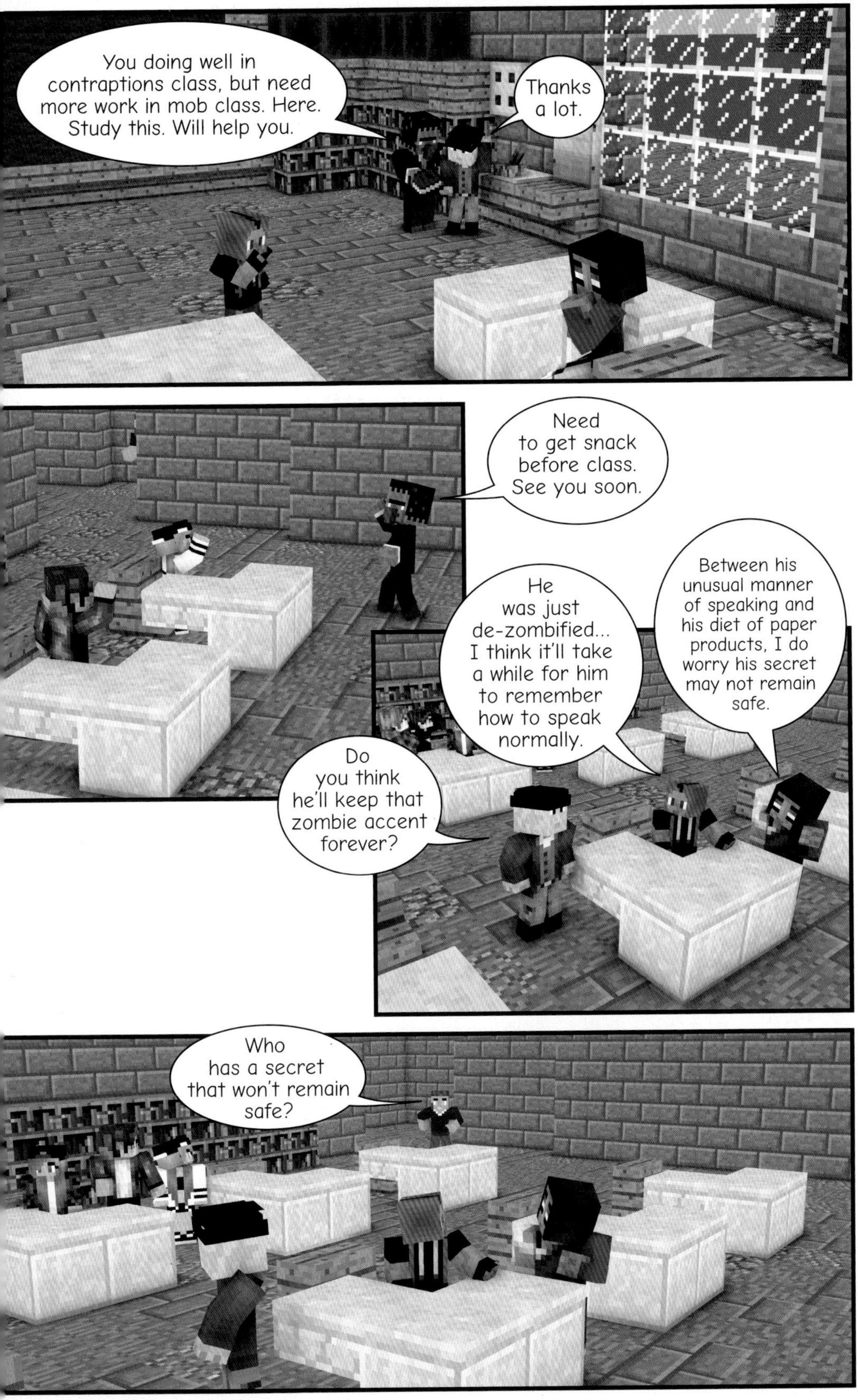
You doing well in contraptions class, but need more work in mob class. Here. Study this. Will help you.
Thanks a lot.
Need to get snack before class. See you soon.
He was just de-zombified... I think it'll take a while for him to remember how to speak normally.
Between his unusual manner of speaking and his diet of paper products, I do worry his secret may not remain safe.
Do you think he'll keep that zombie accent forever?
Who has a secret that won't remain safe?

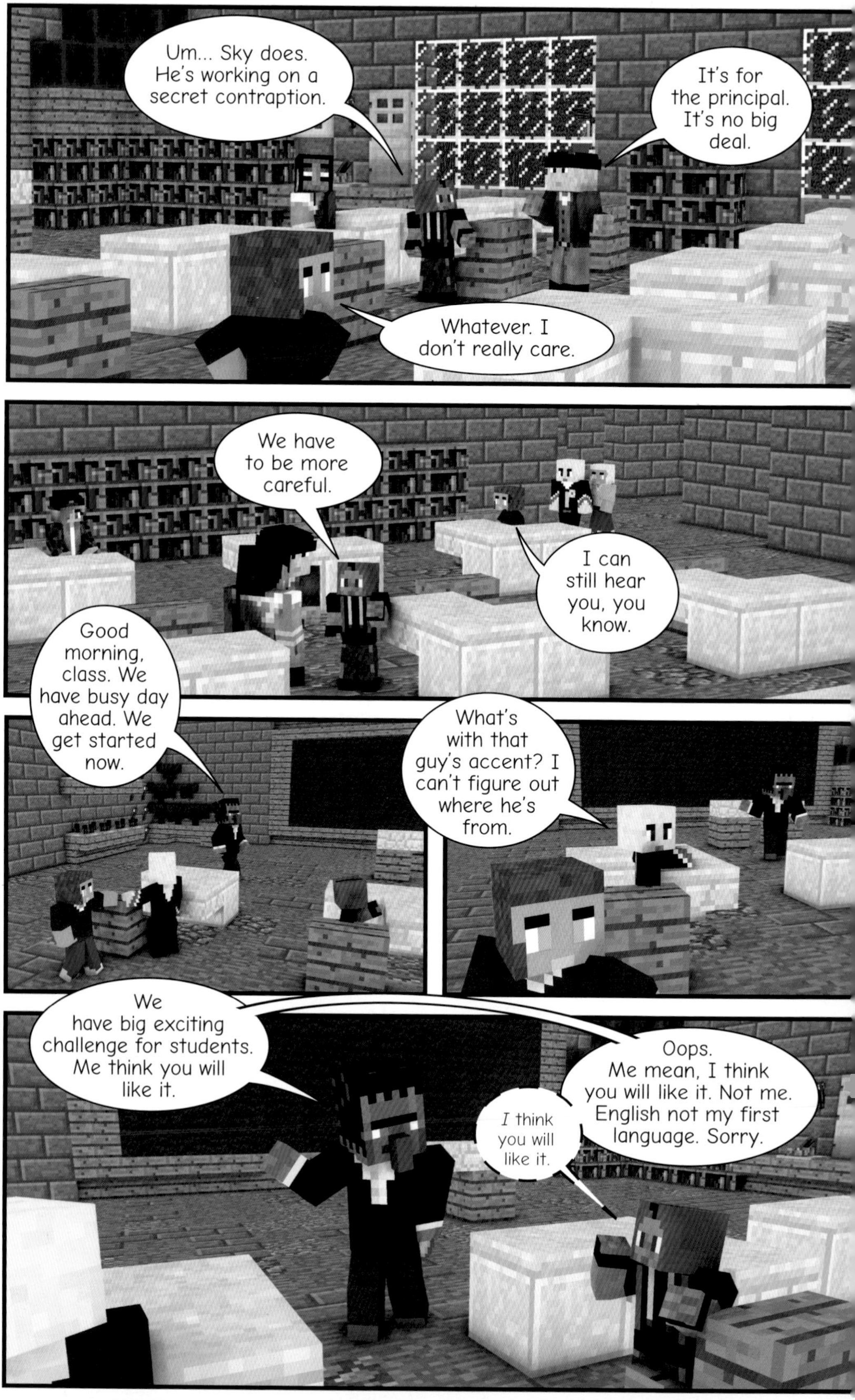
Um... Sky does. He's working on a secret contraption.
It's for the principal. It's no big deal.
Whatever. I don't really care.
We have to be more careful.
I can still hear you, you know.
Good morning, class. We have busy day ahead. We get started now.
What's with that guy's accent? I can't figure out where he's from.
We have big exciting challenge for students. Me think you will like it.
Oops. Me mean, I think you will like it. Not me. English not my first language. Sorry.
I think you will like it.

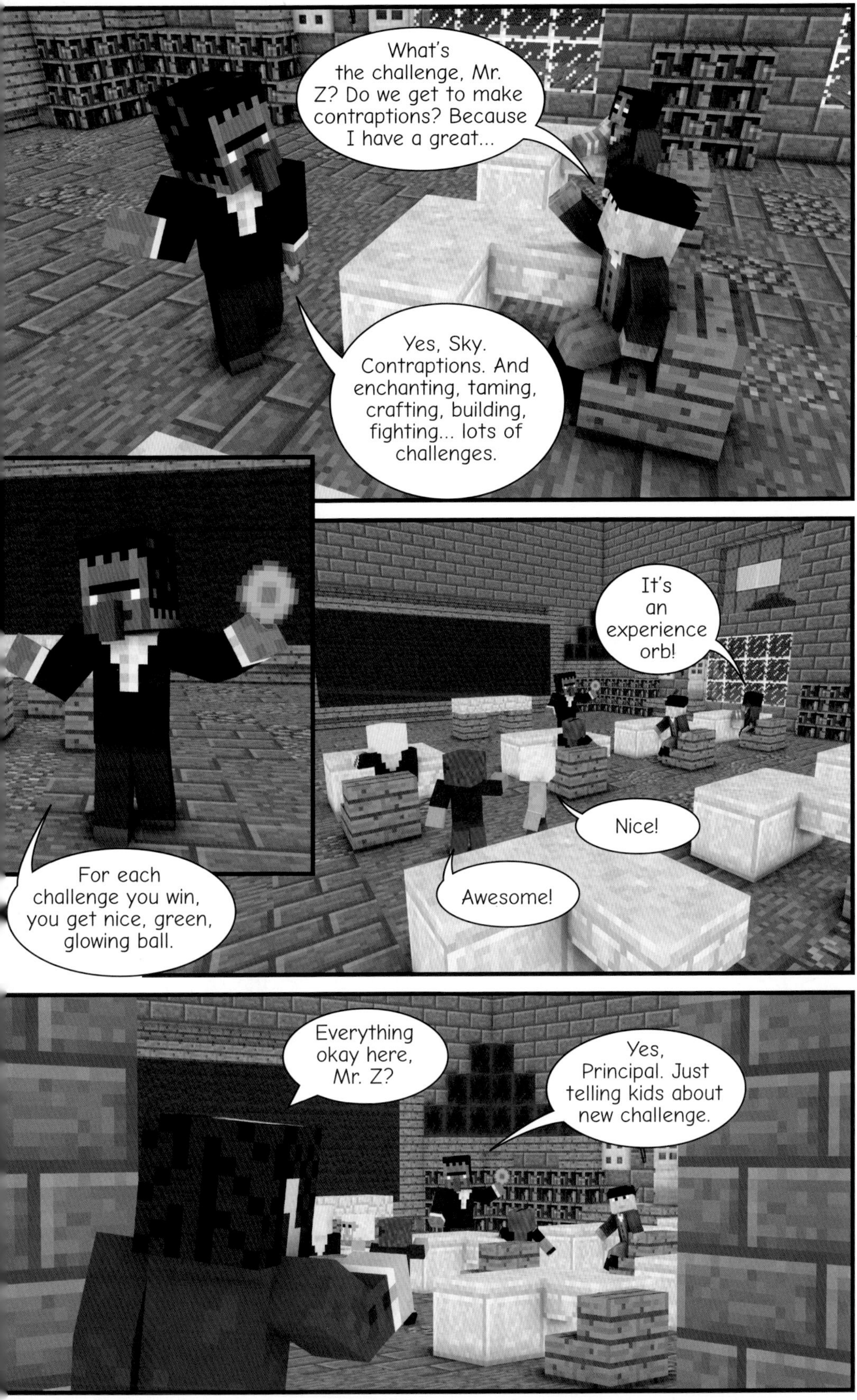
What's the challenge, Mr. Z? Do we get to make contraptions? Because I have a great...
Yes, Sky. Contraptions. And enchanting, taming, crafting, building, fighting... lots of challenges.
For each challenge you win, you get nice, green, glowing ball.
It's an experience orb!
Nice!
Awesome!
Everything okay here, Mr. Z?
Yes, Principal. Just telling kids about new challenge.

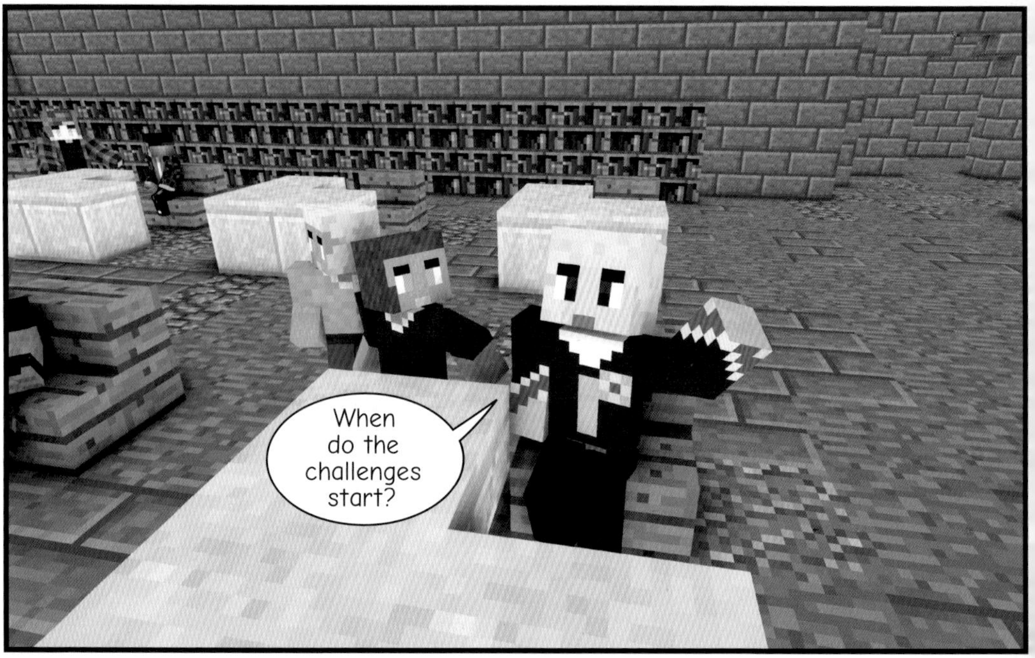
When do the challenges start?

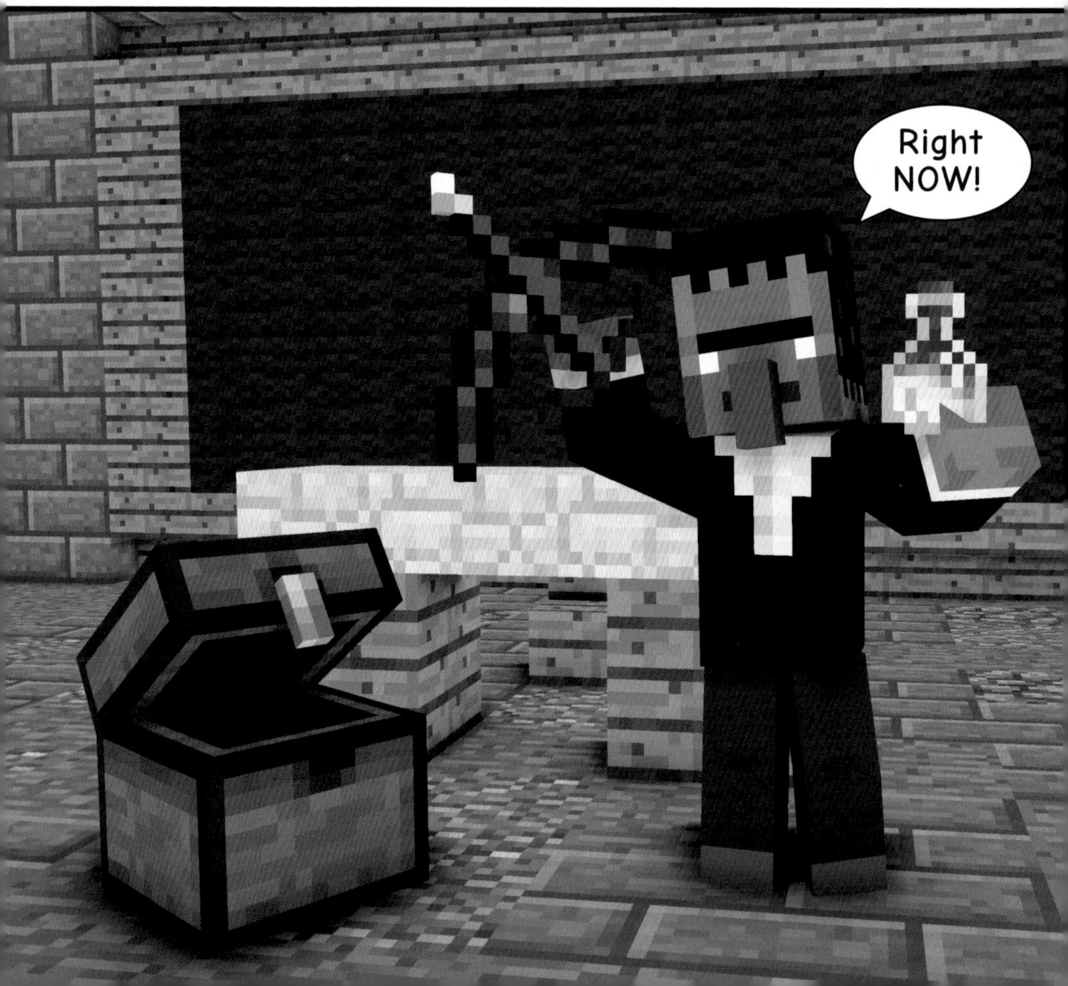
Right NOW!

CHAPTER 4

CHALLENGE ACCEPTED

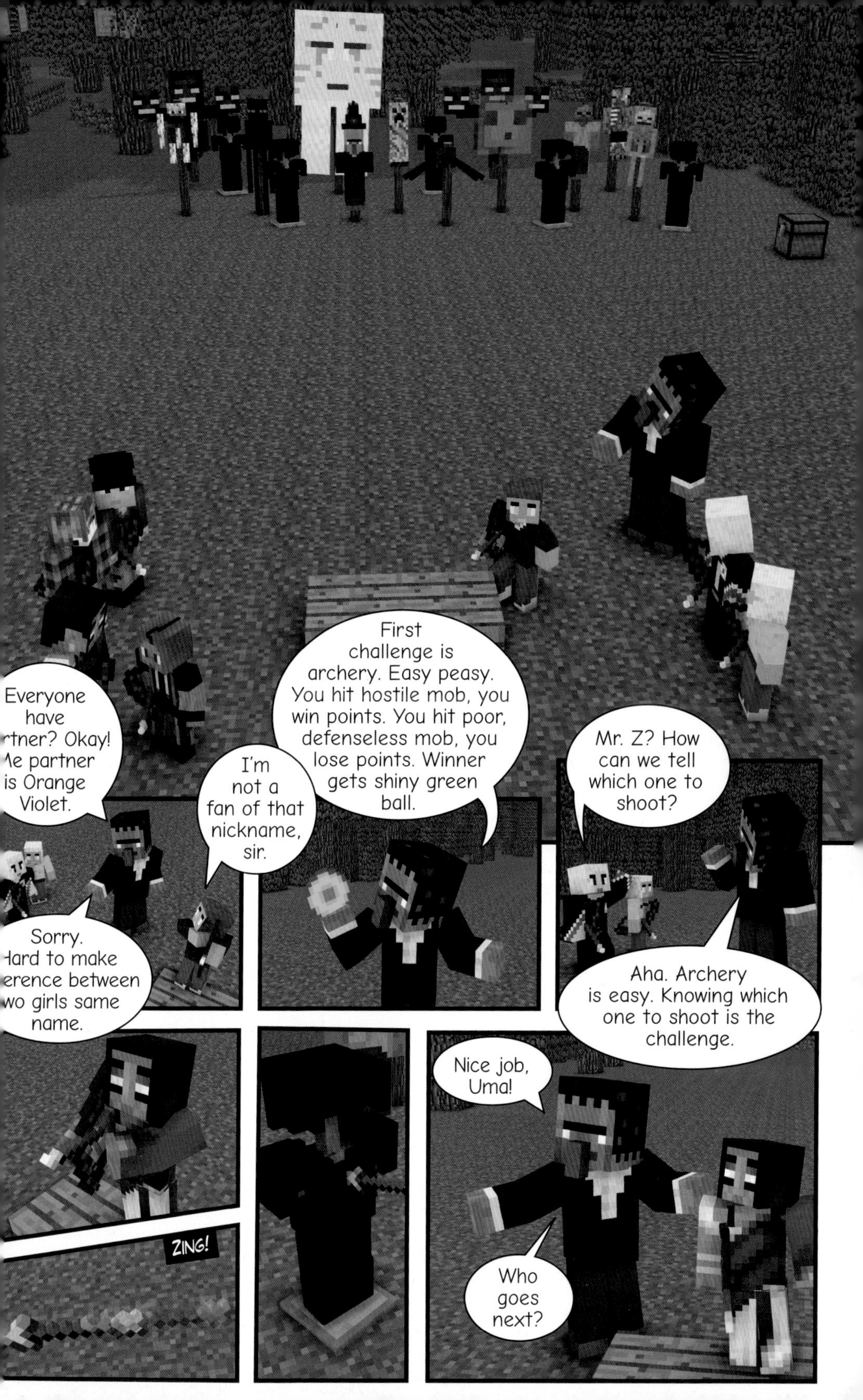

Everyone have ·rtner? Okay! Ae partner is Orange Violet.
I'm not a fan of that nickname, sir.
First challenge is archery. Easy peasy. You hit hostile mob, you win points. You hit poor, defenseless mob, you lose points. Winner gets shiny green ball.
Mr. Z? How can we tell which one to shoot?
Sorry. Hard to make erence between wo girls same name.
Aha. Archery is easy. Knowing which one to shoot is the challenge.
Nice job, Uma!
ZING!
Who goes next?

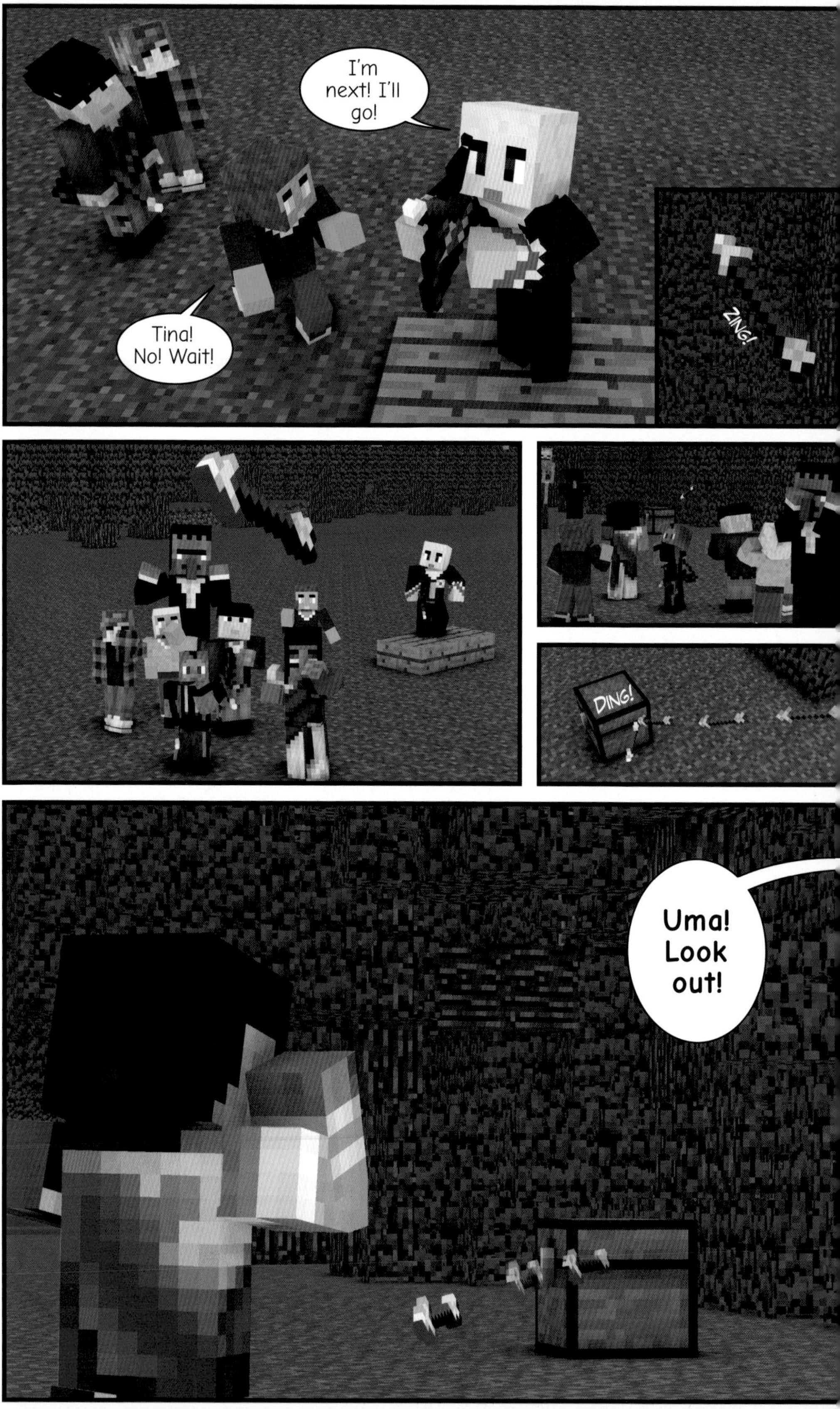
I'm next! I'll go!
Tina! No! Wait!
ZING!
DING!
Uma! Look out!

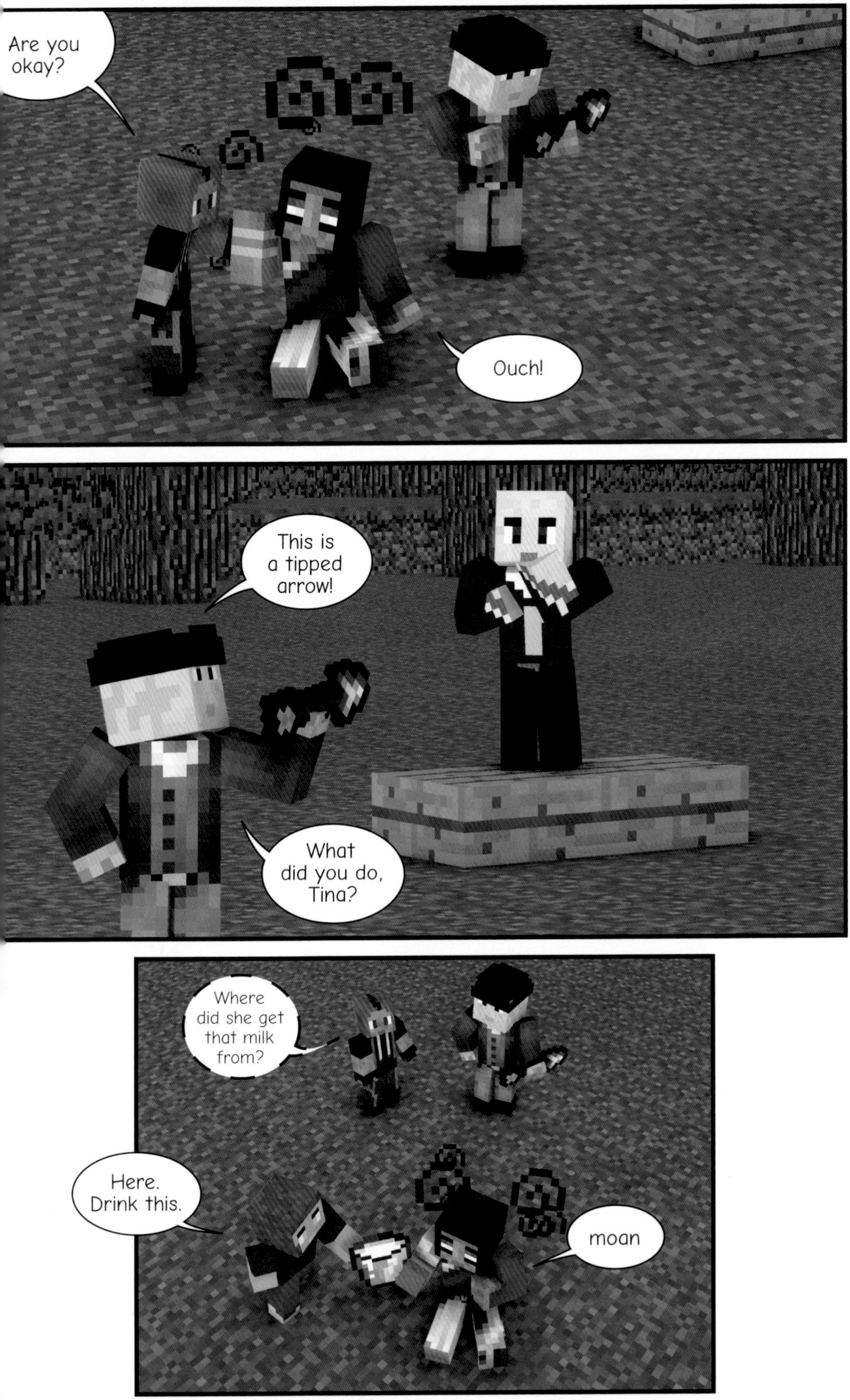
Are you okay?
Ouch!
This is a tipped arrow!
What did you do, Tina?
Where did she get that milk from?
Here. Drink this.
moan

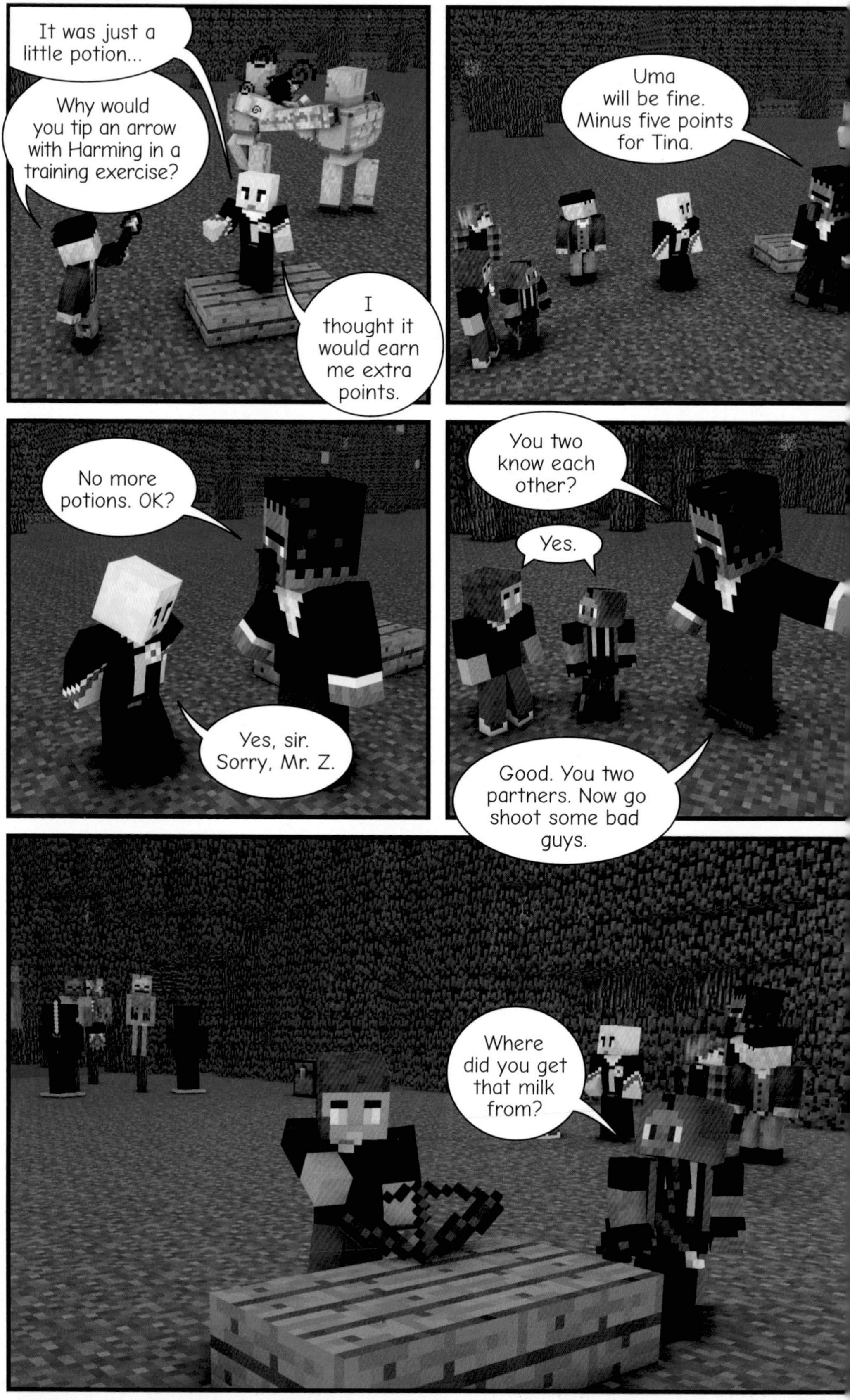
It was just a little potion...
Why would you tip an arrow with Harming in a training exercise?
I thought it would earn me extra points.
Uma will be fine. Minus five points for Tina.
No more potions. OK?
Yes, sir. Sorry, Mr. Z.
You two know each other?
Yes.
Good. You two partners. Now go shoot some bad guys.
Where did you get that milk from?

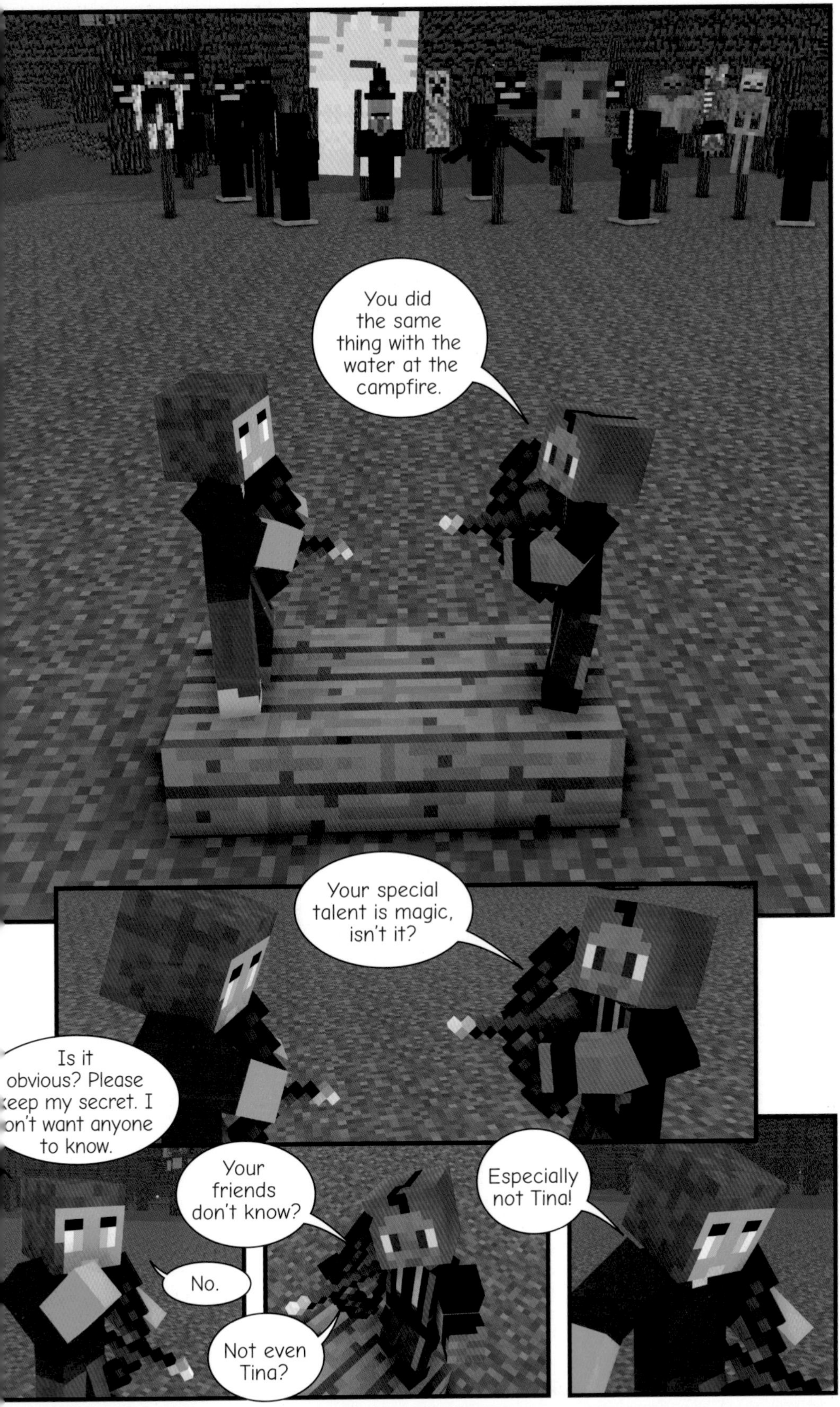
You did the same thing with the water at the campfire.
Your special talent is magic, isn't it?
Is it obvious? Please keep my secret. I don't want anyone to know.
Your friends don't know?
No.
Not even Tina?
Especially not Tina!

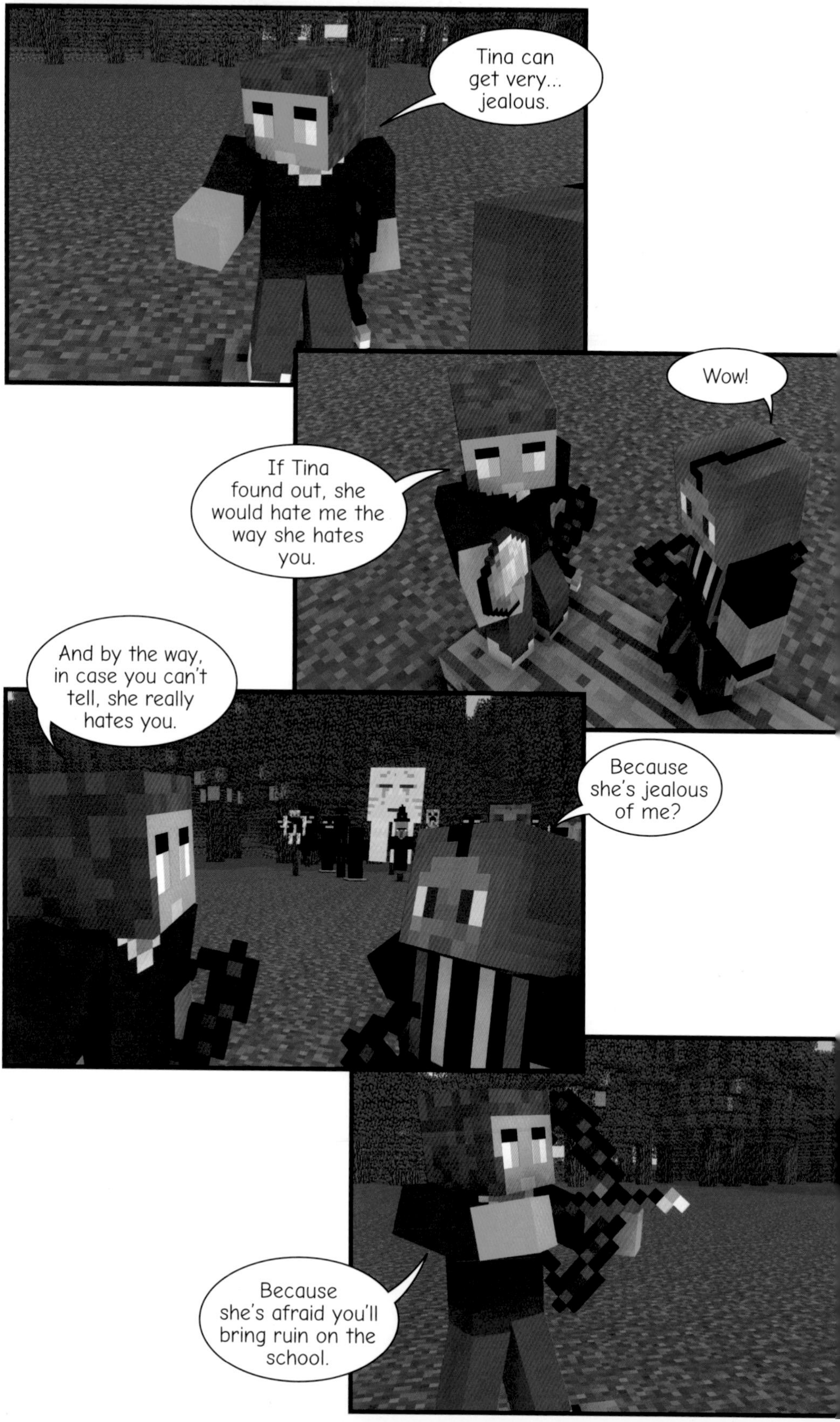
Tina can get very... jealous.
Wow!
If Tina found out, she would hate me the way she hates you.
And by the way, in case you can't tell, she really hates you.
Because she's jealous of me?
Because she's afraid you'll bring ruin on the school.

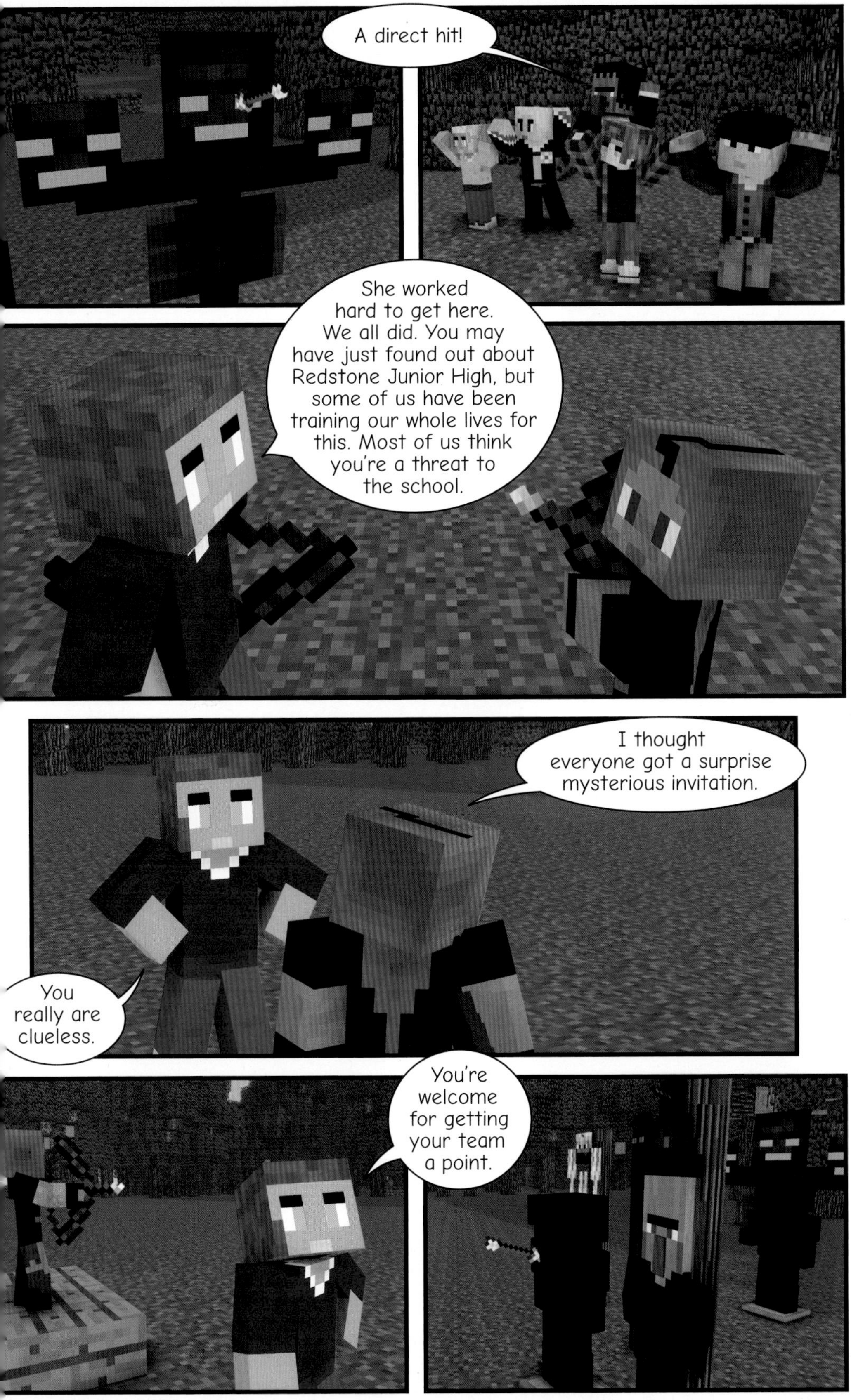
A direct hit!
She worked hard to get here. We all did. You may have just found out about Redstone Junior High, but some of us have been training our whole lives for this. Most of us think you're a threat to the school.
I thought everyone got a surprise mysterious invitation.
You really are clueless.
You're welcome for getting your team a point.

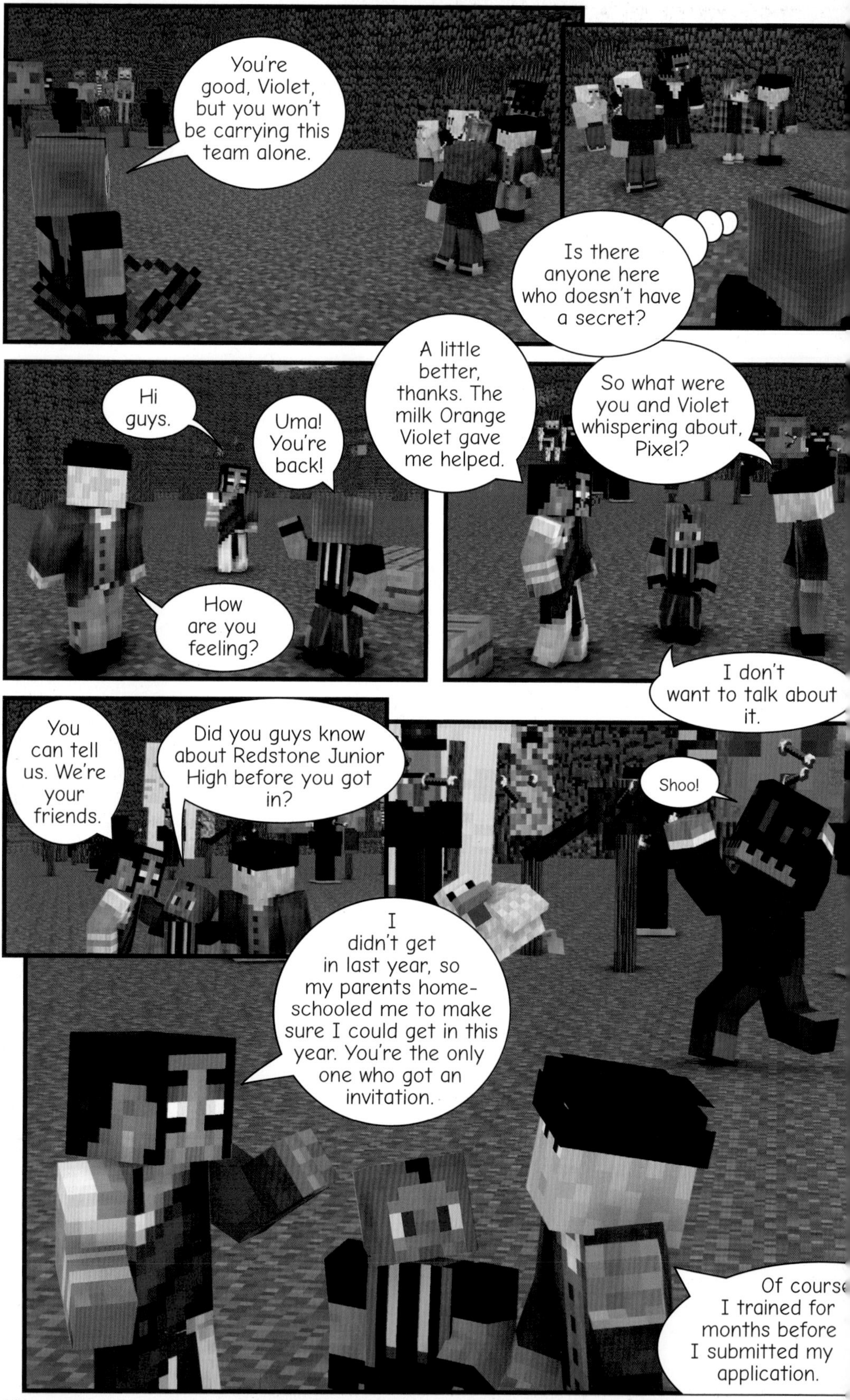
You're good, Violet, but you won't be carrying this team alone.
Is there anyone here who doesn't have a secret?
Hi guys.
Uma! You're back!
How are you feeling?
A little better, thanks. The milk Orange Violet gave me helped.
So what were you and Violet whispering about, Pixel?
I don't want to talk about it.
You can tell us. We're your friends.
Did you guys know about Redstone Junior High before you got in?
Shoo!
I didn't get in last year, so my parents home-schooled me to make sure I could get in this year. You're the only one who got an invitation.
Of course I trained for months before I submitted my application.

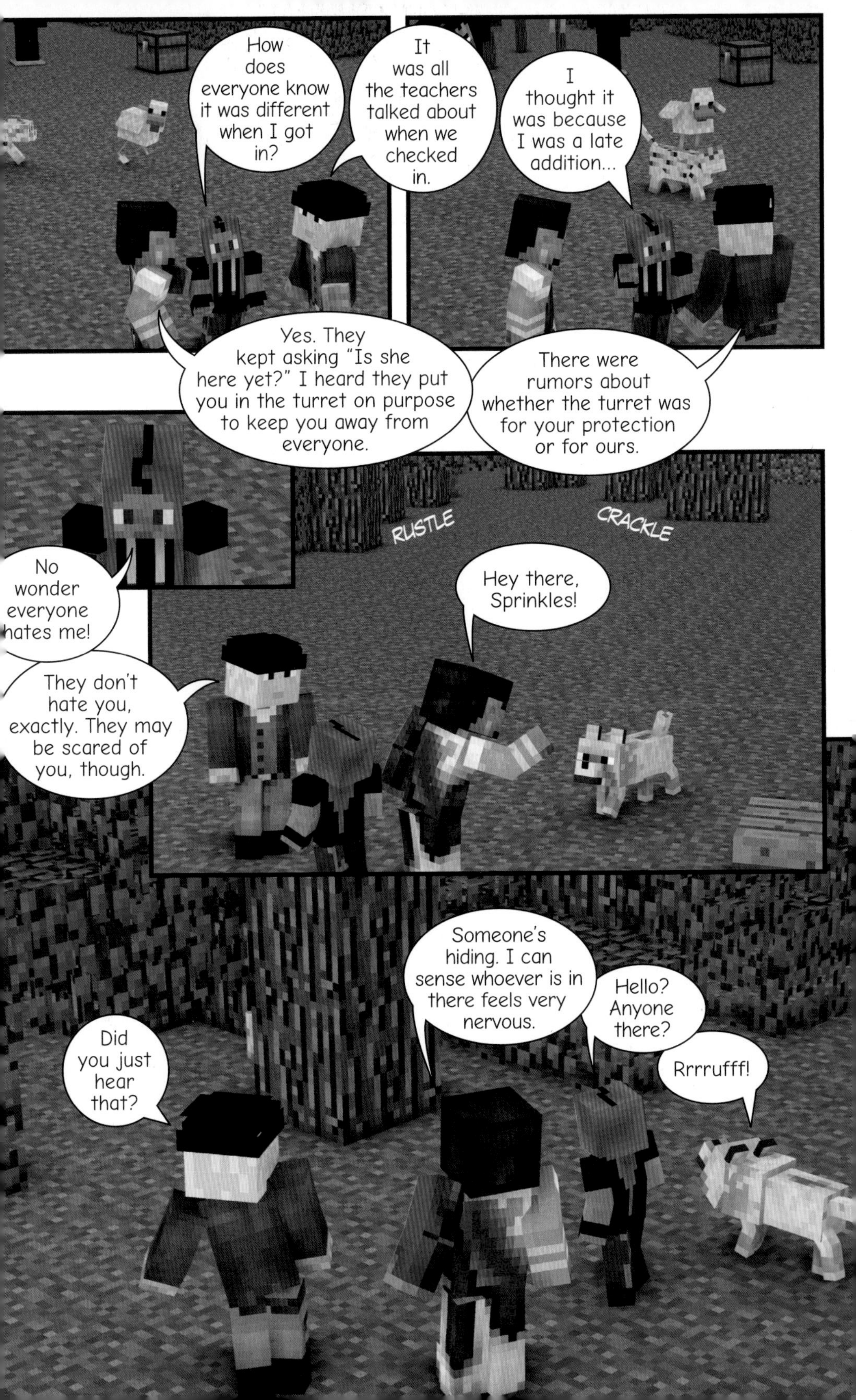
How does everyone know it was different when I got in?
It was all the teachers talked about when we checked in.
Yes. They kept asking "Is she here yet?" I heard they put you in the turret on purpose to keep you away from everyone.
I thought it was because I was a late addition...
There were rumors about whether the turret was for your protection or for ours.
No wonder everyone hates me!
They don't hate you, exactly. They may be scared of you, though.
RUSTLE
CRACKLE
Hey there, Sprinkles!
Did you just hear that?
Someone's hiding. I can sense whoever is in there feels very nervous.
Hello? Anyone there?
Rrrrufff!

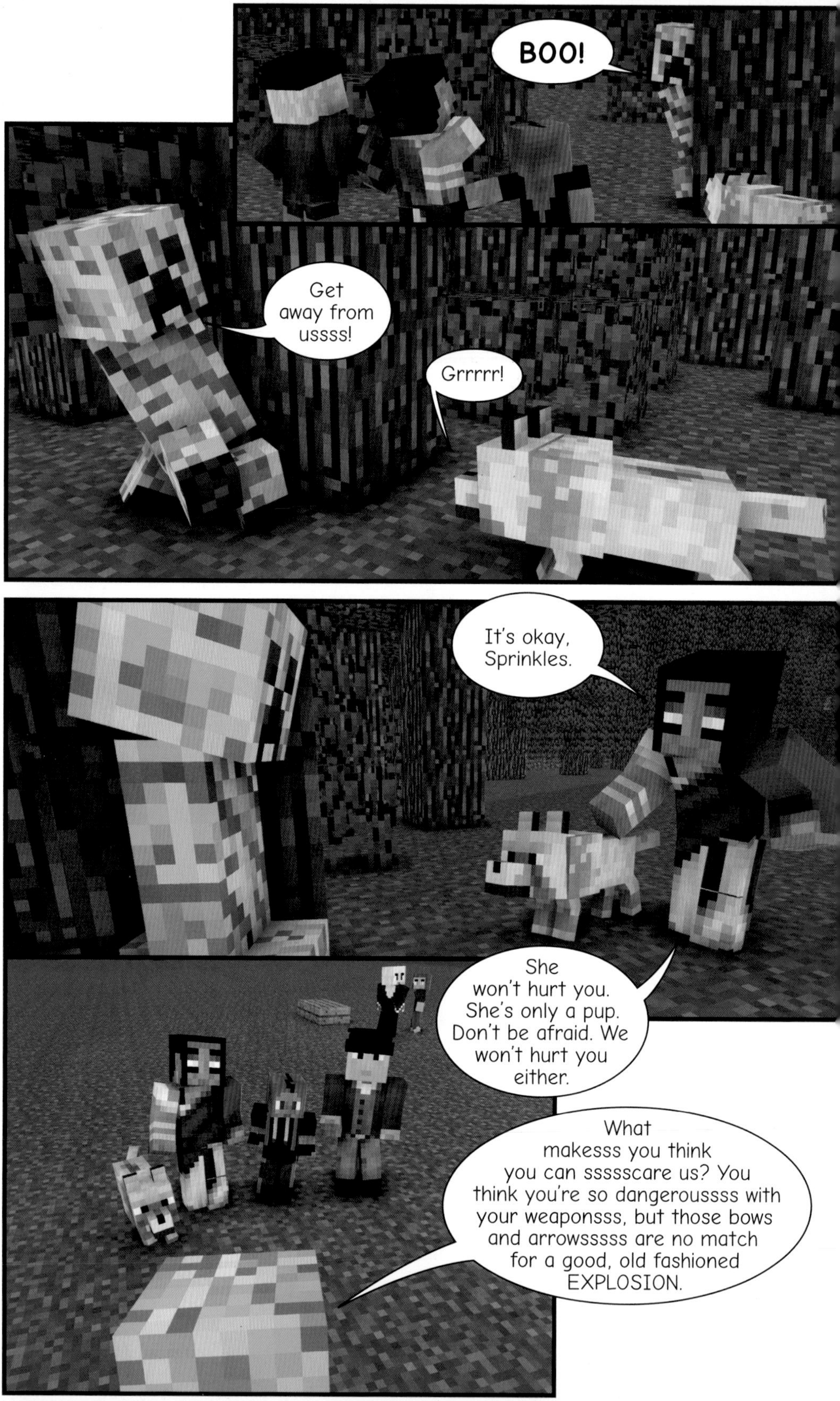
BOO!
Get away from ussss!
Grrrrr!
It's okay, Sprinkles.
She won't hurt you. She's only a pup. Don't be afraid. We won't hurt you either.
What makesss you think you can sssscare us? You think you're so dangeroussss with your weaponsss, but those bows and arrowsssss are no match for a good, old fashioned EXPLOSION.

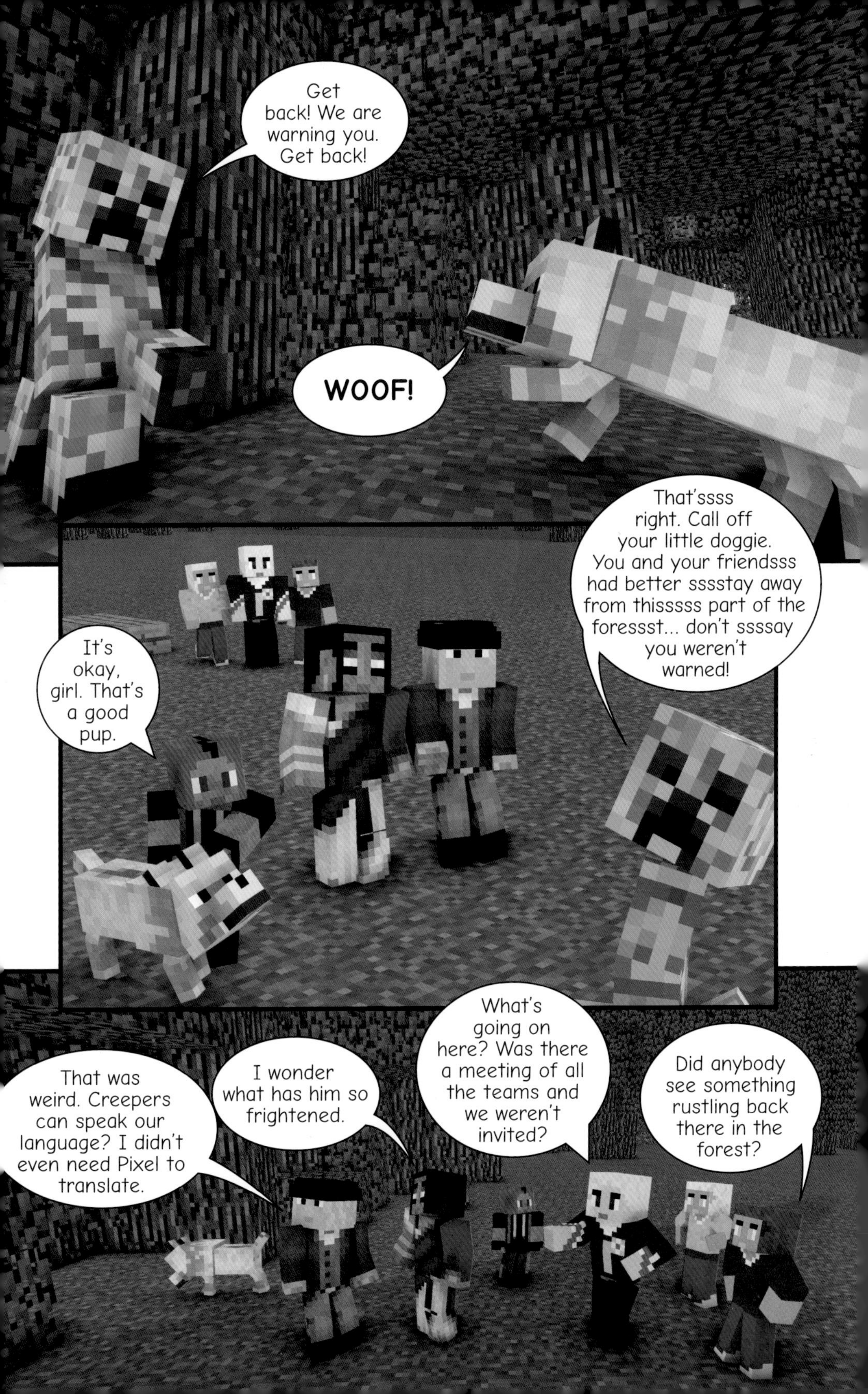
Get back! We are warning you. Get back!
WOOF!
It's okay, girl. That's a good pup.
That'ssss right. Call off your little doggie. You and your friendsss had better sssstay away from thissss part of the foressst... don't ssssay you weren't warned!
That was weird. Creepers can speak our language? I didn't even need Pixel to translate.
I wonder what has him so frightened.
What's going on here? Was there a meeting of all the teams and we weren't invited?
Did anybody see something rustling back there in the forest?

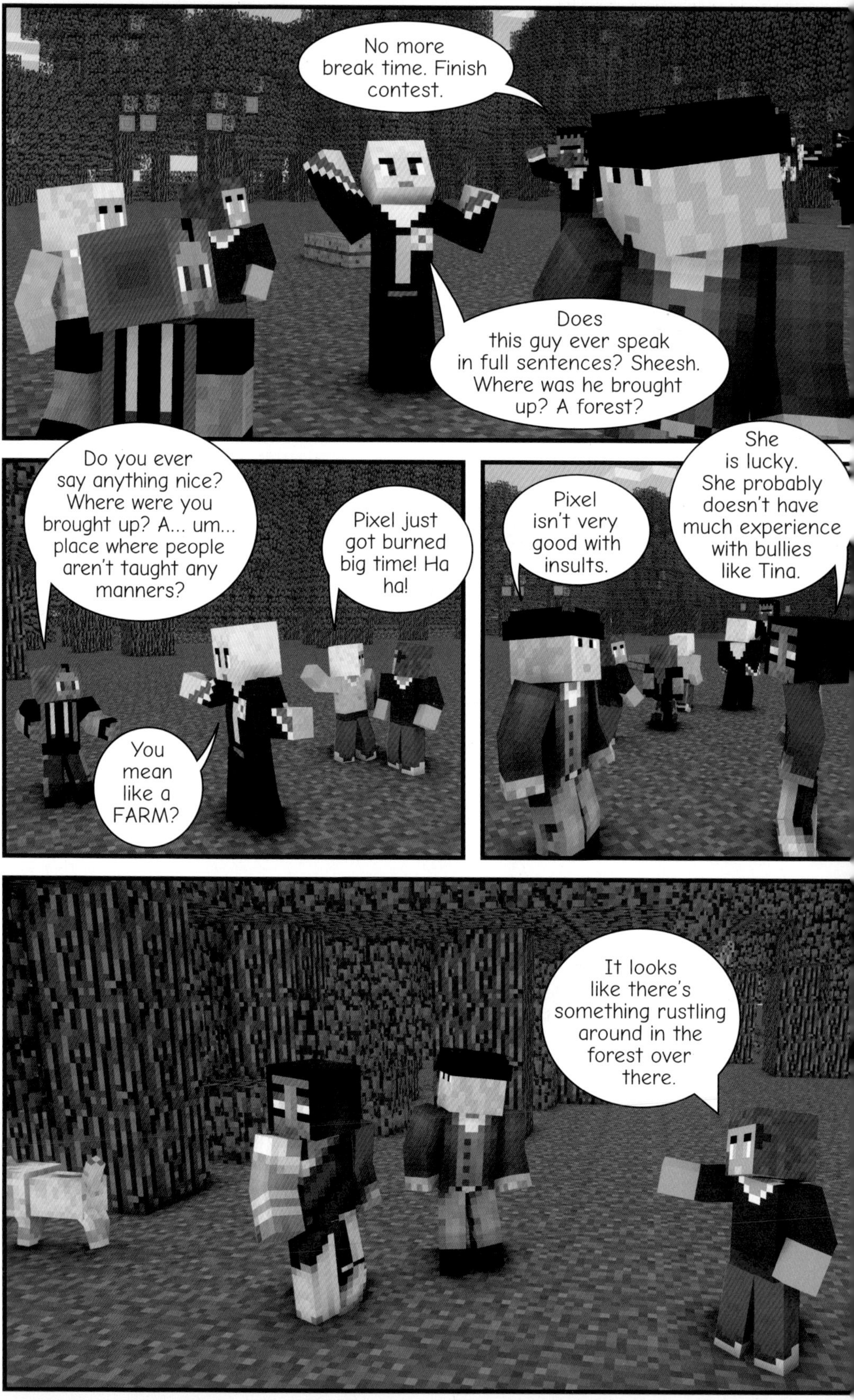
No more break time. Finish contest.
Does this guy ever speak in full sentences? Sheesh. Where was he brought up? A forest?
Do you ever say anything nice? Where were you brought up? A... um... place where people aren't taught any manners?
Pixel just got burned big time! Ha ha!
You mean like a FARM?
Pixel isn't very good with insults.
She is lucky. She probably doesn't have much experience with bullies like Tina.
It looks like there's something rustling around in the forest over there.

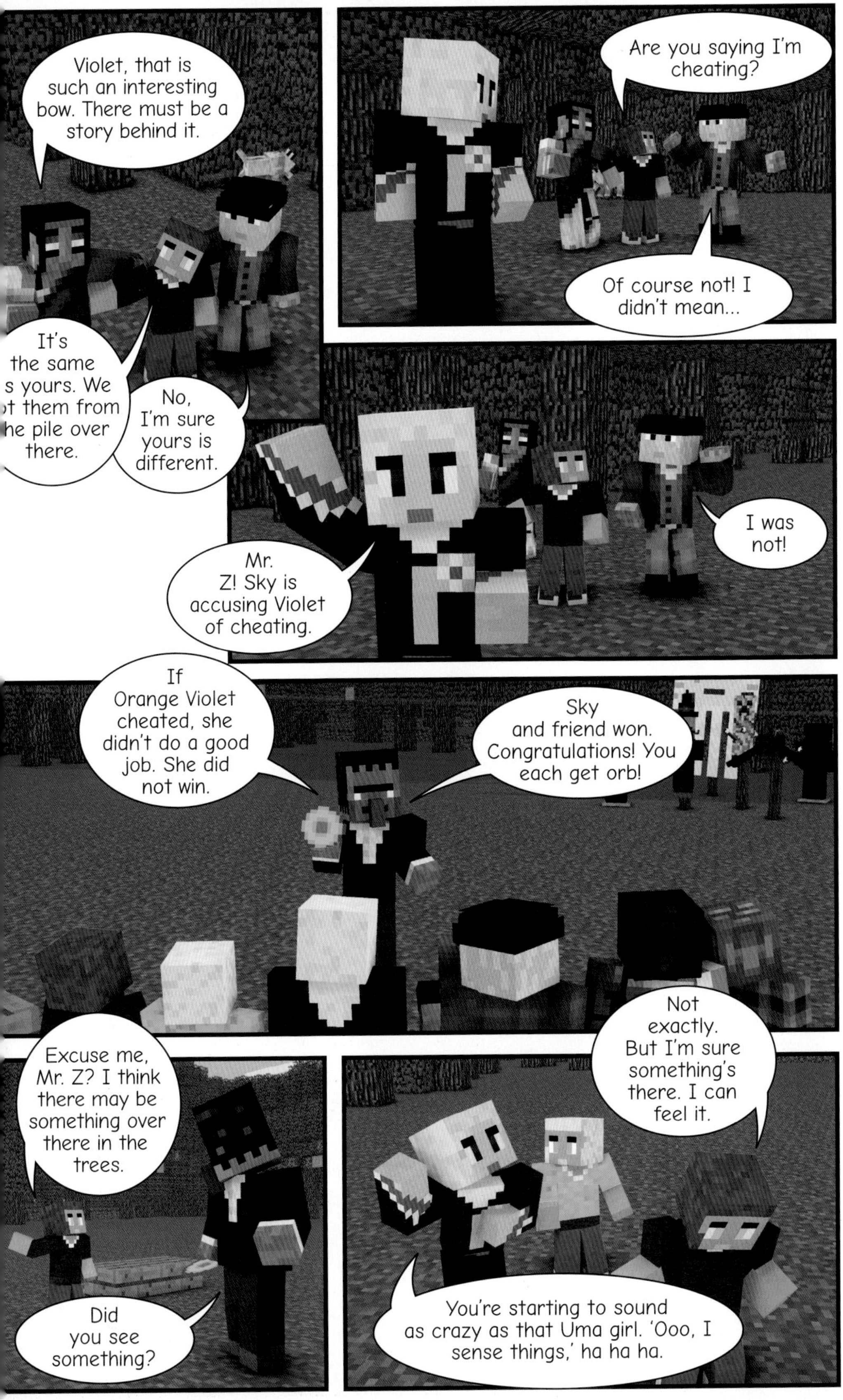

Violet, that is such an interesting bow. There must be a story behind it.
It's the same s yours. We ot them from he pile over there.
No, I'm sure yours is different.
Are you saying I'm cheating?
Of course not! I didn't mean...
Mr. Z! Sky is accusing Violet of cheating.
I was not!
If Orange Violet cheated, she didn't do a good job. She did not win.
Sky and friend won. Congratulations! You each get orb!
Excuse me, Mr. Z? I think there may be something over there in the trees.
Did you see something?
Not exactly. But I'm sure something's there. I can feel it.
You're starting to sound as crazy as that Uma girl. 'Ooo, I sense things,' ha ha ha.

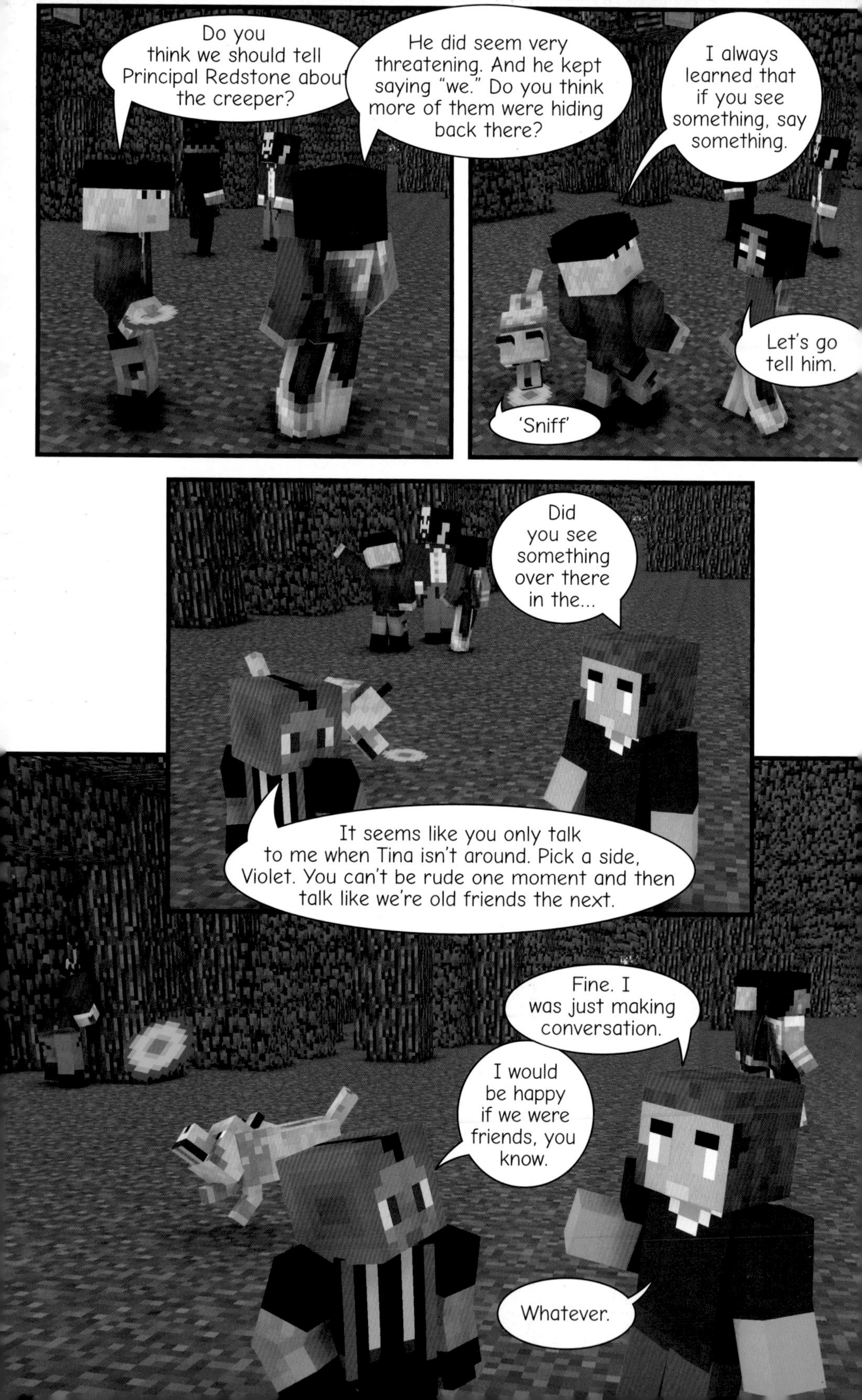

Do you think we should tell Principal Redstone about the creeper?
He did seem very threatening. And he kept saying "we." Do you think more of them were hiding back there?
I always learned that if you see something, say something.
Let's go tell him.
'Sniff'
Did you see something over there in the...
It seems like you only talk to me when Tina isn't around. Pick a side, Violet. You can't be rude one moment and then talk like we're old friends the next.
Fine. I was just making conversation.
I would be happy if we were friends, you know.
Whatever.

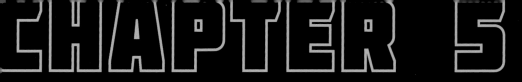

CHAPTER 5

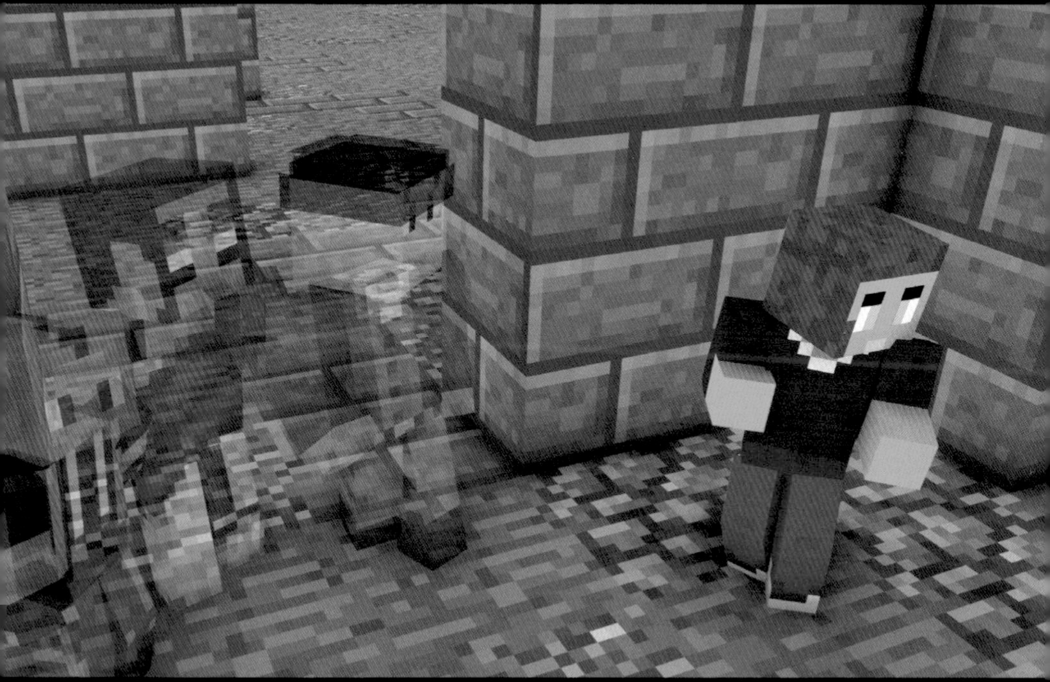

SECRETS

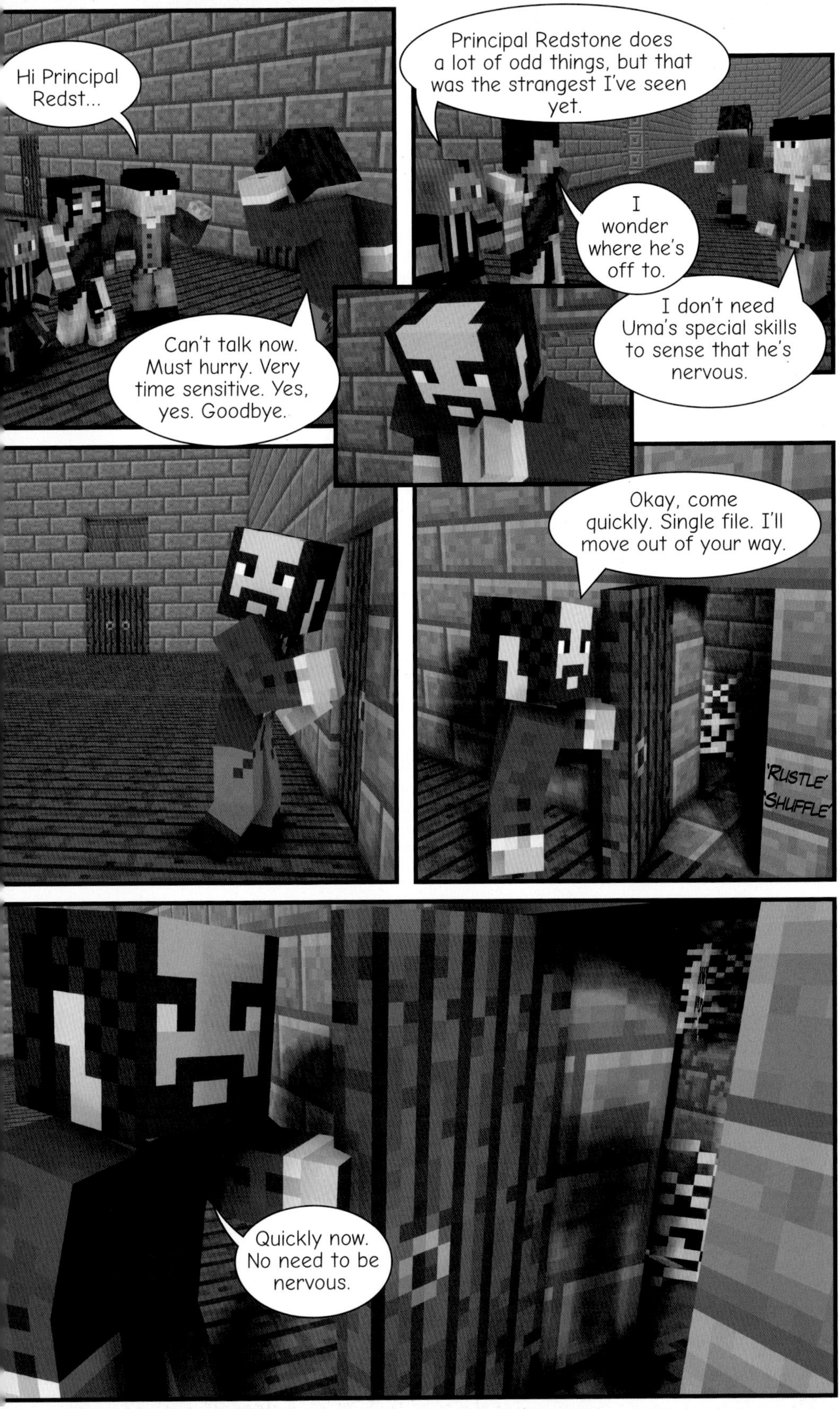
Hi Principal Redst...
Can't talk now. Must hurry. Very time sensitive. Yes, yes. Goodbye.
Principal Redstone does a lot of odd things, but that was the strangest I've seen yet.
I wonder where he's off to.
I don't need Uma's special skills to sense that he's nervous.
Okay, come quickly. Single file. I'll move out of your way.
'Rustle'
'Shuffle'
Quickly now. No need to be nervous.

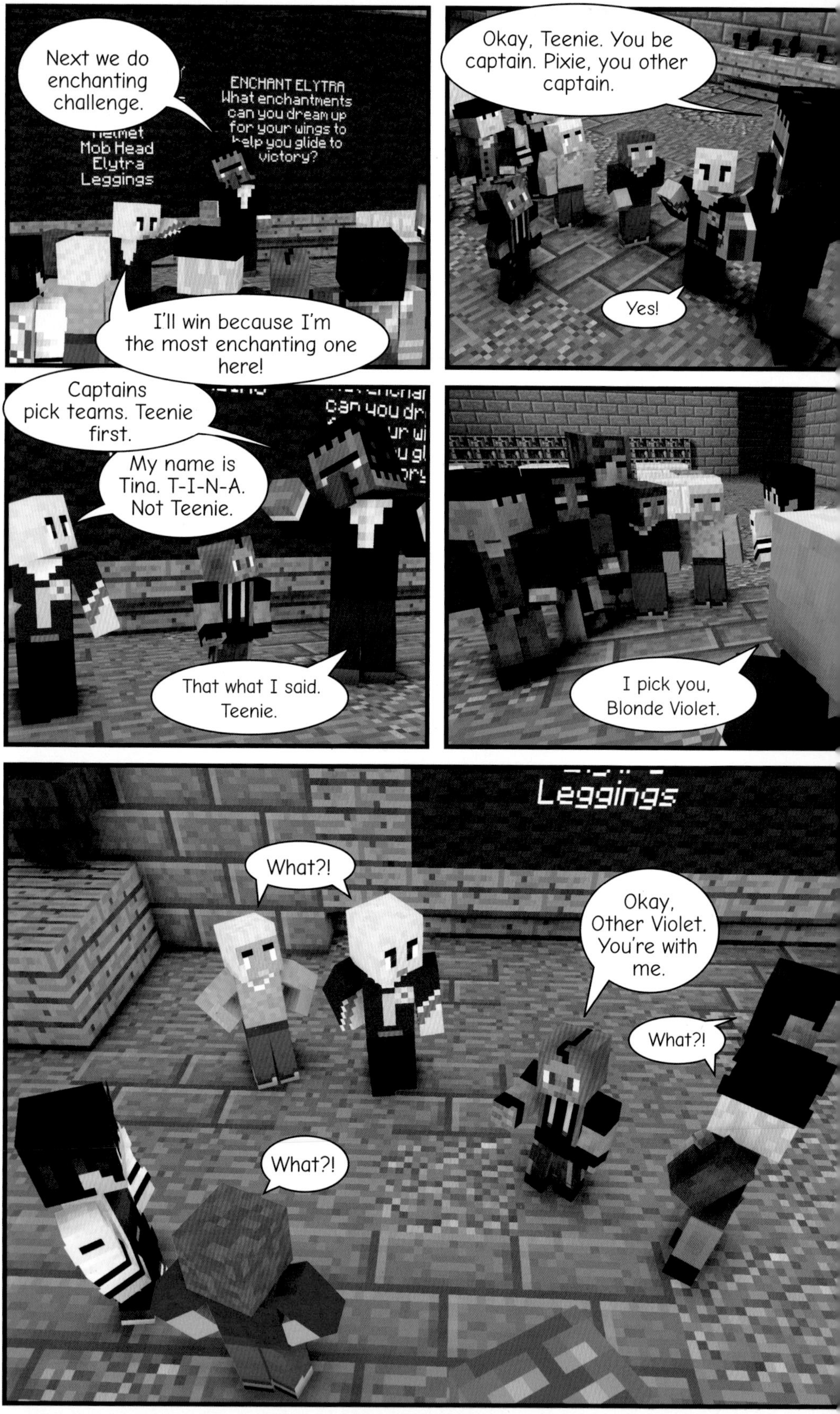
Next we do enchanting challenge.
ENCHANT ELYTRA
What enchantments can you dream up for your wings to
victory?
Mob Head
Elytra
Leggings
I'll win because I'm the most enchanting one here!
Okay, Teenie. You be captain. Pixie, you other captain.
Yes!
Captains pick teams. Teenie first.
My name is Tina. T-I-N-A. Not Teenie.
That what I said. Teenie.
I pick you, Blonde Violet.
Leggings
What?!
Okay, Other Violet. You're with me.
What?!
What?!

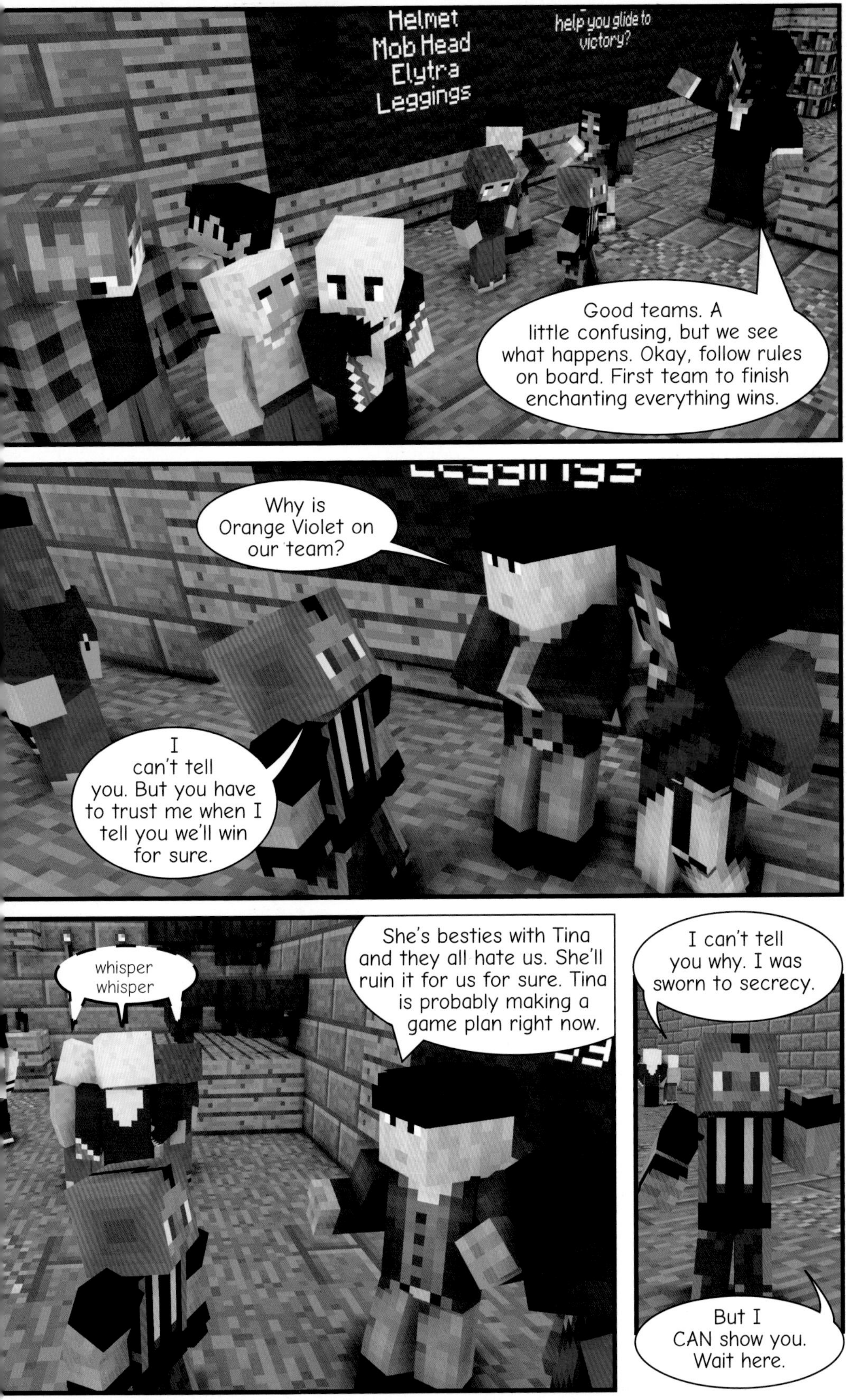
Helmet
Mob Head
Elytra
Leggings
help you glide to victory?
Good teams. A little confusing, but we see what happens. Okay, follow rules on board. First team to finish enchanting everything wins.
Why is Orange Violet on our team?
I can't tell you. But you have to trust me when I tell you we'll win for sure.
whisper whisper
She's besties with Tina and they all hate us. She'll ruin it for us for sure. Tina is probably making a game plan right now.
I can't tell you why. I was sworn to secrecy.
But I CAN show you. Wait here.

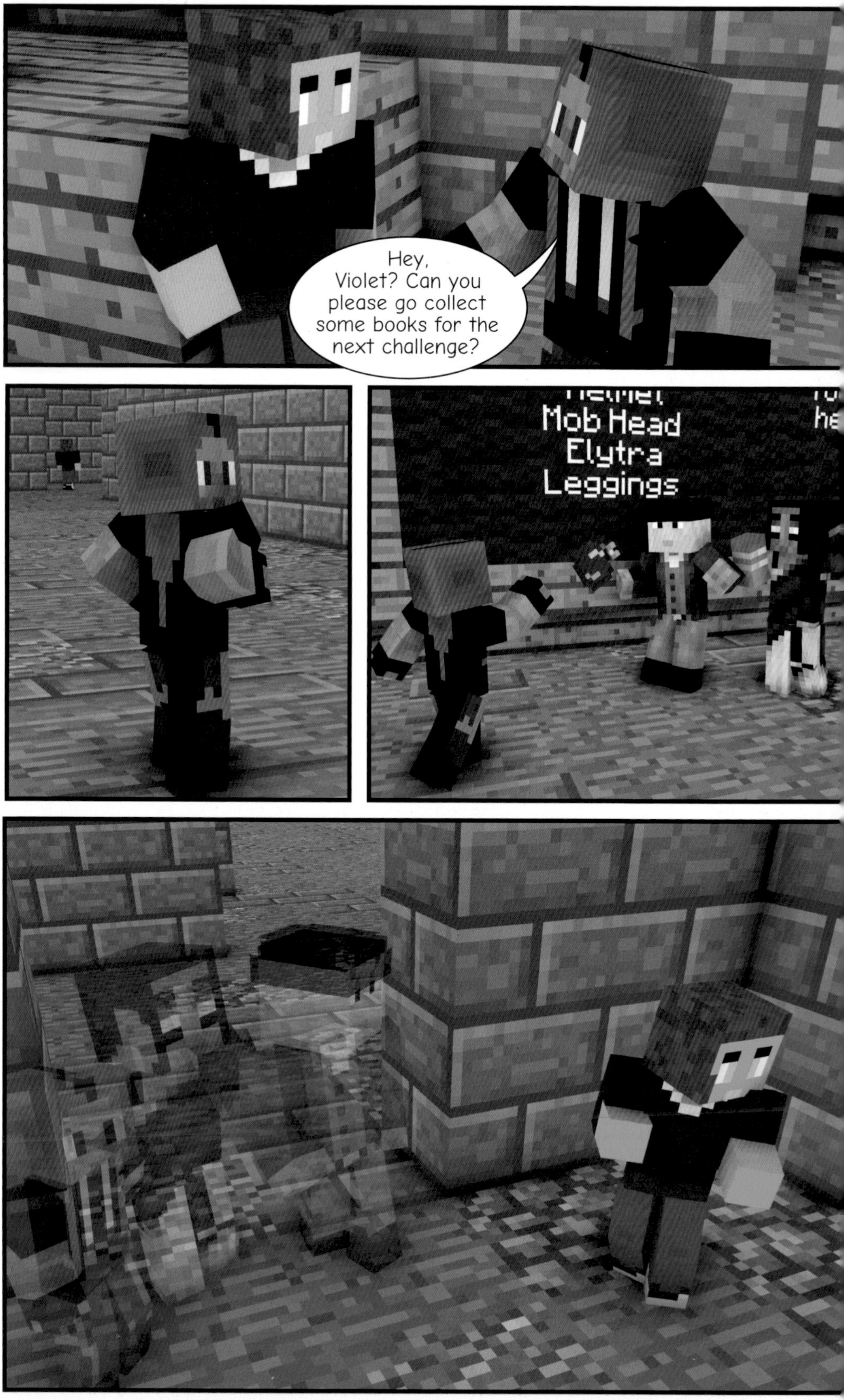
Hey, Violet? Can you please go collect some books for the next challenge?
Mob Head
Elytra
Leggings

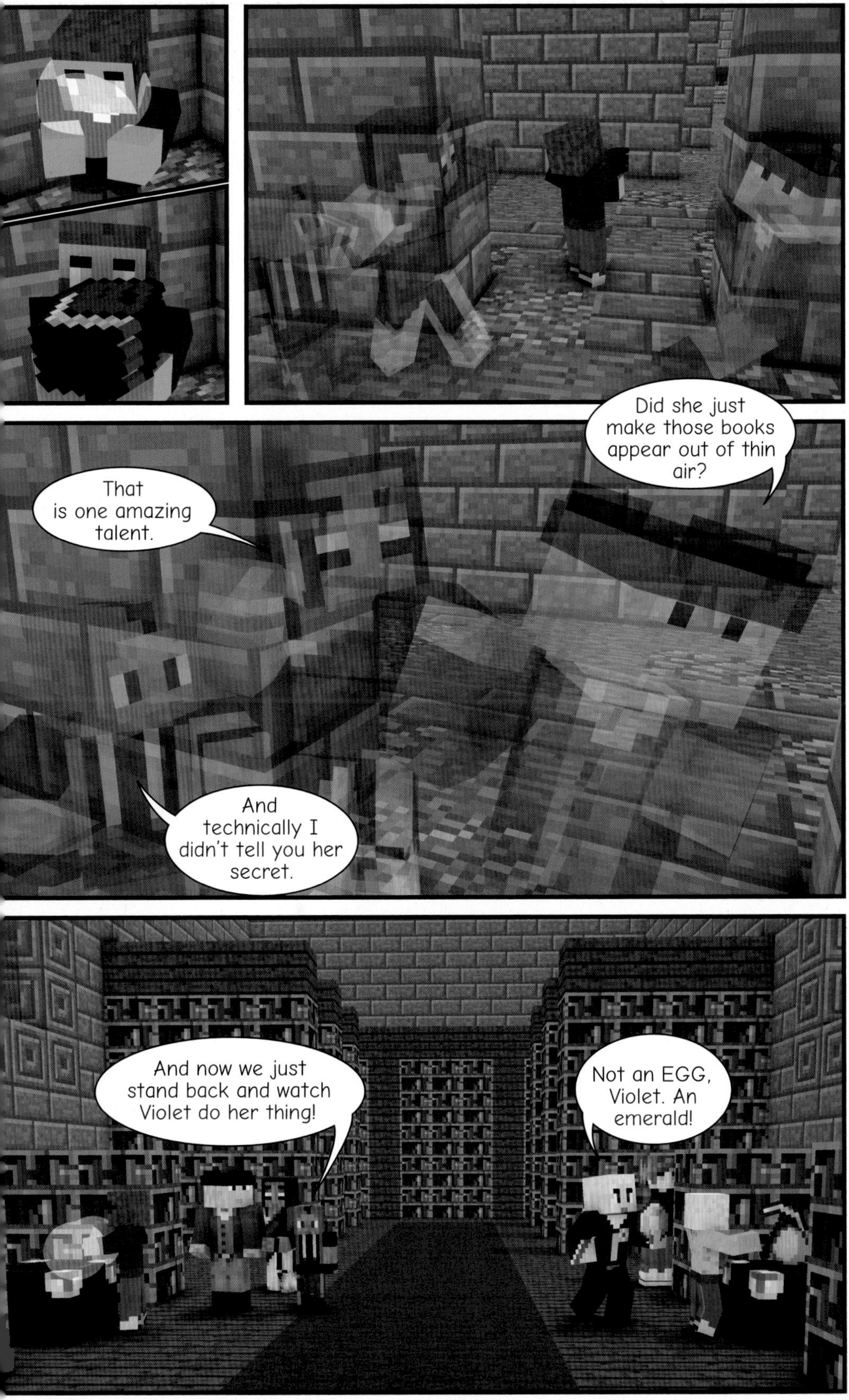
Did she just make those books appear out of thin air?
That is one amazing talent.
And technically I didn't tell you her secret.
And now we just stand back and watch Violet do her thing!
Not an EGG, Violet. An emerald!

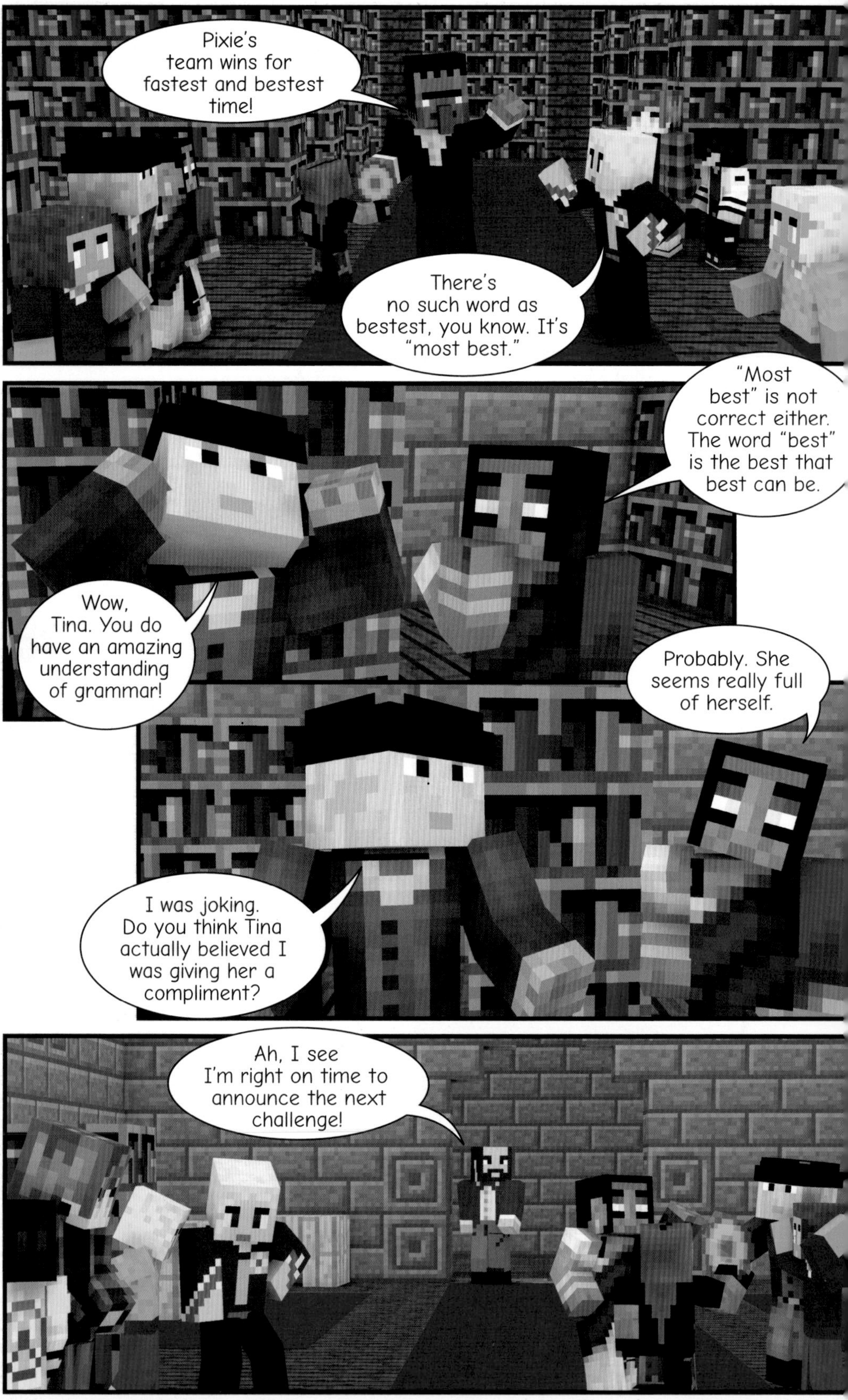
Pixie's team wins for fastest and bestest time!
There's no such word as bestest, you know. It's "most best."
"Most best" is not correct either. The word "best" is the best that best can be.
Wow, Tina. You do have an amazing understanding of grammar!
Probably. She seems really full of herself.
I was joking. Do you think Tina actually believed I was giving her a compliment?
Ah, I see I'm right on time to announce the next challenge!

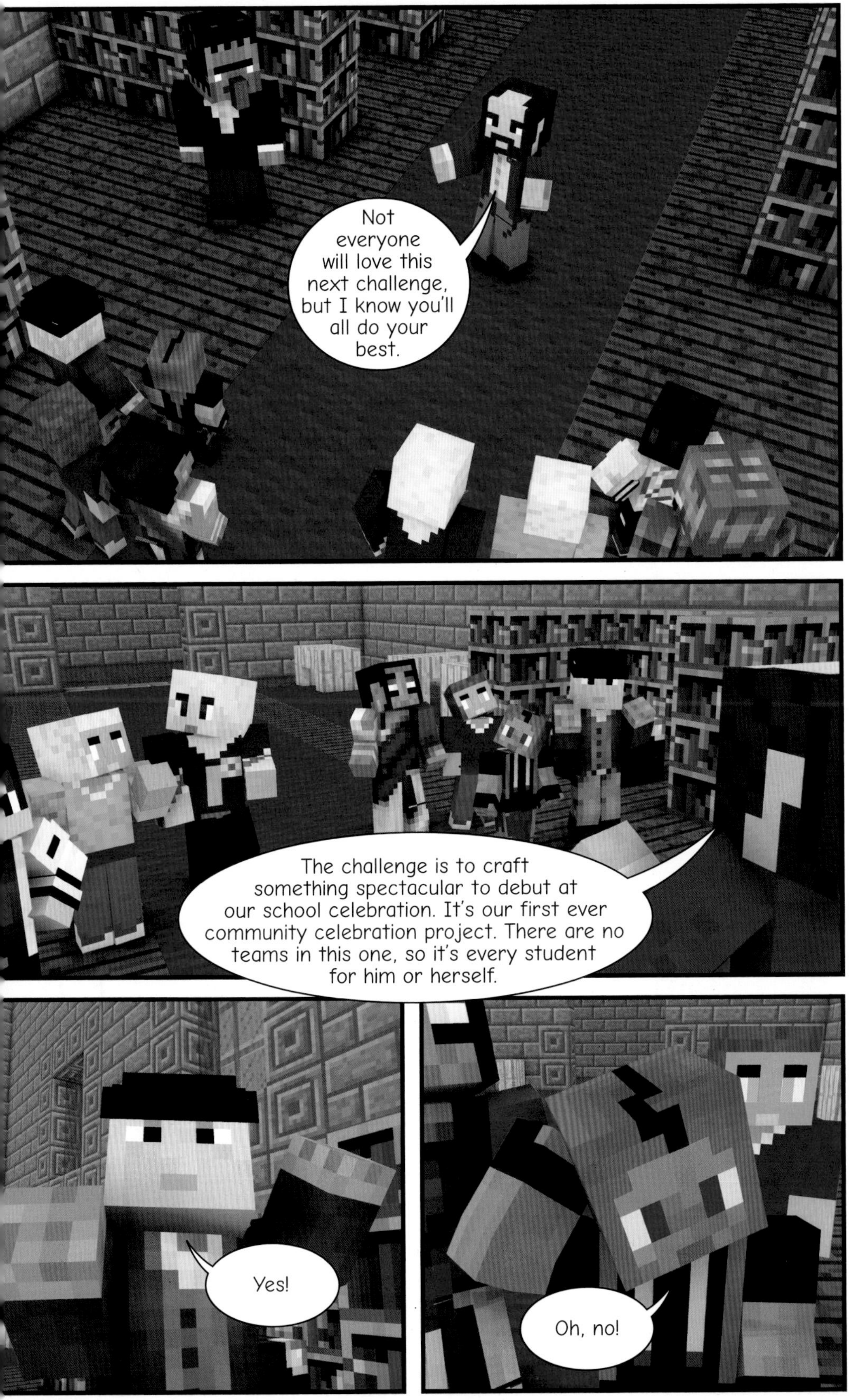
Not everyone will love this next challenge, but I know you'll all do your best.
The challenge is to craft something spectacular to debut at our school celebration. It's our first ever community celebration project. There are no teams in this one, so it's every student for him or herself.
Yes!
Oh, no!

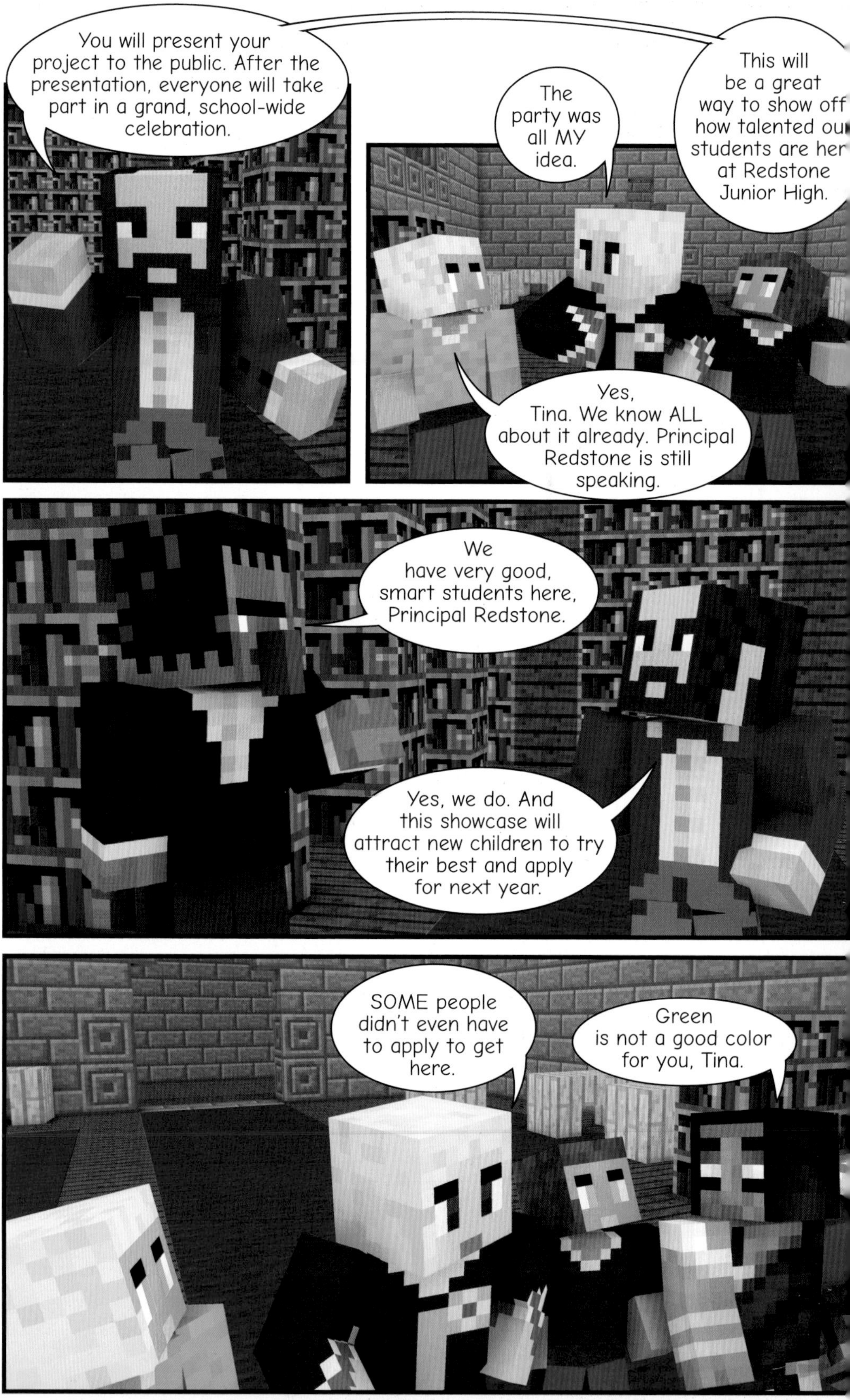
You will present your project to the public. After the presentation, everyone will take part in a grand, school-wide celebration.
This will be a great way to show off how talented ou students are her at Redstone Junior High.
The party was all MY idea.
Yes, Tina. We know ALL about it already. Principal Redstone is still speaking.
We have very good, smart students here, Principal Redstone.
Yes, we do. And this showcase will attract new children to try their best and apply for next year.
SOME people didn't even have to apply to get here.
Green is not a good color for you, Tina.

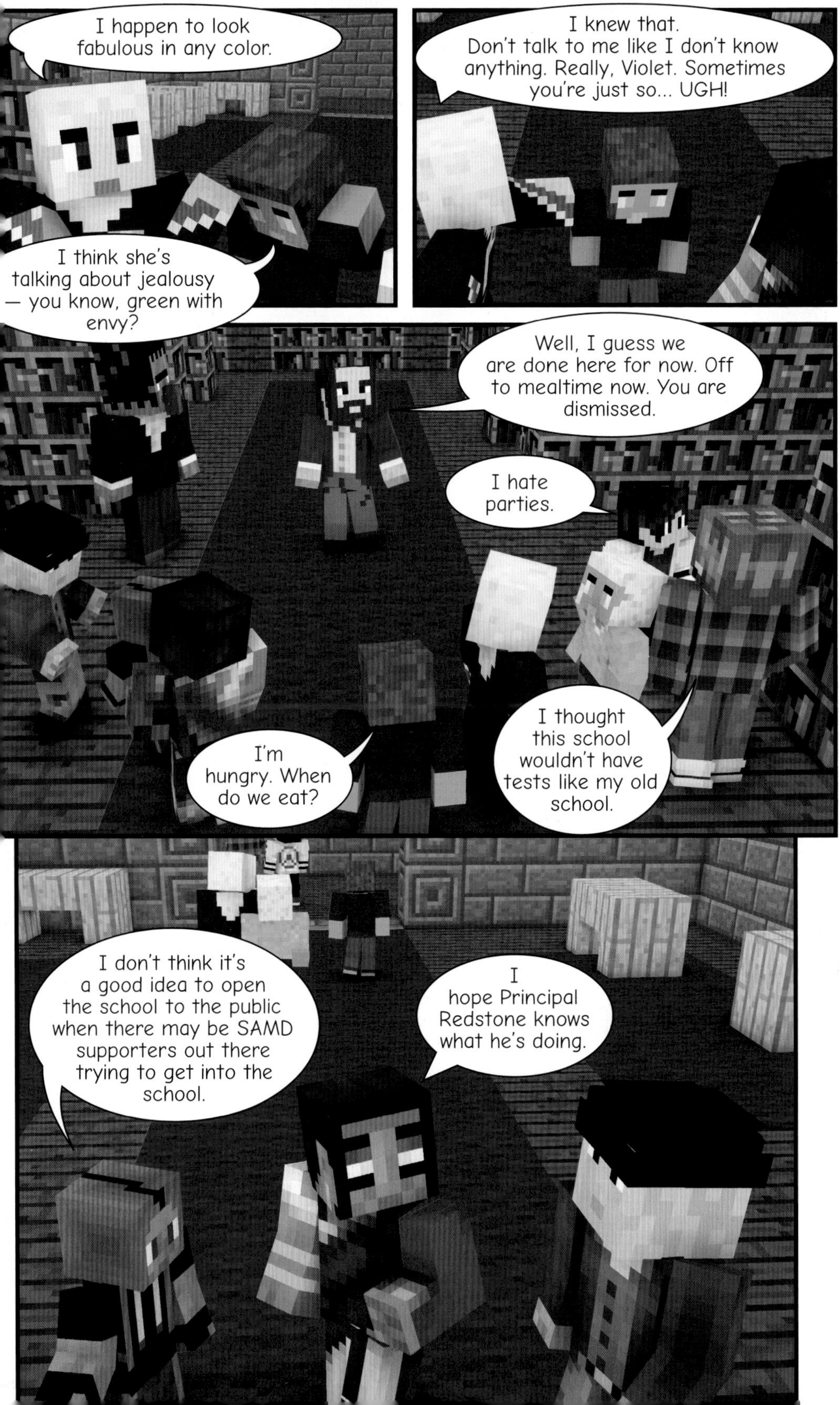
I happen to look fabulous in any color.
I think she's talking about jealousy — you know, green with envy?
I knew that. Don't talk to me like I don't know anything. Really, Violet. Sometimes you're just so... UGH!
Well, I guess we are done here for now. Off to mealtime now. You are dismissed.
I hate parties.
I'm hungry. When do we eat?
I thought this school wouldn't have tests like my old school.
I don't think it's a good idea to open the school to the public when there may be SAMD supporters out there trying to get into the school.
I hope Principal Redstone knows what he's doing.

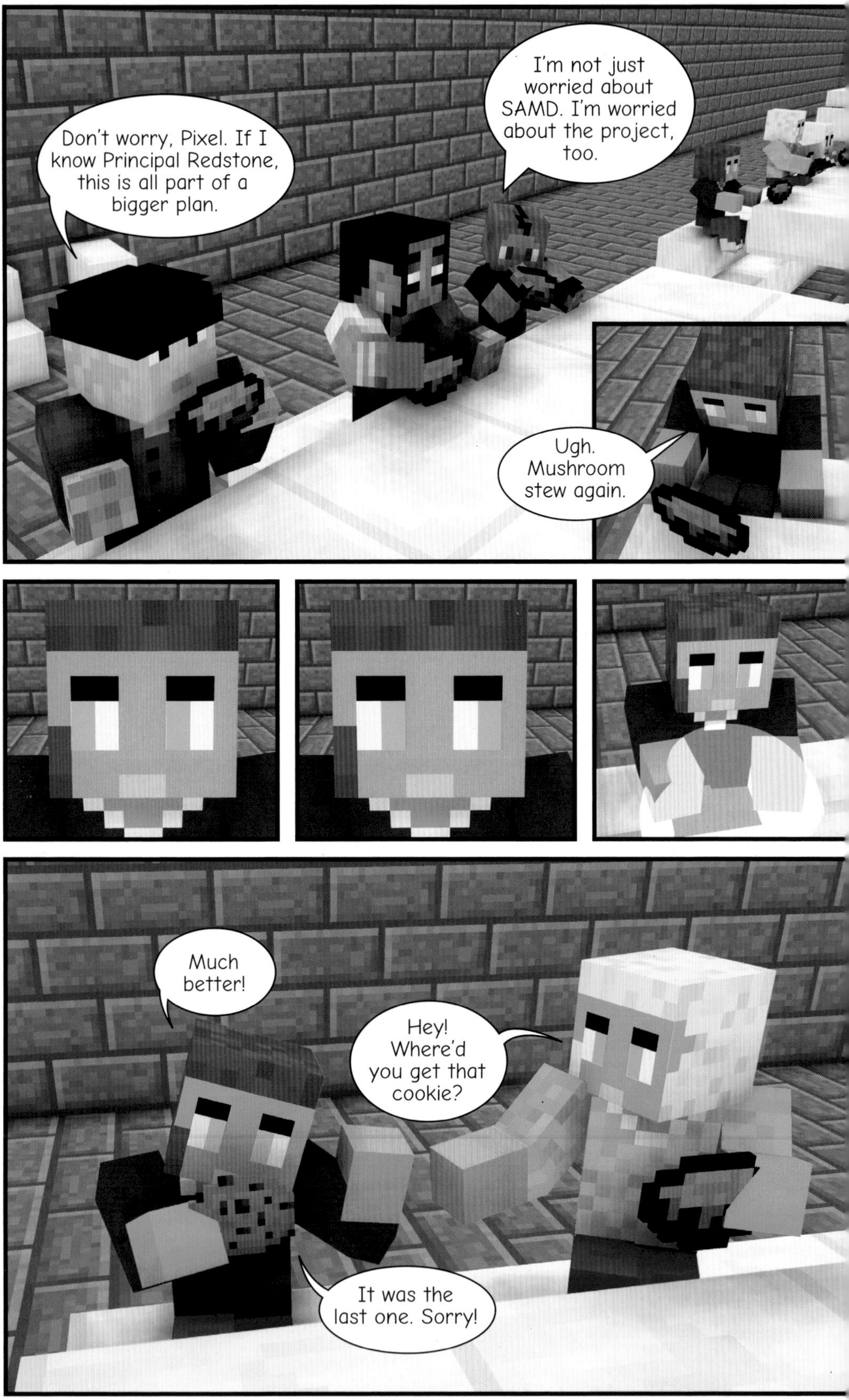
Don't worry, Pixel. If I know Principal Redstone, this is all part of a bigger plan.
I'm not just worried about SAMD. I'm worried about the project, too.
Ugh. Mushroom stew again.
Much better!
Hey! Where'd you get that cookie?
It was the last one. Sorry!

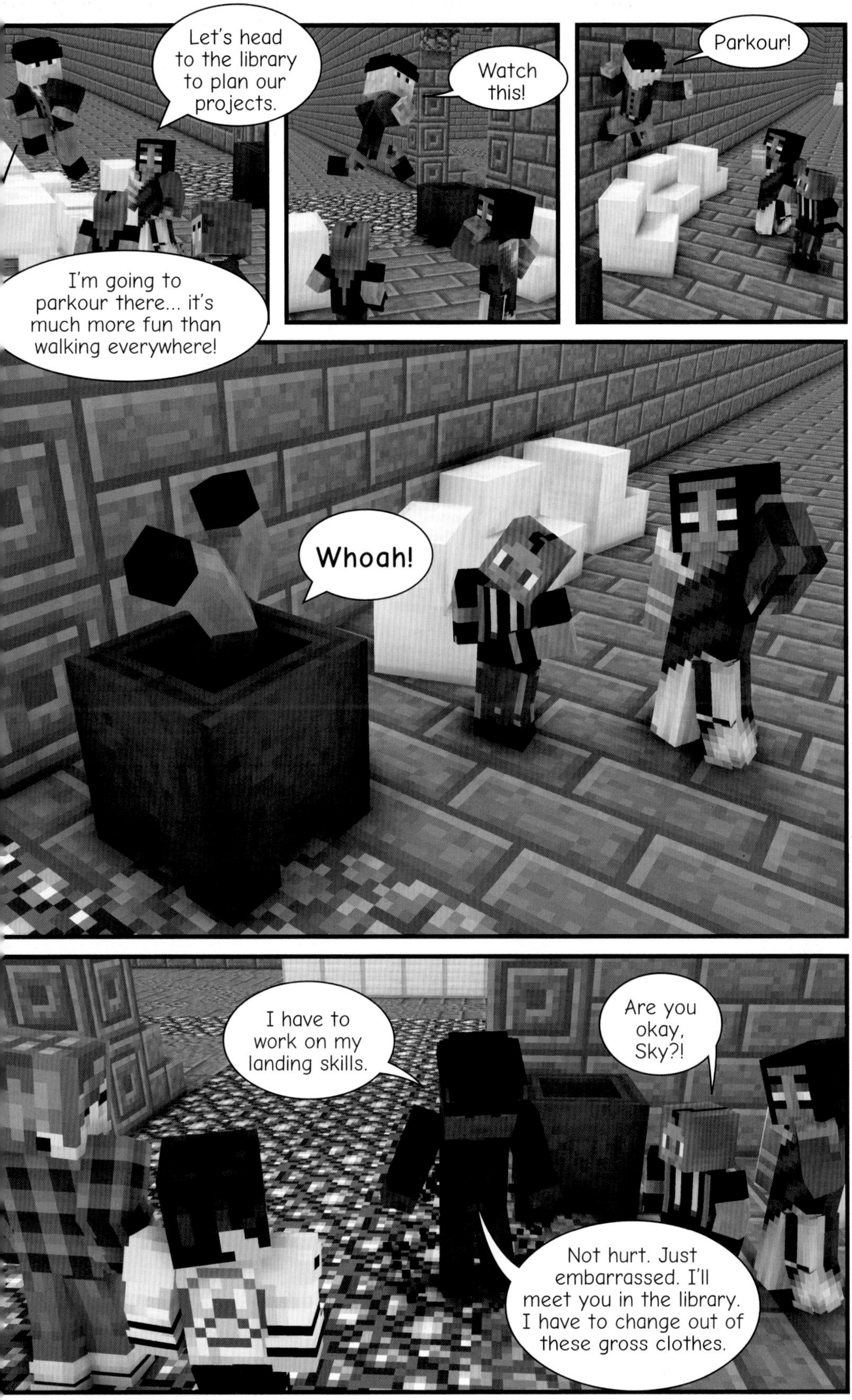
Let's head to the library to plan our projects.
I'm going to parkour there... it's much more fun than walking everywhere!
Watch this!
Parkour!
Whoah!
I have to work on my landing skills.
Are you okay, Sky?!
Not hurt. Just embarrassed. I'll meet you in the library. I have to change out of these gross clothes.

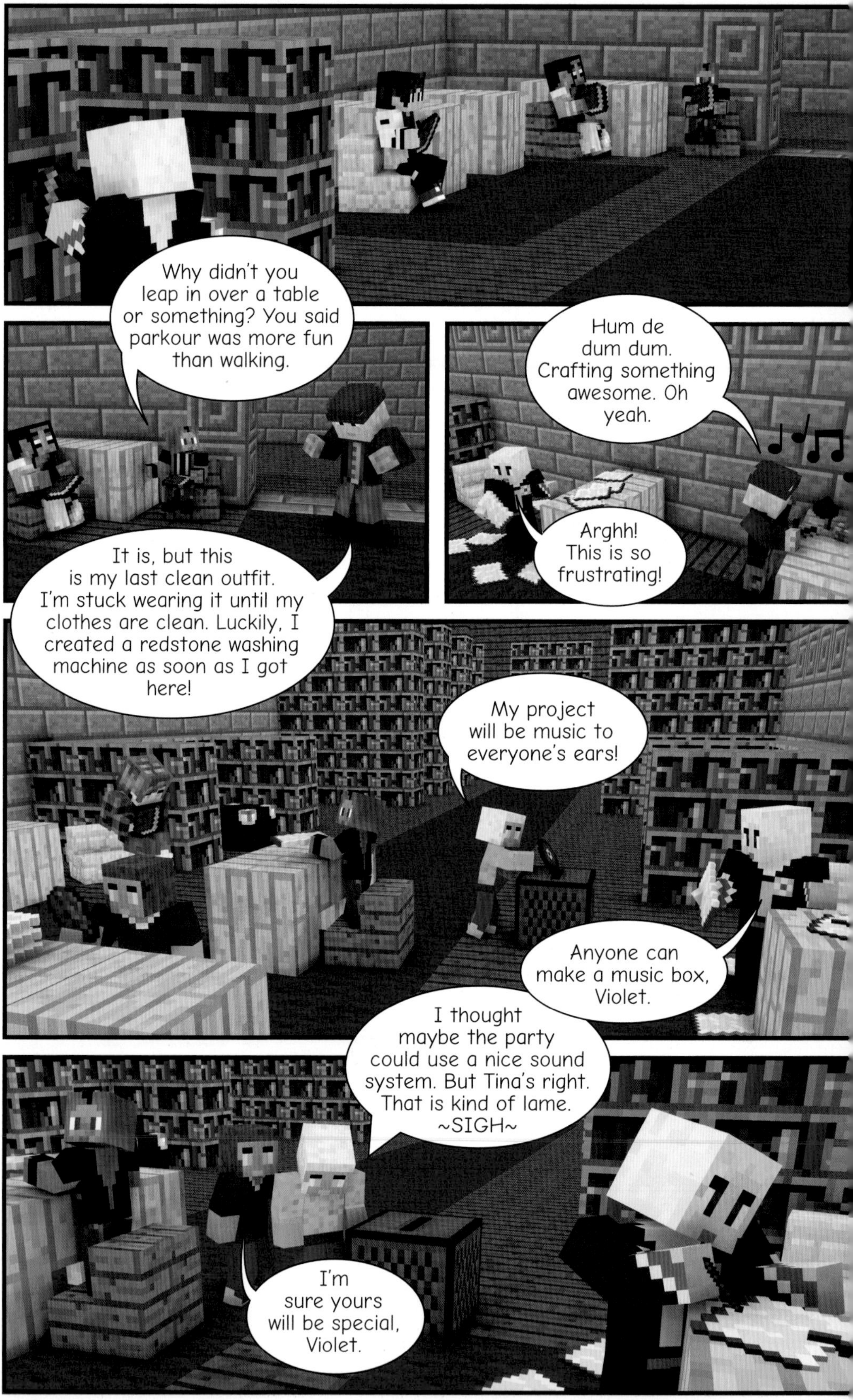

Why didn't you leap in over a table or something? You said parkour was more fun than walking.
It is, but this is my last clean outfit. I'm stuck wearing it until my clothes are clean. Luckily, I created a redstone washing machine as soon as I got here!
Hum de dum dum. Crafting something awesome. Oh yeah.
Arghh! This is so frustrating!
My project will be music to everyone's ears!
Anyone can make a music box, Violet.
I thought maybe the party could use a nice sound system. But Tina's right. That is kind of lame. ~SIGH~
I'm sure yours will be special, Violet.

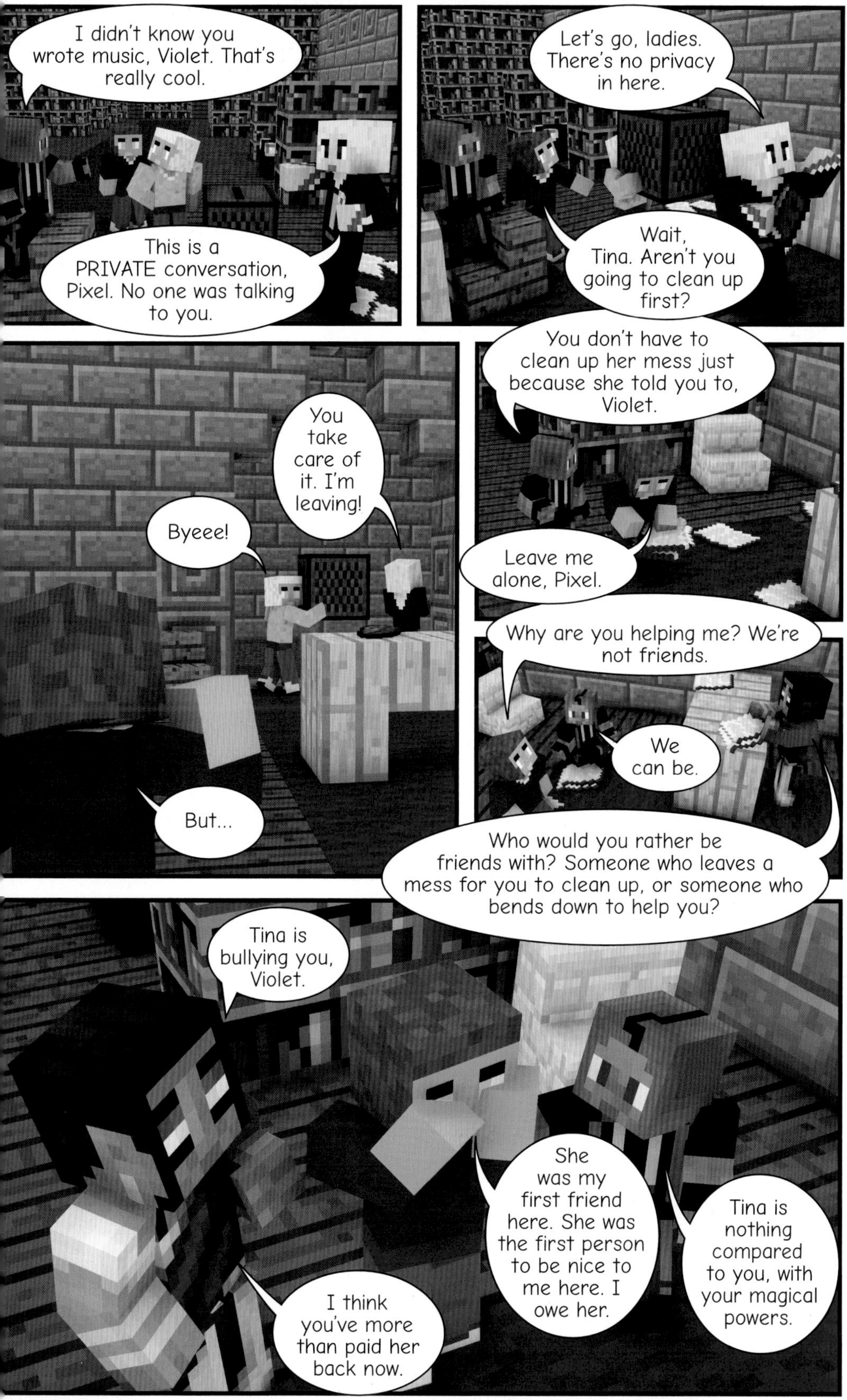
I didn't know you wrote music, Violet. That's really cool.
This is a PRIVATE conversation, Pixel. No one was talking to you.
Let's go, ladies. There's no privacy in here.
Wait, Tina. Aren't you going to clean up first?
You take care of it. I'm leaving!
Byeee!
But...
You don't have to clean up her mess just because she told you to, Violet.
Leave me alone, Pixel.
Why are you helping me? We're not friends.
We can be.
Who would you rather be friends with? Someone who leaves a mess for you to clean up, or someone who bends down to help you?
Tina is bullying you, Violet.
She was my first friend here. She was the first person to be nice to me here. I owe her.
Tina is nothing compared to you, with your magical powers.
I think you've more than paid her back now.

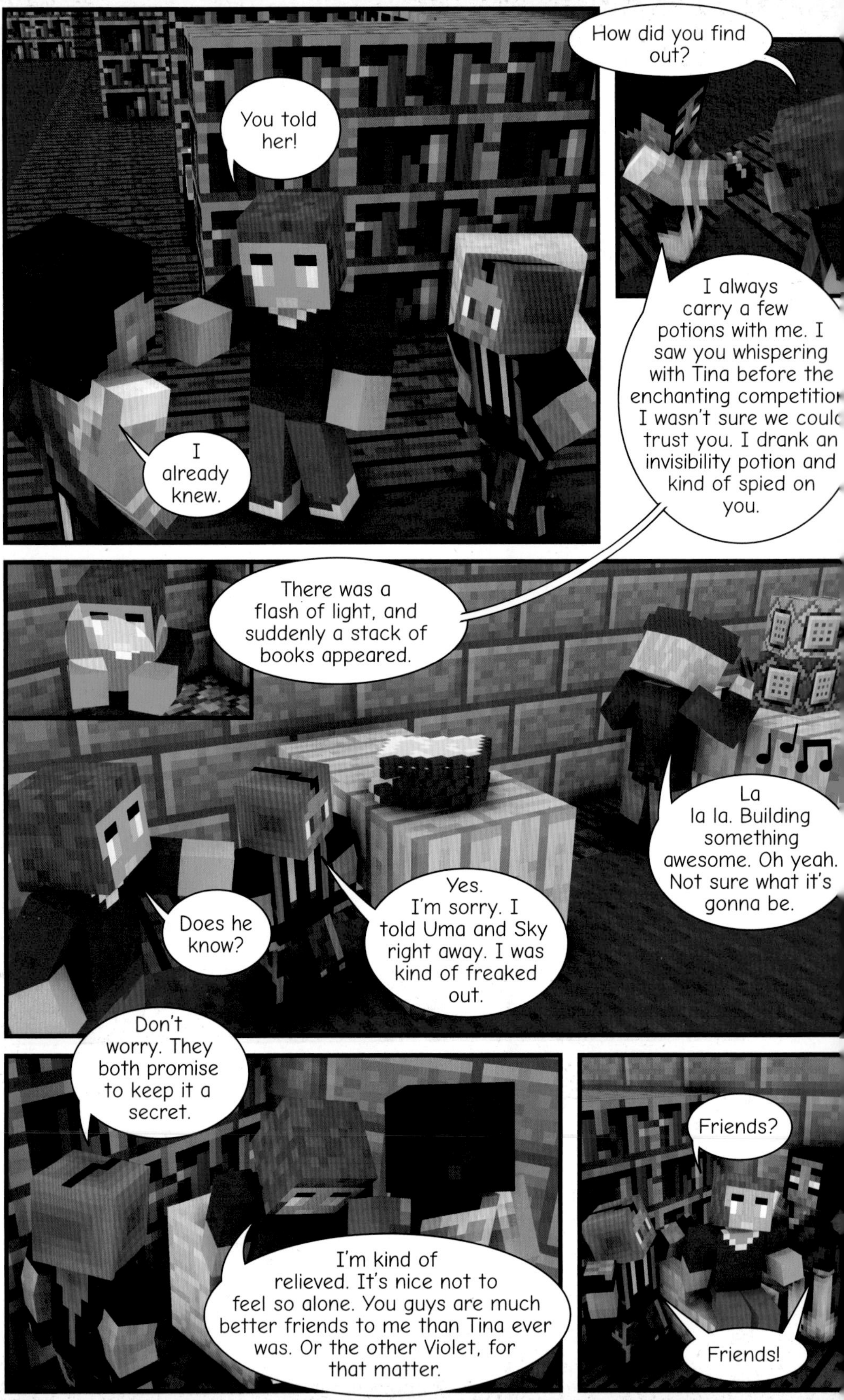
You told her!
I already knew.
How did you find out?
I always carry a few potions with me. I saw you whispering with Tina before the enchanting competitio
I wasn't sure we coul
trust you. I drank an invisibility potion and kind of spied on you.
There was a flash of light, and suddenly a stack of books appeared.
La la la. Building something awesome. Oh yeah. Not sure what it's gonna be.
Does he know?
Yes. I'm sorry. I told Uma and Sky right away. I was kind of freaked out.
Don't worry. They both promise to keep it a secret.
I'm kind of relieved. It's nice not to feel so alone. You guys are much better friends to me than Tina ever was. Or the other Violet, for that matter.
Friends?
Friends!

CHAPTER 6

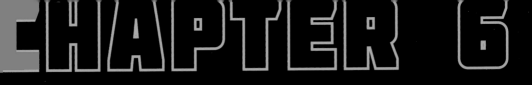

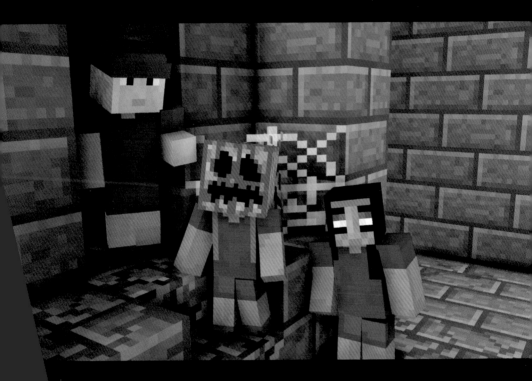

DOWN IN THE DARK

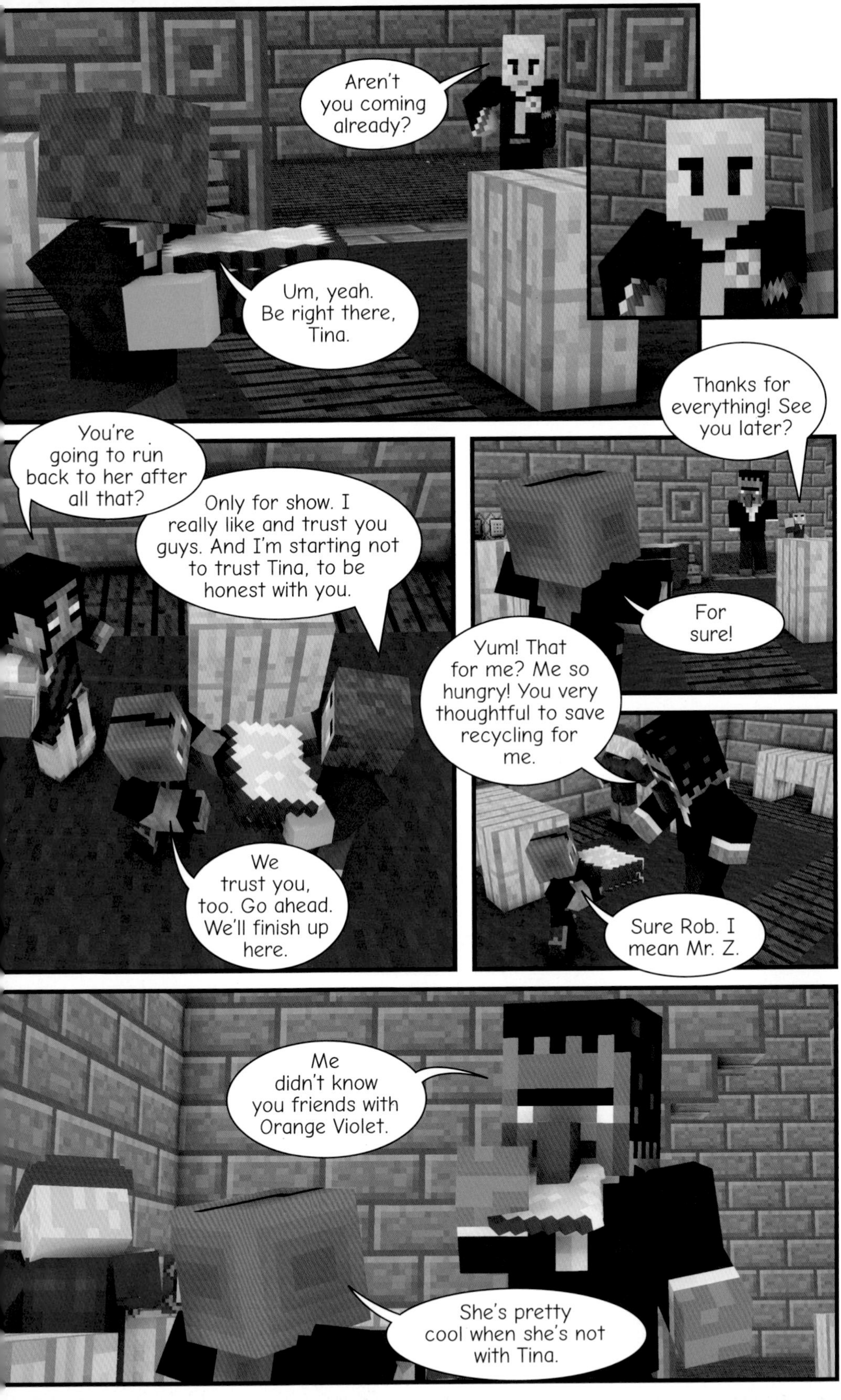
Aren't you coming already?
Um, yeah. Be right there, Tina.
You're going to run back to her after all that?
Only for show. I really like and trust you guys. And I'm starting not to trust Tina, to be honest with you.
We trust you, too. Go ahead. We'll finish up here.
Thanks for everything! See you later?
For sure!
Yum! That for me? Me so hungry! You very thoughtful to save recycling for me.
Sure Rob. I mean Mr. Z.
Me didn't know you friends with Orange Violet.
She's pretty cool when she's not with Tina.

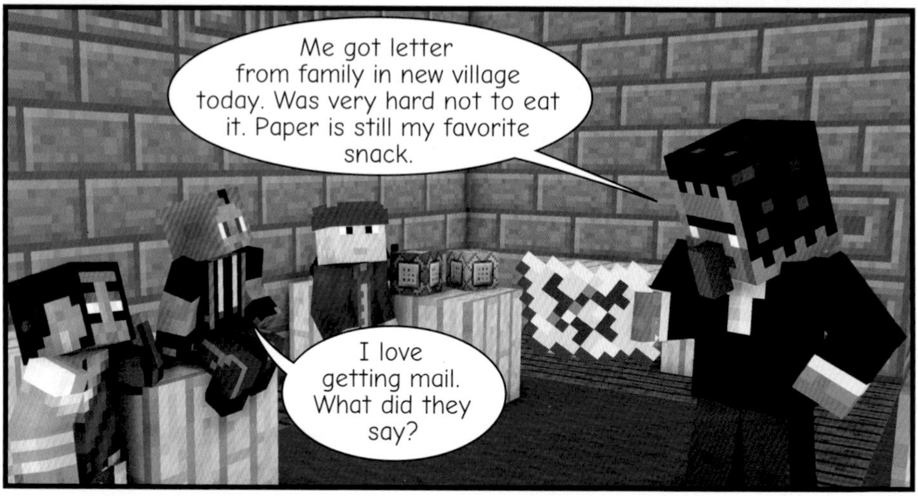
Me got letter from family in new village today. Was very hard not to eat it. Paper is still my favorite snack.
I love getting mail. What did they say?

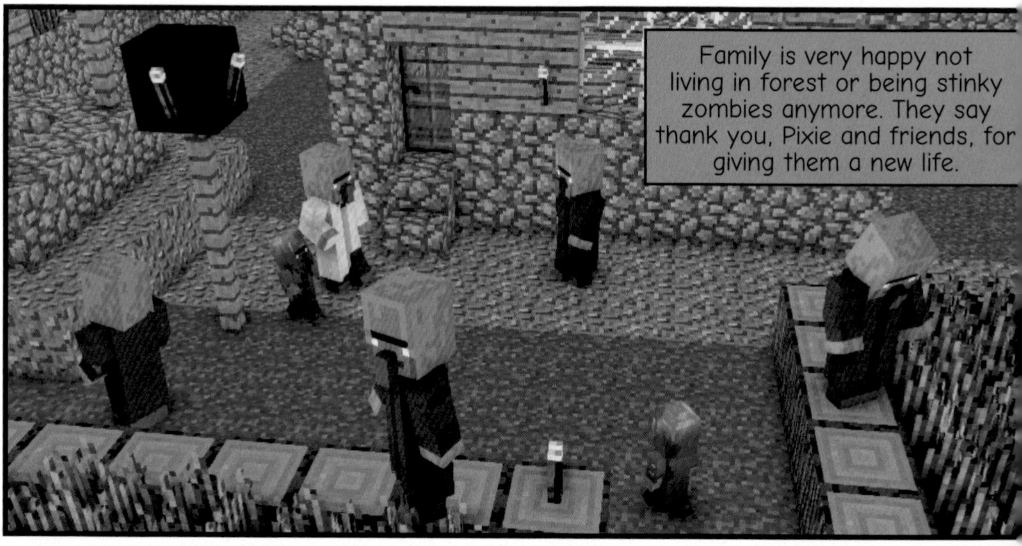
Family is very happy not living in forest or being stinky zombies anymore. They say thank you, Pixie and friends, for giving them a new life.

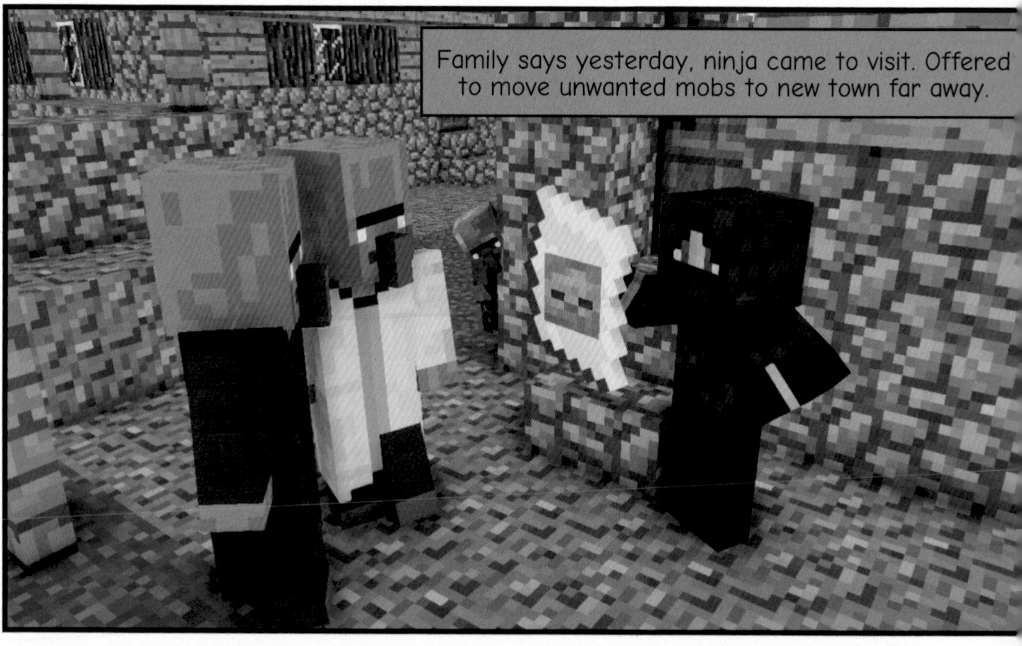
Family says yesterday, ninja came to visit. Offered to move unwanted mobs to new town far away.

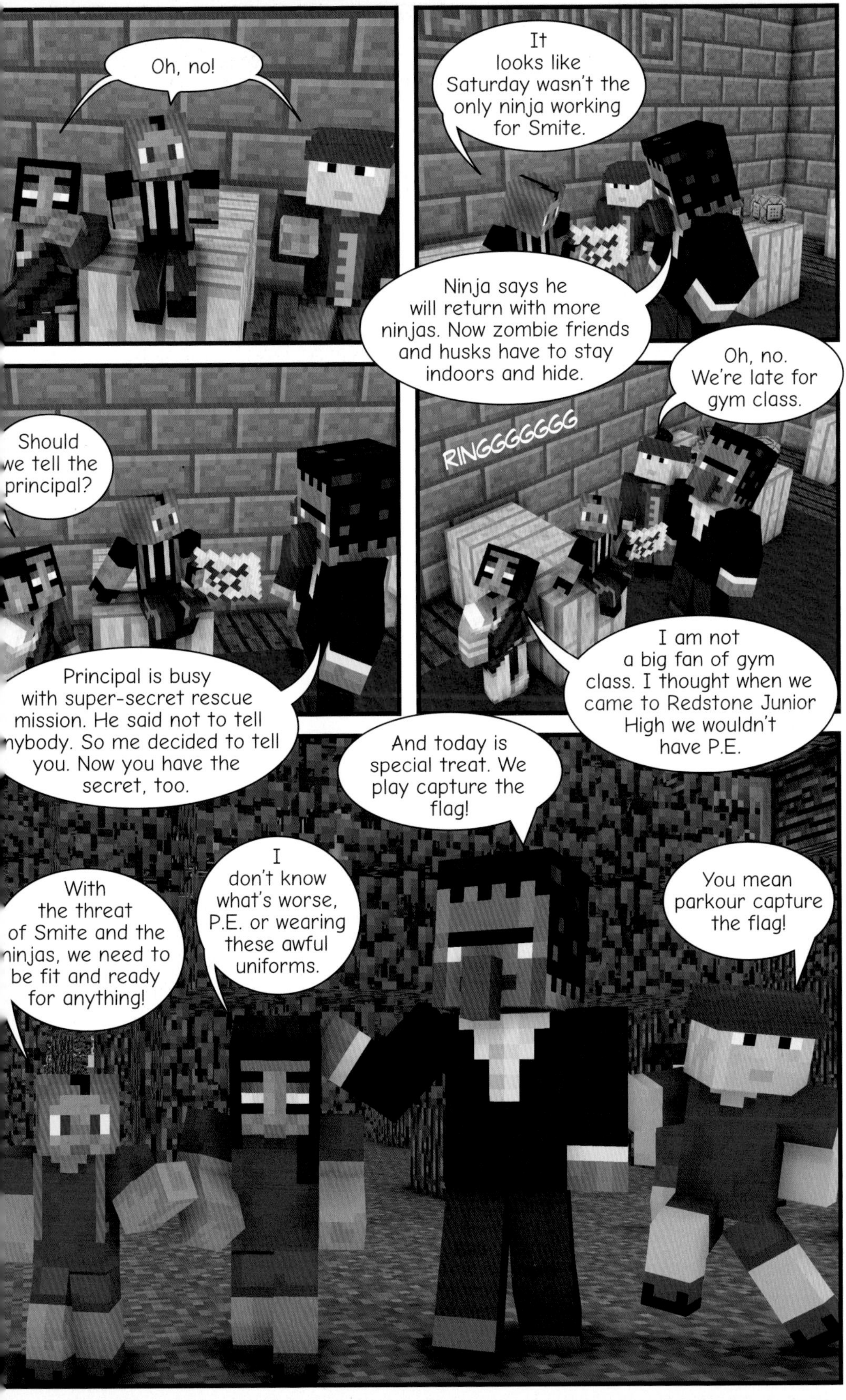
Oh, no!
It looks like Saturday wasn't the only ninja working for Smite.
Ninja says he will return with more ninjas. Now zombie friends and husks have to stay indoors and hide.
Should we tell the principal?
Principal is busy with super-secret rescue mission. He said not to tell nybody. So me decided to tell you. Now you have the secret, too.
RINGGGGGGG
Oh, no. We're late for gym class.
I am not a big fan of gym class. I thought when we came to Redstone Junior High we wouldn't have P.E.
And today is special treat. We play capture the flag!
With the threat of Smite and the ninjas, we need to be fit and ready for anything!
I don't know what's worse, P.E. or wearing these awful uniforms.
You mean parkour capture the flag!

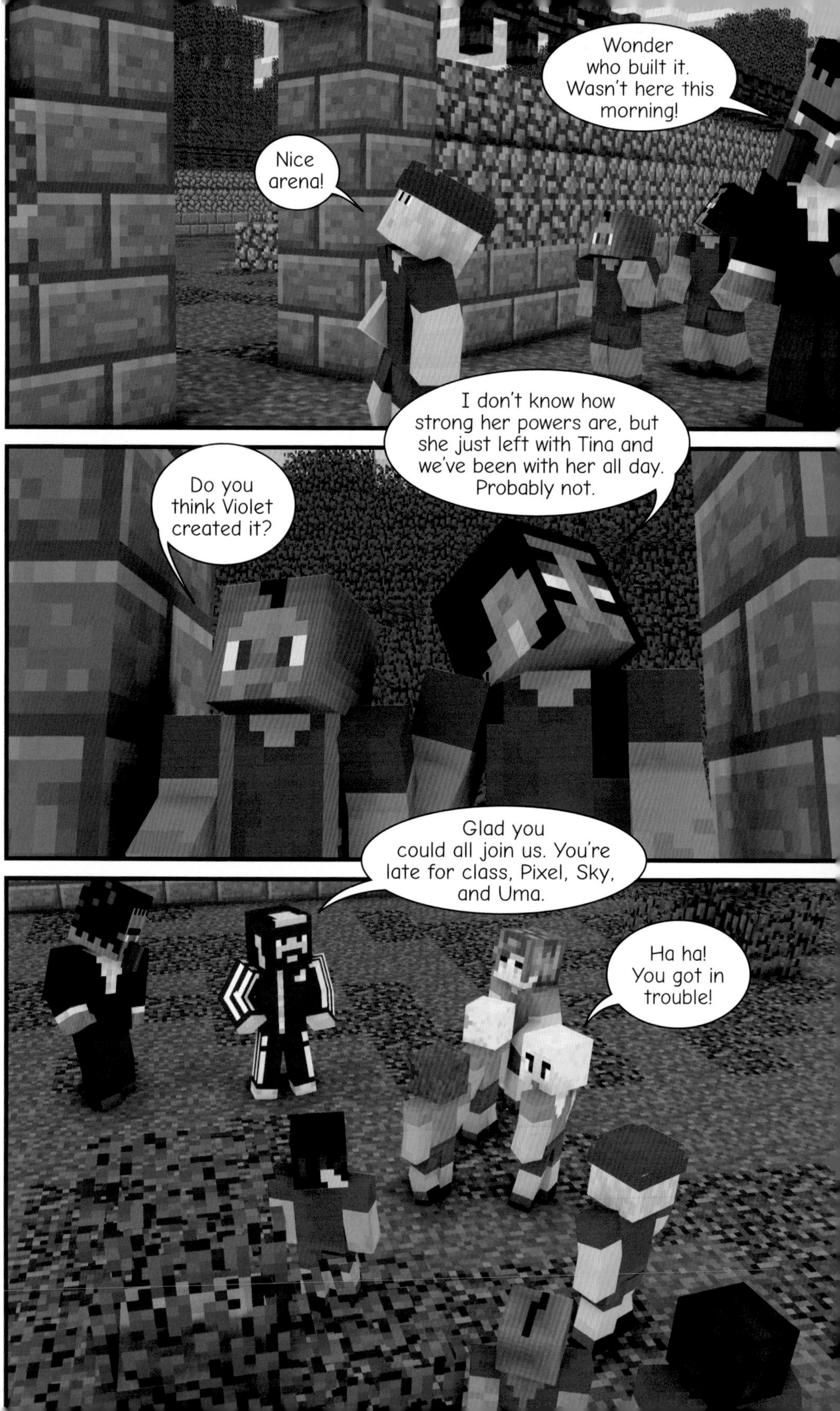
Wonder who built it. Wasn't here this morning!
Nice arena!
Do you think Violet created it?
I don't know how strong her powers are, but she just left with Tina and we've been with her all day. Probably not.
Glad you could all join us. You're late for class, Pixel, Sky, and Uma.
Ha ha! You got in trouble!

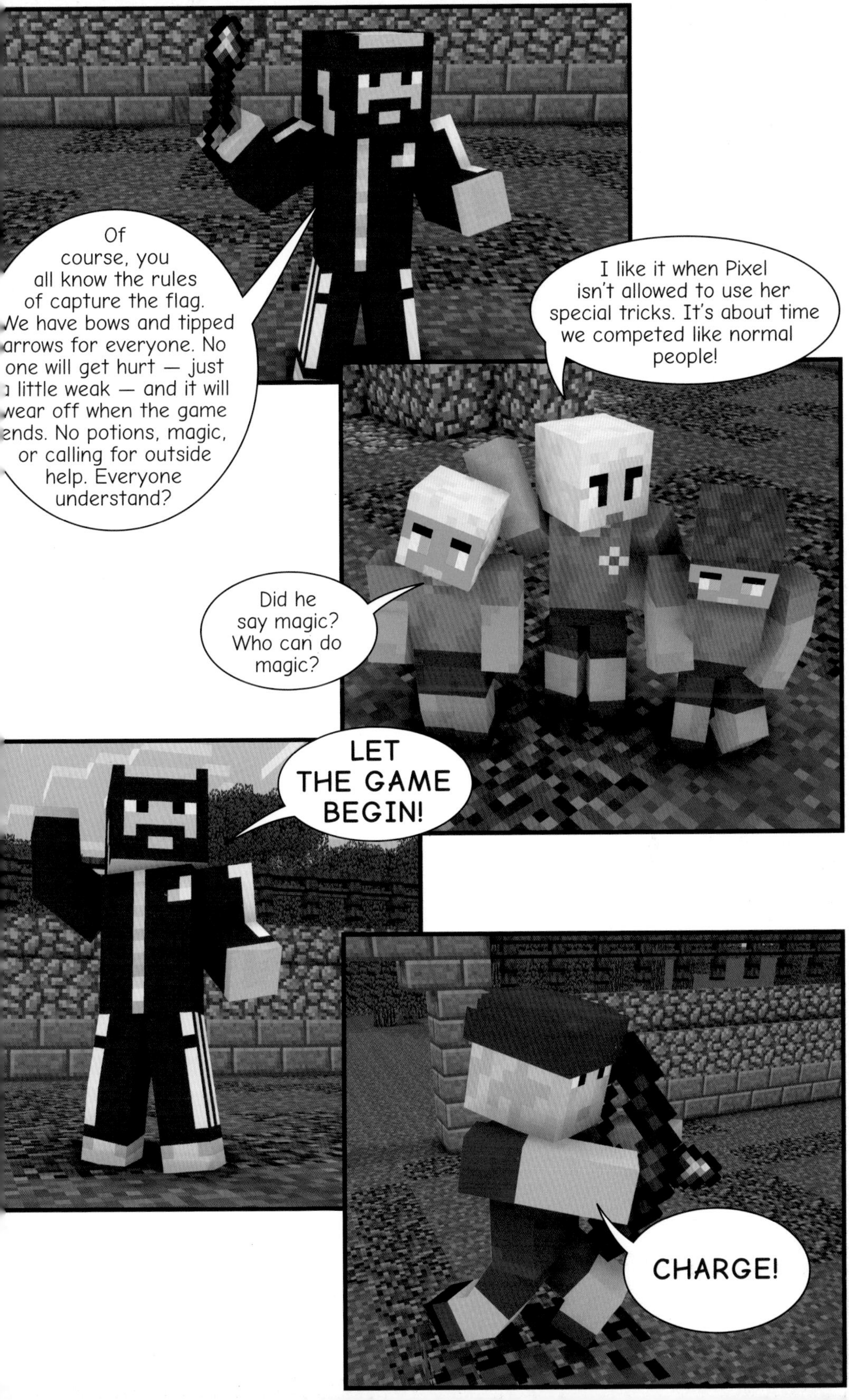
Of course, you all know the rules of capture the flag. We have bows and tipped arrows for everyone. No one will get hurt — just a little weak — and it will wear off when the game ends. No potions, magic, or calling for outside help. Everyone understand?
I like it when Pixel isn't allowed to use her special tricks. It's about time we competed like normal people!
Did he say magic? Who can do magic?
LET THE GAME BEGIN!
CHARGE!

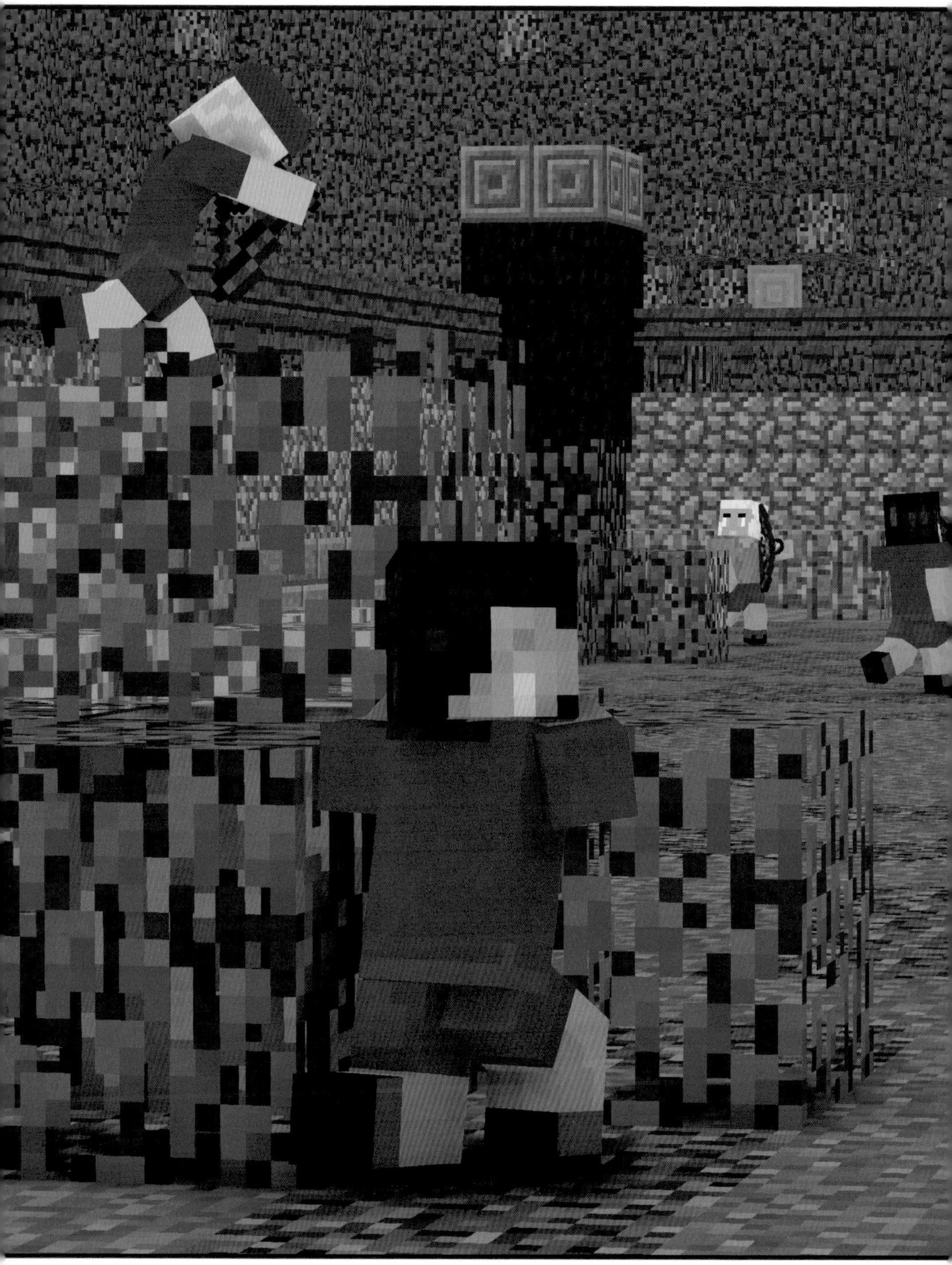

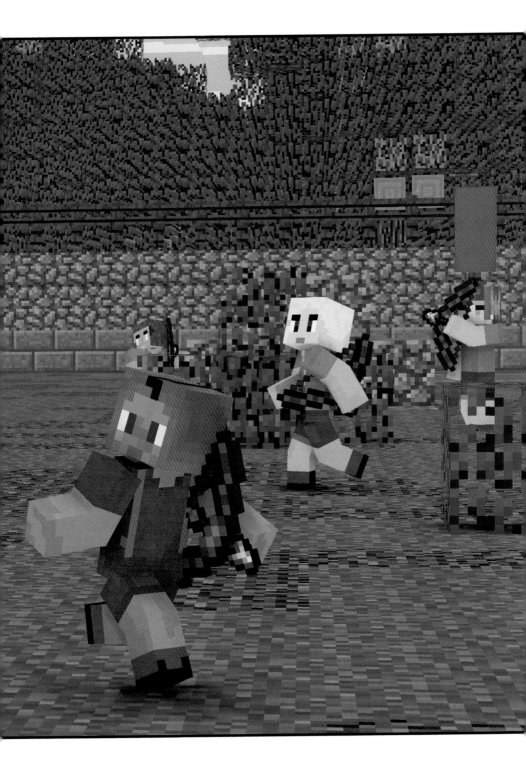

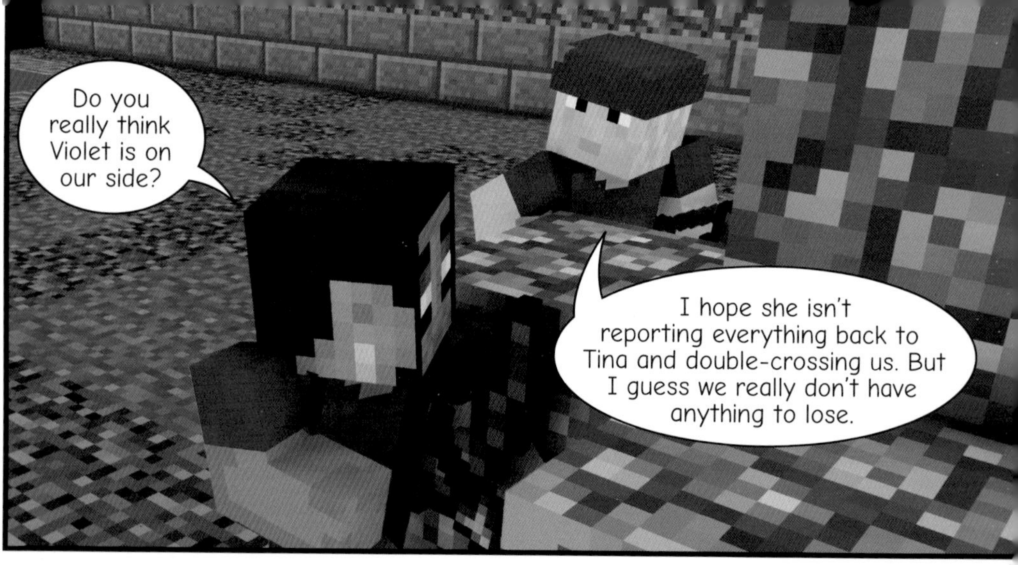
Do you really think Violet is on our side?
I hope she isn't reporting everything back to Tina and double-crossing us. But I guess we really don't have anything to lose.

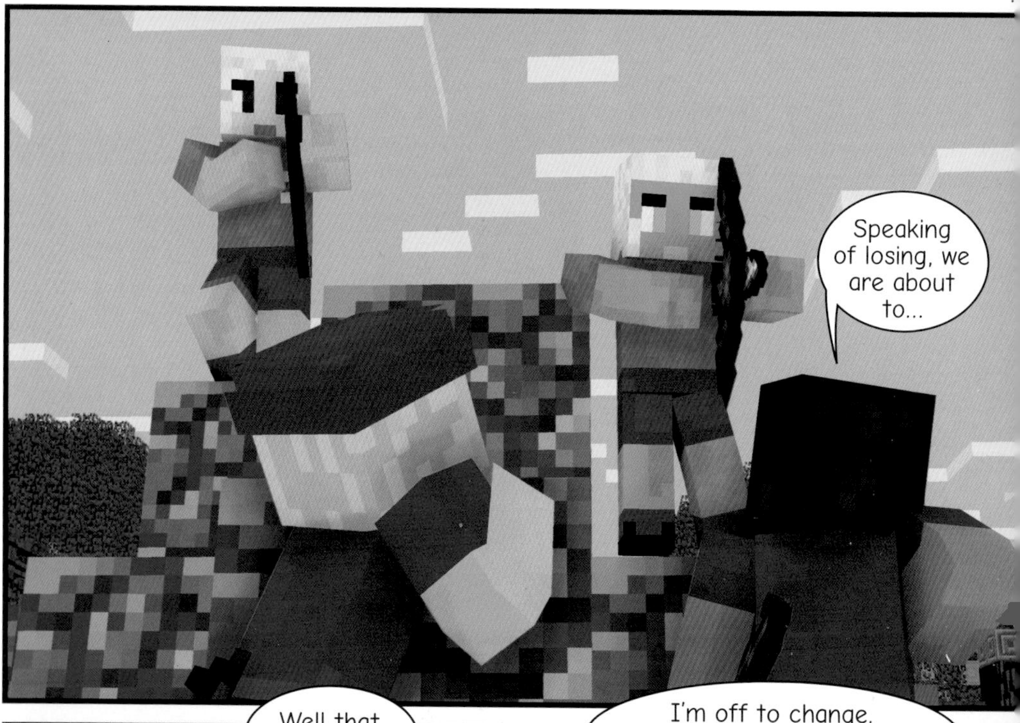
Speaking of losing, we are about to...

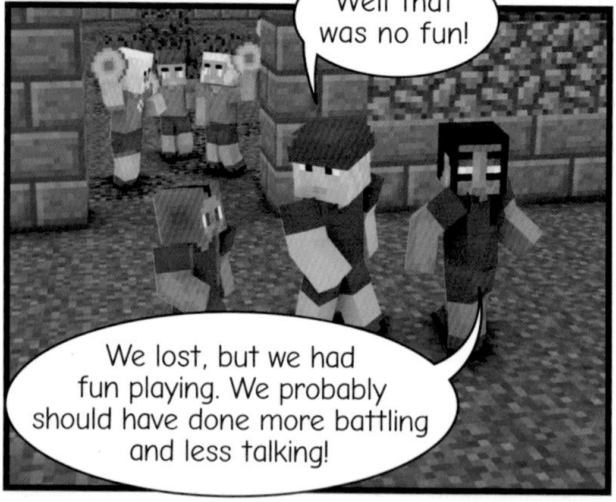
Well that was no fun!
We lost, but we had fun playing. We probably should have done more battling and less talking!

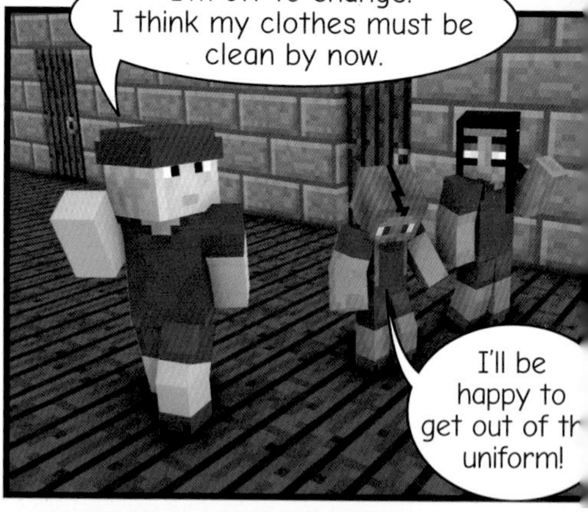
I'm off to change. I think my clothes must be clean by now.
I'll be happy to get out of th
uniform!

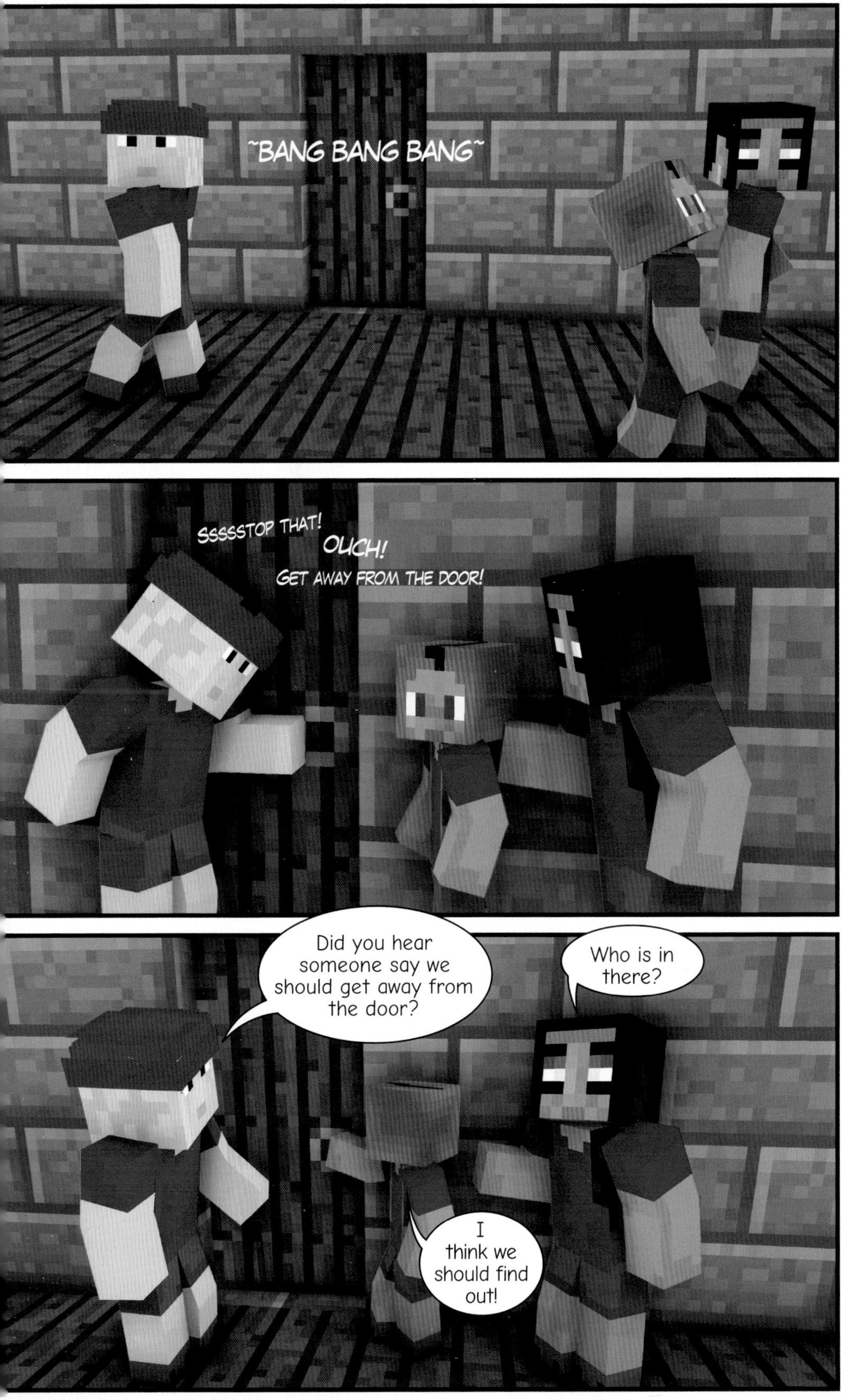
~BANG BANG BANG~
SSSSSTOP THAT!
OUCH!
GET AWAY FROM THE DOOR!
Did you hear someone say we should get away from the door?
Who is in there?
I think we should find out!

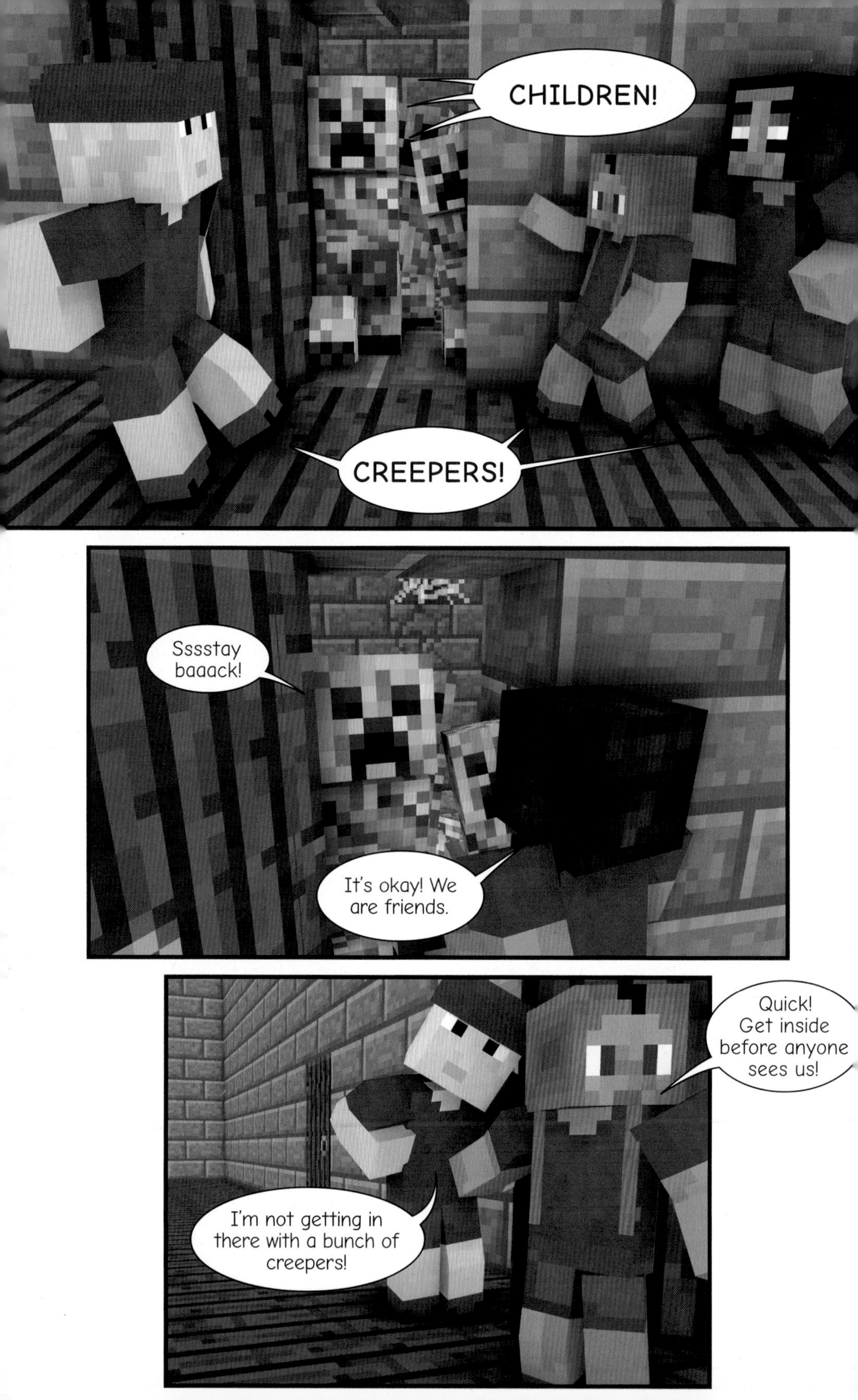
CHILDREN!
CREEPERS!
Sssstay baaack!
It's okay! We are friends.
Quick! Get inside before anyone sees us!
I'm not getting in there with a bunch of creepers!

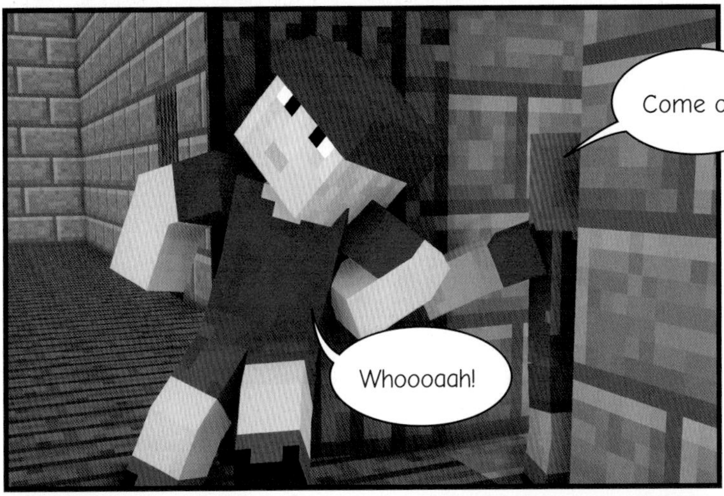
Come on!
Whoooaah!

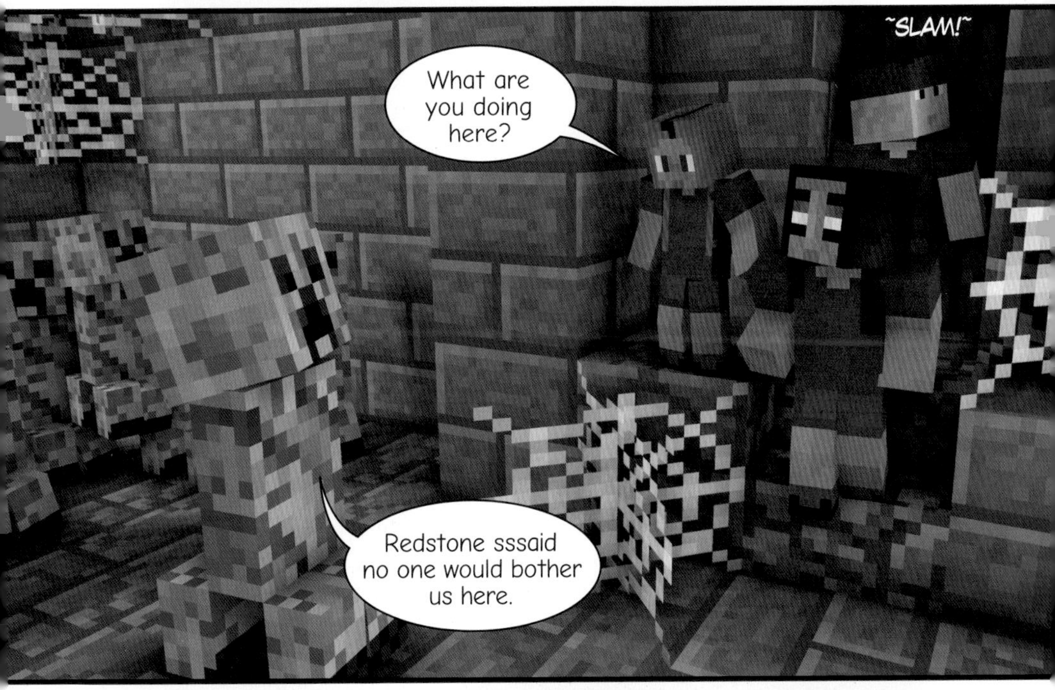
~SLAM!~
What are you doing here?
Redstone sssaid no one would bother us here.

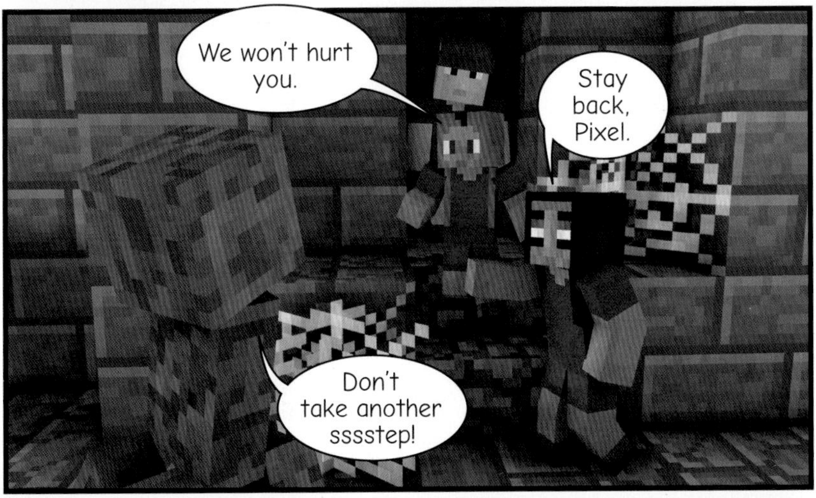
We won't hurt you.
Stay back, Pixel.
Don't take another sssstep!

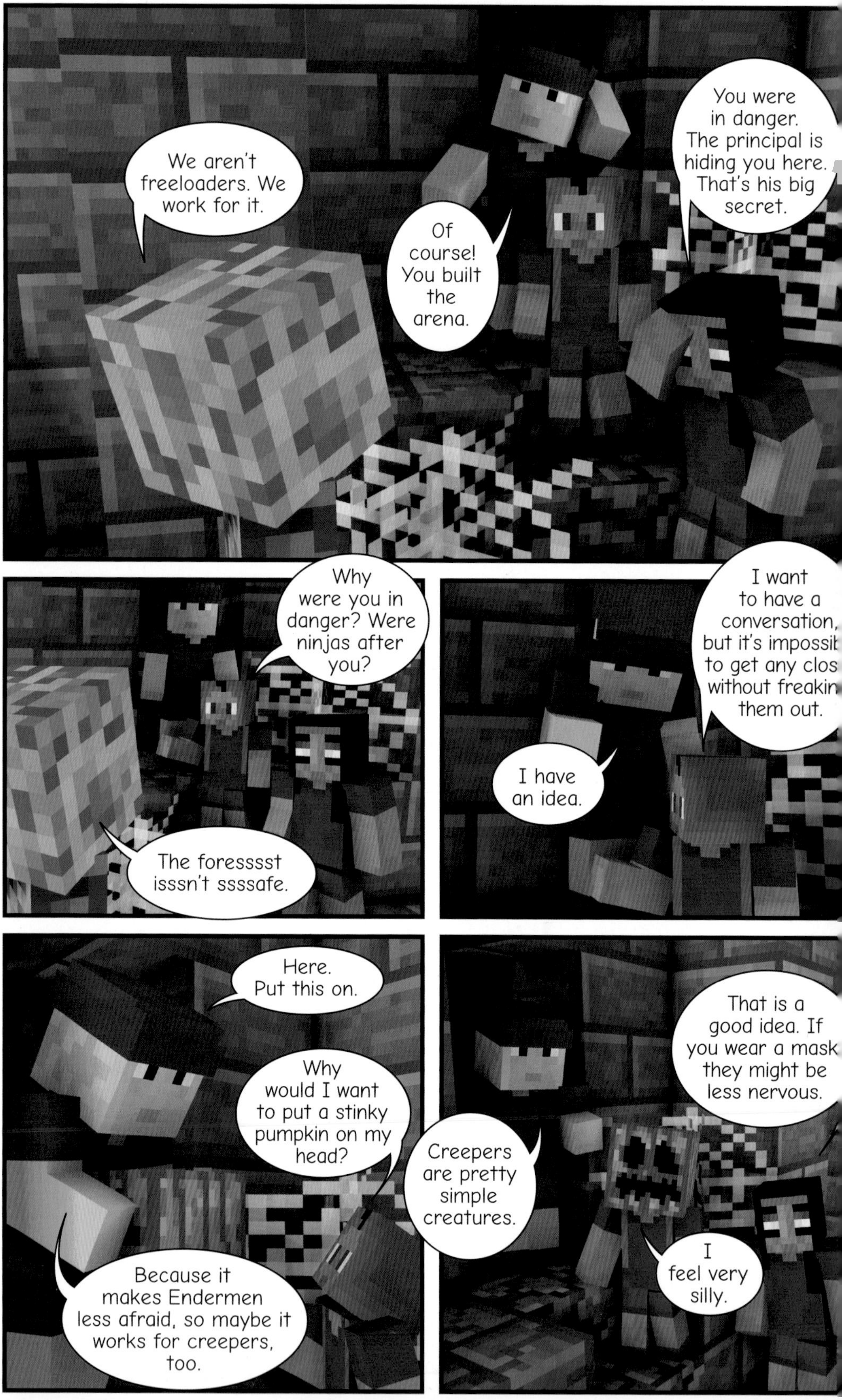
We aren't freeloaders. We work for it.
Of course! You built the arena.
You were in danger. The principal is hiding you here. That's his big secret.
Why were you in danger? Were ninjas after you?
The foresssst isssn't ssssafe.
I want to have a conversation, but it's impossib to get any clos without freakin them out.
I have an idea.
Here. Put this on.
Why would I want to put a stinky pumpkin on my head?
Because it makes Endermen less afraid, so maybe it works for creepers, too.
That is a good idea. If you wear a mask they might be less nervous.
Creepers are pretty simple creatures.
I feel very silly.

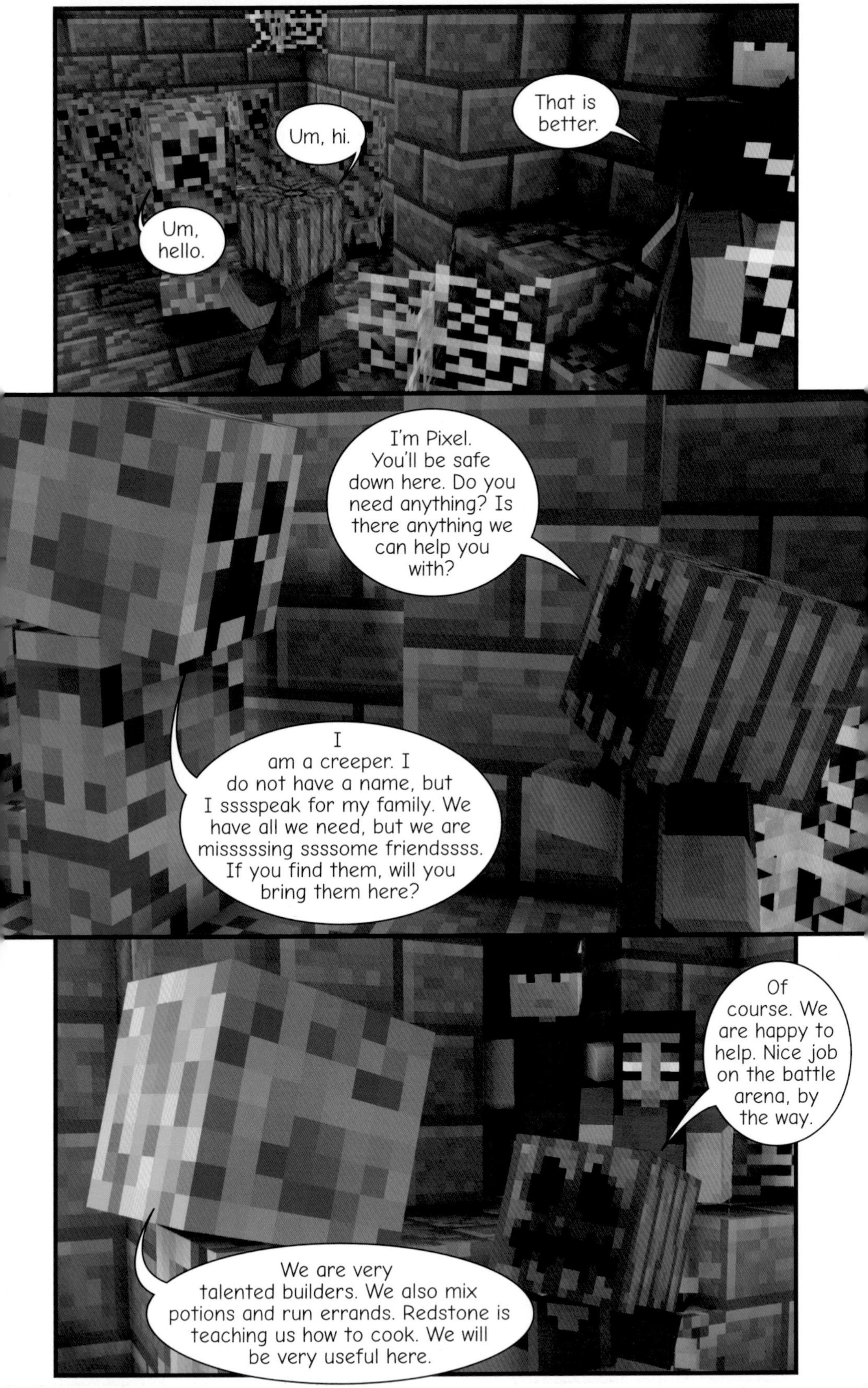
Um, hi.
Um, hello.
That is better.
I'm Pixel. You'll be safe down here. Do you need anything? Is there anything we can help you with?
I am a creeper. I do not have a name, but I sssspeak for my family. We have all we need, but we are missssssing sssome friendssss. If you find them, will you bring them here?
Of course. We are happy to help. Nice job on the battle arena, by the way.
We are very talented builders. We also mix potions and run errands. Redstone is teaching us how to cook. We will be very useful here.

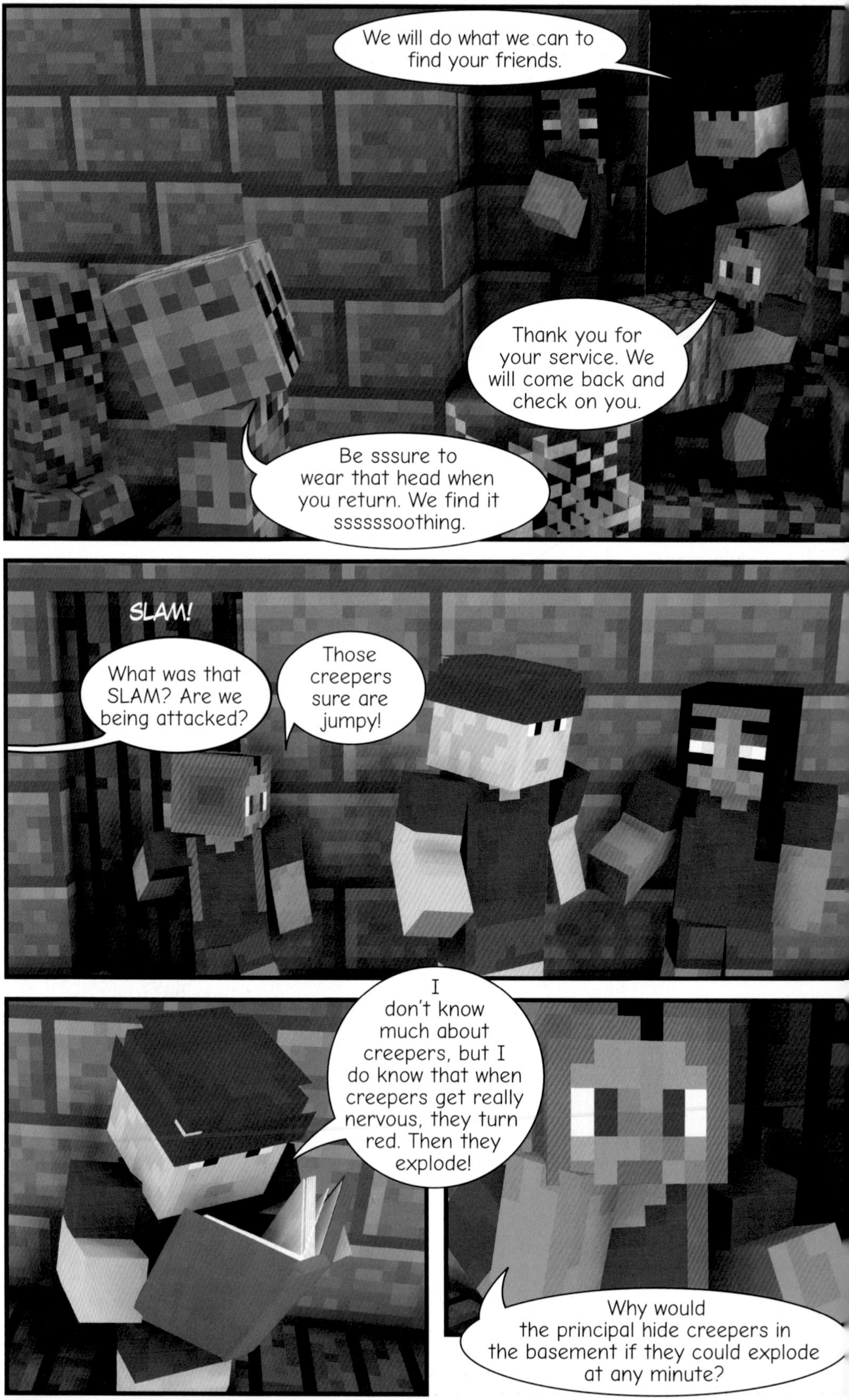
We will do what we can to find your friends.
Thank you for your service. We will come back and check on you.
Be sssure to wear that head when you return. We find it sssssssoothing.
SLAM!
What was that SLAM? Are we being attacked?
Those creepers sure are jumpy!
I don't know much about creepers, but I do know that when creepers get really nervous, they turn red. Then they explode!
Why would the principal hide creepers in the basement if they could explode at any minute?

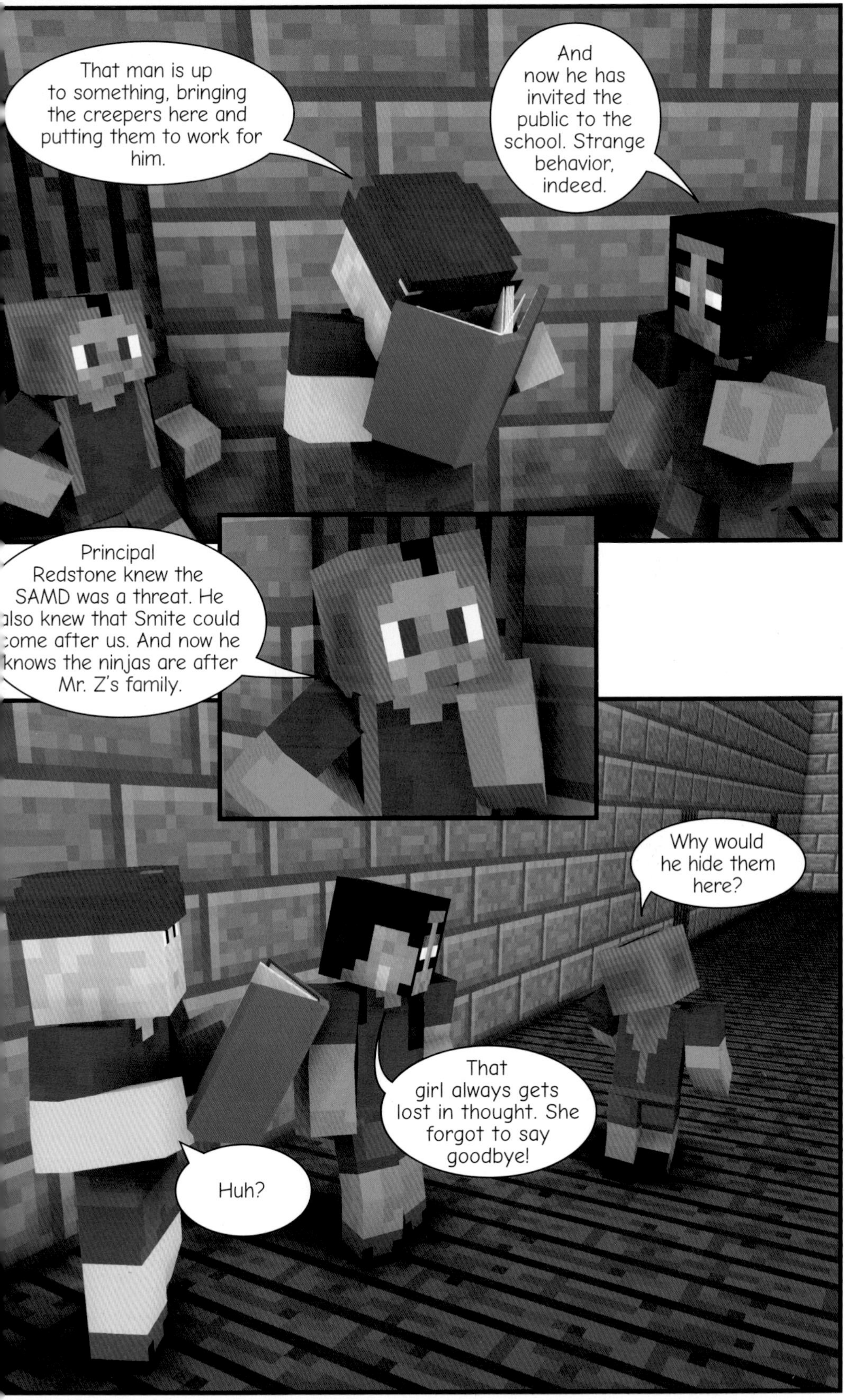
That man is up to something, bringing the creepers here and putting them to work for him.
And now he has invited the public to the school. Strange behavior, indeed.
Principal Redstone knew the SAMD was a threat. He also knew that Smite could come after us. And now he knows the ninjas are after Mr. Z's family.
Why would he hide them here?
That girl always gets lost in thought. She forgot to say goodbye!
Huh?

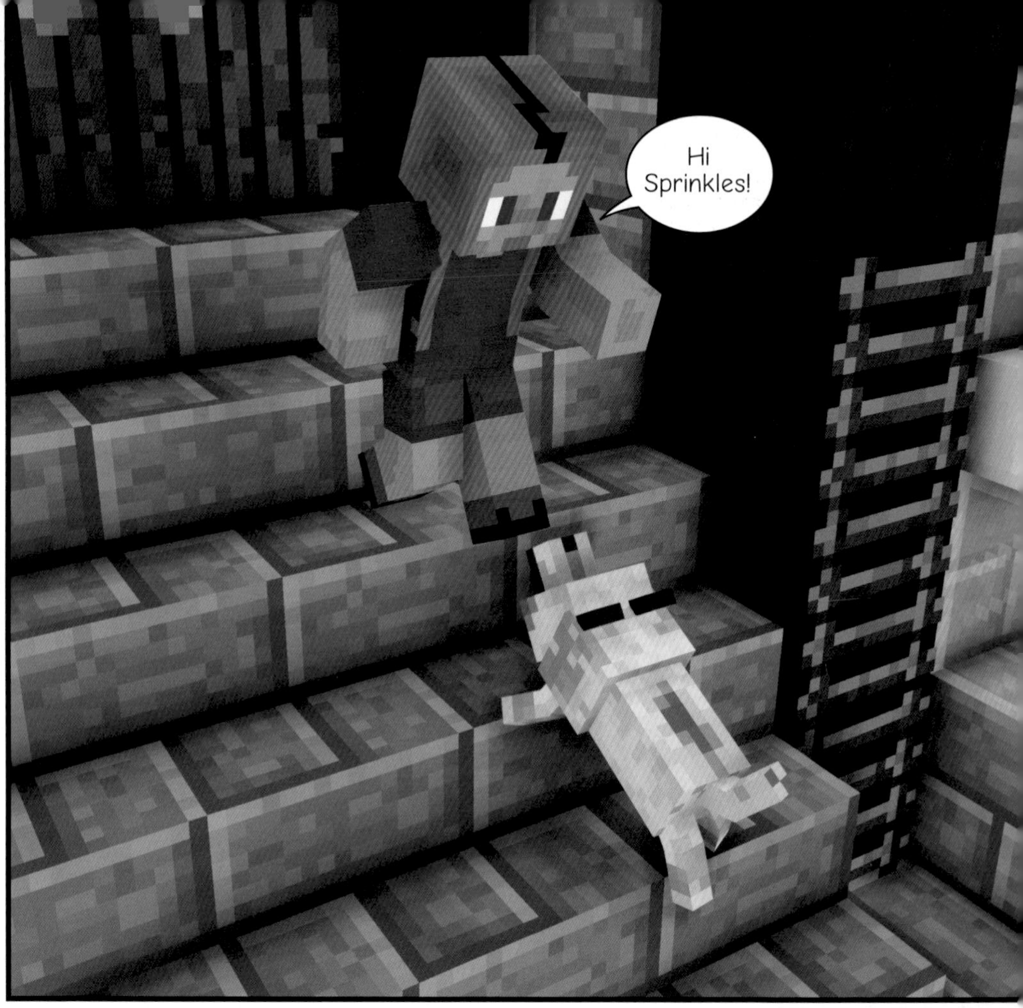
Hi Sprinkles!

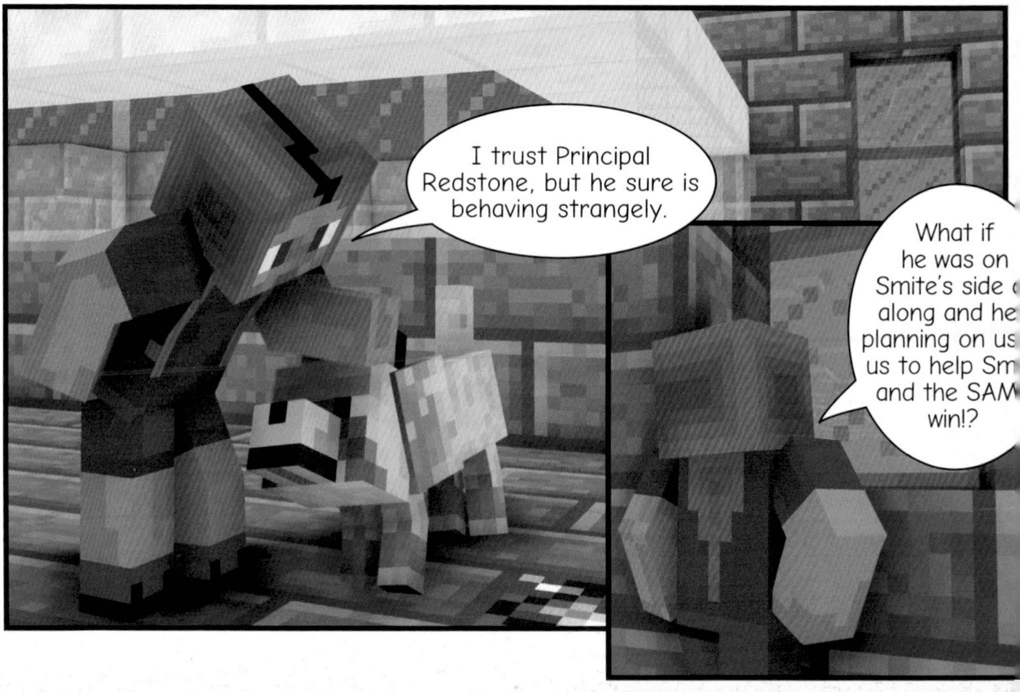
I trust Principal Redstone, but he sure is behaving strangely.
What if he was on Smite's side along and he planning on us us to help Sm and the SAM win!?

CHAPTER 7

BUILDING PLANS

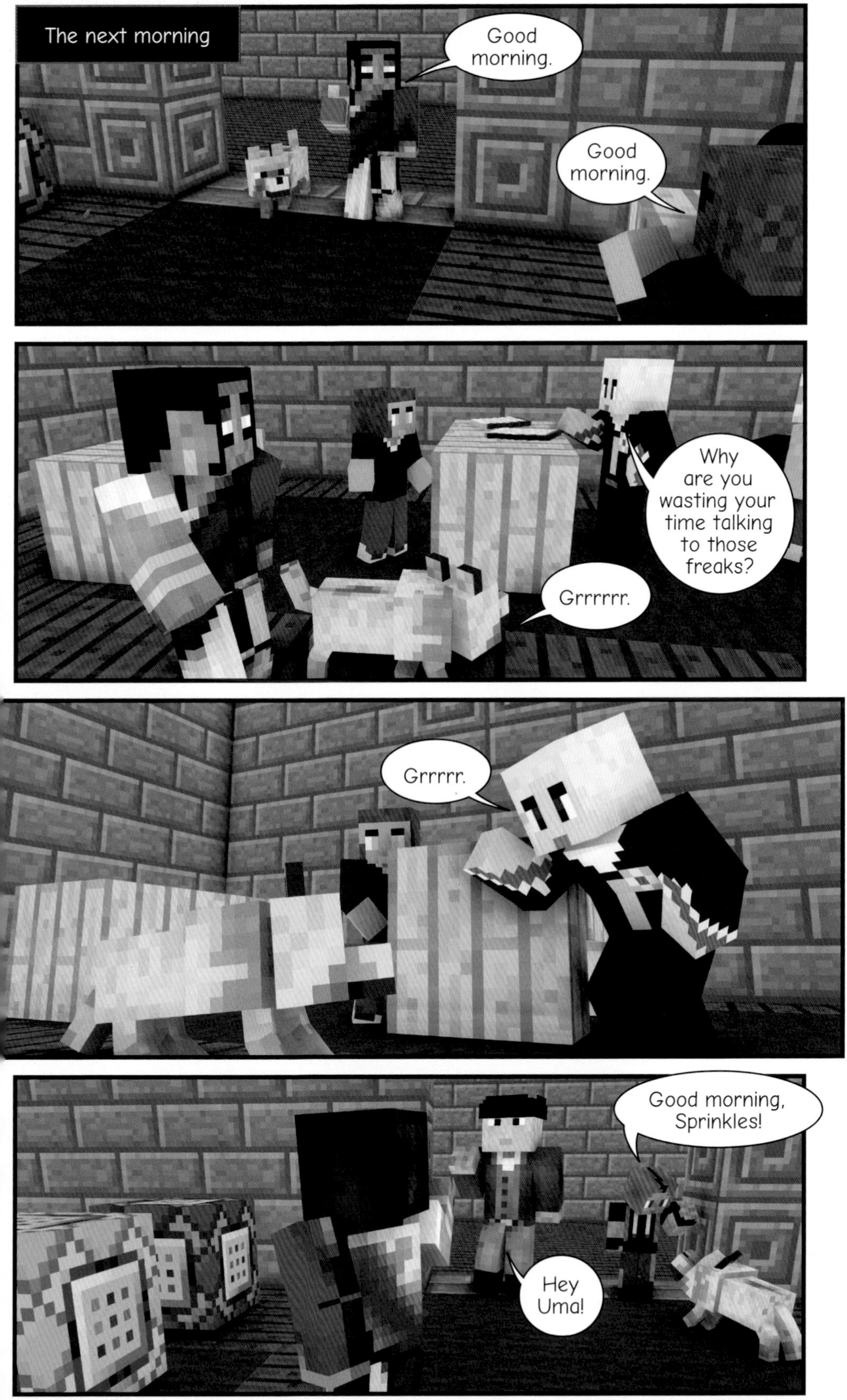
The next morning
Good morning.
Good morning.
Why are you wasting your time talking to those freaks?
Grrrrrr.
Grrrrr.
Good morning, Sprinkles!
Hey Uma!

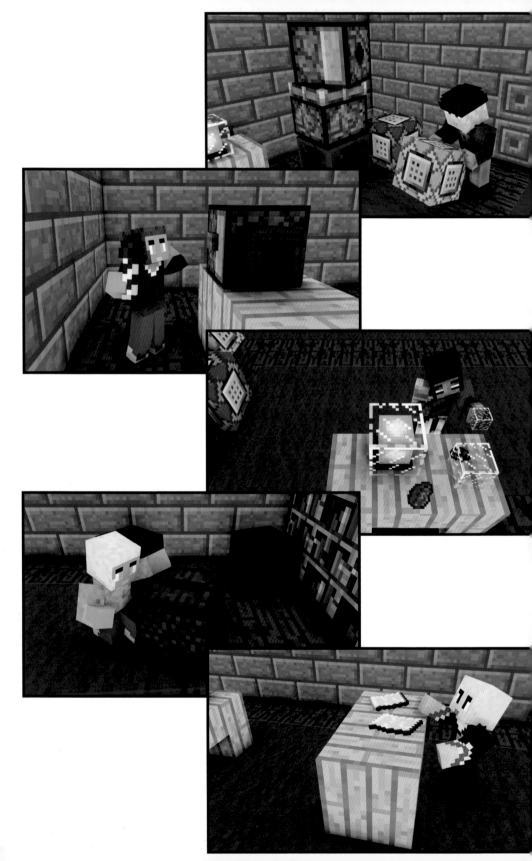

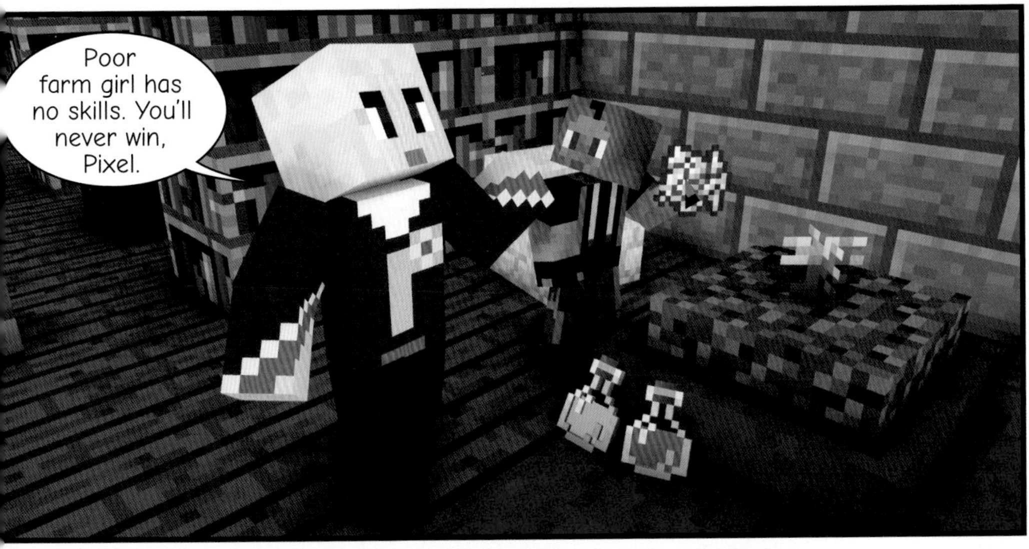
Poor farm girl has no skills. You'll never win, Pixel.

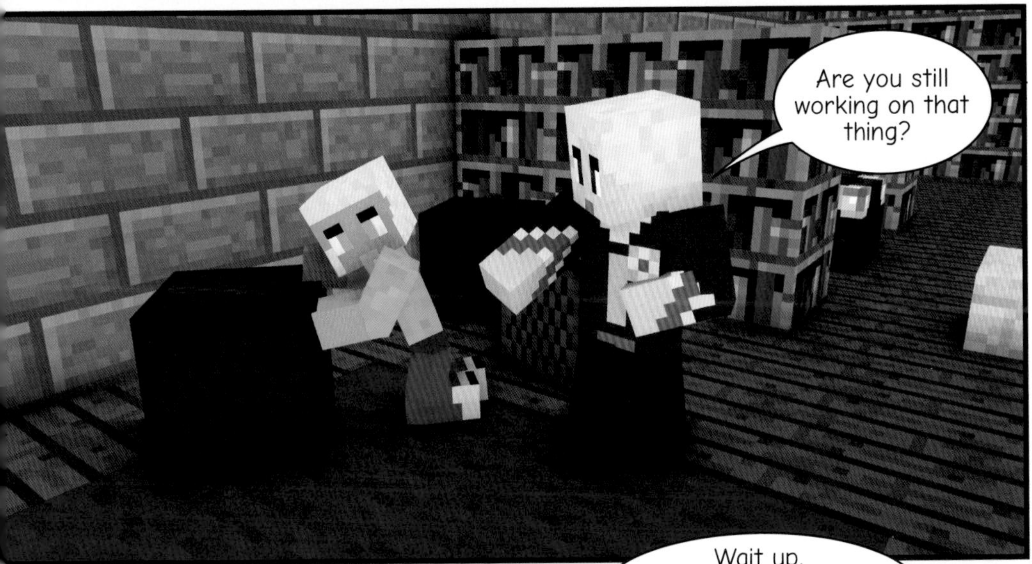
Are you still working on that thing?

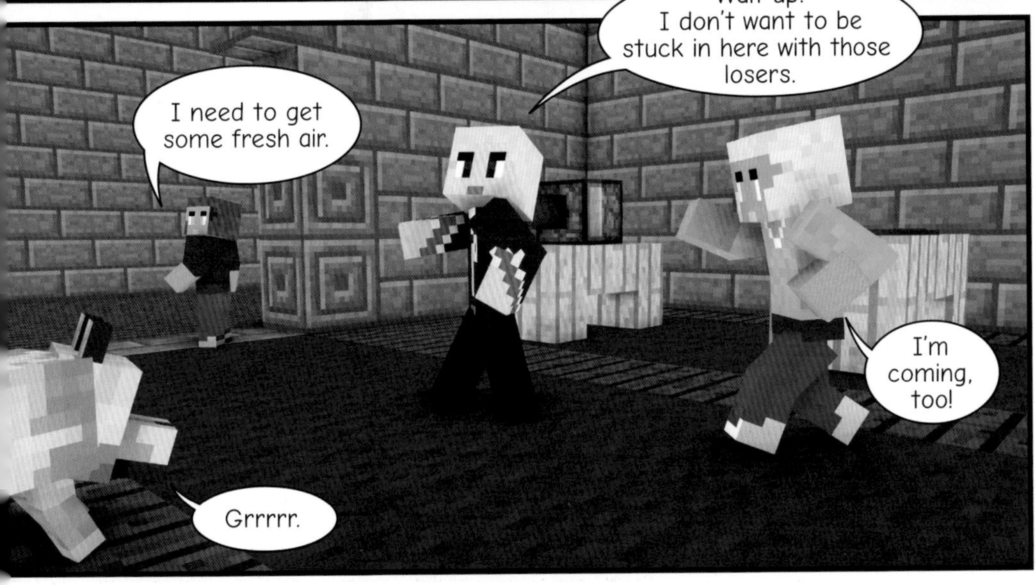
I need to get some fresh air.
Wait up. I don't want to be stuck in here with those losers.
I'm coming, too!
Grrrrr.

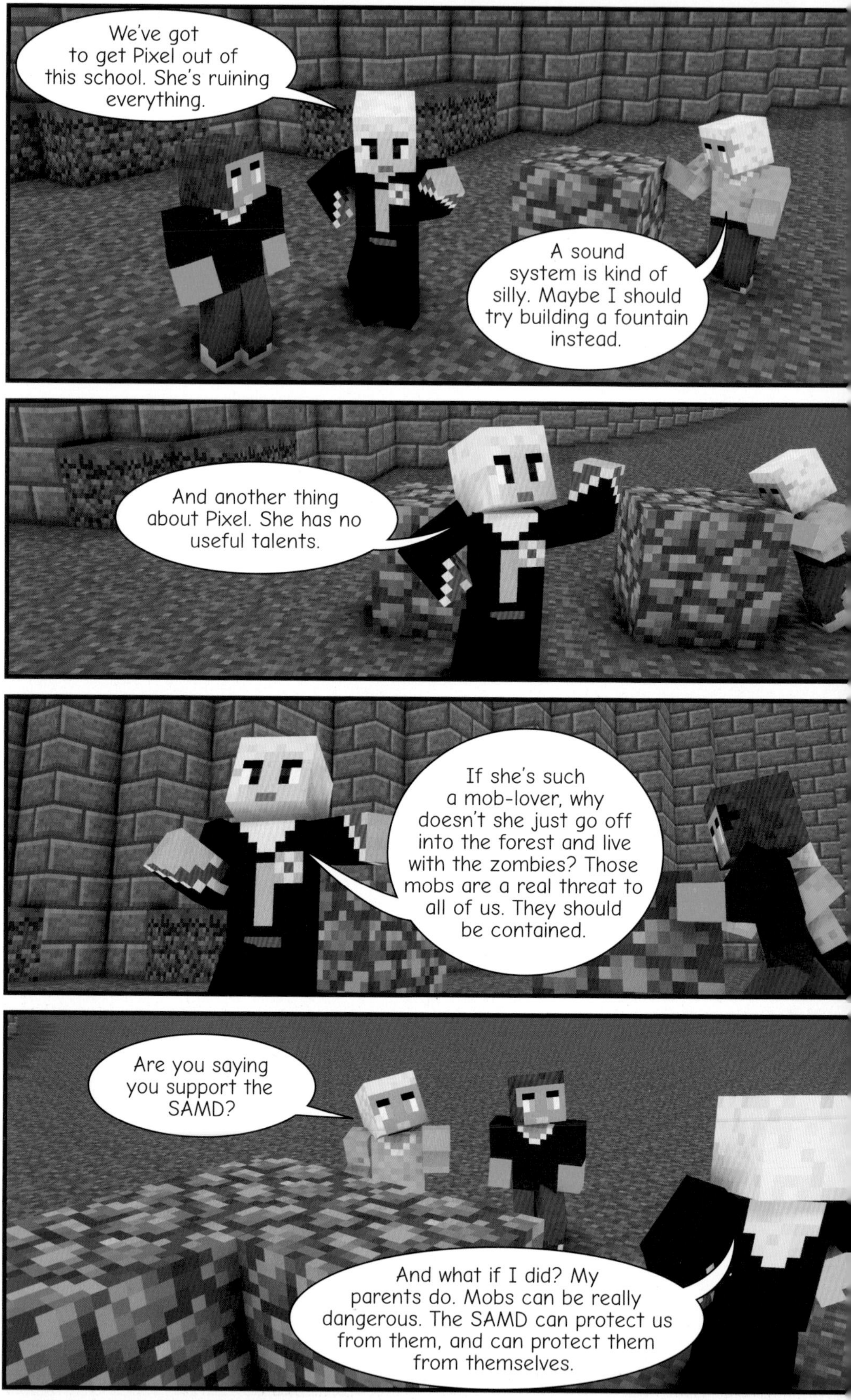
We've got to get Pixel out of this school. She's ruining everything.
A sound system is kind of silly. Maybe I should try building a fountain instead.
And another thing about Pixel. She has no useful talents.
If she's such a mob-lover, why doesn't she just go off into the forest and live with the zombies? Those mobs are a real threat to all of us. They should be contained.
Are you saying you support the SAMD?
And what if I did? My parents do. Mobs can be really dangerous. The SAMD can protect us from them, and can protect them from themselves.

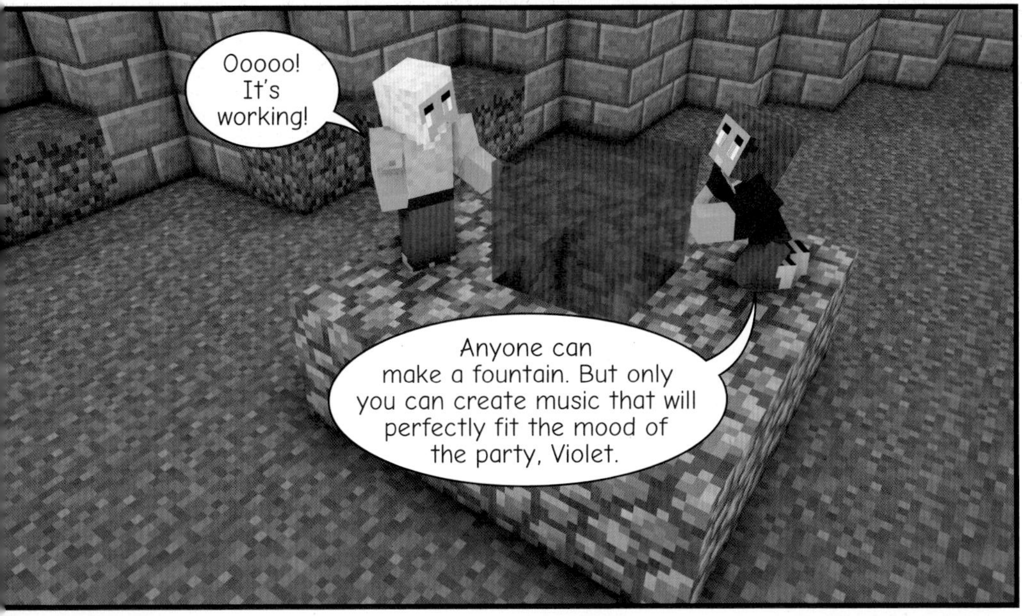
Ooooo! It's working!
Anyone can make a fountain. But only you can create music that will perfectly fit the mood of the party, Violet.

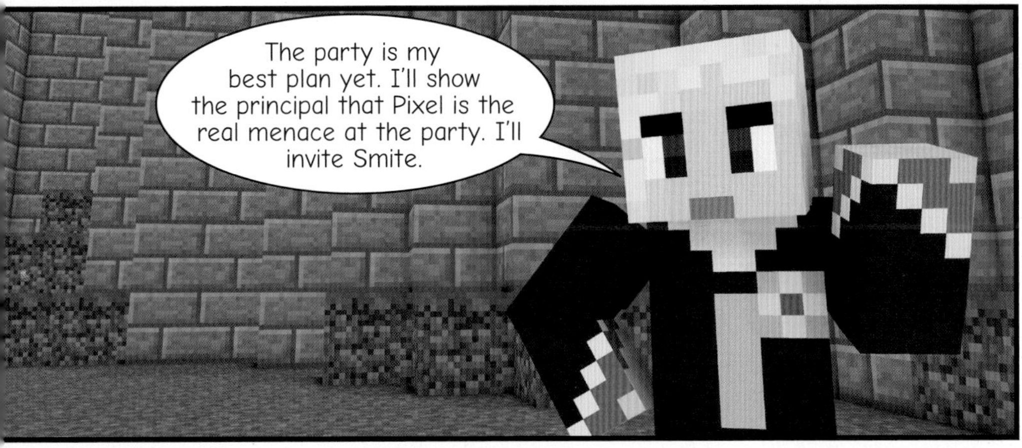
The party is my best plan yet. I'll show the principal that Pixel is the real menace at the party. I'll invite Smite.

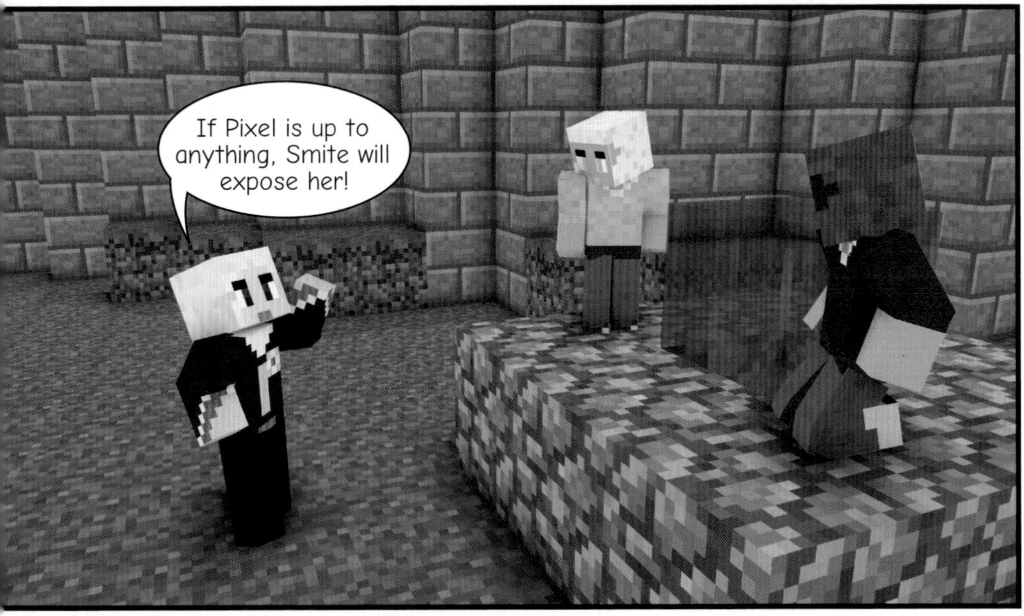
If Pixel is up to anything, Smite will expose her!

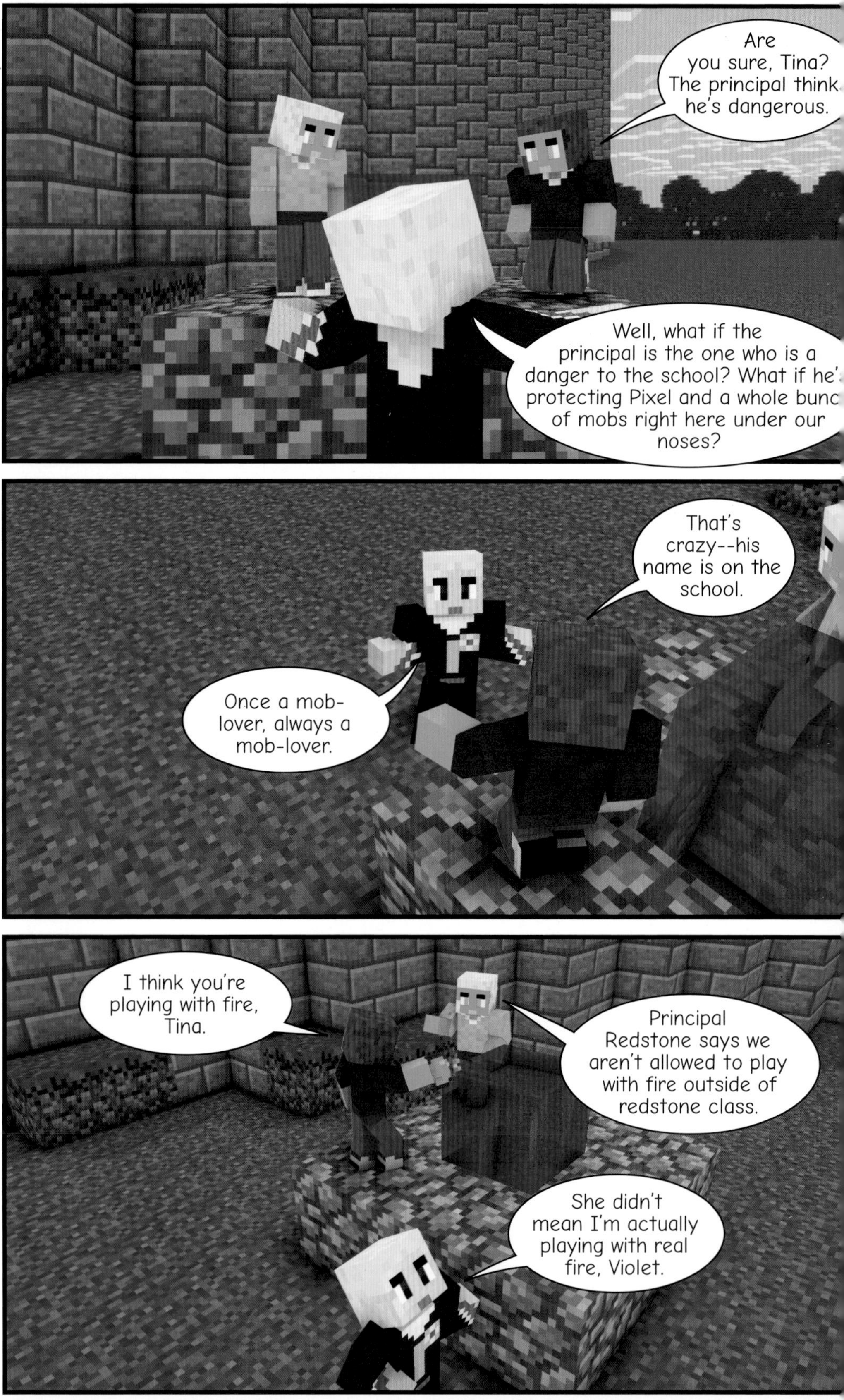
Are you sure, Tina? The principal think he's dangerous.
Well, what if the principal is the one who is a danger to the school? What if he' protecting Pixel and a whole bunc of mobs right here under our noses?
That's crazy--his name is on the school.
Once a mob-lover, always a mob-lover.
I think you're playing with fire, Tina.
Principal Redstone says we aren't allowed to play with fire outside of redstone class.
She didn't mean I'm actually playing with real fire, Violet.

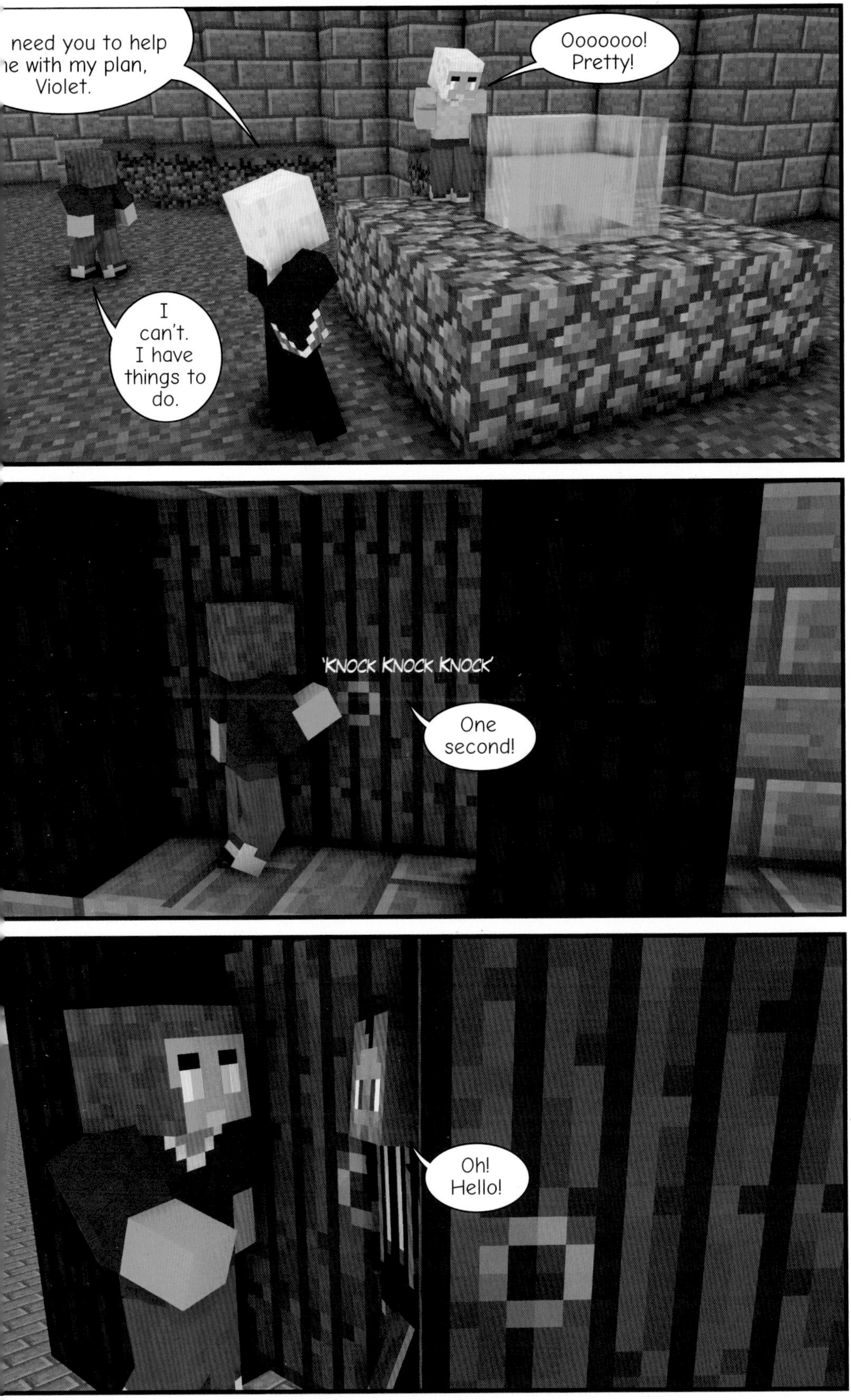
need you to help with my plan, Violet.
Ooooooo! Pretty!
I can't. I have things to do.
'KNOCK KNOCK KNOCK'
One second!
Oh! Hello!

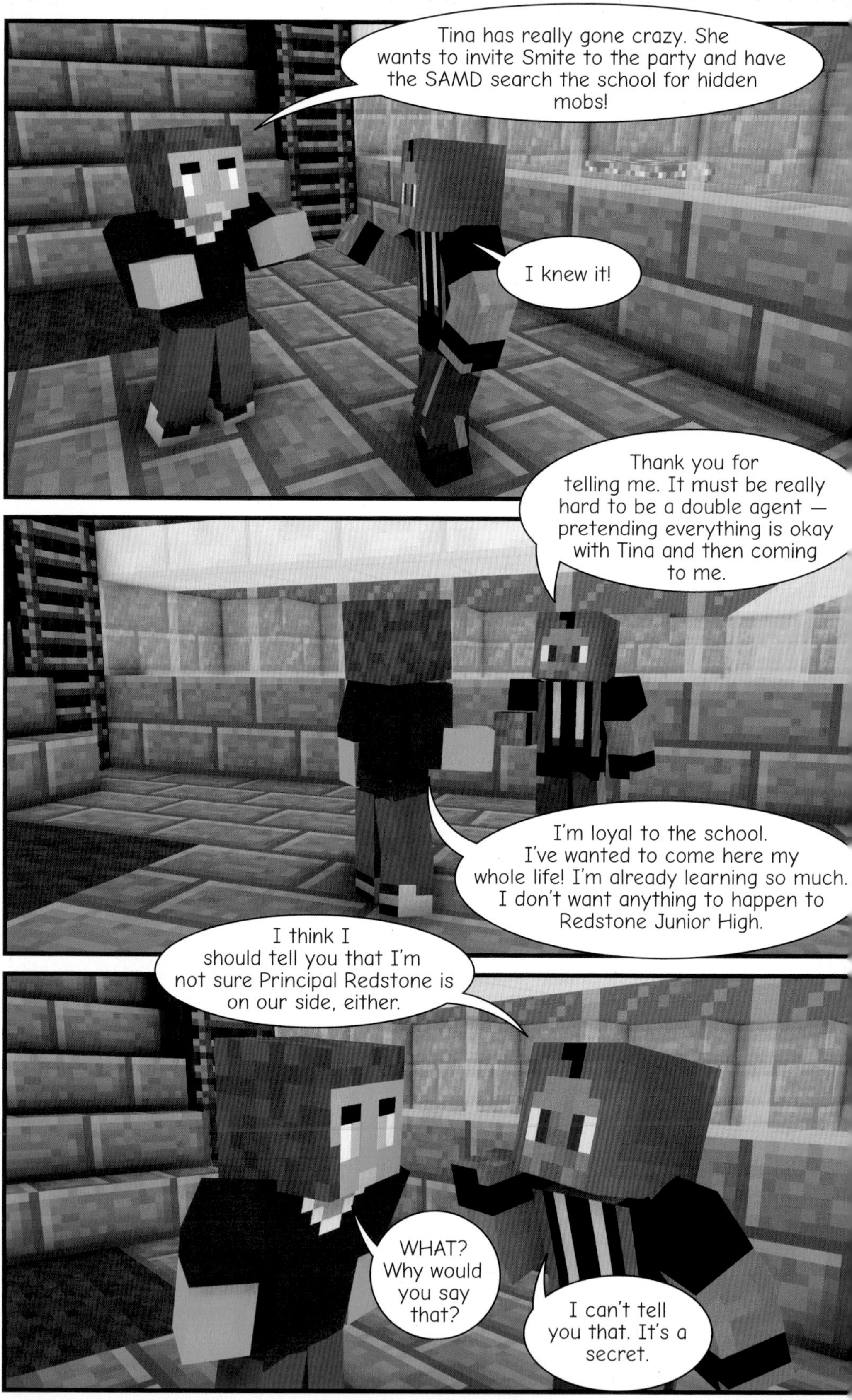
Tina has really gone crazy. She wants to invite Smite to the party and have the SAMD search the school for hidden mobs!
I knew it!
Thank you for telling me. It must be really hard to be a double agent — pretending everything is okay with Tina and then coming to me.
I'm loyal to the school. I've wanted to come here my whole life! I'm already learning so much. I don't want anything to happen to Redstone Junior High.
I think I should tell you that I'm not sure Principal Redstone is on our side, either.
WHAT? Why would you say that?
I can't tell you that. It's a secret.

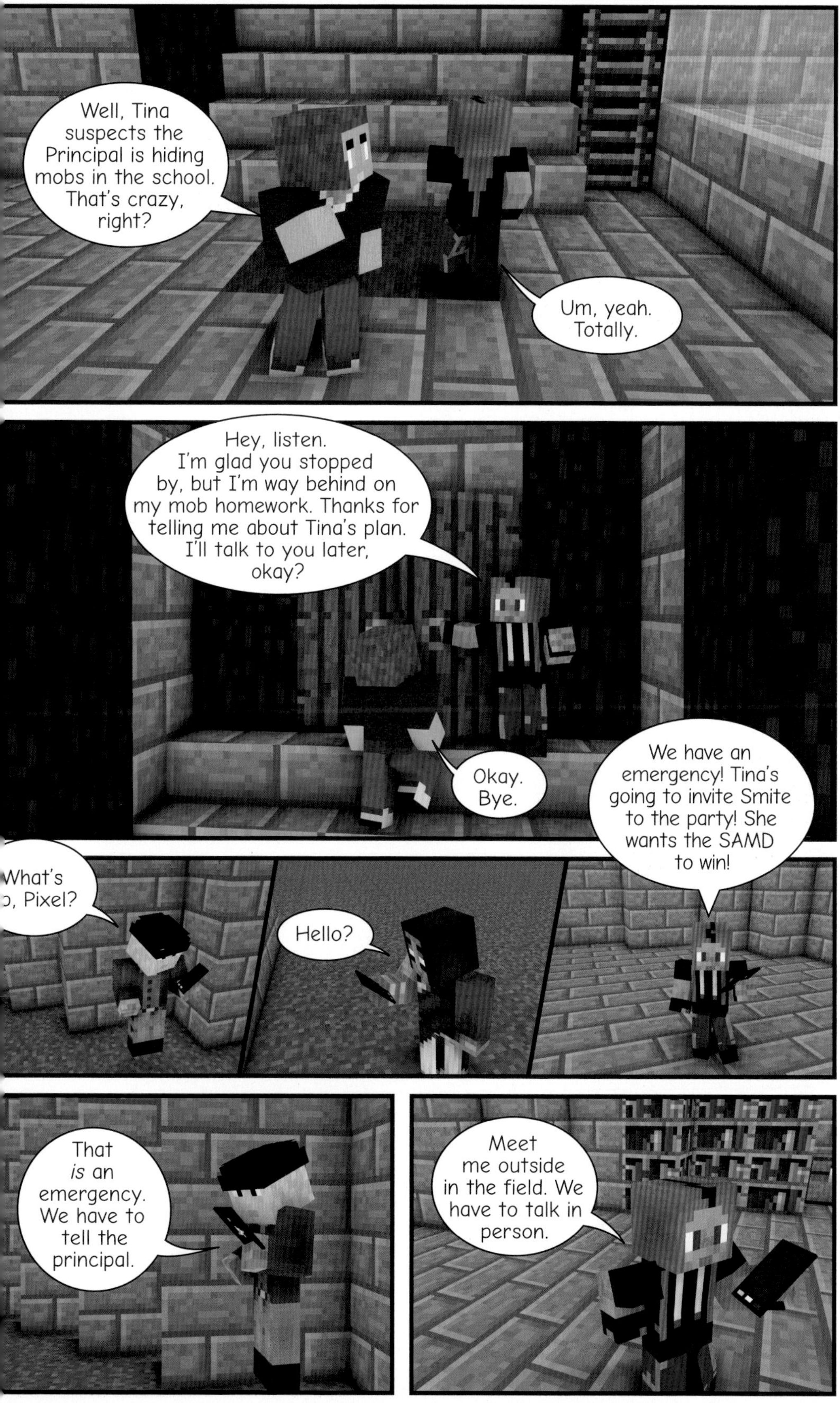
Well, Tina suspects the Principal is hiding mobs in the school. That's crazy, right?
Um, yeah. Totally.
Hey, listen. I'm glad you stopped by, but I'm way behind on my mob homework. Thanks for telling me about Tina's plan. I'll talk to you later, okay?
Okay. Bye.
What's
, Pixel?
Hello?
We have an emergency! Tina's going to invite Smite to the party! She wants the SAMD to win!
That *is* an emergency. We have to tell the principal.
Meet me outside in the field. We have to talk in person.

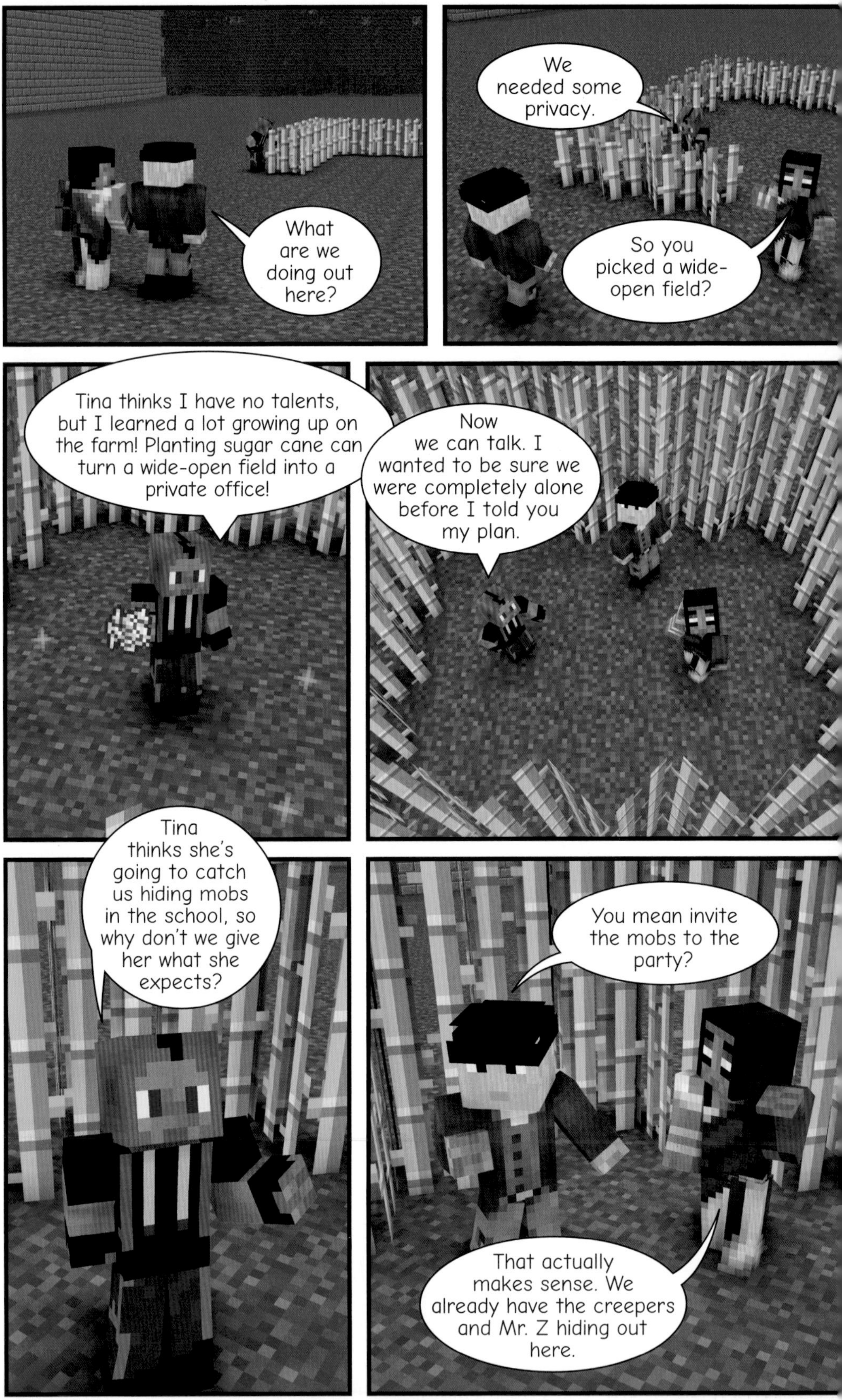

What are we doing out here?
We needed some privacy.
So you picked a wide-open field?
Tina thinks I have no talents, but I learned a lot growing up on the farm! Planting sugar cane can turn a wide-open field into a private office!
Now we can talk. I wanted to be sure we were completely alone before I told you my plan.
Tina thinks she's going to catch us hiding mobs in the school, so why don't we give her what she expects?
You mean invite the mobs to the party?
That actually makes sense. We already have the creepers and Mr. Z hiding out here.

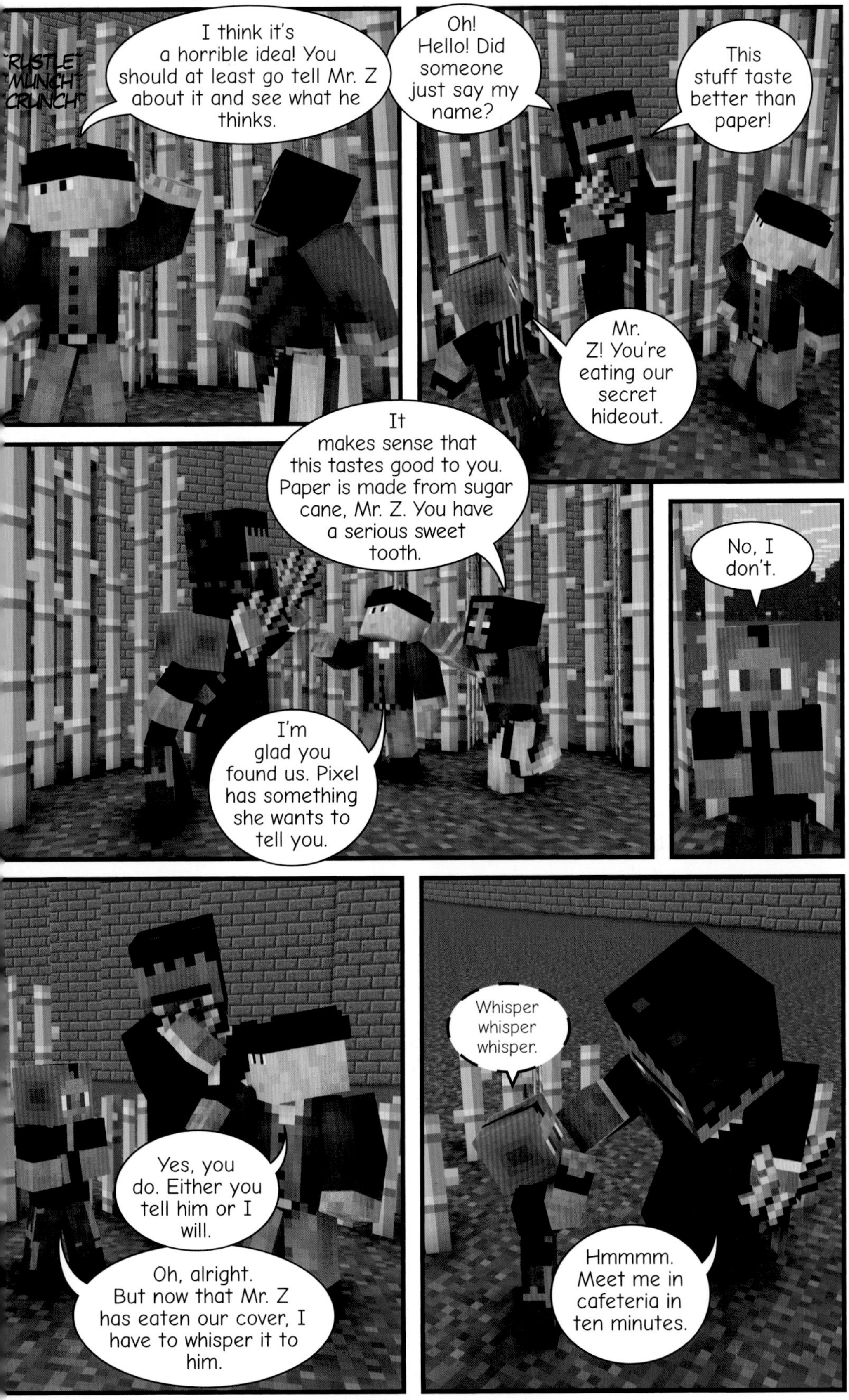
RUSTLE MUNCH CRUNCH
I think it's a horrible idea! You should at least go tell Mr. Z about it and see what he thinks.
Oh! Hello! Did someone just say my name?
This stuff taste better than paper!
Mr. Z! You're eating our secret hideout.
It makes sense that this tastes good to you. Paper is made from sugar cane, Mr. Z. You have a serious sweet tooth.
I'm glad you found us. Pixel has something she wants to tell you.
No, I don't.
Yes, you do. Either you tell him or I will.
Oh, alright. But now that Mr. Z has eaten our cover, I have to whisper it to him.
Whisper whisper whisper.
Hmmmm. Meet me in cafeteria in ten minutes.

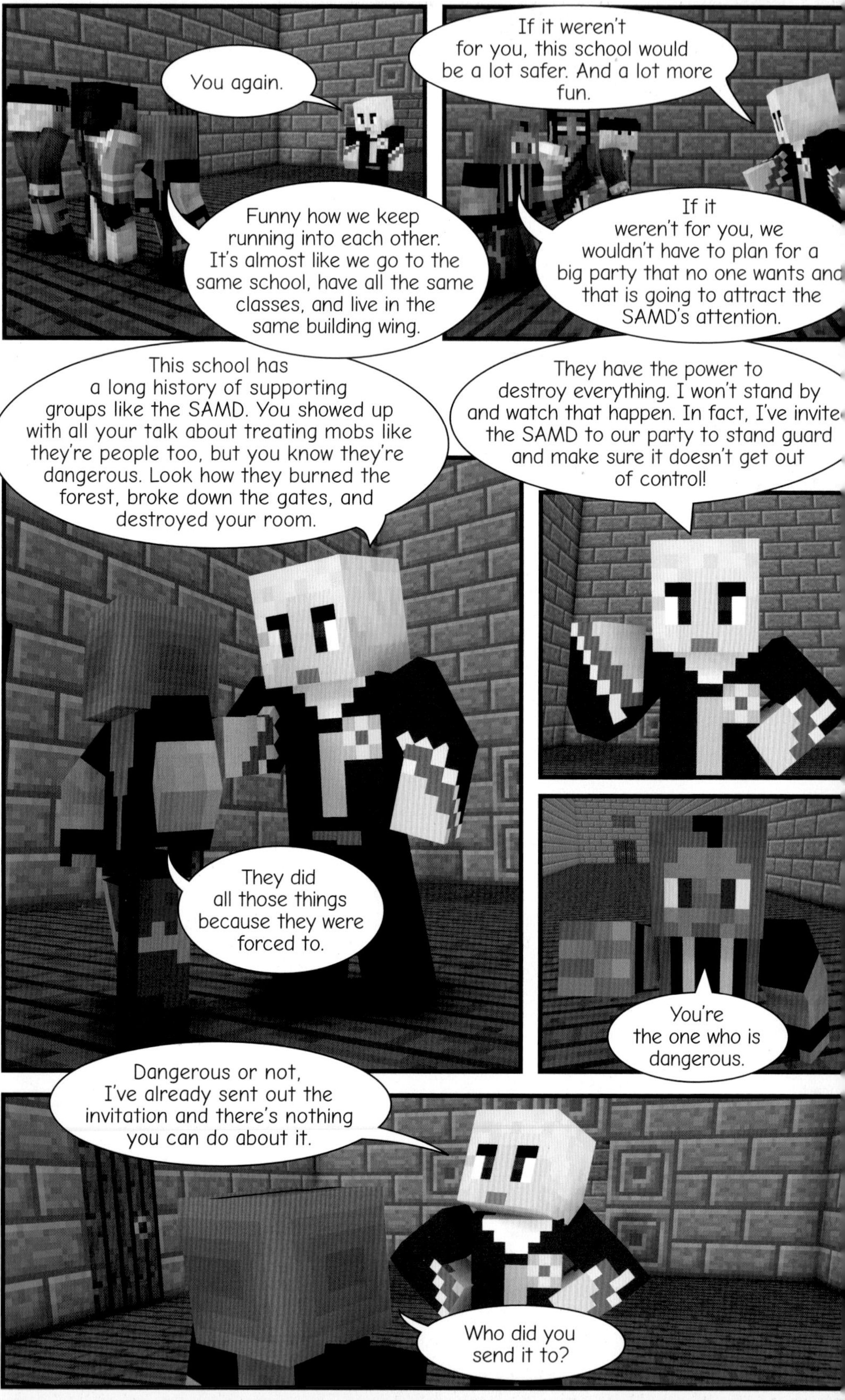
You again.
Funny how we keep running into each other. It's almost like we go to the same school, have all the same classes, and live in the same building wing.
If it weren't for you, this school would be a lot safer. And a lot more fun.
If it weren't for you, we wouldn't have to plan for a big party that no one wants and that is going to attract the SAMD's attention.
This school has a long history of supporting groups like the SAMD. You showed up with all your talk about treating mobs like they're people too, but you know they're dangerous. Look how they burned the forest, broke down the gates, and destroyed your room.
They did all those things because they were forced to.
They have the power to destroy everything. I won't stand by and watch that happen. In fact, I've invite the SAMD to our party to stand guard and make sure it doesn't get out of control!
You're the one who is dangerous.
Dangerous or not, I've already sent out the invitation and there's nothing you can do about it.
Who did you send it to?

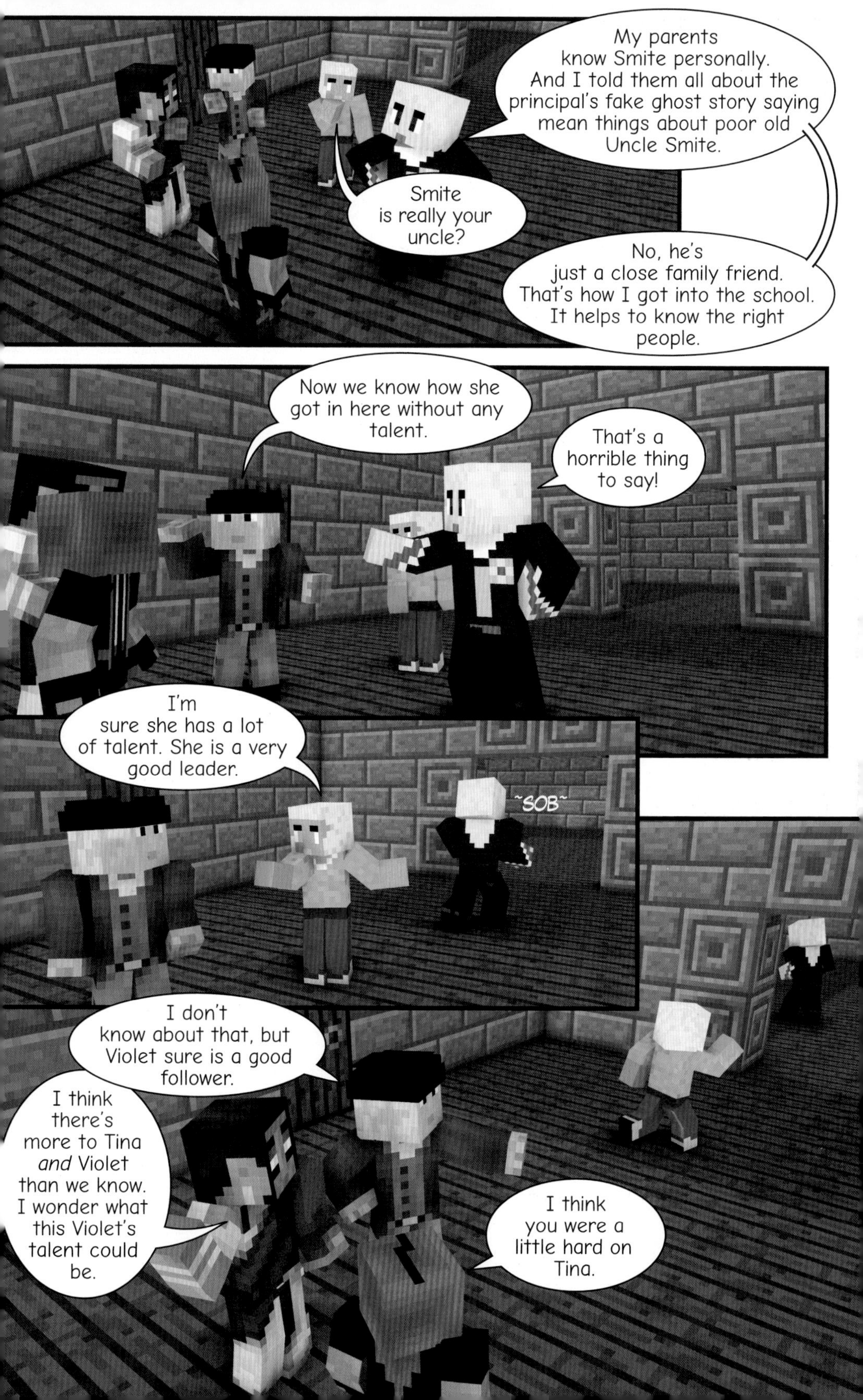
My parents know Smite personally. And I told them all about the principal's fake ghost story saying mean things about poor old Uncle Smite.
Smite is really your uncle?
No, he's just a close family friend. That's how I got into the school. It helps to know the right people.
Now we know how she got in here without any talent.
That's a horrible thing to say!
I'm sure she has a lot of talent. She is a very good leader.
~SOB~
I don't know about that, but Violet sure is a good follower.
I think there's more to Tina *and* Violet than we know. I wonder what this Violet's talent could be.
I think you were a little hard on Tina.

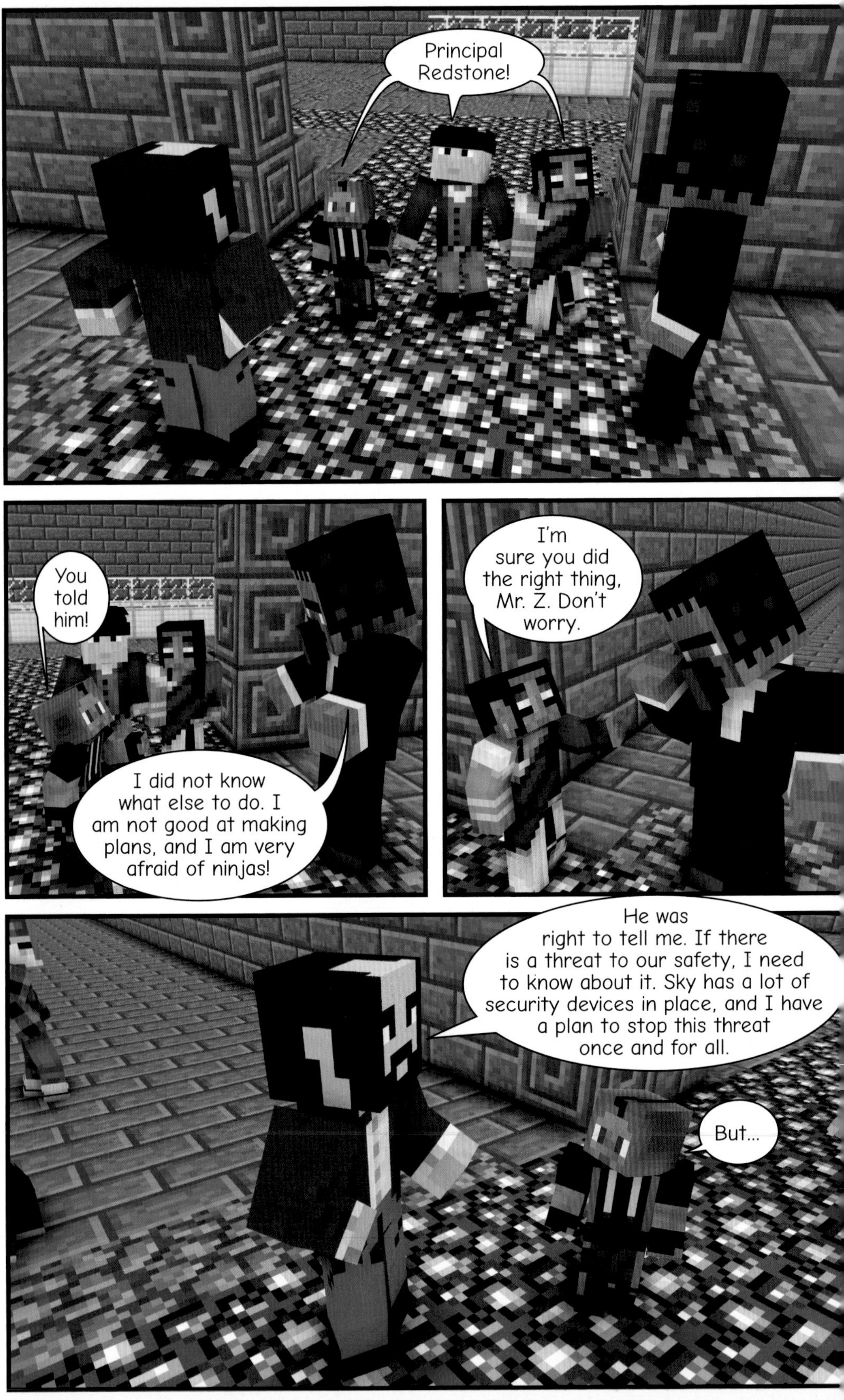
Principal Redstone!
You told him!
I did not know what else to do. I am not good at making plans, and I am very afraid of ninjas!
I'm sure you did the right thing, Mr. Z. Don't worry.
He was right to tell me. If there is a threat to our safety, I need to know about it. Sky has a lot of security devices in place, and I have a plan to stop this threat once and for all.
But...

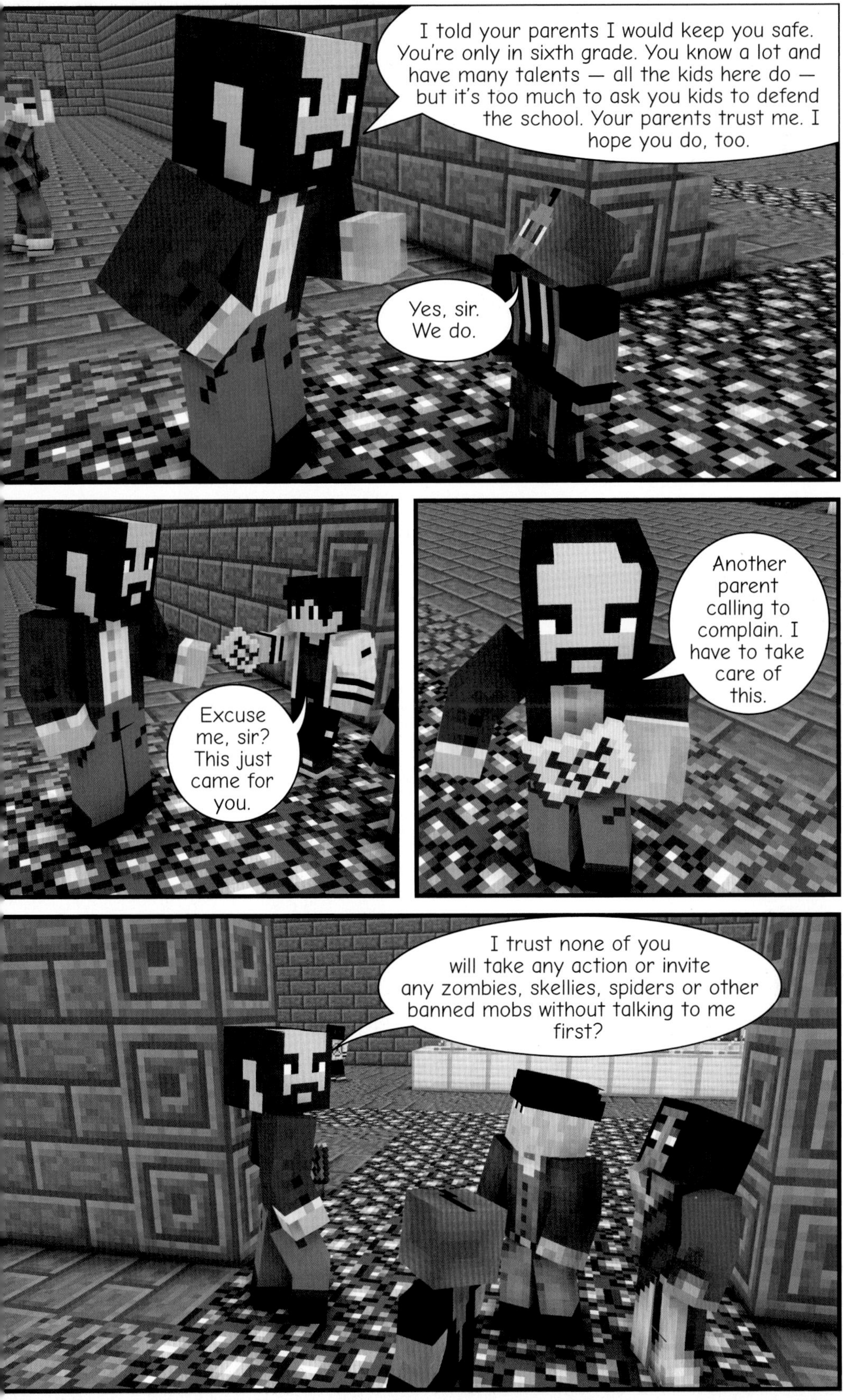
I told your parents I would keep you safe. You're only in sixth grade. You know a lot and have many talents — all the kids here do — but it's too much to ask you kids to defend the school. Your parents trust me. I hope you do, too.
Yes, sir. We do.
Excuse me, sir? This just came for you.
Another parent calling to complain. I have to take care of this.
I trust none of you will take any action or invite any zombies, skellies, spiders or other banned mobs without talking to me first?

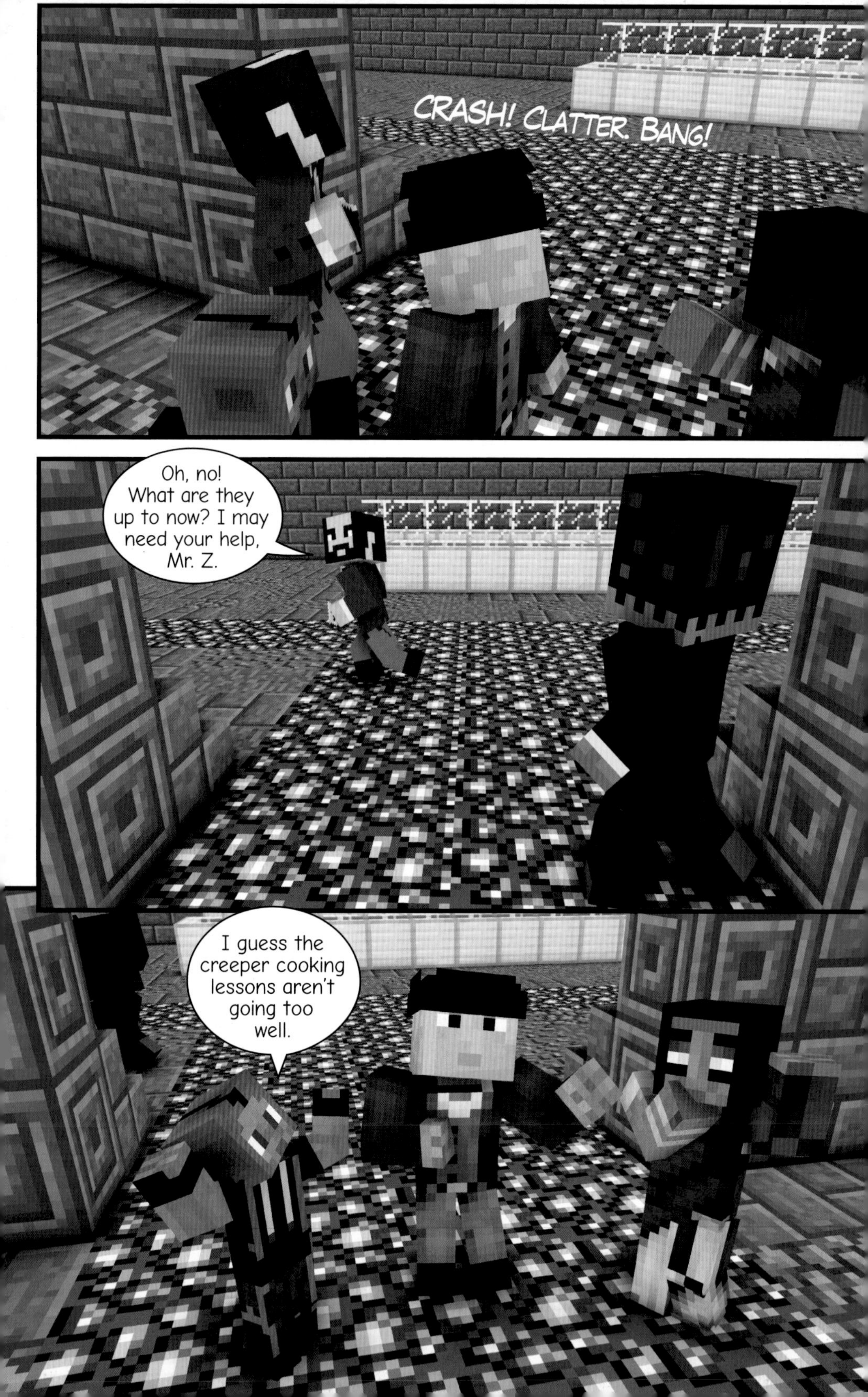
CRASH! CLATTER. BANG!
Oh, no! What are they up to now? I may need your help, Mr. Z.
I guess the creeper cooking lessons aren't going too well.

CHAPTER 8

Food
Milk
Dust
Cake Plates
Apples
PARKLE!
Watermelon
plates

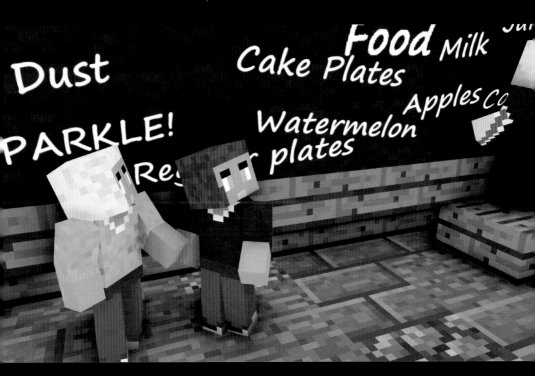

THE PARTY FAIRIES

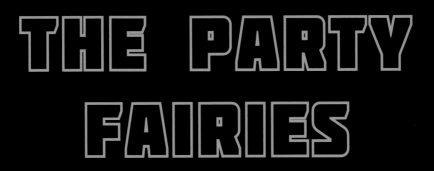

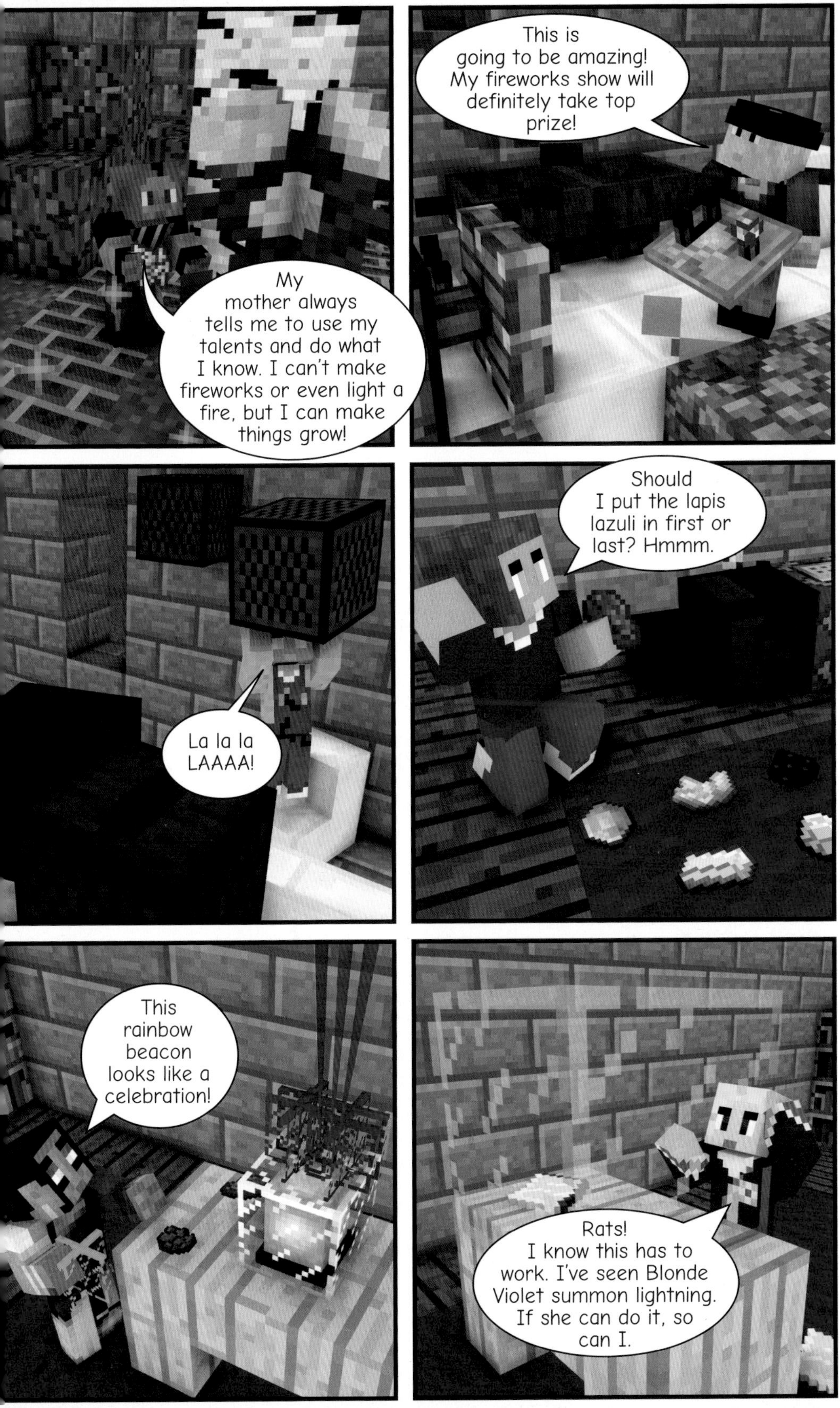
My mother always tells me to use my talents and do what I know. I can't make fireworks or even light a fire, but I can make things grow!
This is going to be amazing! My fireworks show will definitely take top prize!
La la la LAAAA!
Should I put the lapis lazuli in first or last? Hmmm.
This rainbow beacon looks like a celebration!
Rats! I know this has to work. I've seen Blonde Violet summon lightning. If she can do it, so can I.

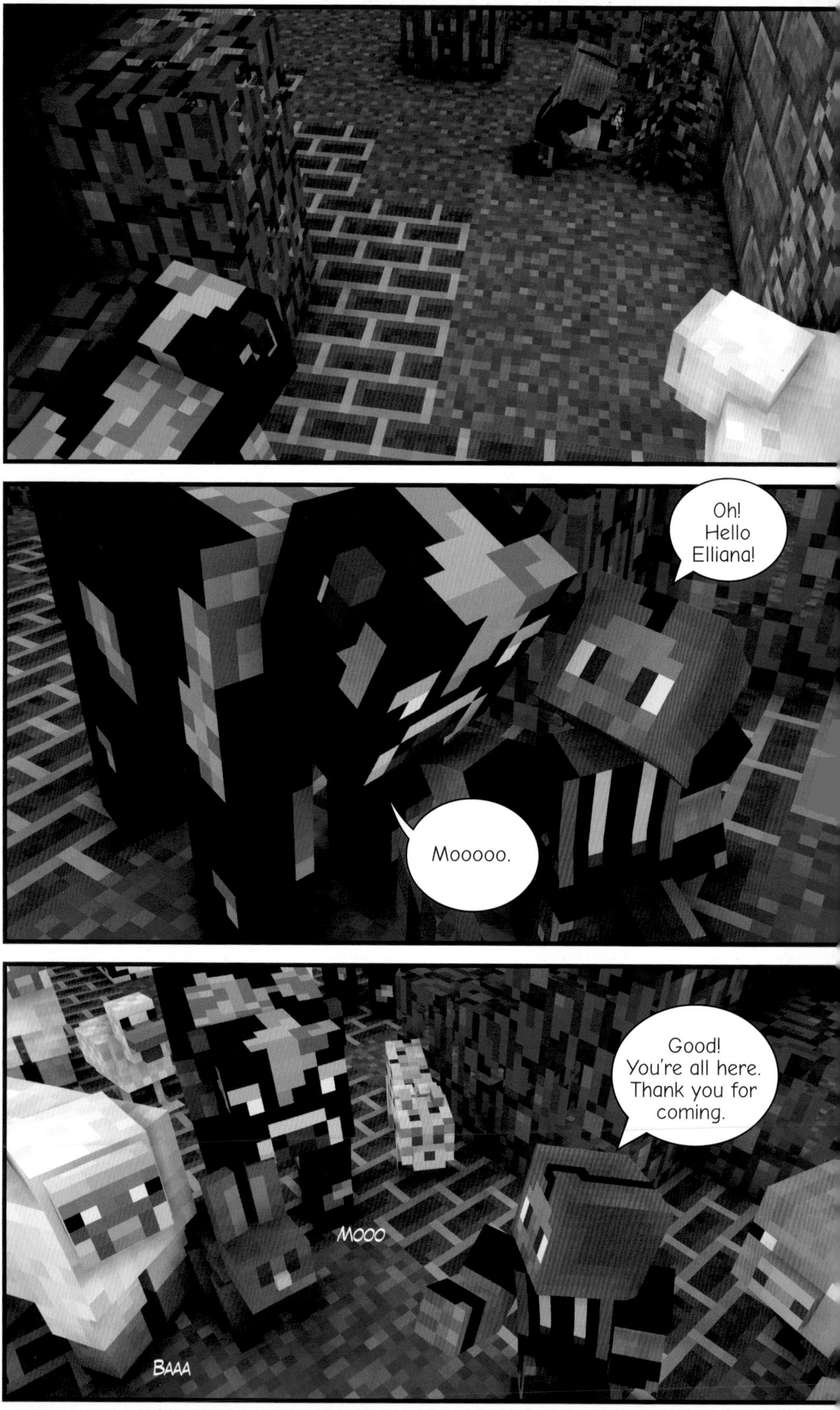
Oh!
Hello
Elliana!
Mooooo.
Good!
You're all here.
Thank you for
coming.
MOOO
BAAA

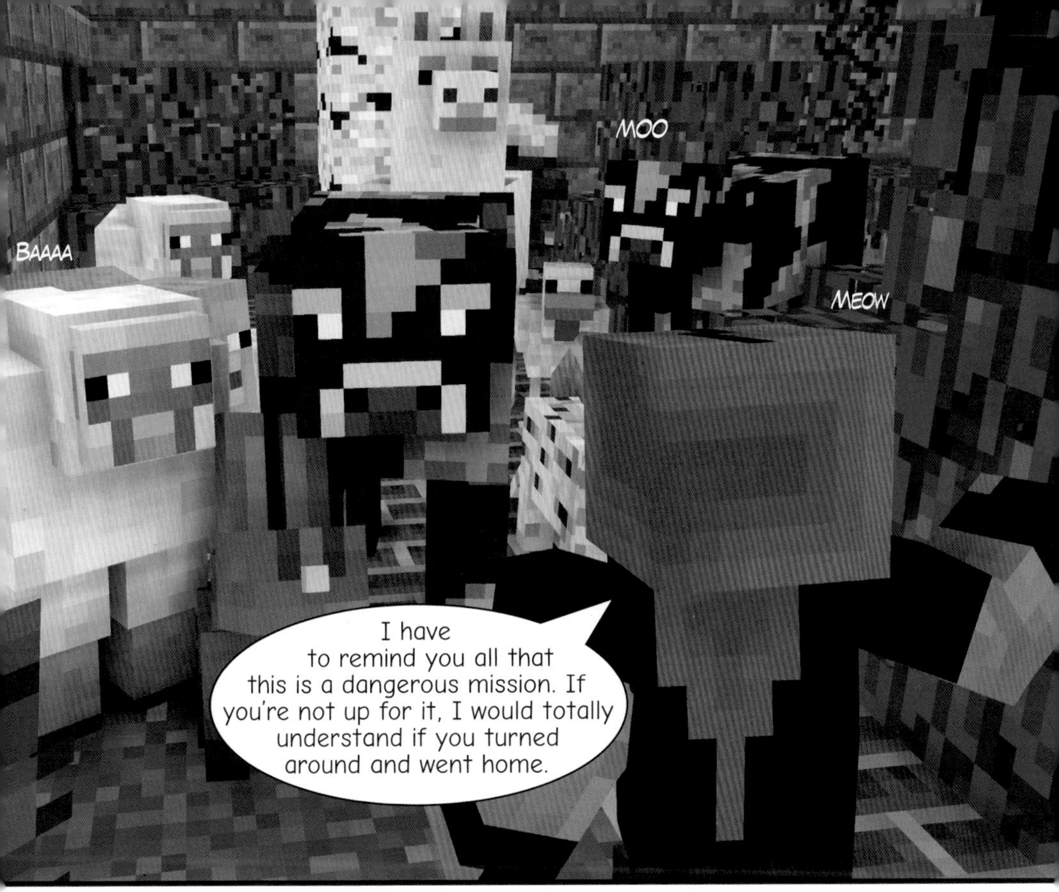
MOO
BAAAA
MEOW
I have to remind you all that this is a dangerous mission. If you're not up for it, I would totally understand if you turned around and went home.

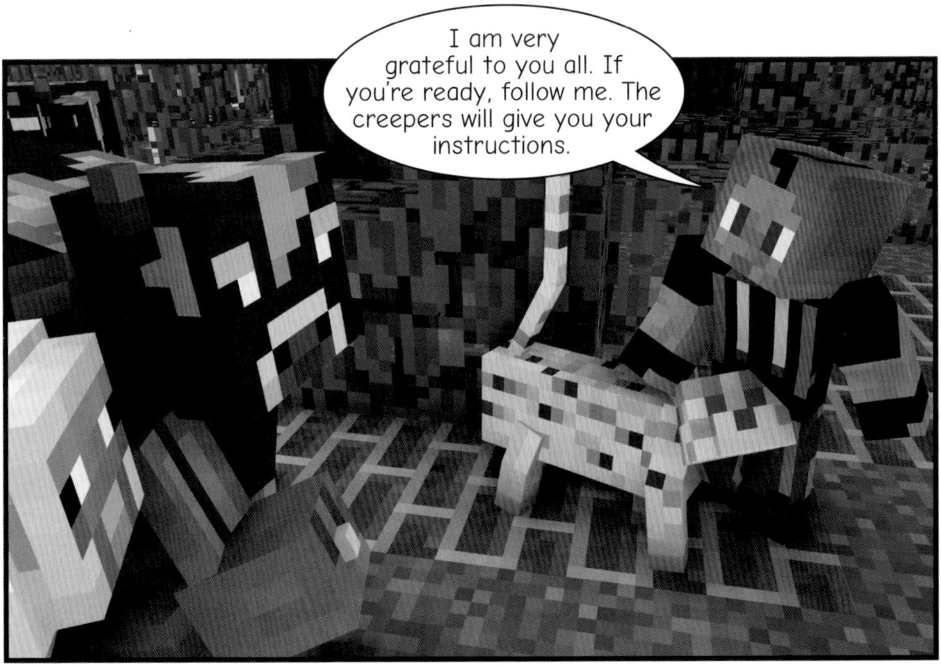
I am very grateful to you all. If you're ready, follow me. The creepers will give you your instructions.

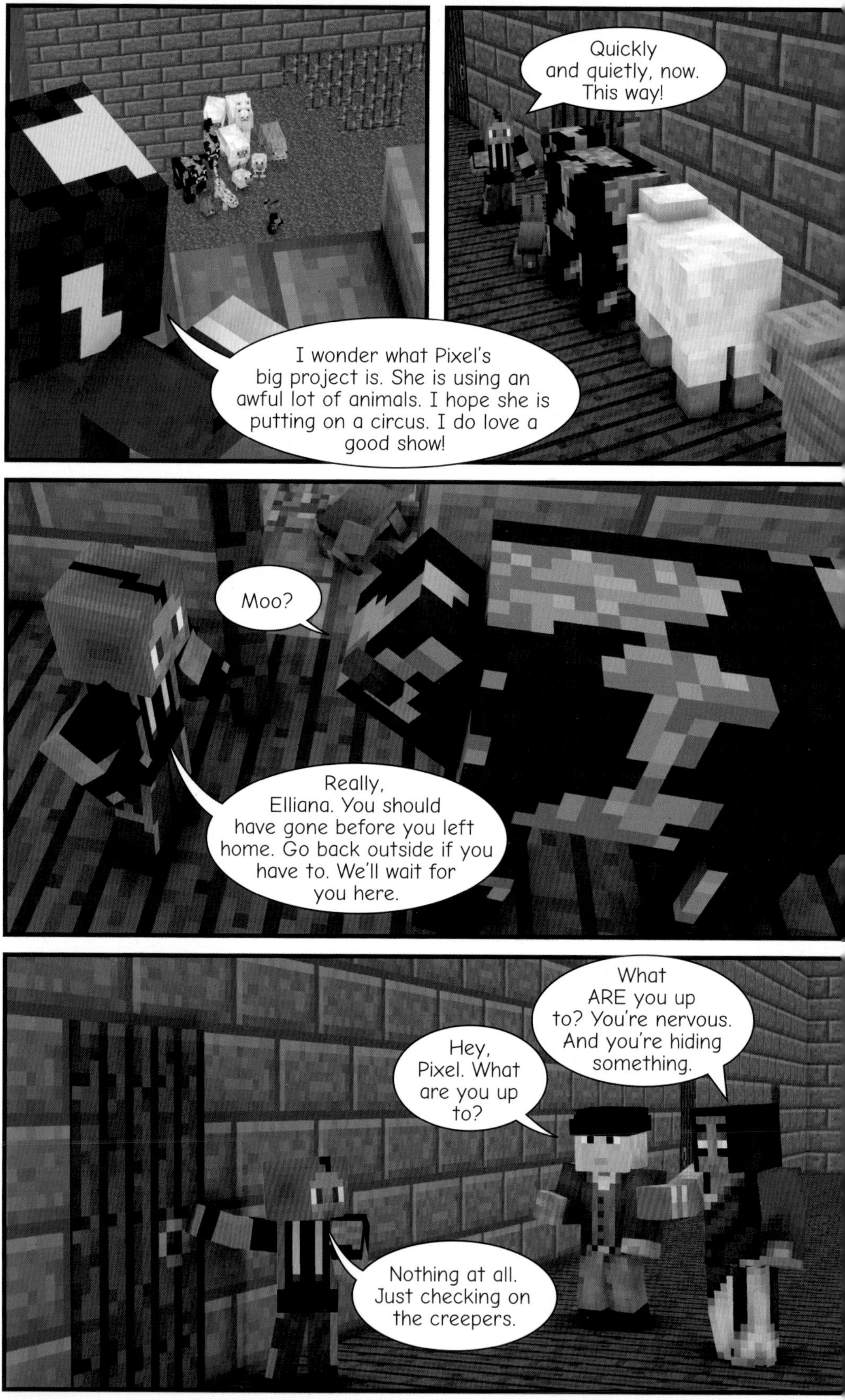

I wonder what Pixel's big project is. She is using an awful lot of animals. I hope she is putting on a circus. I do love a good show!
Quickly and quietly, now. This way!
Moo?
Really, Elliana. You should have gone before you left home. Go back outside if you have to. We'll wait for you here.
Hey, Pixel. What are you up to?
What ARE you up to? You're nervous. And you're hiding something.
Nothing at all. Just checking on the creepers.

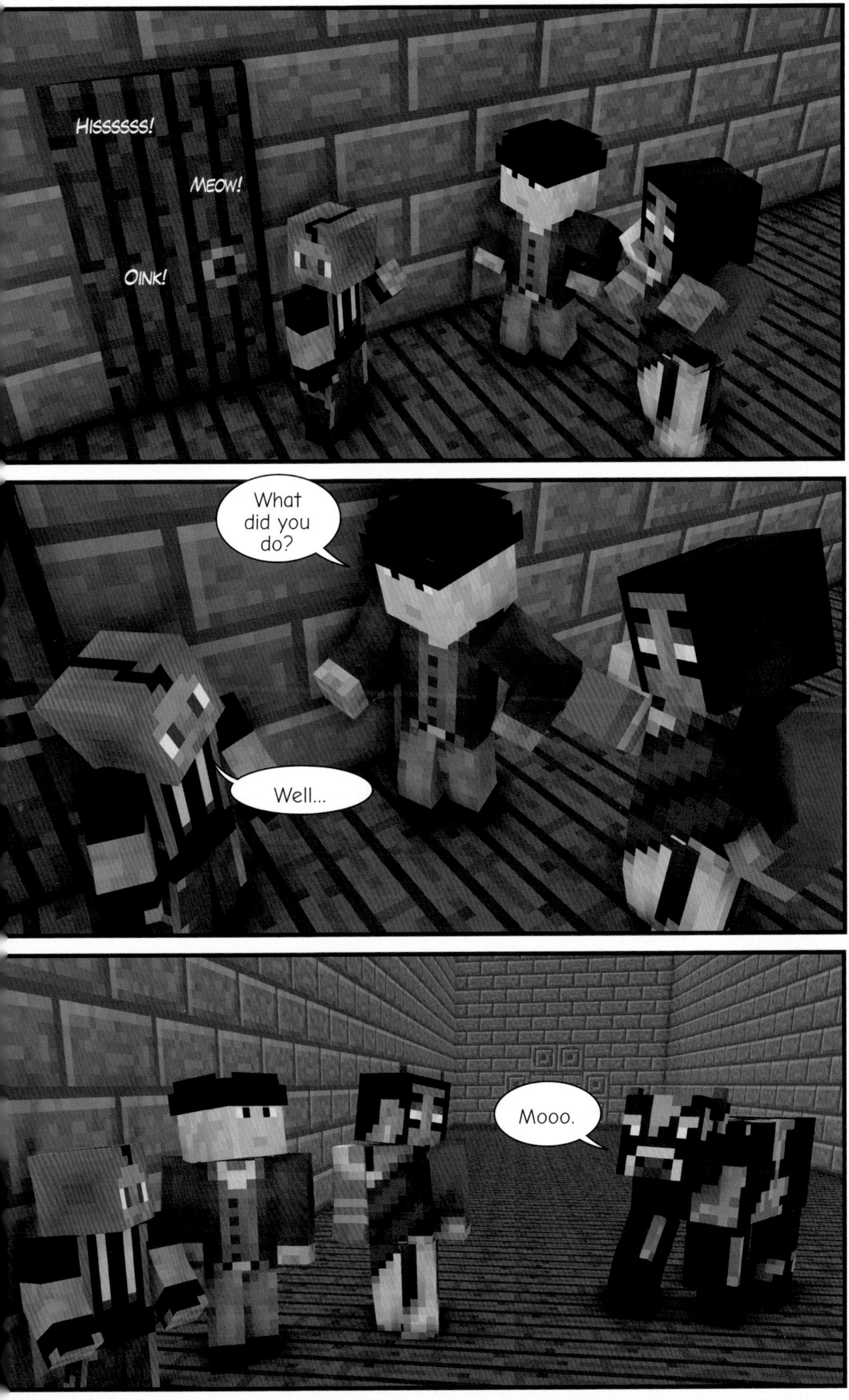
HISSSSSS!
MEOW!
OINK!
What did you do?
Well...
Mooo.

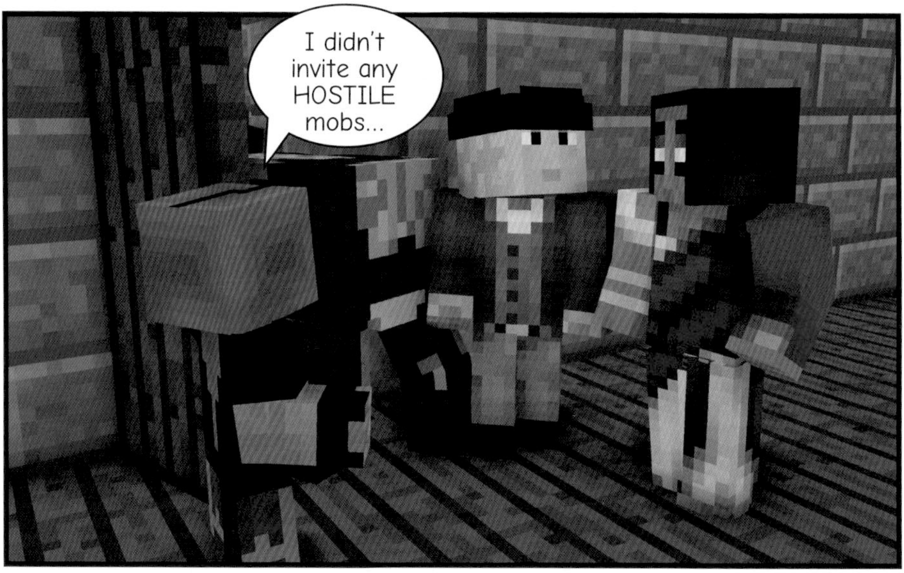
I didn't invite any HOSTILE mobs...

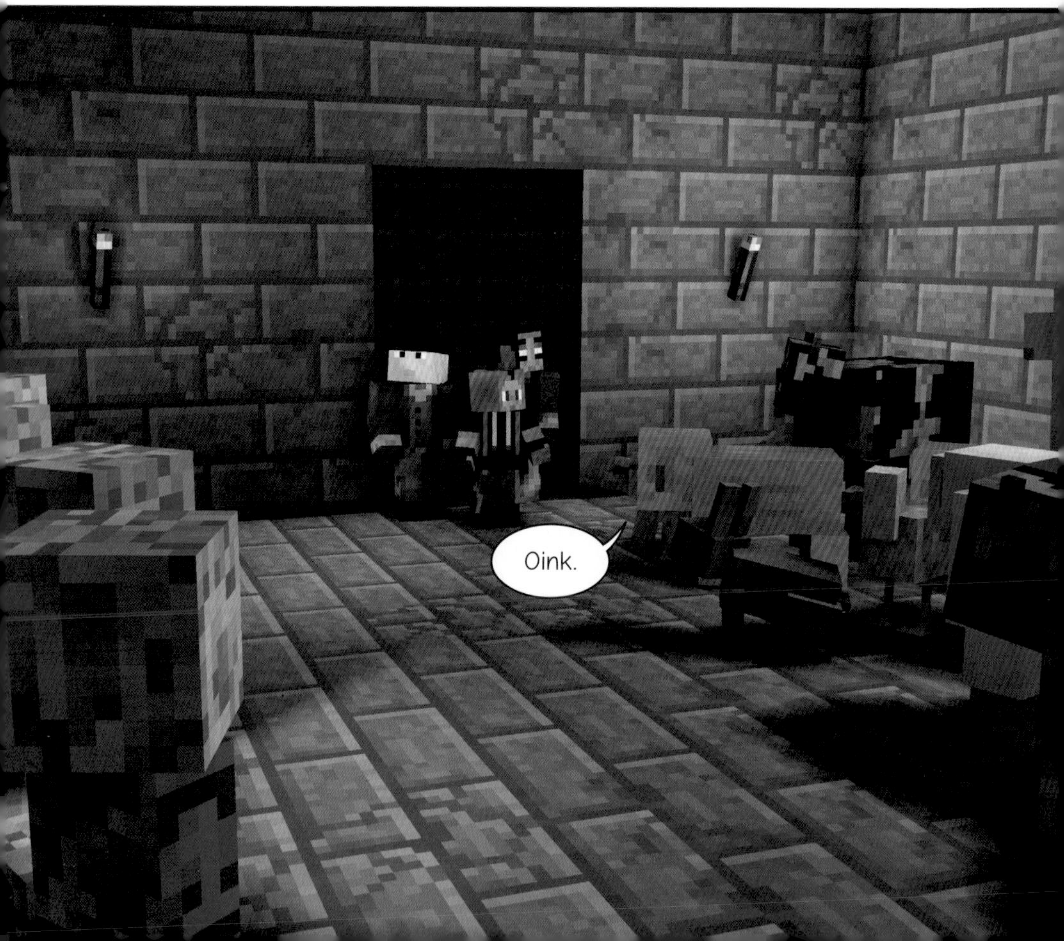
Oink.

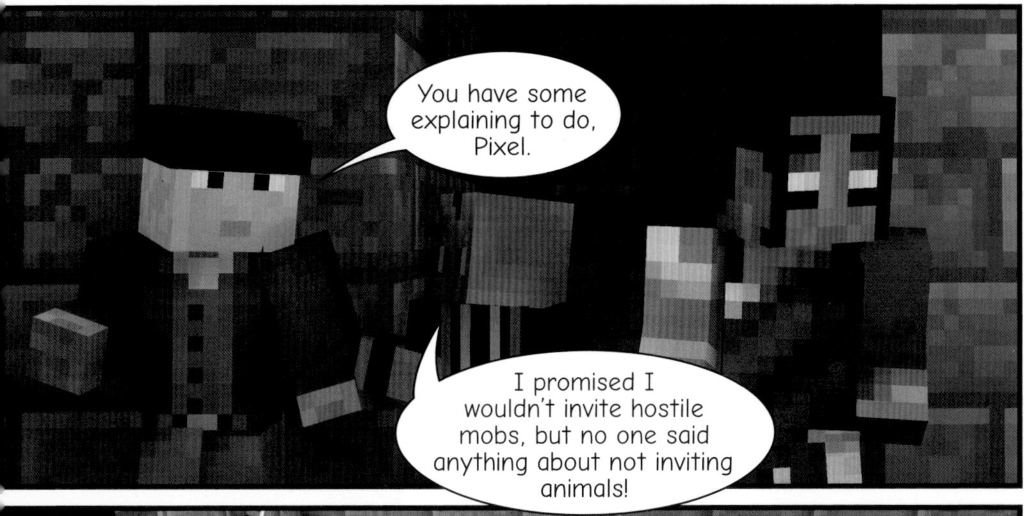
You have some explaining to do, Pixel.
I promised I wouldn't invite hostile mobs, but no one said anything about not inviting animals!

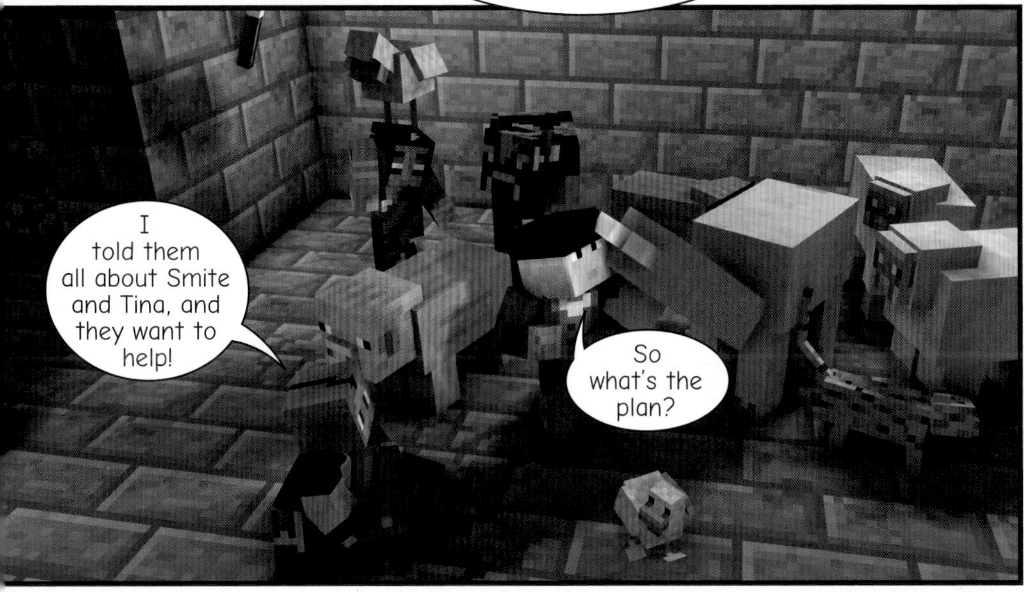
I told them all about Smite and Tina, and they want to help!
So what's the plan?

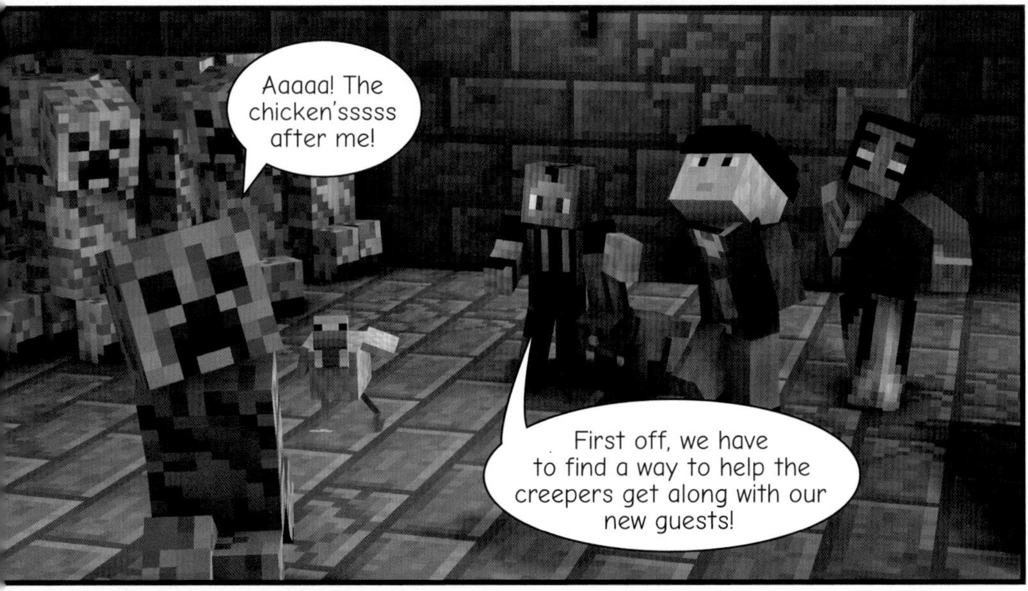
Aaaaa! The chicken'sssss after me!
First off, we have to find a way to help the creepers get along with our new guests!

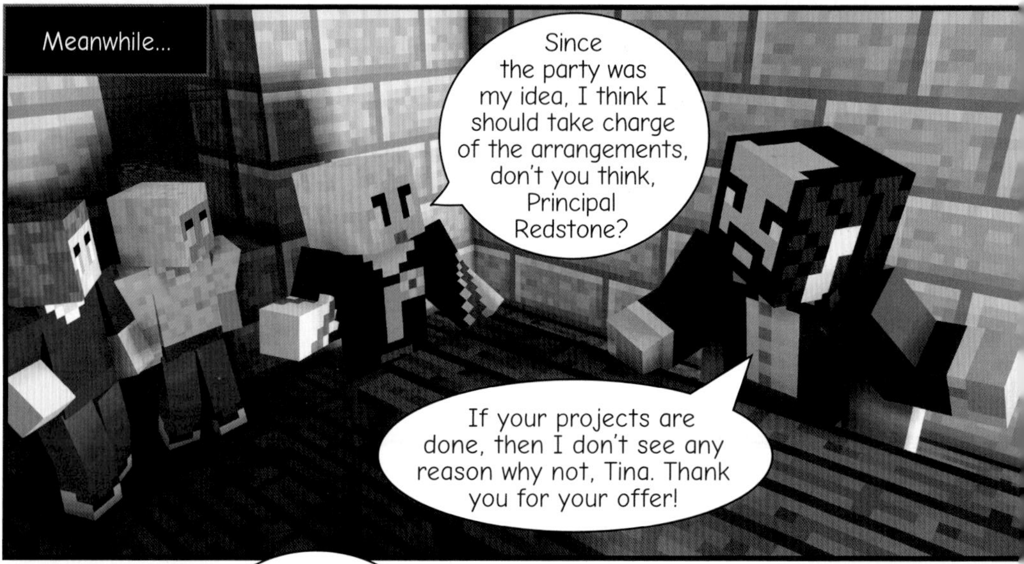
Meanwhile...
Since the party was my idea, I think I should take charge of the arrangements, don't you think, Principal Redstone?
If your projects are done, then I don't see any reason why not, Tina. Thank you for your offer!

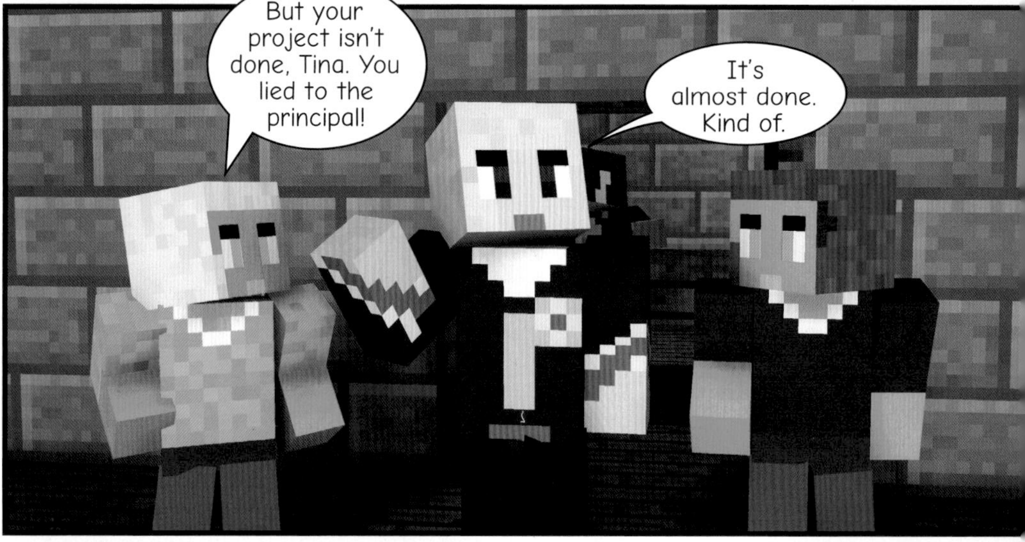
But your project isn't done, Tina. You lied to the principal!
It's almost done. Kind of.

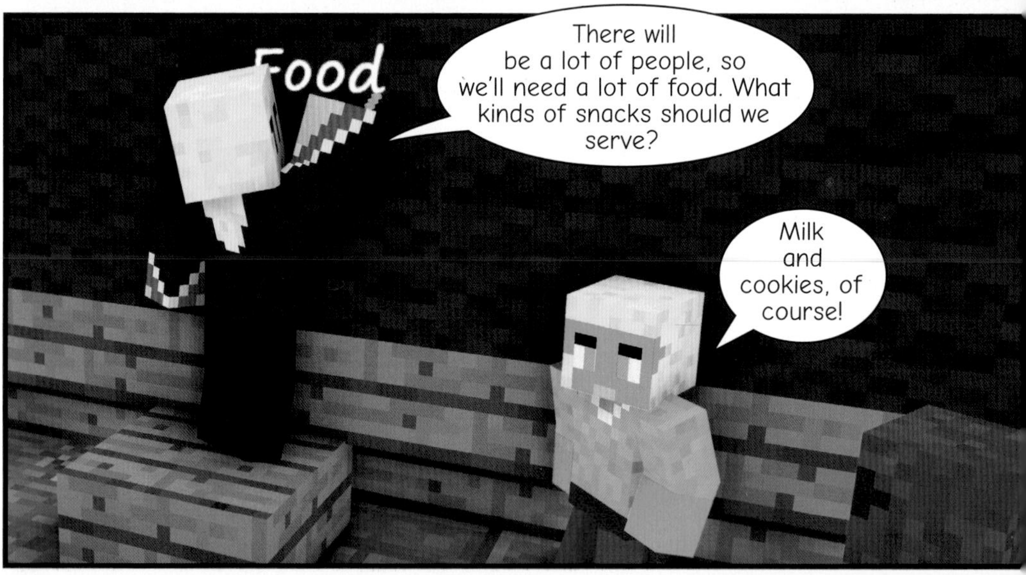
Food
There will be a lot of people, so we'll need a lot of food. What kinds of snacks should we serve?
Milk and cookies, of course!

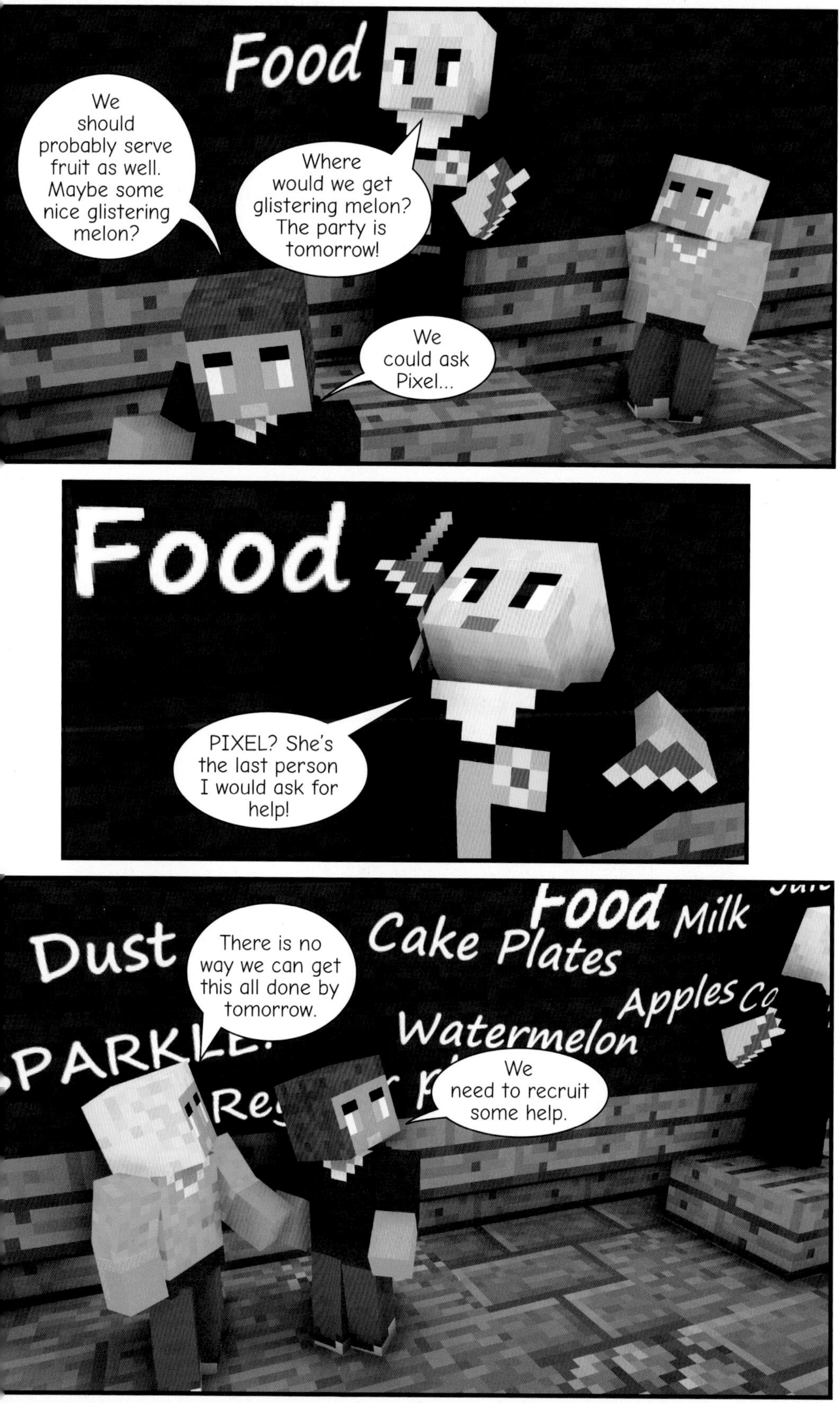
Food
We should probably serve fruit as well. Maybe some nice glistering melon?
Where would we get glistering melon? The party is tomorrow!
We could ask Pixel...
Food
PIXEL? She's the last person I would ask for help!
Dust
Cake Plates
Food Milk
Apples
Watermelon
There is no way we can get this all done by tomorrow.
We need to recruit some help.

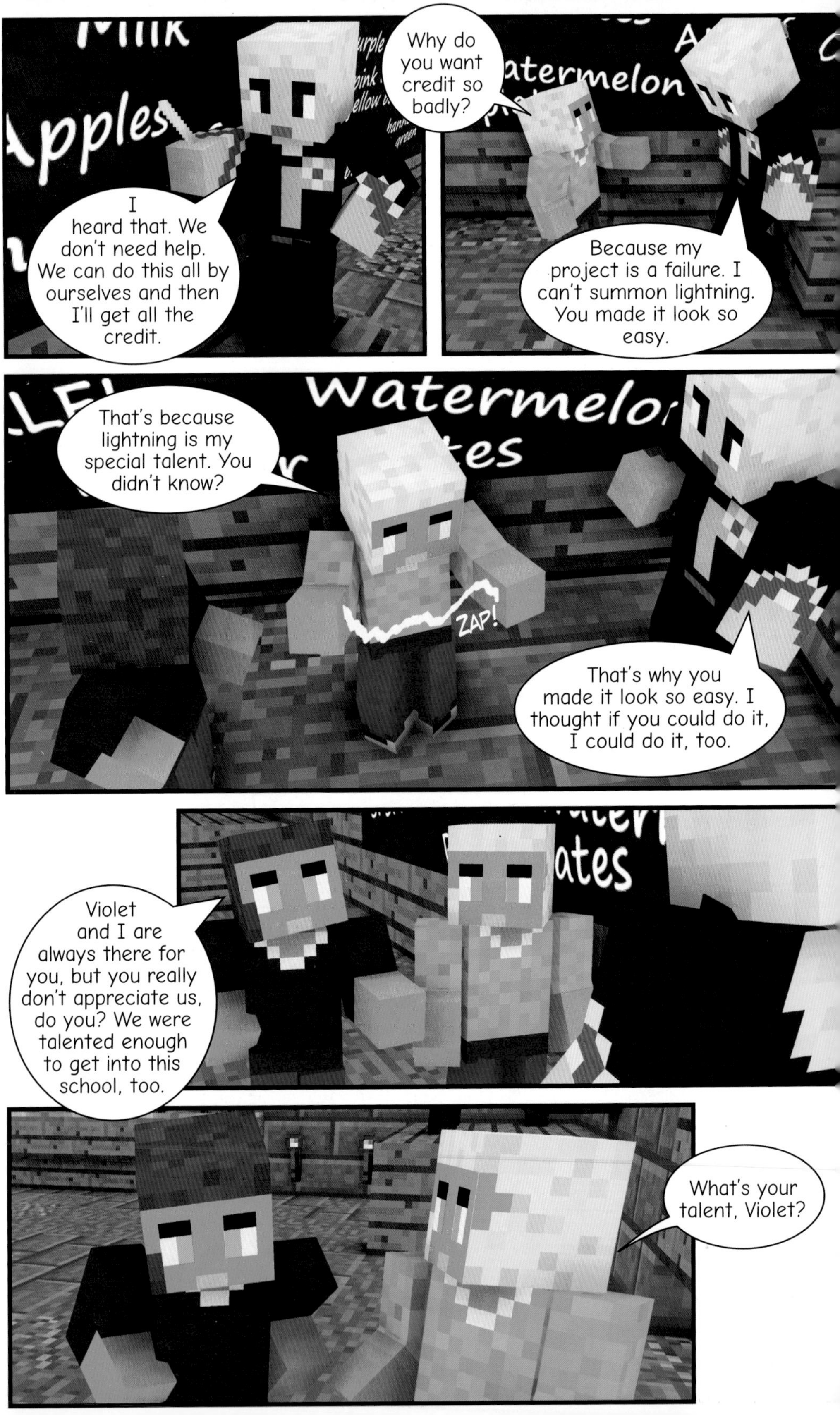
I heard that. We don't need help. We can do this all by ourselves and then I'll get all the credit.
Why do you want credit so badly?
Because my project is a failure. I can't summon lightning. You made it look so easy.
That's because lightning is my special talent. You didn't know?
ZAP!
That's why you made it look so easy. I thought if you could do it, I could do it, too.
Violet and I are always there for you, but you really don't appreciate us, do you? We were talented enough to get into this school, too.
What's your talent, Violet?

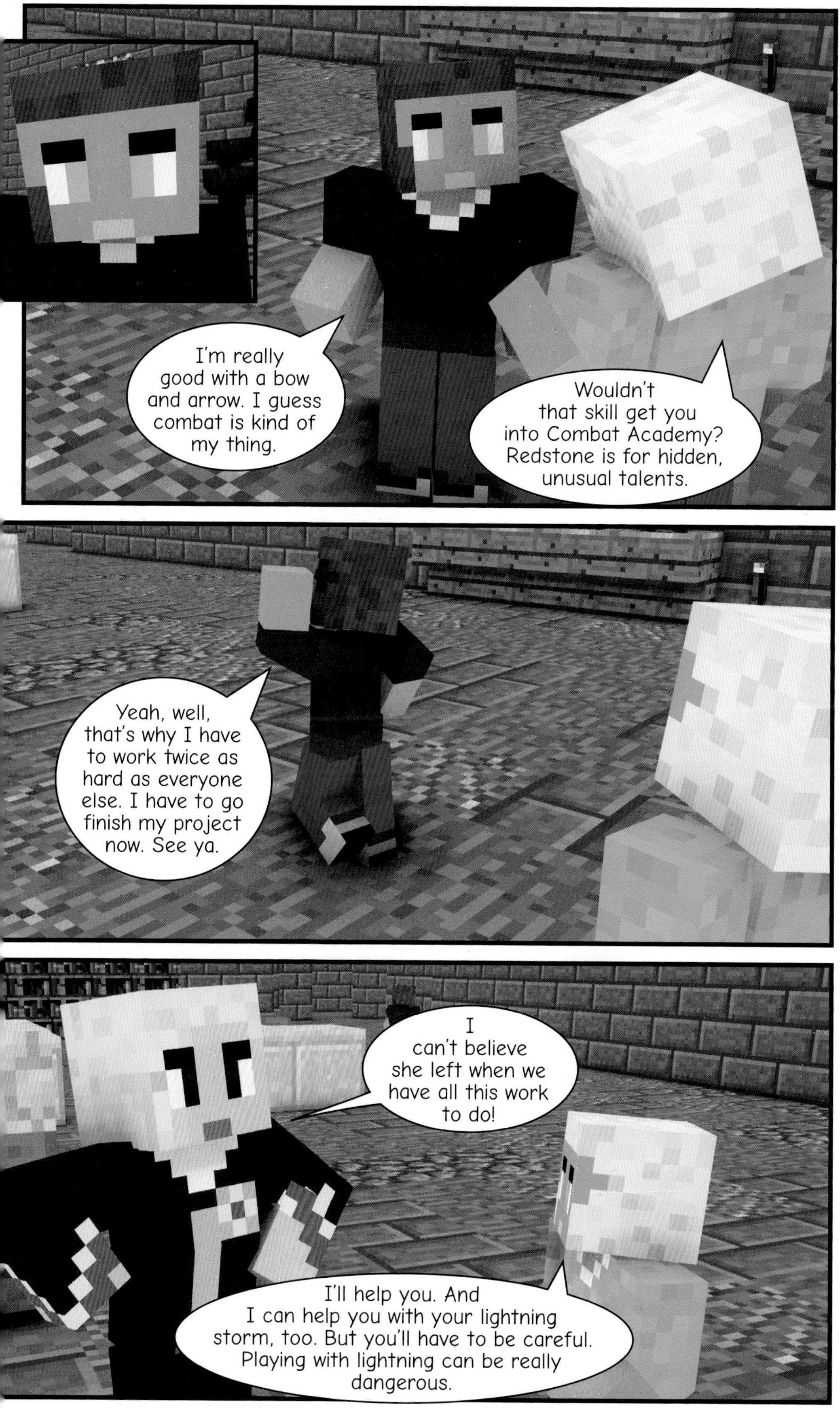
I'm really good with a bow and arrow. I guess combat is kind of my thing.
Wouldn't that skill get you into Combat Academy? Redstone is for hidden, unusual talents.
Yeah, well, that's why I have to work twice as hard as everyone else. I have to go finish my project now. See ya.
I can't believe she left when we have all this work to do!
I'll help you. And I can help you with your lightning storm, too. But you'll have to be careful. Playing with lightning can be really dangerous.

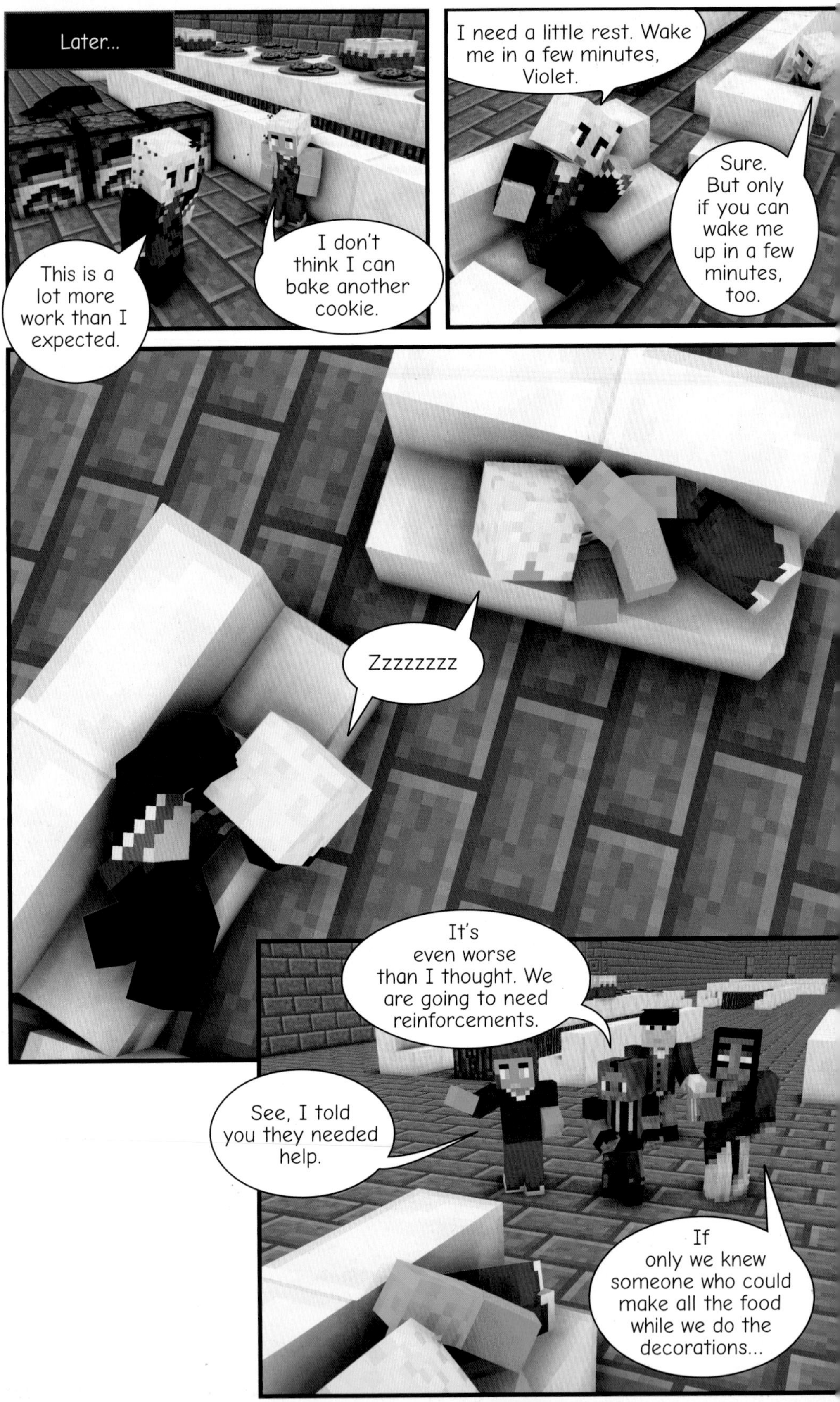
Later...
This is a lot more work than I expected.
I don't think I can bake another cookie.
I need a little rest. Wake me in a few minutes, Violet.
Sure. But only if you can wake me up in a few minutes, too.
Zzzzzzzz
It's even worse than I thought. We are going to need reinforcements.
See, I told you they needed help.
If only we knew someone who could make all the food while we do the decorations...

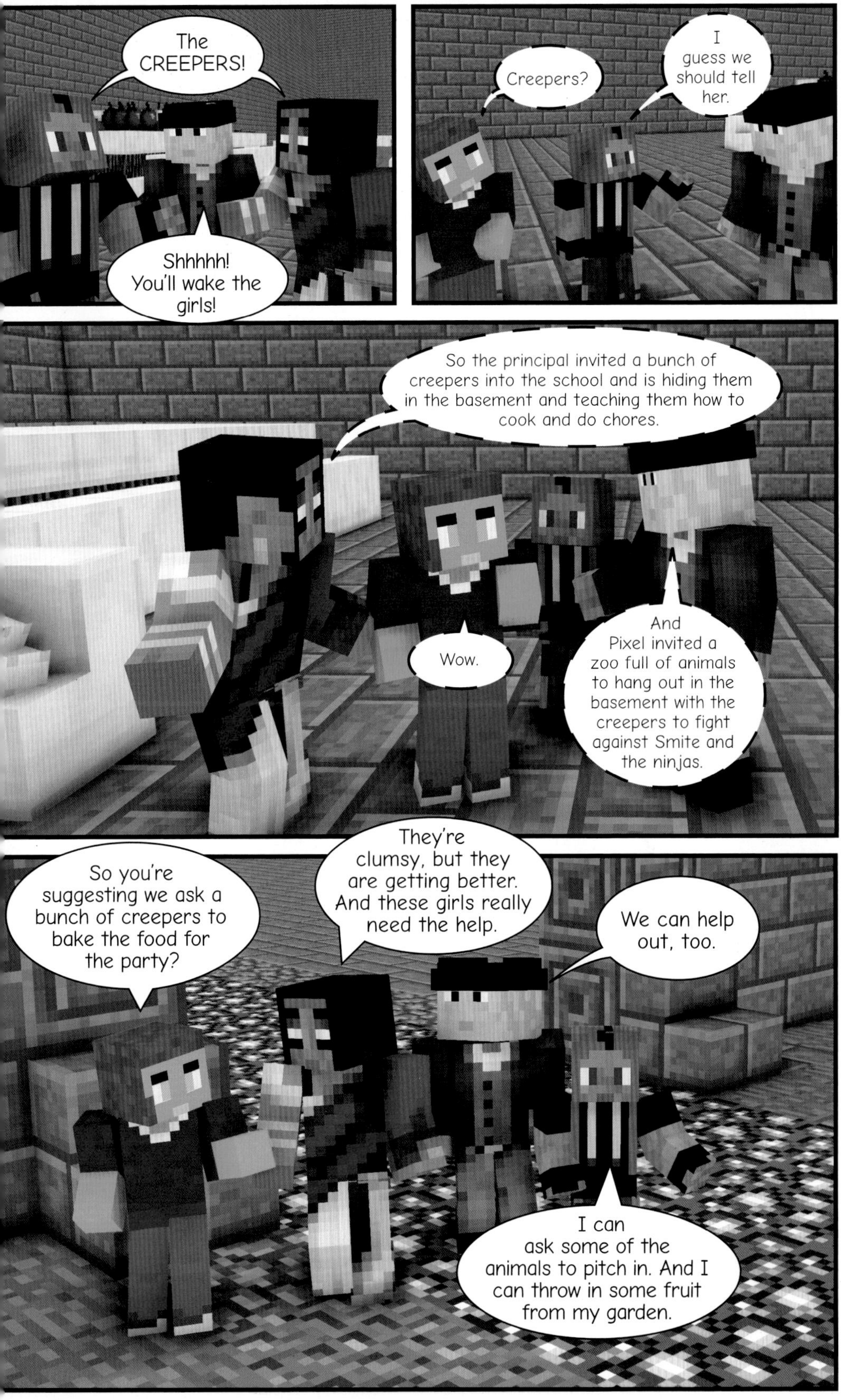
The CREEPERS!
Shhhhh! You'll wake the girls!
Creepers?
I guess we should tell her.
So the principal invited a bunch of creepers into the school and is hiding them in the basement and teaching them how to cook and do chores.
Wow.
And Pixel invited a zoo full of animals to hang out in the basement with the creepers to fight against Smite and the ninjas.
So you're suggesting we ask a bunch of creepers to bake the food for the party?
They're clumsy, but they are getting better. And these girls really need the help.
We can help out, too.
I can ask some of the animals to pitch in. And I can throw in some fruit from my garden.

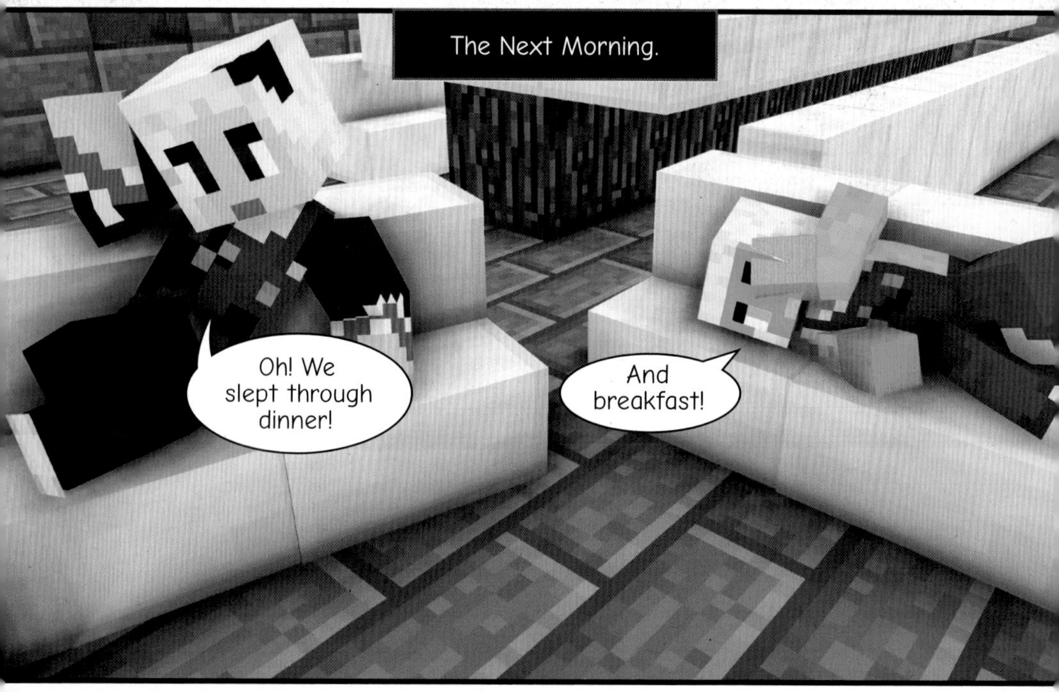
The Next Morning.
Oh! We slept through dinner!
And breakfast!

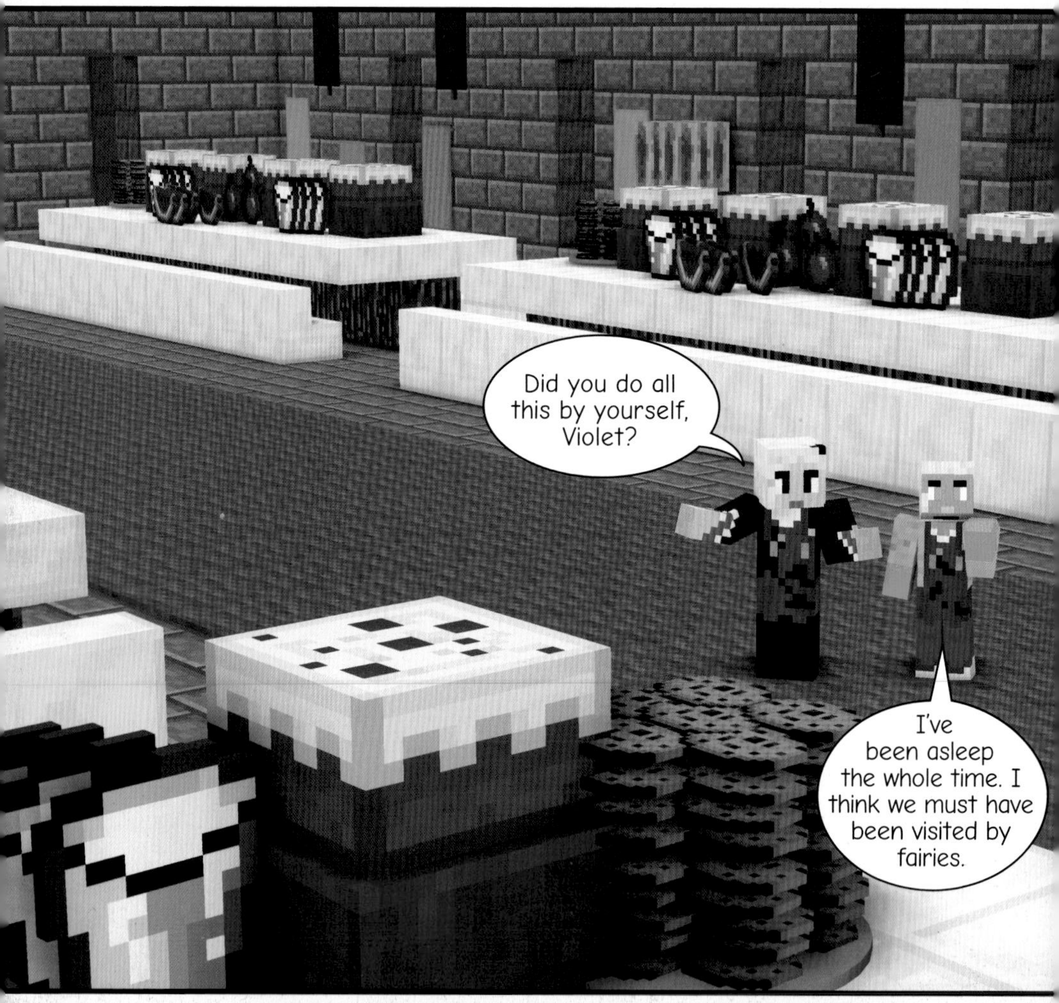
Did you do all this by yourself, Violet?
I've been asleep the whole time. I think we must have been visited by fairies.

CHAPTER 9

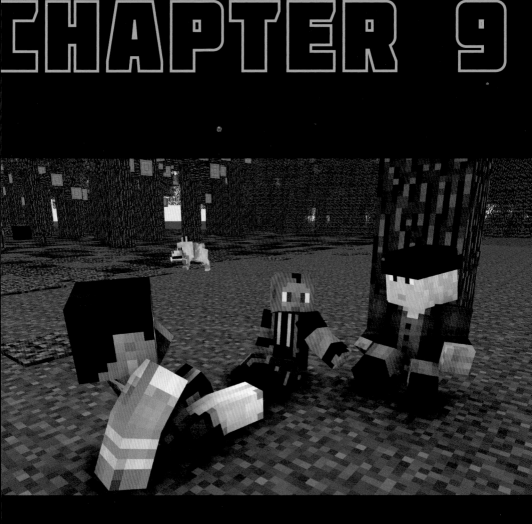

THE MAIN EVENT

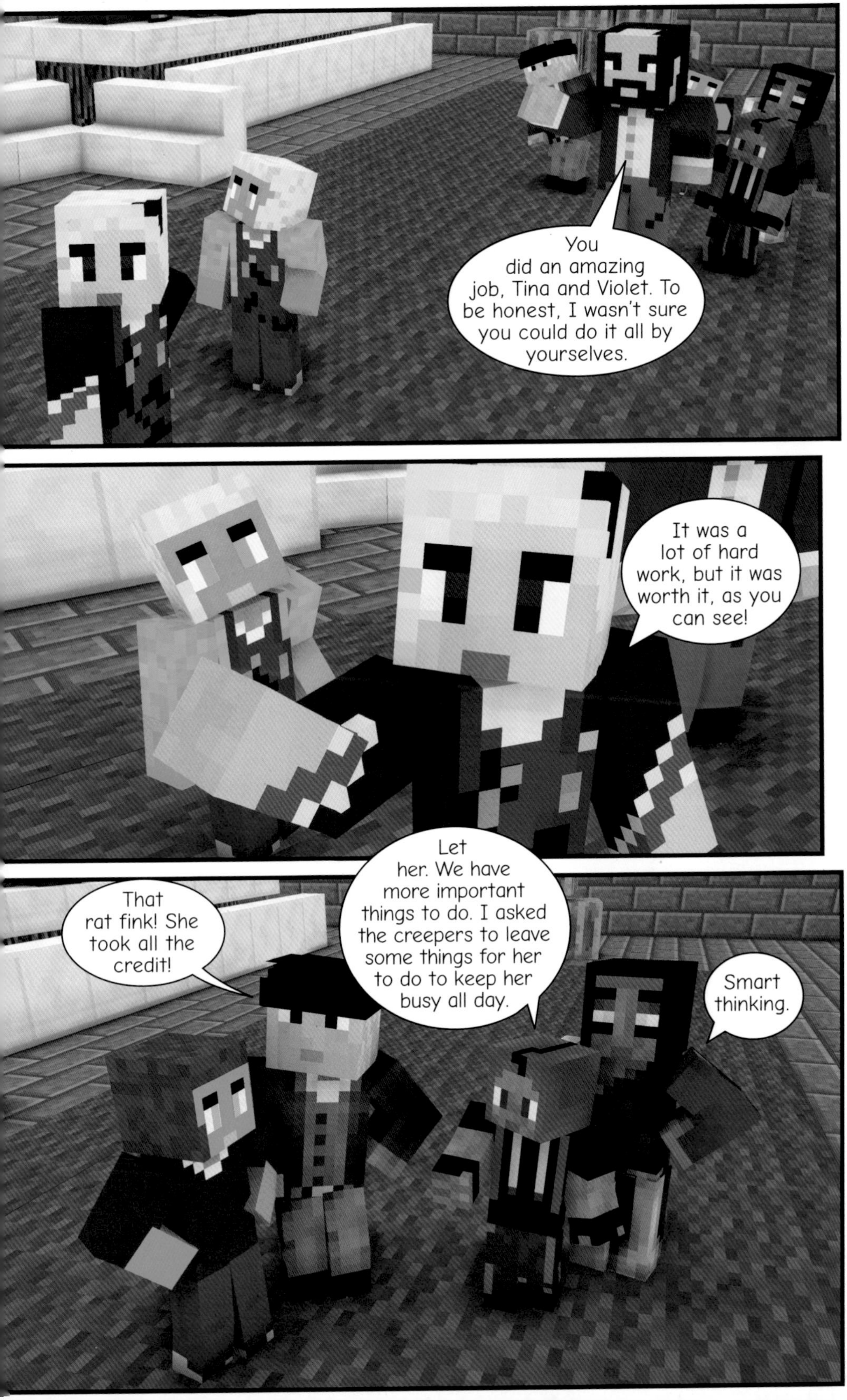
You did an amazing job, Tina and Violet. To be honest, I wasn't sure you could do it all by yourselves.
It was a lot of hard work, but it was worth it, as you can see!
That rat fink! She took all the credit!
Let her. We have more important things to do. I asked the creepers to leave some things for her to do to keep her busy all day.
Smart thinking.

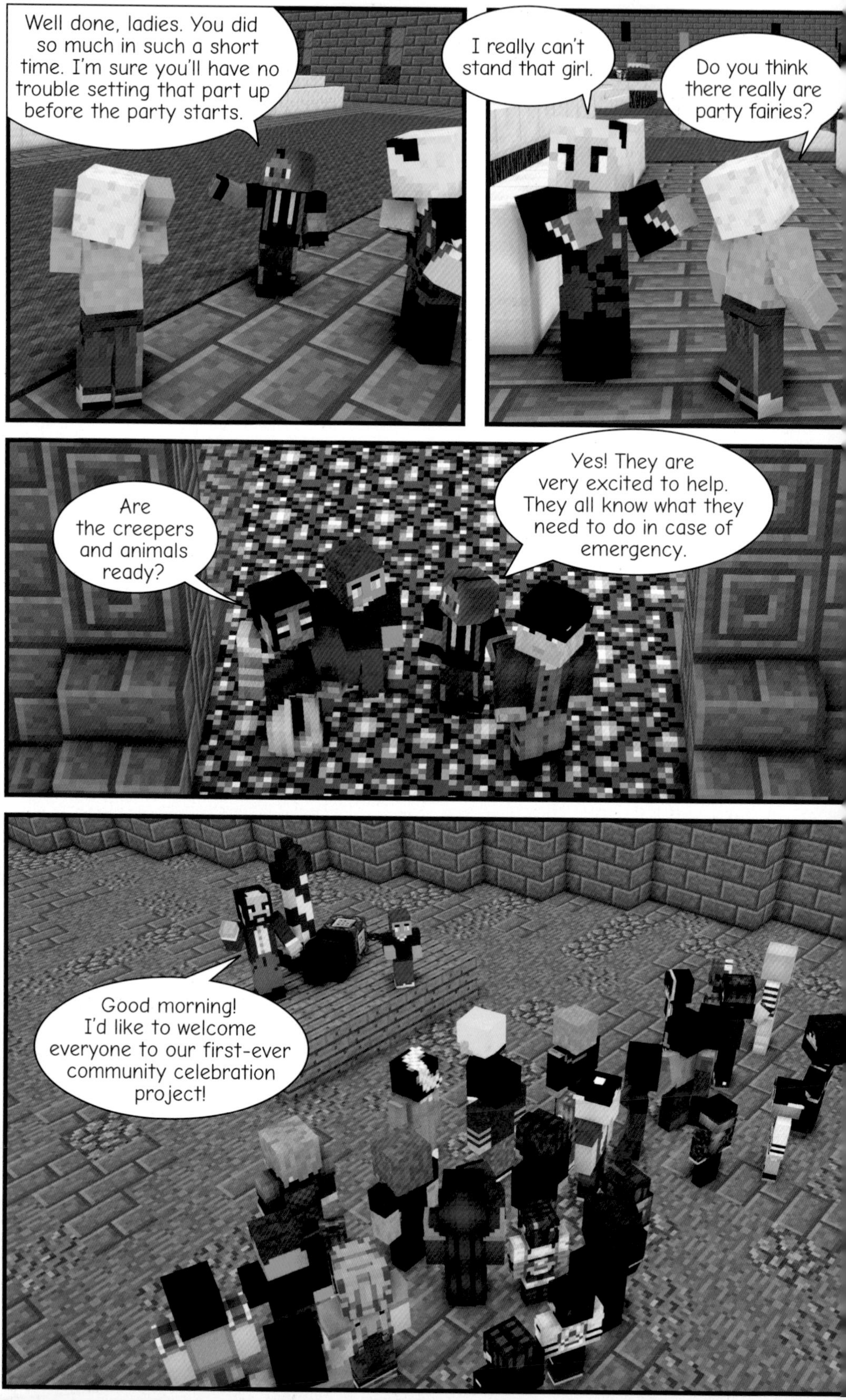
Well done, ladies. You did so much in such a short time. I'm sure you'll have no trouble setting that part up before the party starts.
I really can't stand that girl.
Do you think there really are party fairies?
Are the creepers and animals ready?
Yes! They are very excited to help. They all know what they need to do in case of emergency.
Good morning! I'd like to welcome everyone to our first-ever community celebration project!

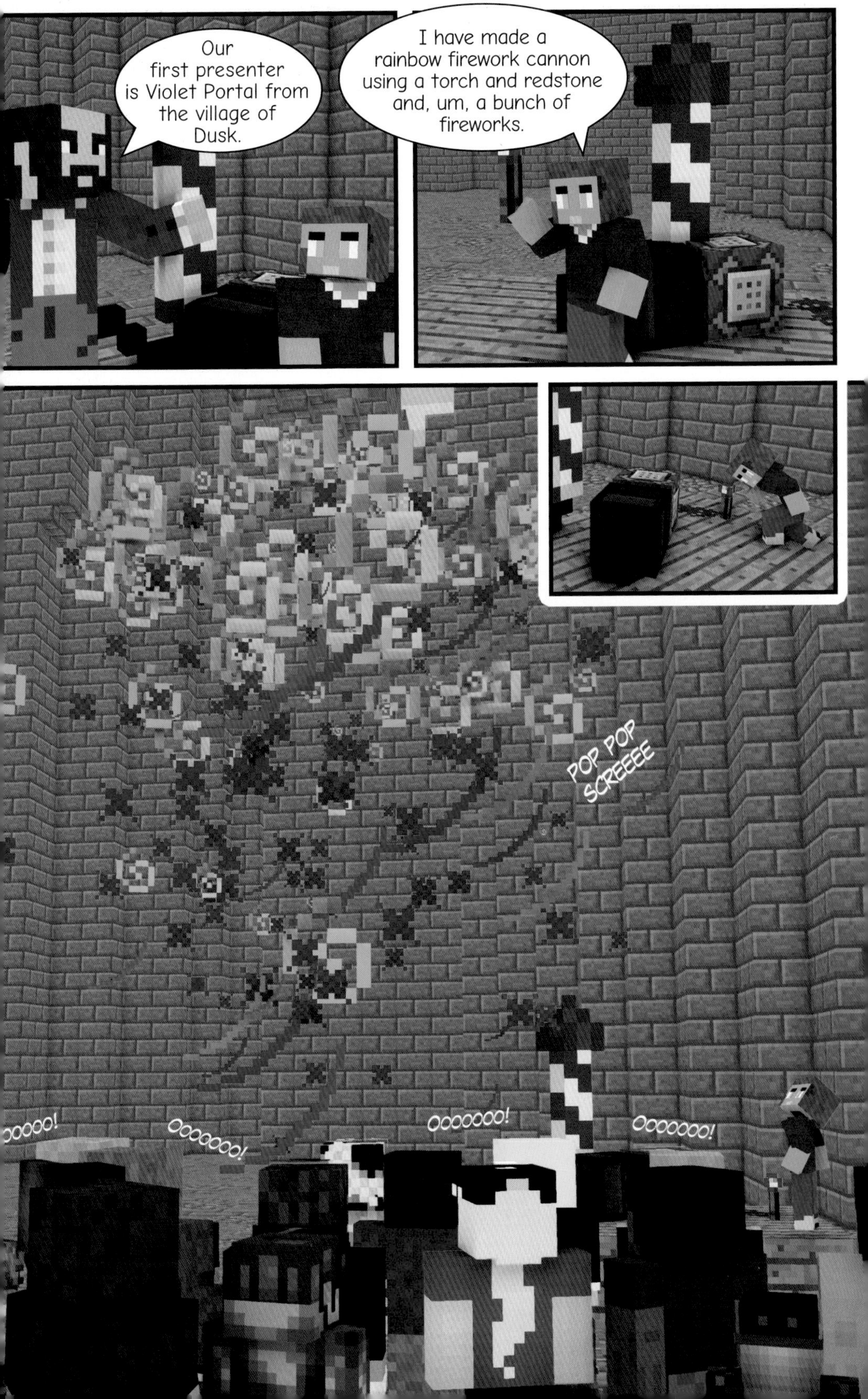
Our first presenter is Violet Portal from the village of Dusk.
I have made a rainbow firework cannon using a torch and redstone and, um, a bunch of fireworks.
POP POP SCREEEE
OOOOO!
OOOOOOO!
OOOOOOO!
OOOOOOO!

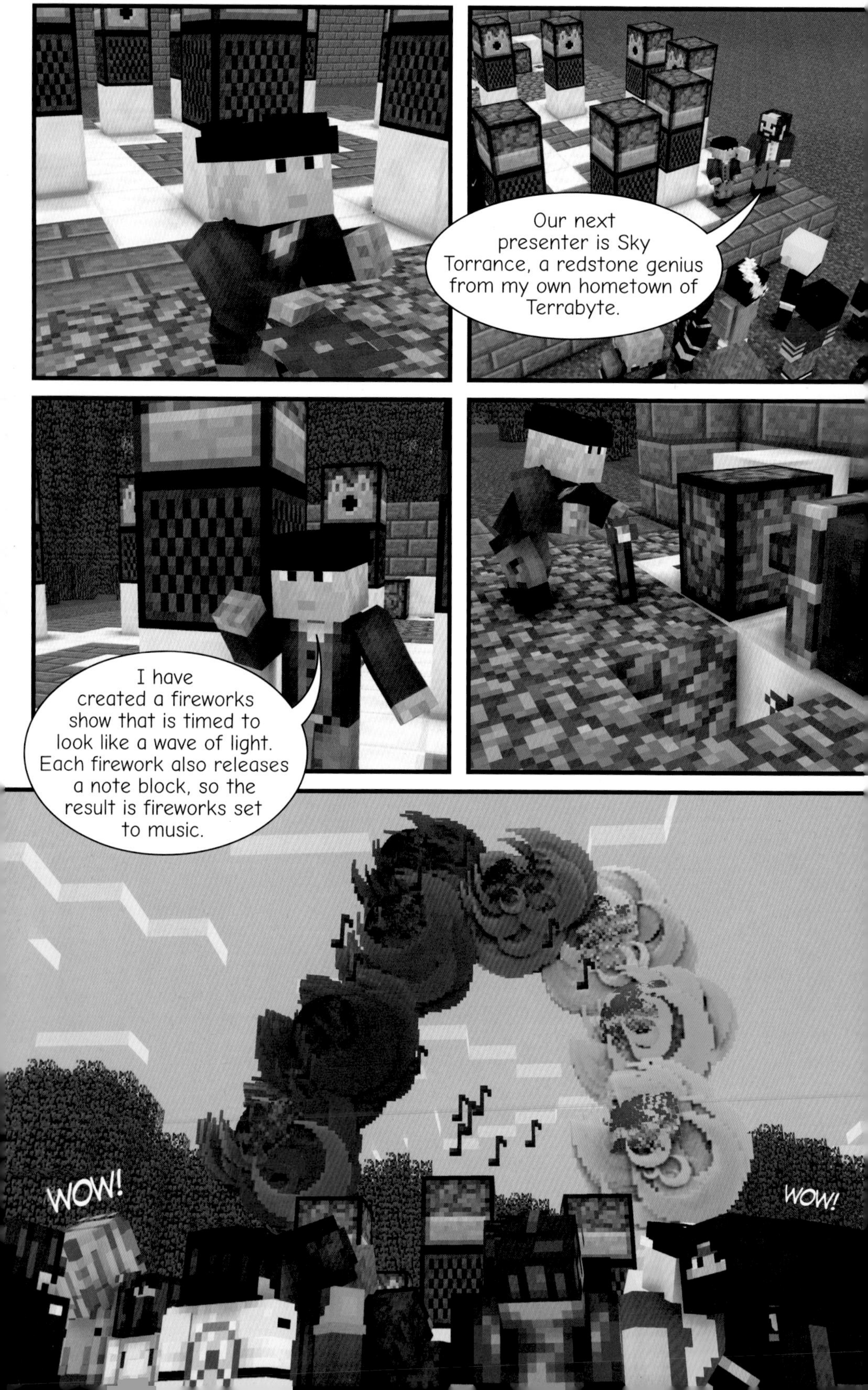
Our next presenter is Sky Torrance, a redstone genius from my own hometown of Terrabyte.
I have created a fireworks show that is timed to look like a wave of light. Each firework also releases a note block, so the result is fireworks set to music.
WOW!
WOW!

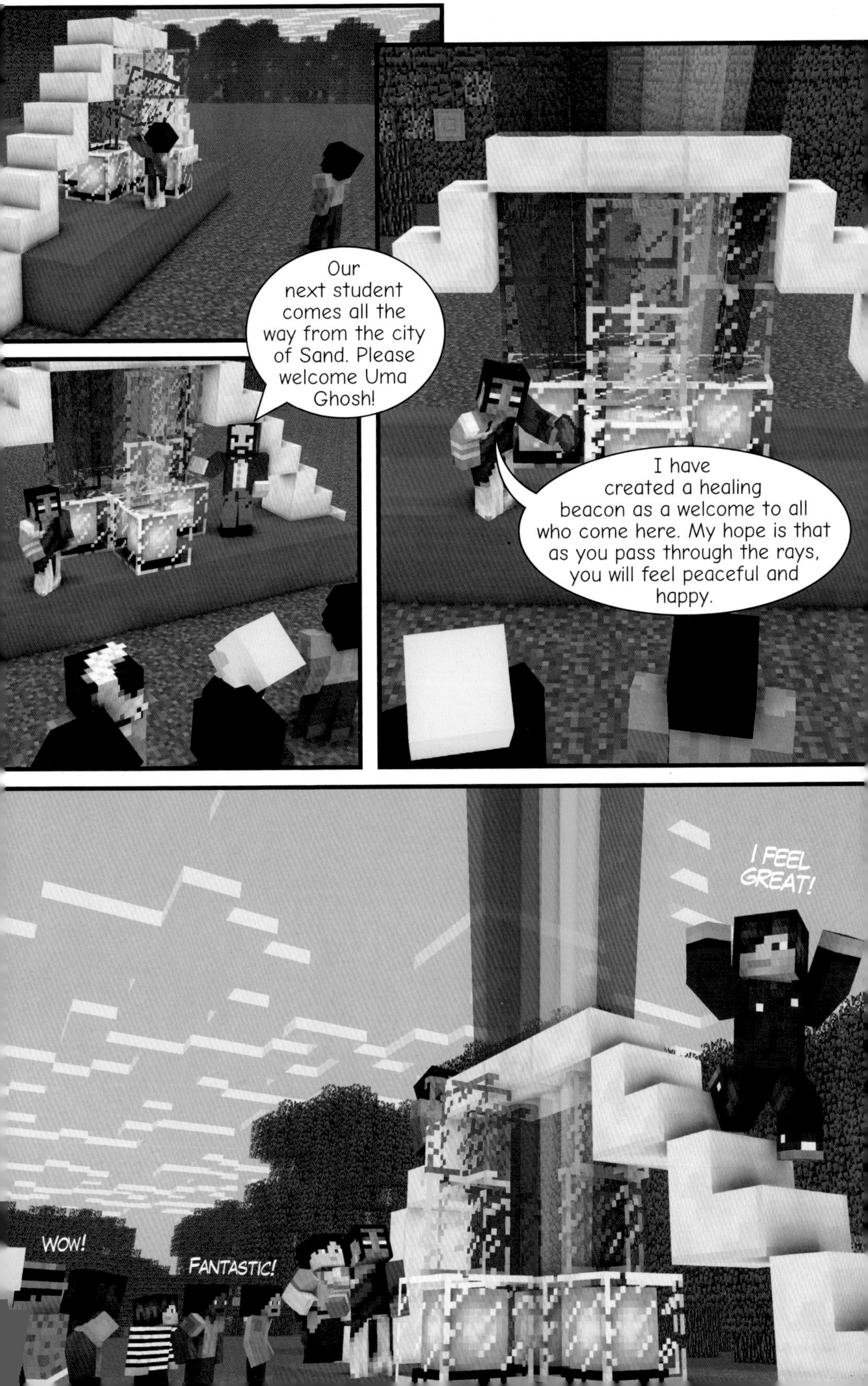
Our next student comes all the way from the city of Sand. Please welcome Uma Ghosh!
I have created a healing beacon as a welcome to all who come here. My hope is that as you pass through the rays, you will feel peaceful and happy.
I FEEL GREAT!
WOW!
FANTASTIC!

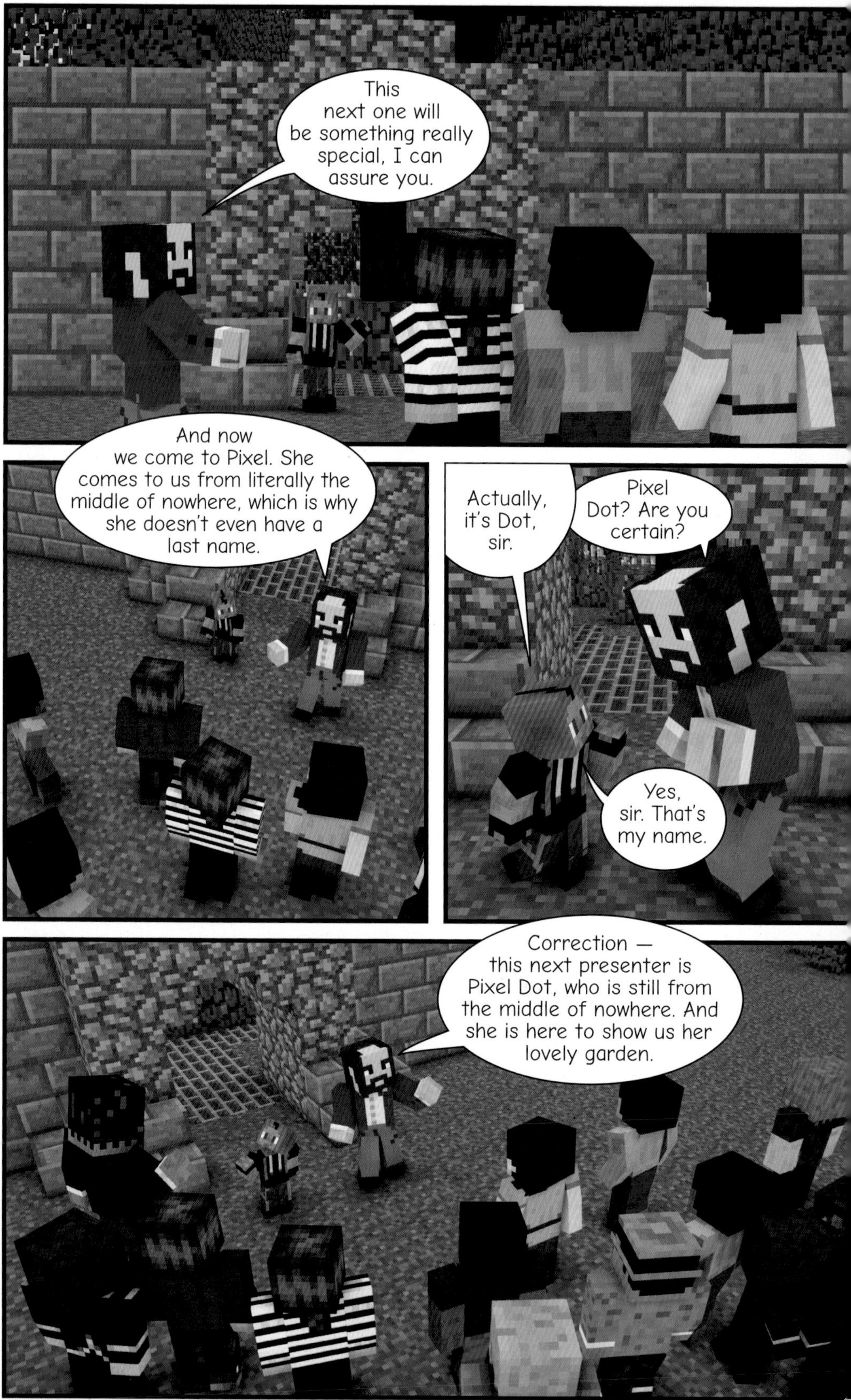
This next one will be something really special, I can assure you.
And now we come to Pixel. She comes to us from literally the middle of nowhere, which is why she doesn't even have a last name.
Actually, it's Dot, sir.
Pixel Dot? Are you certain?
Yes, sir. That's my name.
Correction — this next presenter is Pixel Dot, who is still from the middle of nowhere. And she is here to show us her lovely garden.

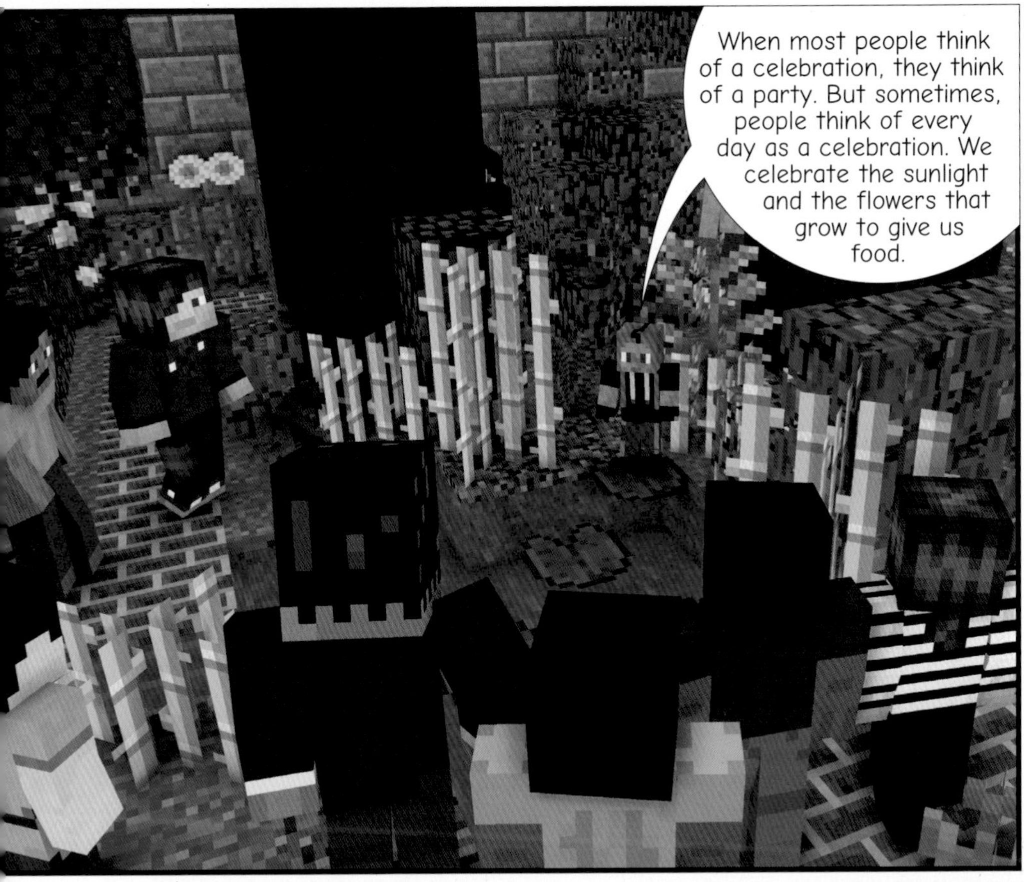
When most people think of a celebration, they think of a party. But sometimes, people think of every day as a celebration. We celebrate the sunlight and the flowers that grow to give us food.

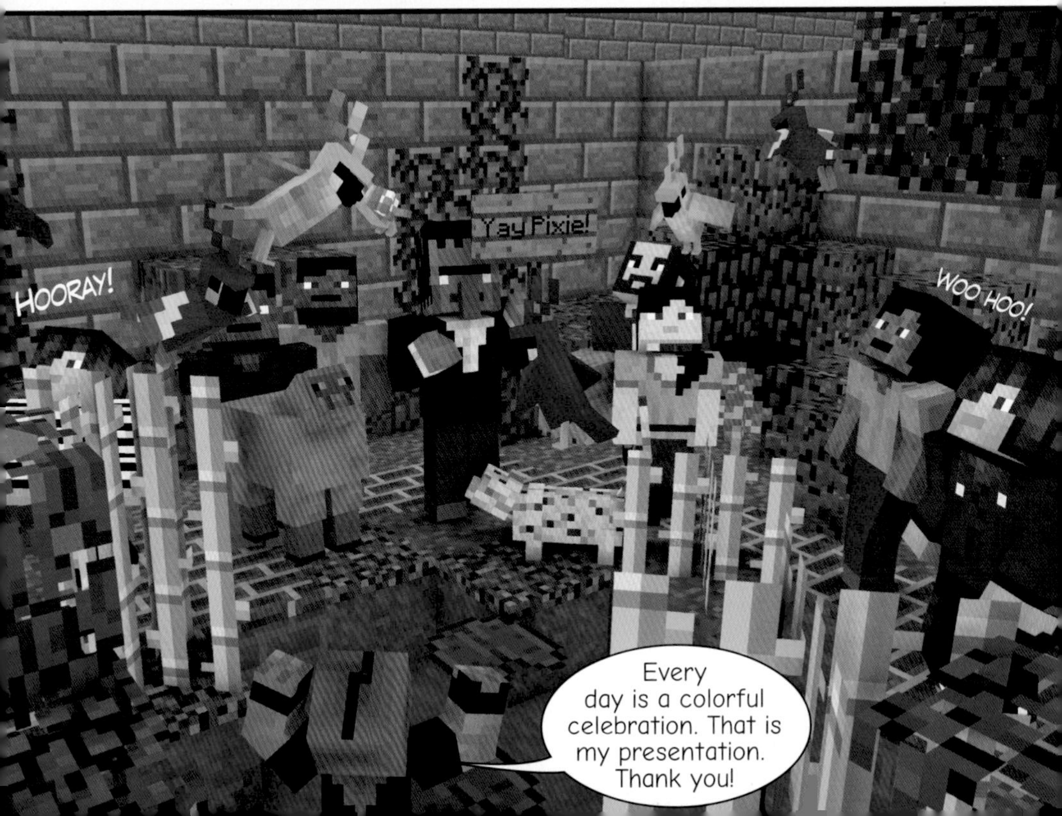
Yay Pixie!
HOORAY!
WOO HOO!
Every day is a colorful celebration. That is my presentation. Thank you!

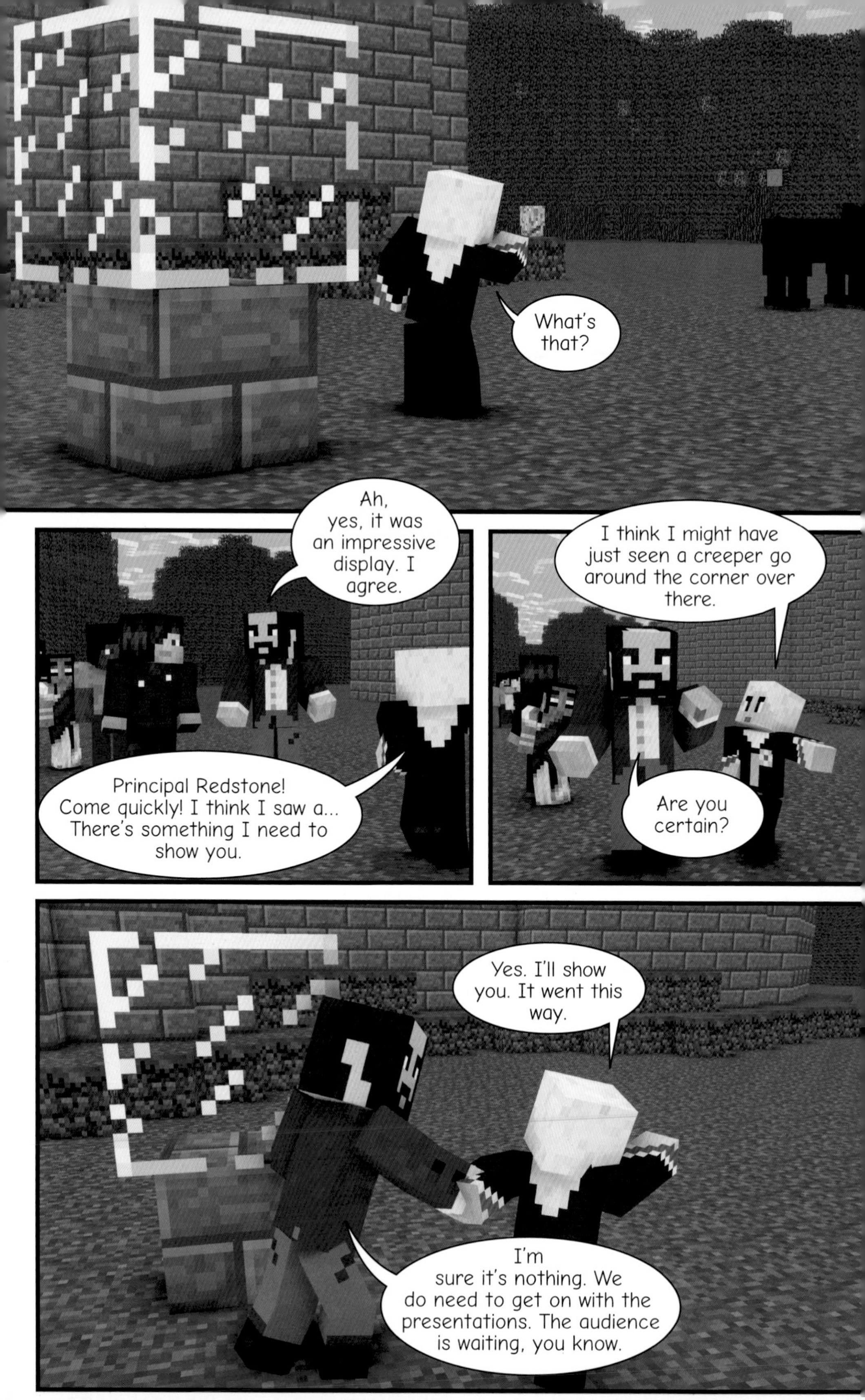
What's that?
Ah, yes, it was an impressive display. I agree.
Principal Redstone! Come quickly! I think I saw a... There's something I need to show you.
I think I might have just seen a creeper go around the corner over there.
Are you certain?
Yes. I'll show you. It went this way.
I'm sure it's nothing. We do need to get on with the presentations. The audience is waiting, you know.

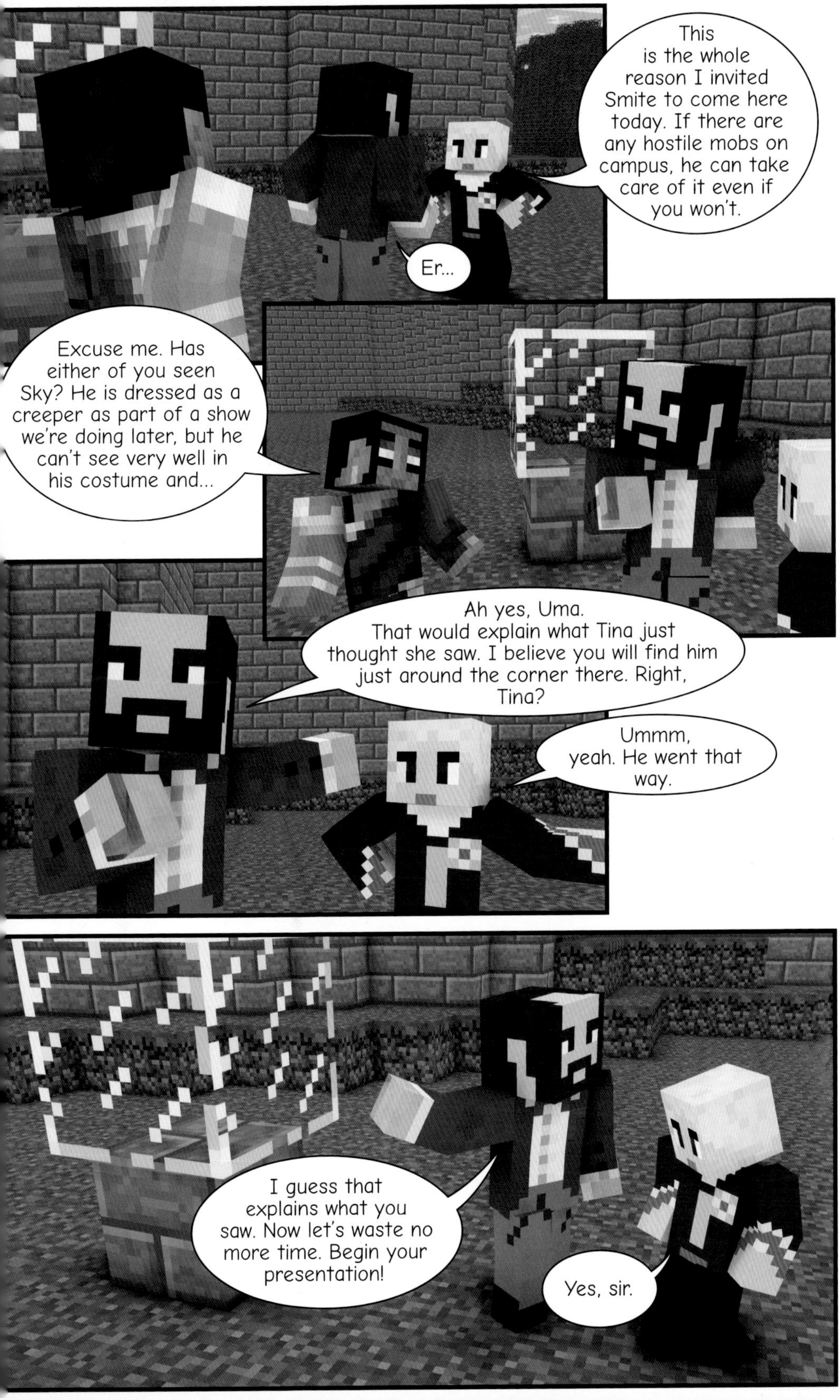
This is the whole reason I invited Smite to come here today. If there are any hostile mobs on campus, he can take care of it even if you won't.
Er...
Excuse me. Has either of you seen Sky? He is dressed as a creeper as part of a show we're doing later, but he can't see very well in his costume and...
Ah yes, Uma. That would explain what Tina just thought she saw. I believe you will find him just around the corner there. Right, Tina?
Ummm, yeah. He went that way.
I guess that explains what you saw. Now let's waste no more time. Begin your presentation!
Yes, sir.

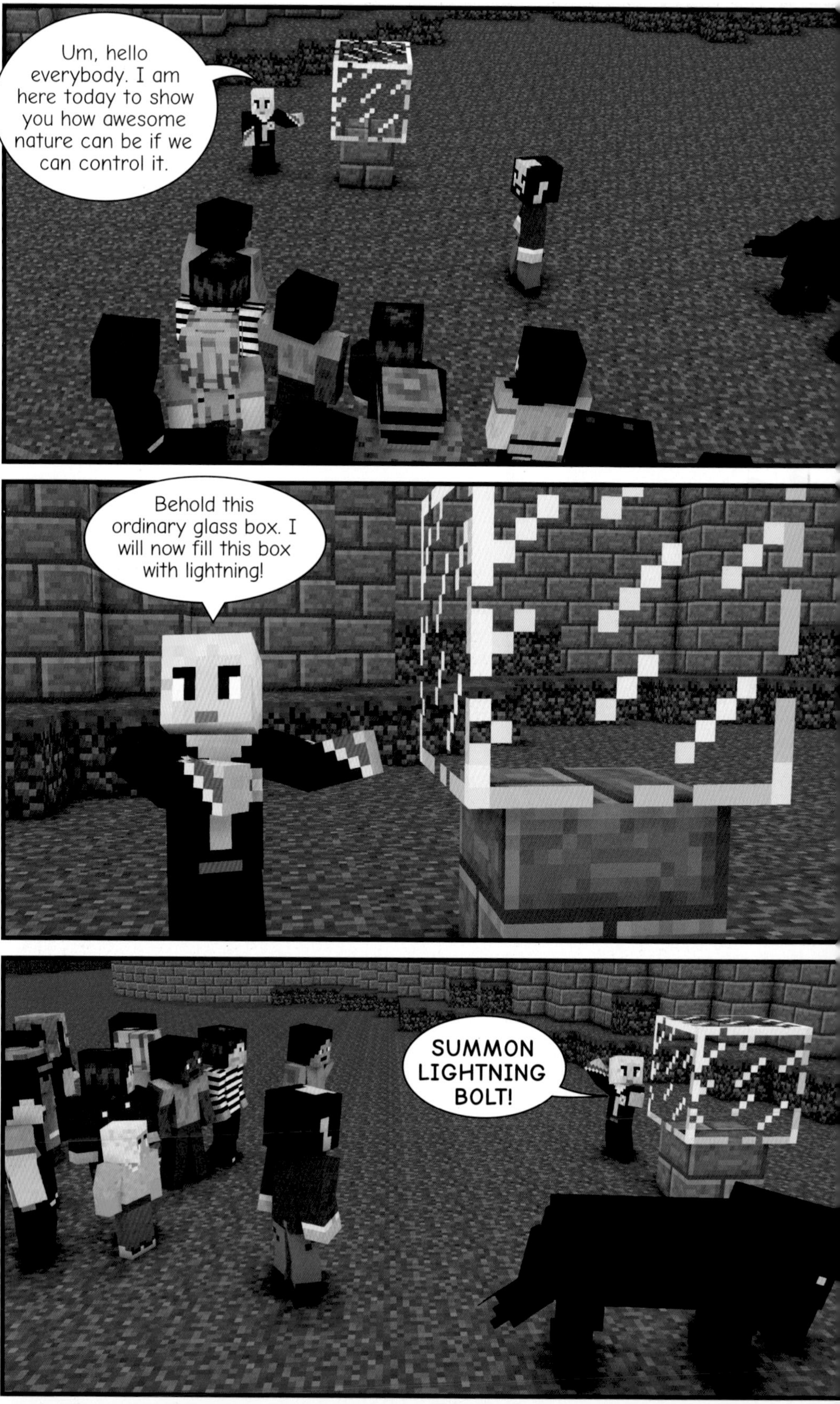
Um, hello everybody. I am here today to show you how awesome nature can be if we can control it.
Behold this ordinary glass box. I will now fill this box with lightning!
SUMMON LIGHTNING BOLT!

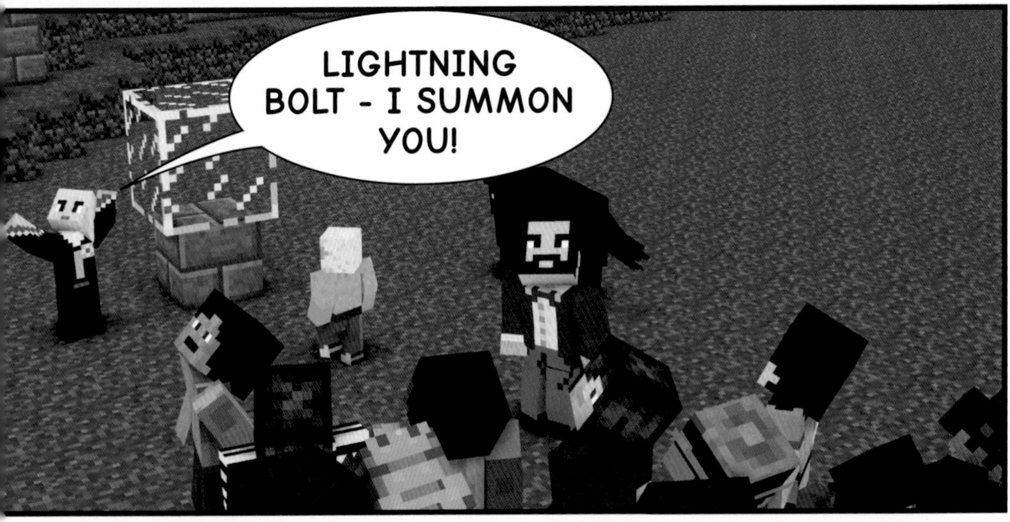
LIGHTNING BOLT - I SUMMON YOU!

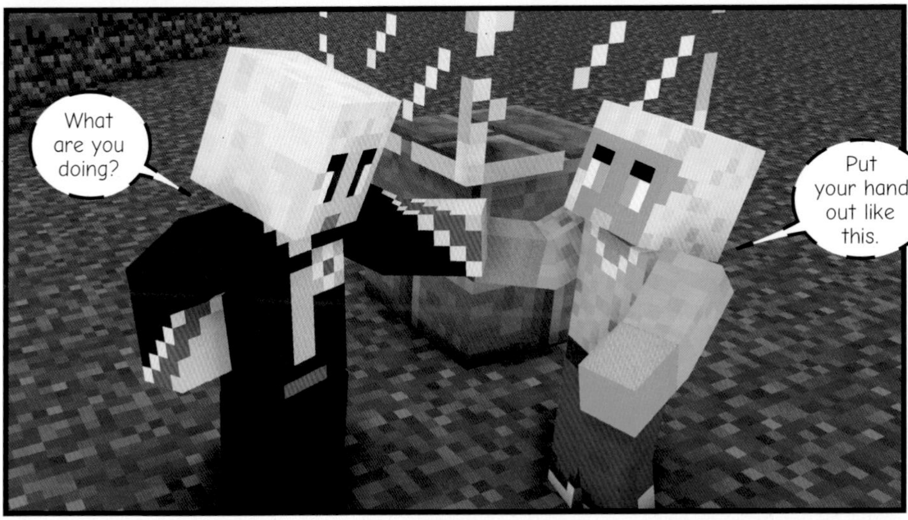
What are you doing?
Put your hand out like this.

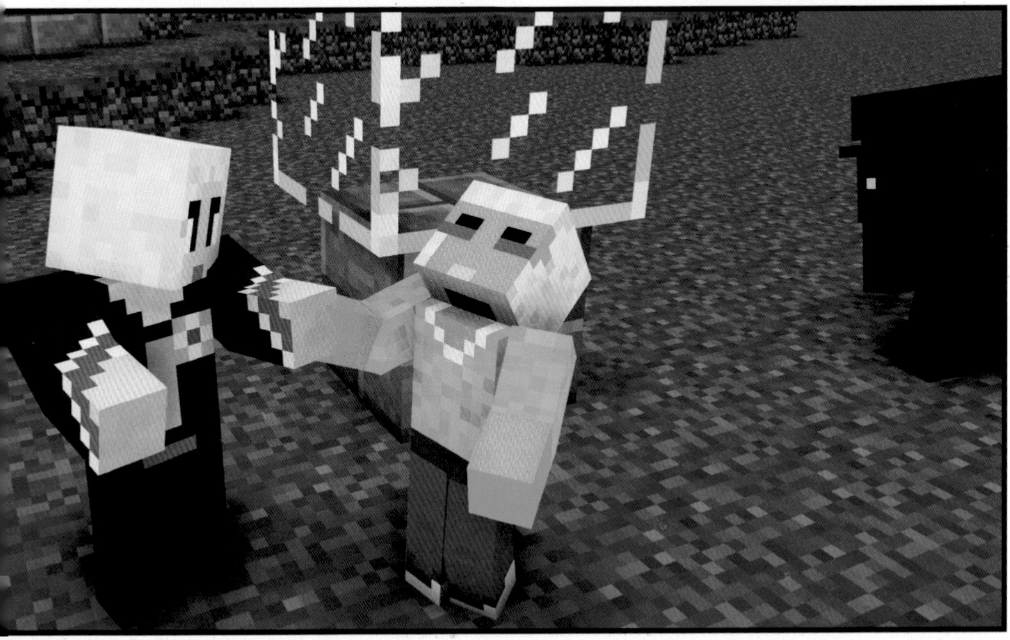

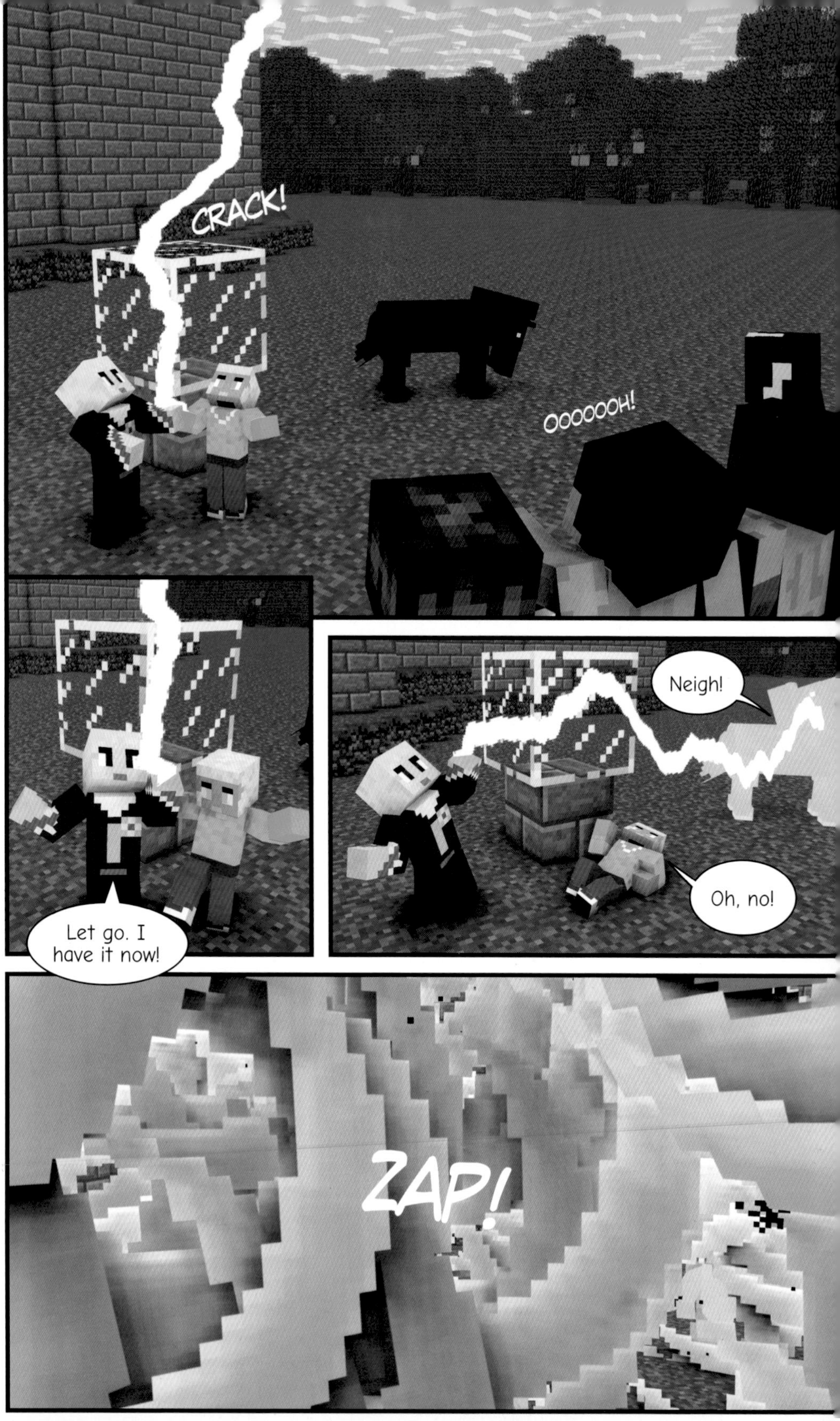
CRACK!
OOOOOOH!
Let go. I have it now!
Neigh!
Oh, no!
ZAP!

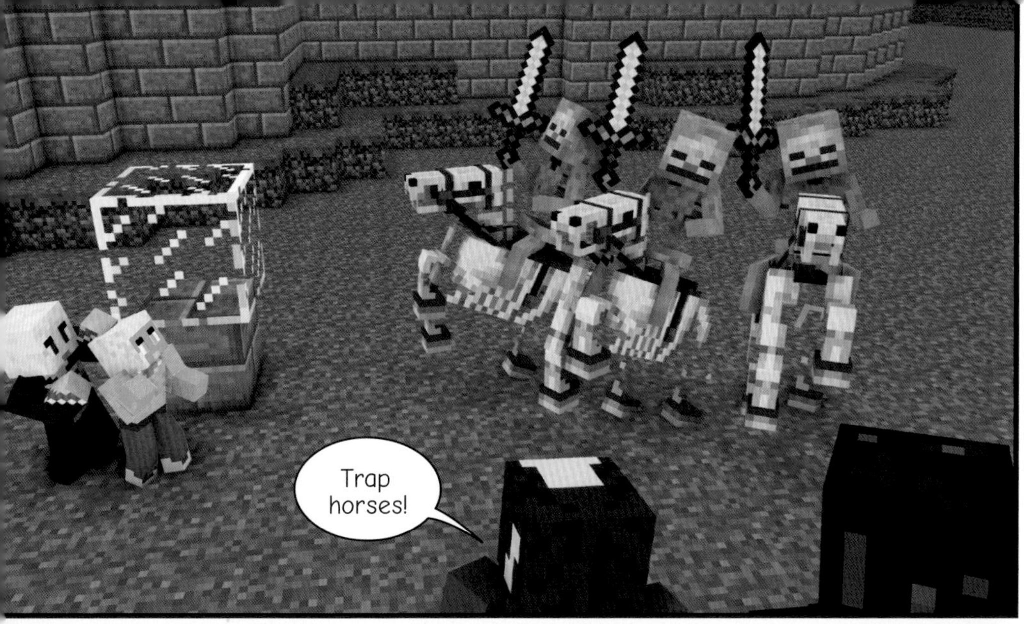
Trap horses!

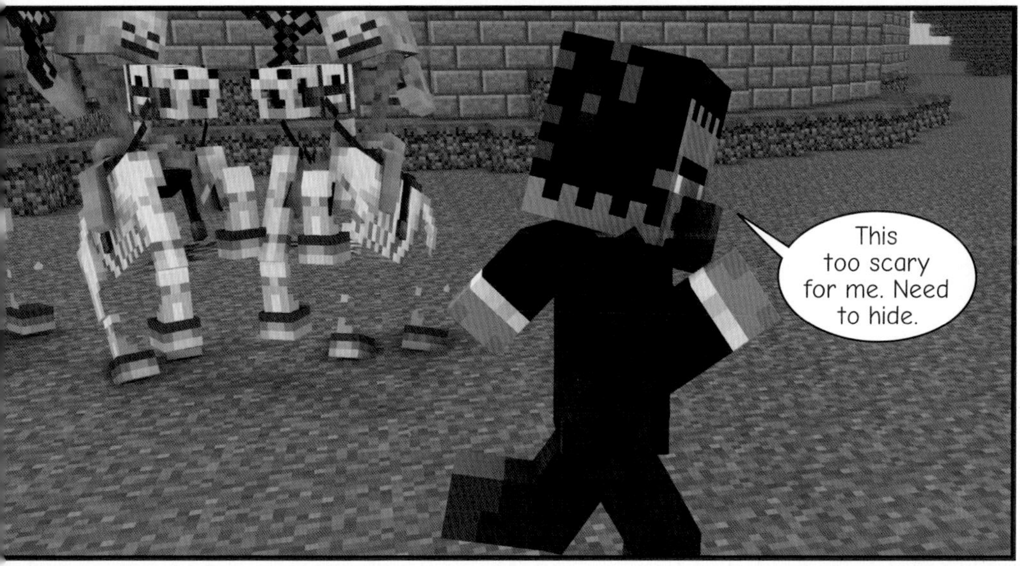
This too scary for me. Need to hide.

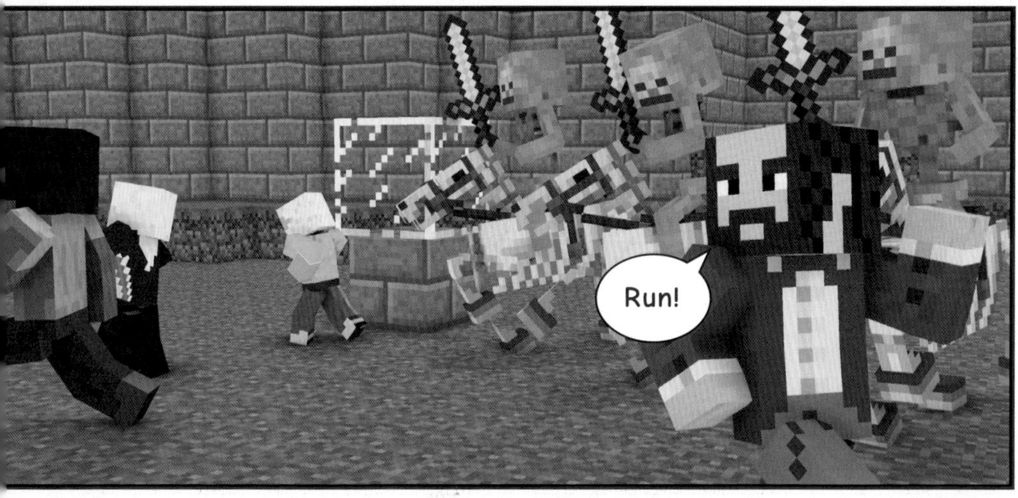
Run!

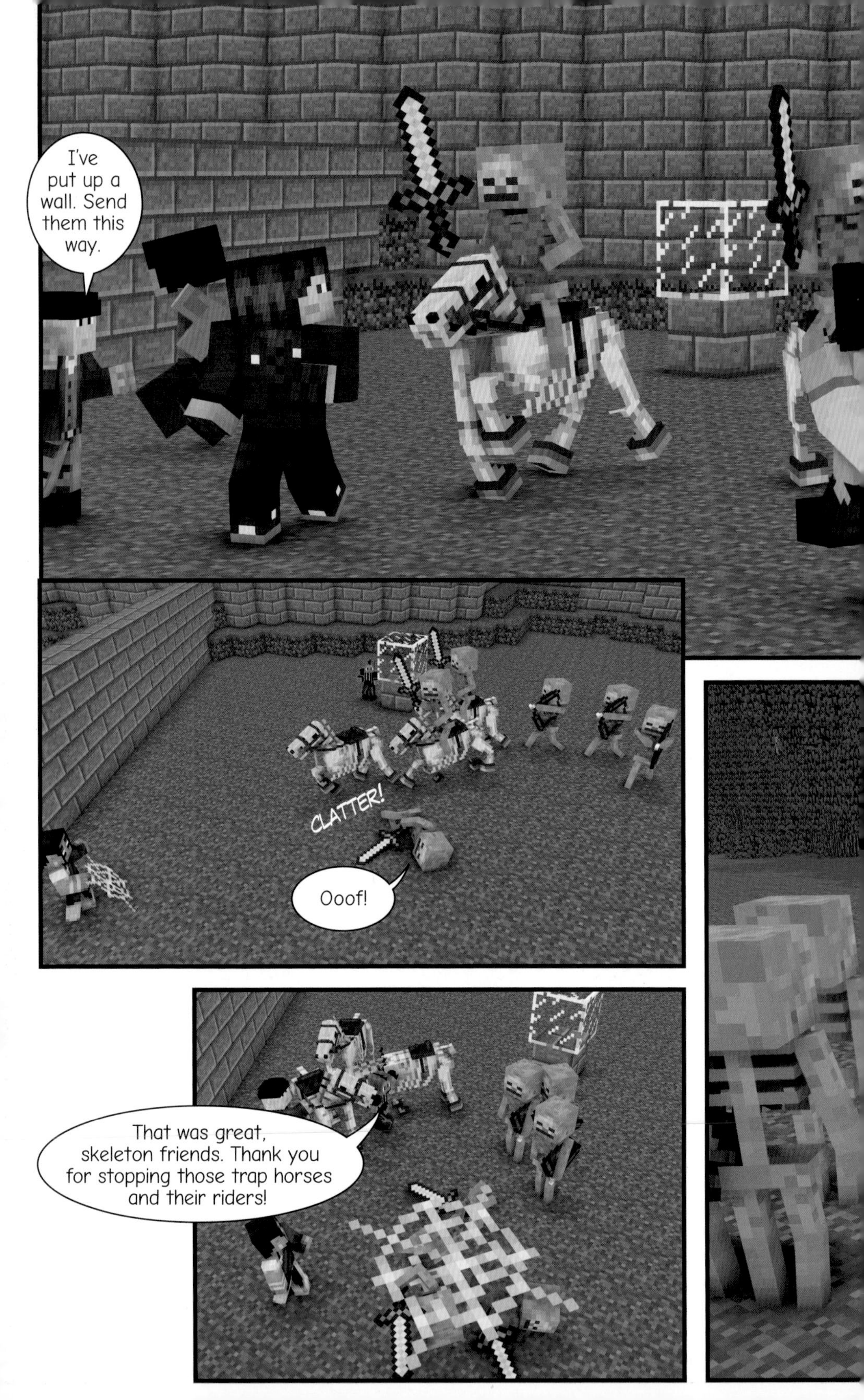
I've put up a wall. Send them this way.
CLATTER!
Ooof!
That was great, skeleton friends. Thank you for stopping those trap horses and their riders!

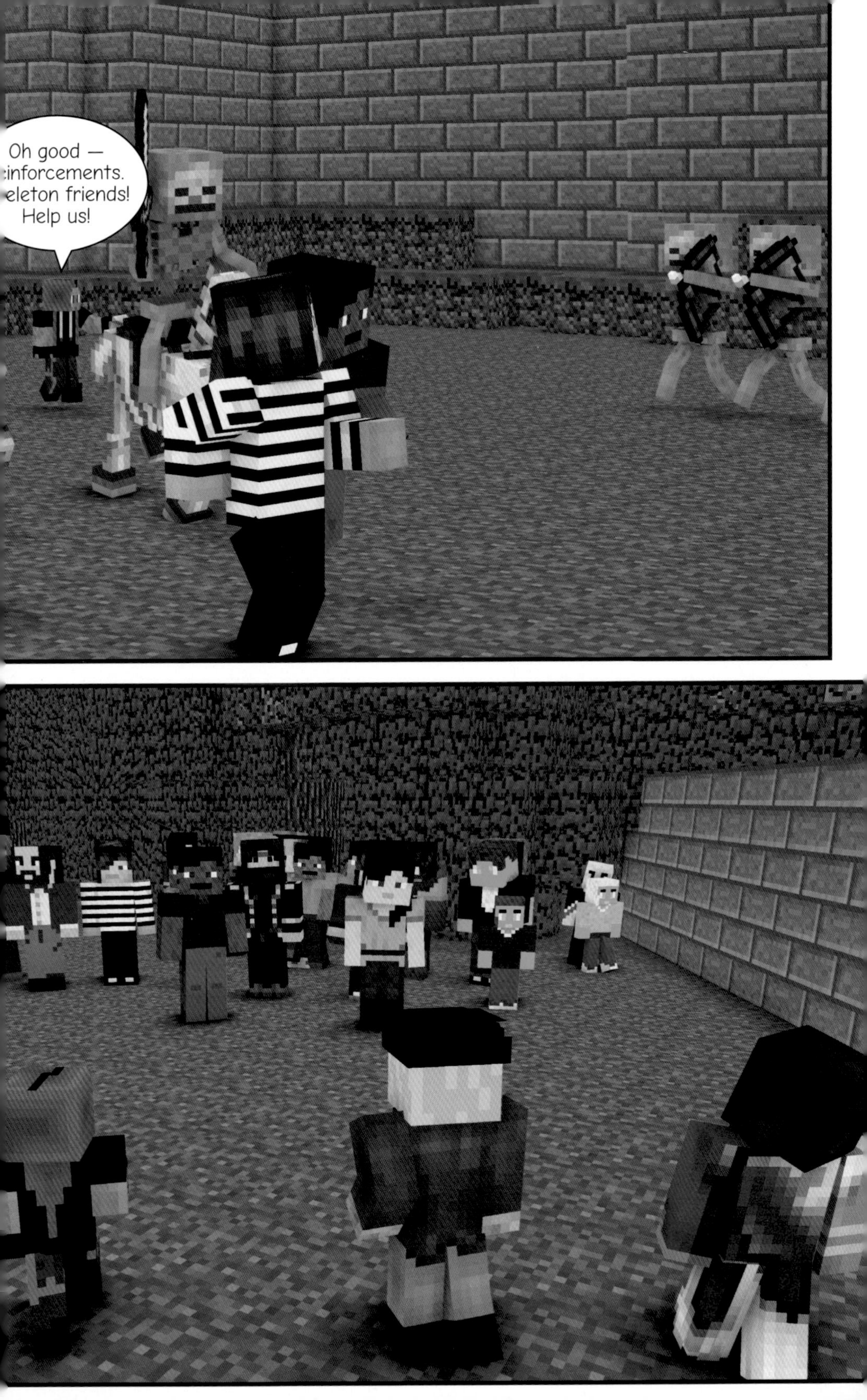
Oh good — inforcements. eleton friends! Help us!

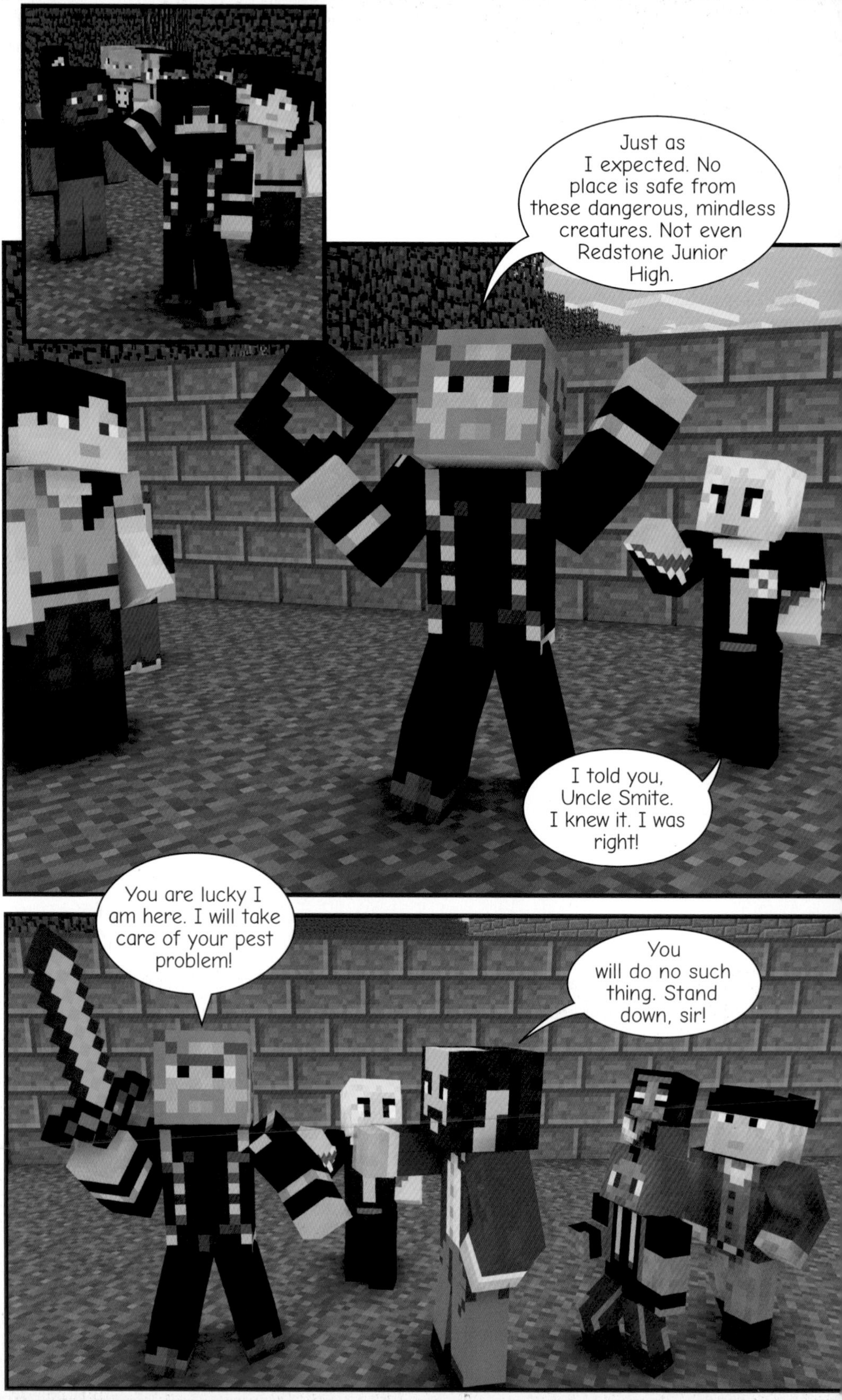
Just as I expected. No place is safe from these dangerous, mindless creatures. Not even Redstone Junior High.
I told you, Uncle Smite. I knew it. I was right!
You are lucky I am here. I will take care of your pest problem!
You will do no such thing. Stand down, sir!

CHAPTER 10

PARTY

CRASHERS

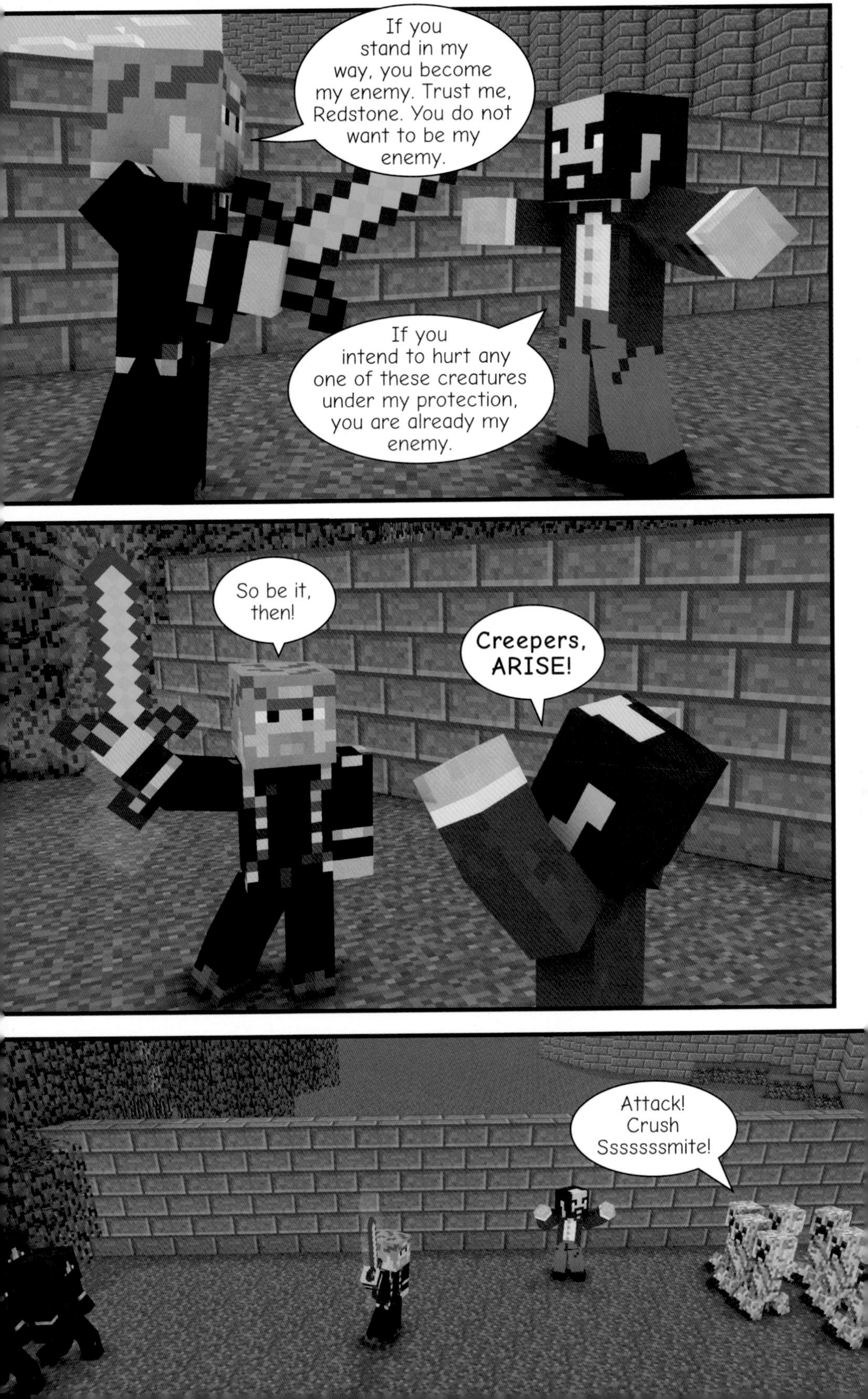
If you stand in my way, you become my enemy. Trust me, Redstone. You do not want to be my enemy.
If you intend to hurt any one of these creatures under my protection, you are already my enemy.
So be it, then!
Creepers, ARISE!
Attack! Crush Sssssssmite!

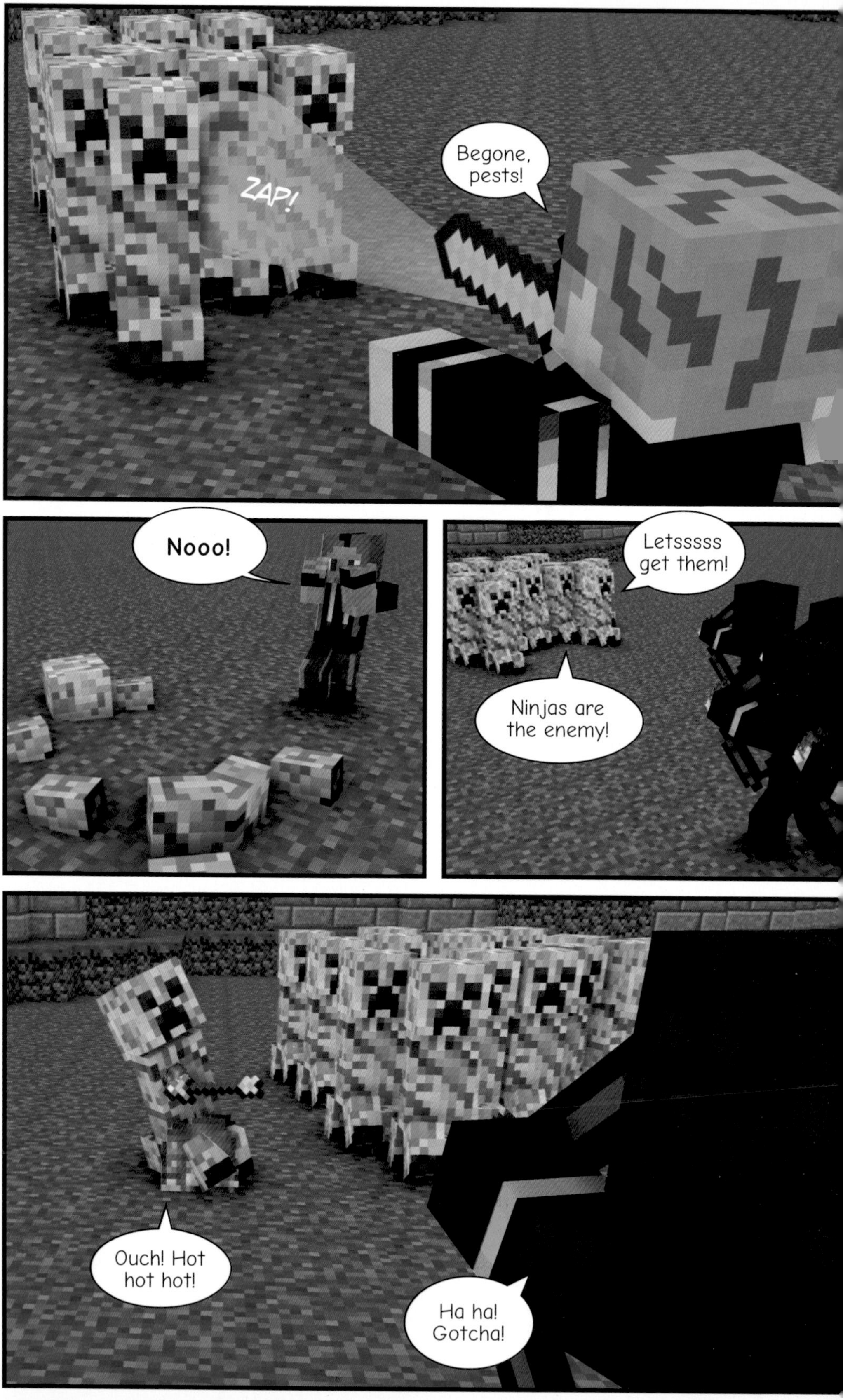

Begone, pests!
ZAP!
Nooo!
Letssssss get them!
Ninjas are the enemy!
Ouch! Hot hot hot!
Ha ha! Gotcha!

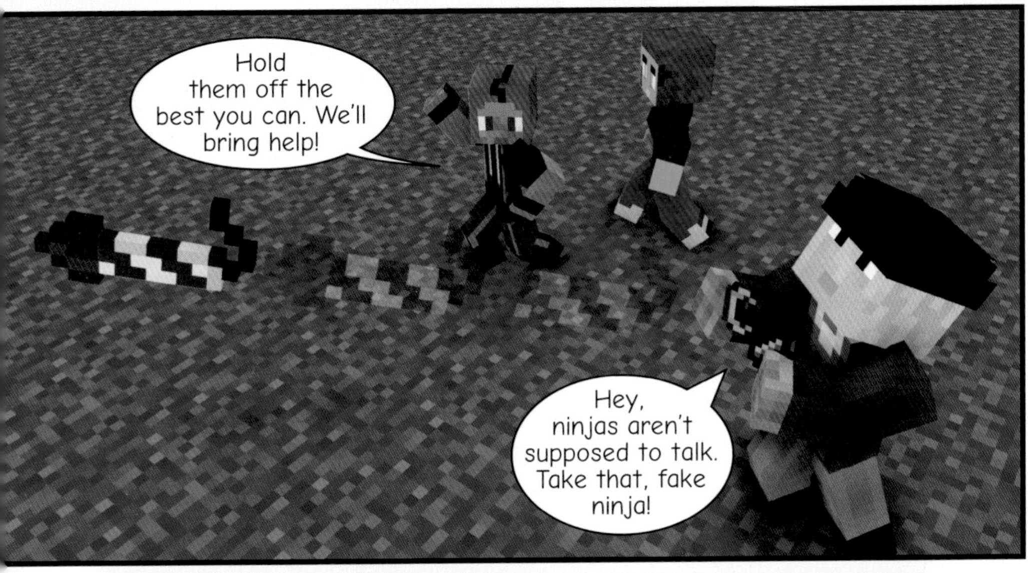
Hold them off the best you can. We'll bring help!
Hey, ninjas aren't supposed to talk. Take that, fake ninja!

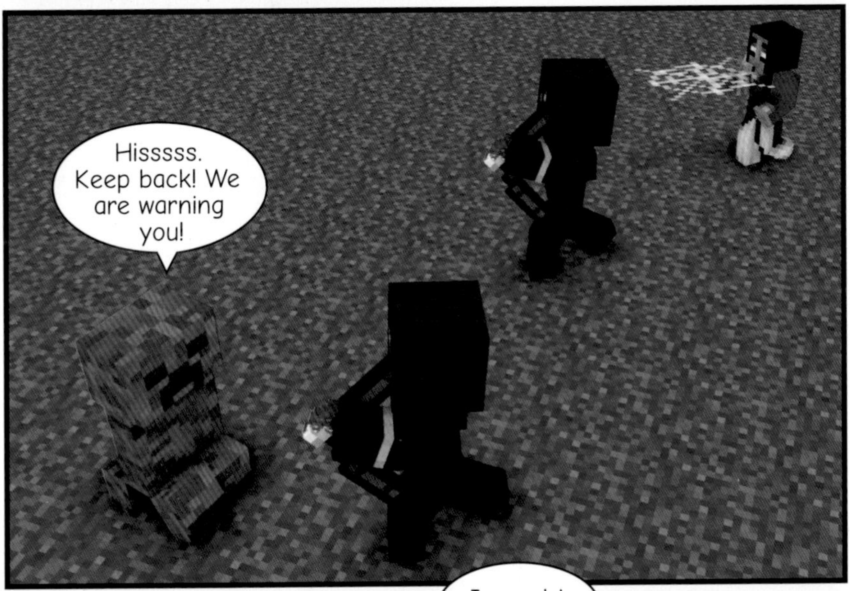
Hissssss. Keep back! We are warning you!

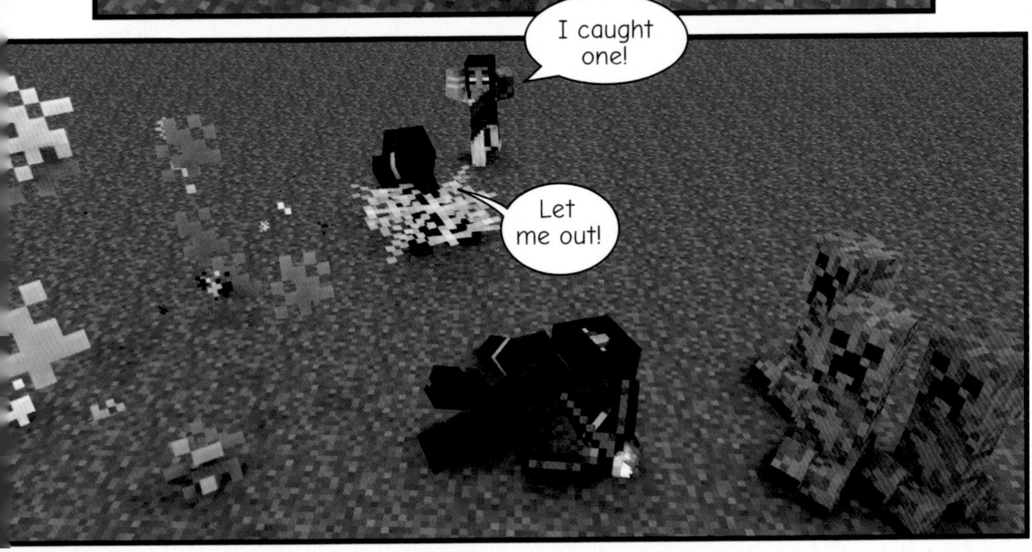
I caught one!
Let me out!

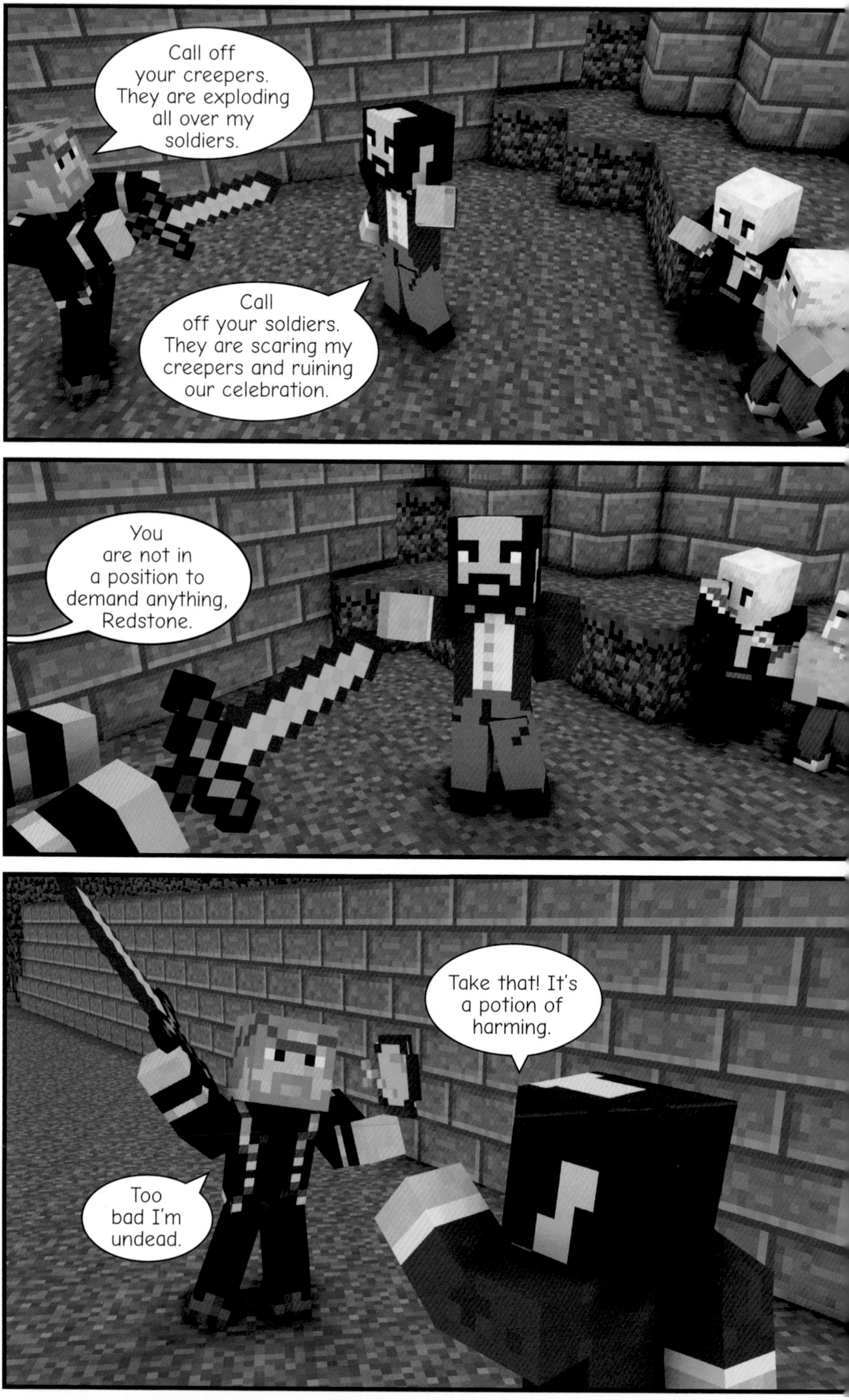
Call off your creepers. They are exploding all over my soldiers.
Call off your soldiers. They are scaring my creepers and ruining our celebration.
You are not in a position to demand anything, Redstone.
Take that! It's a potion of harming.
Too bad I'm undead.

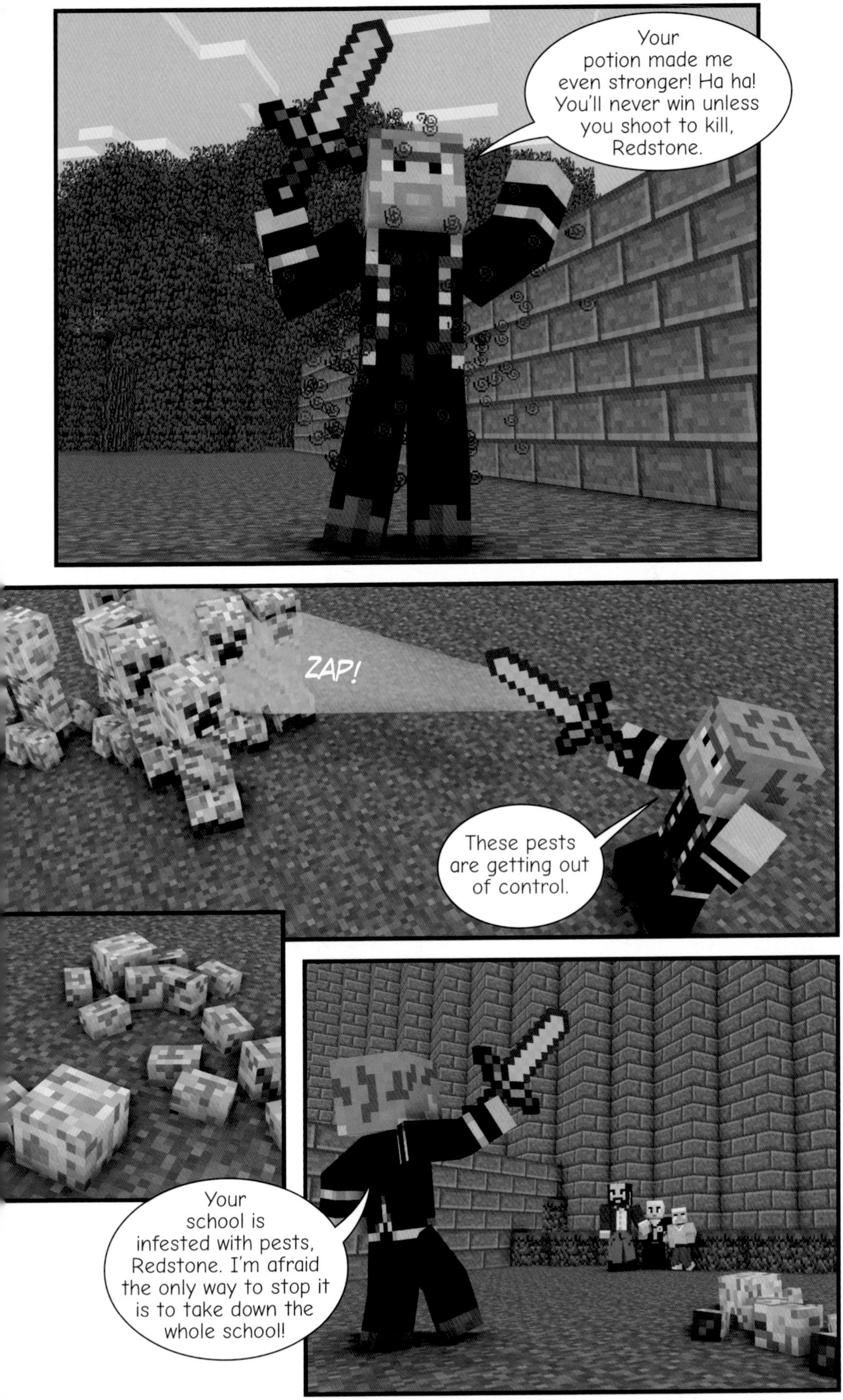
Your potion made me even stronger! Ha ha! You'll never win unless you shoot to kill, Redstone.
ZAP!
These pests are getting out of control.
Your school is infested with pests, Redstone. I'm afraid the only way to stop it is to take down the whole school!

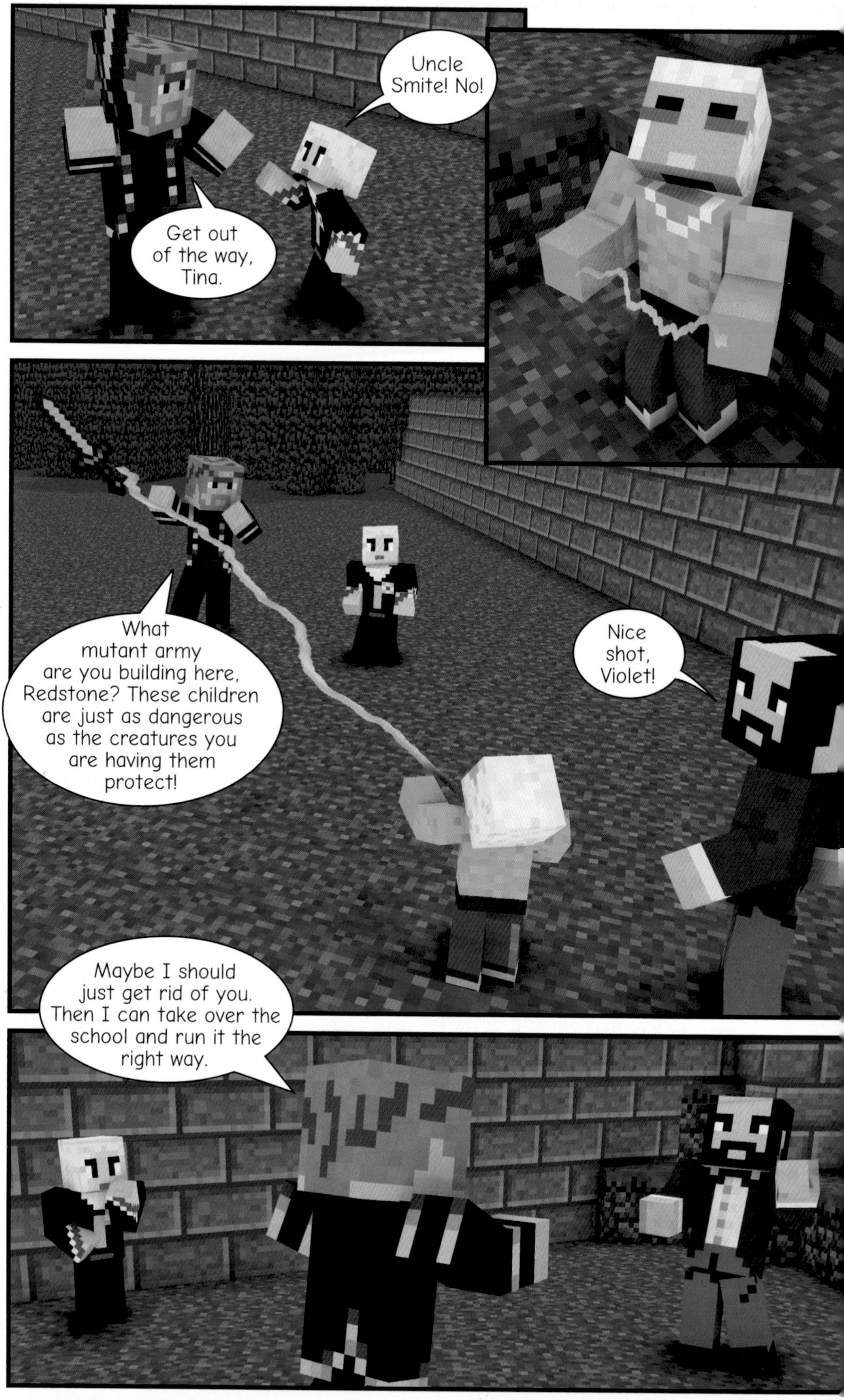
Uncle Smite! No!
Get out of the way, Tina.
What mutant army are you building here, Redstone? These children are just as dangerous as the creatures you are having them protect!
Nice shot, Violet!
Maybe I should just get rid of you. Then I can take over the school and run it the right way.

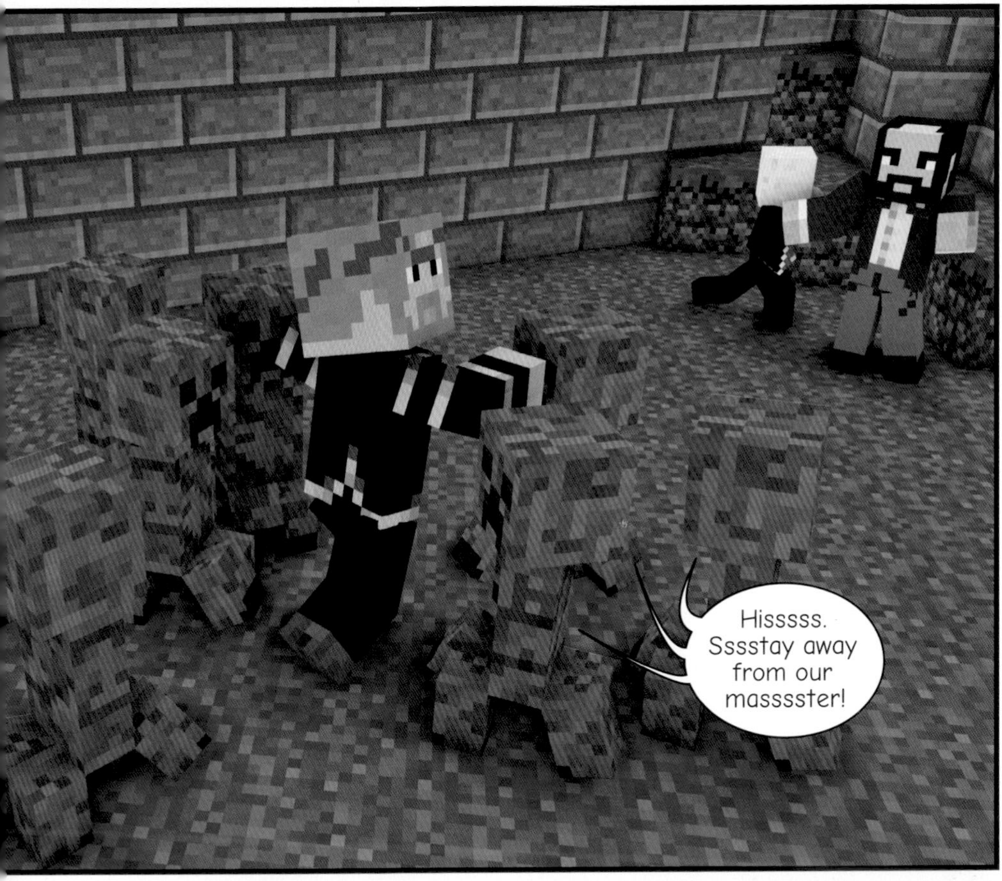
Hisssss. Sssstay away from our massssster!

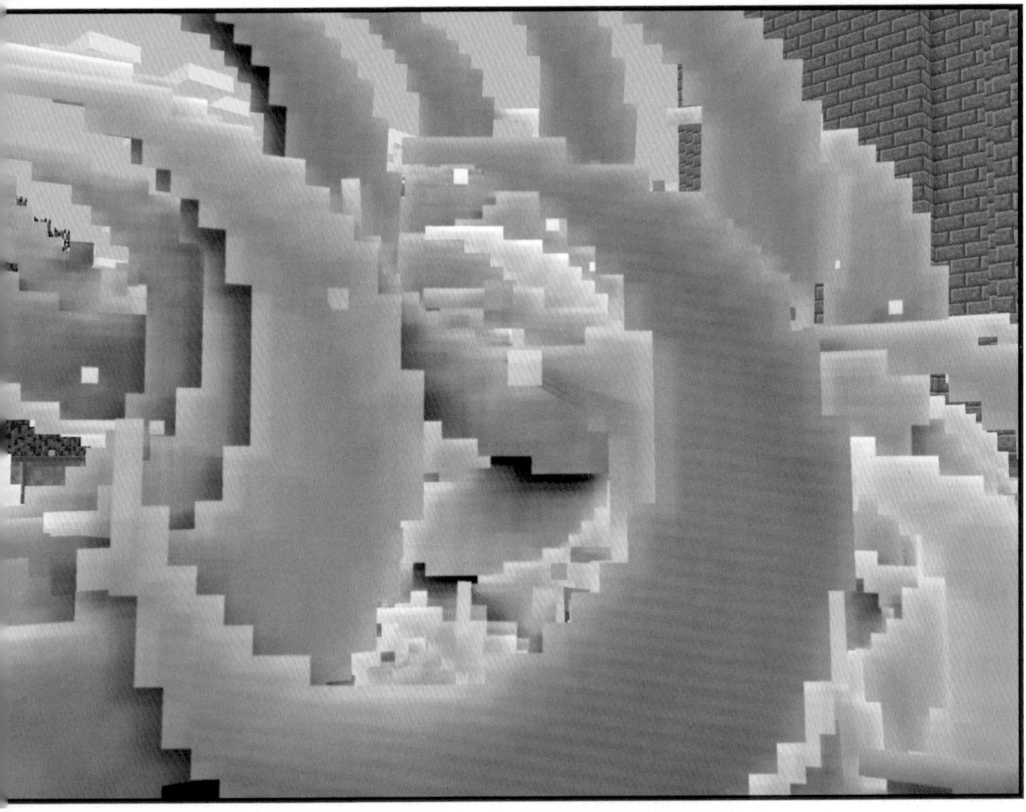

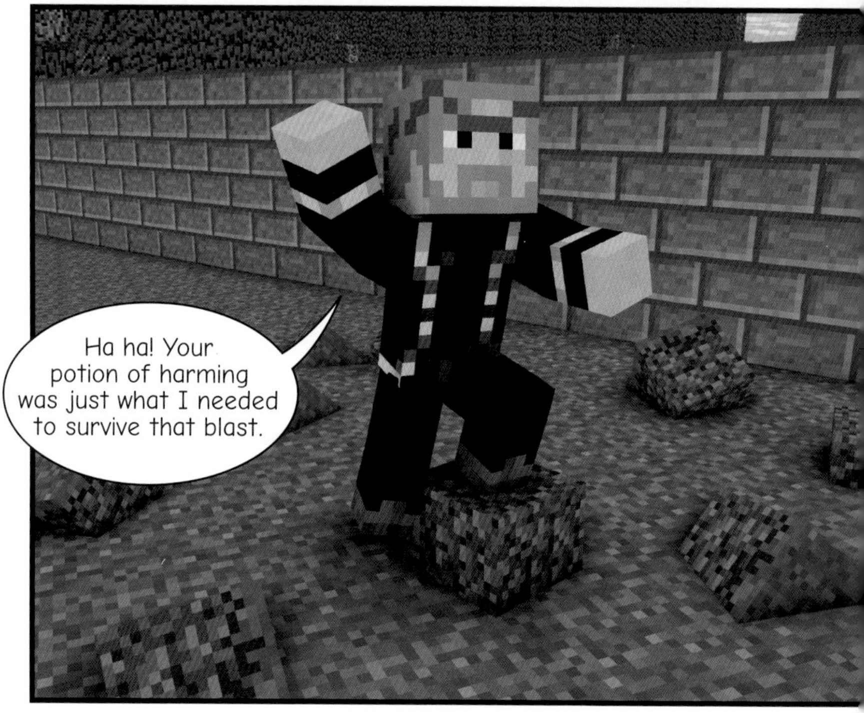
Ha ha! Your potion of harming was just what I needed to survive that blast.

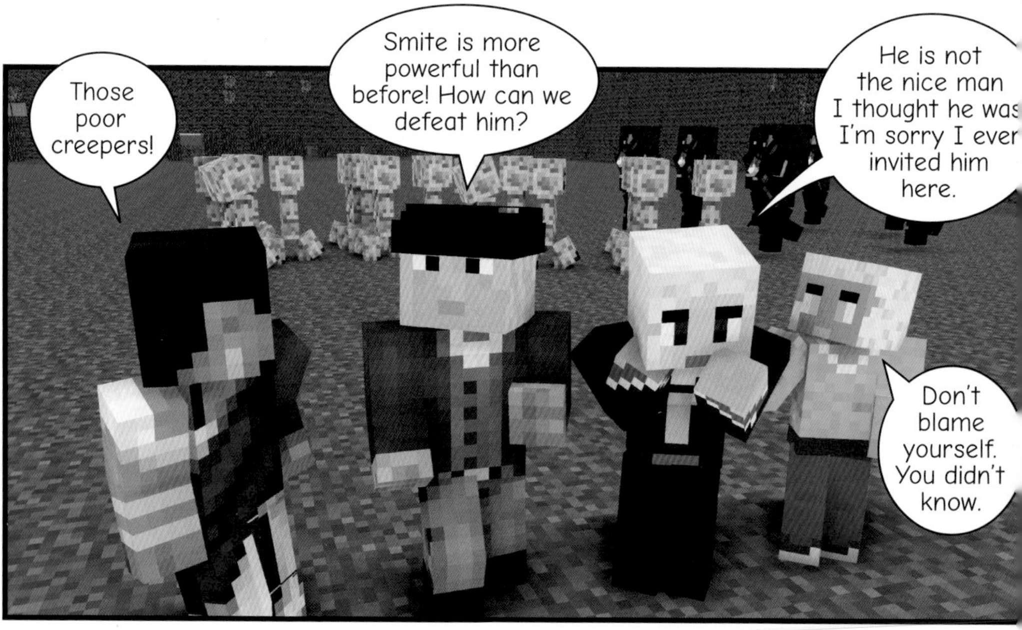
Those poor creepers!
Smite is more powerful than before! How can we defeat him?
He is not the nice man I thought he was I'm sorry I ever invited him here.
Don't blame yourself. You didn't know.

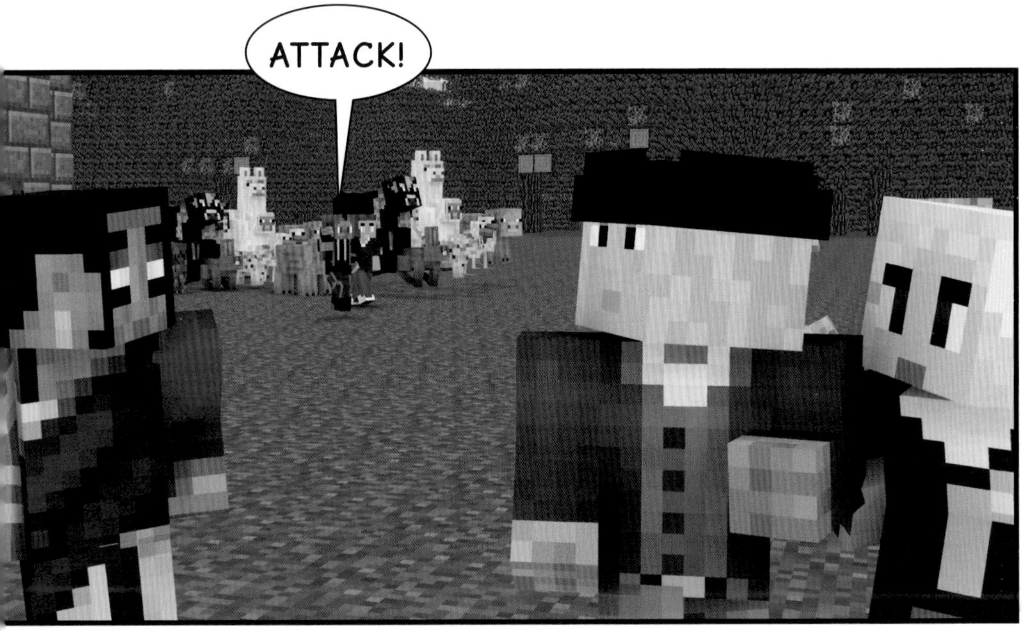
ATTACK!

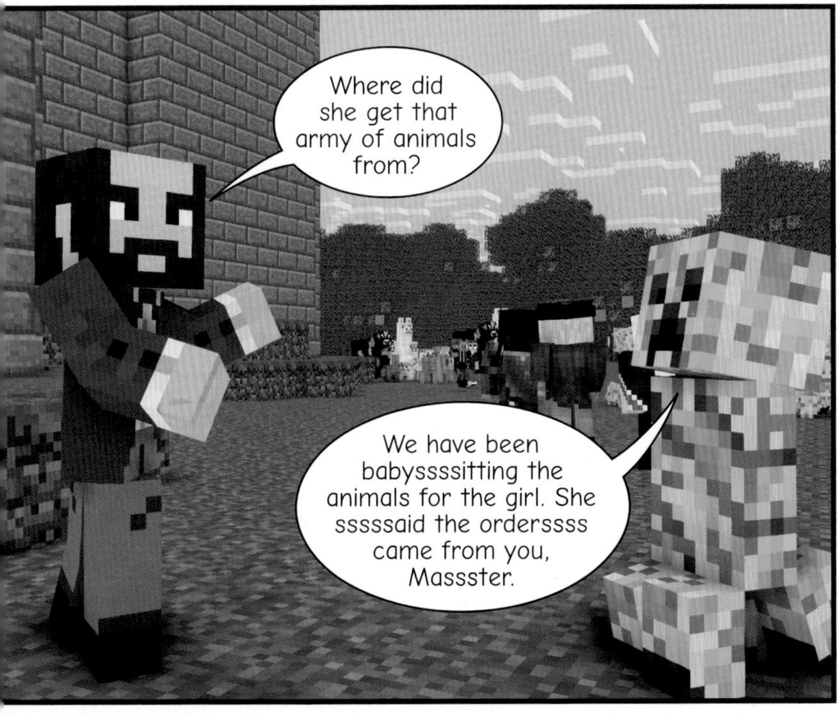
Where did she get that army of animals from?
We have been babyssssitting the animals for the girl. She sssssaid the orderssss came from you, Masssster.

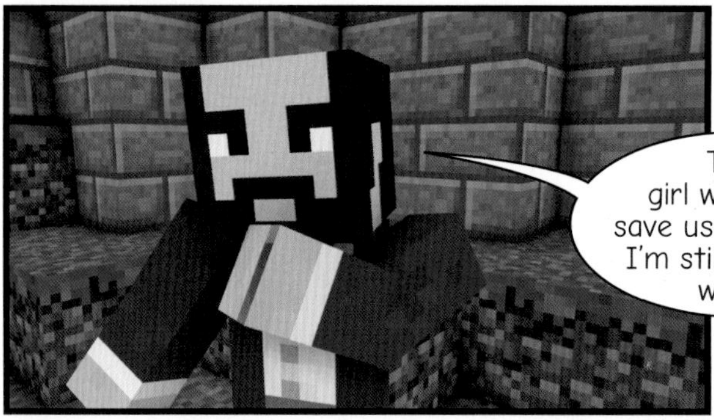
That girl will either save us or ruin us. I'm still not sure which.

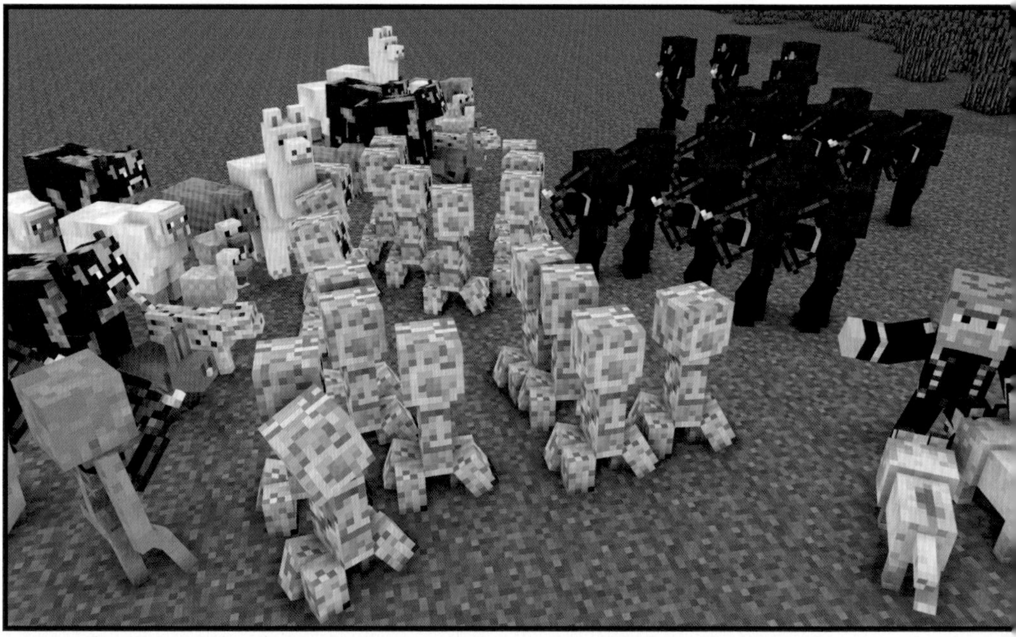

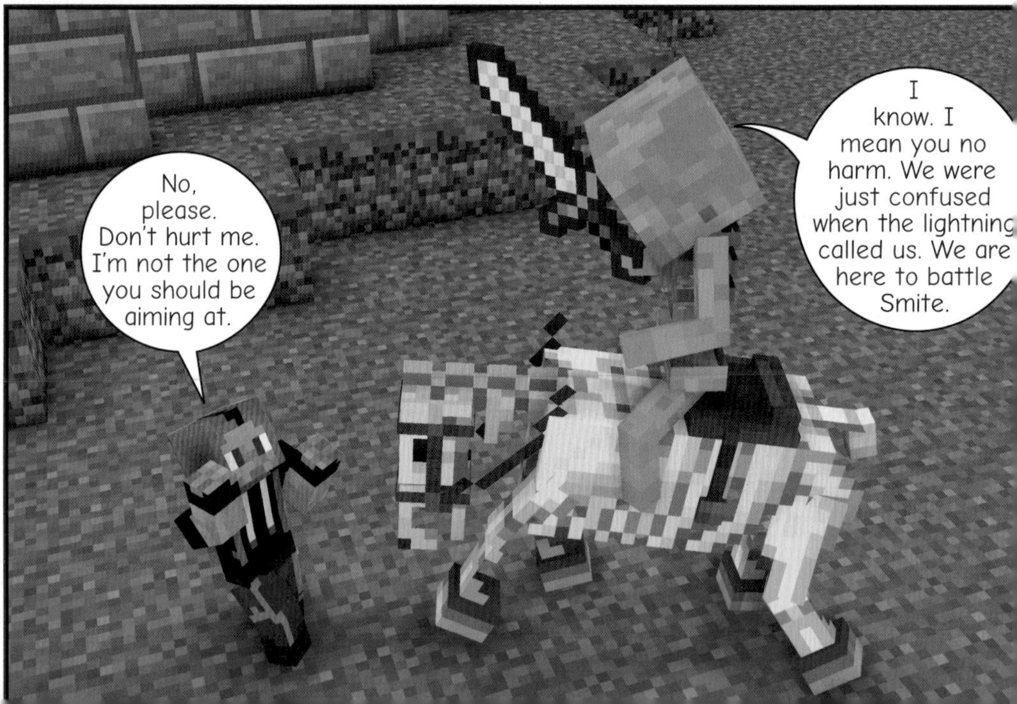
No, please. Don't hurt me. I'm not the one you should be aiming at.
I know. I mean you no harm. We were just confused when the lightning called us. We are here to battle Smite.

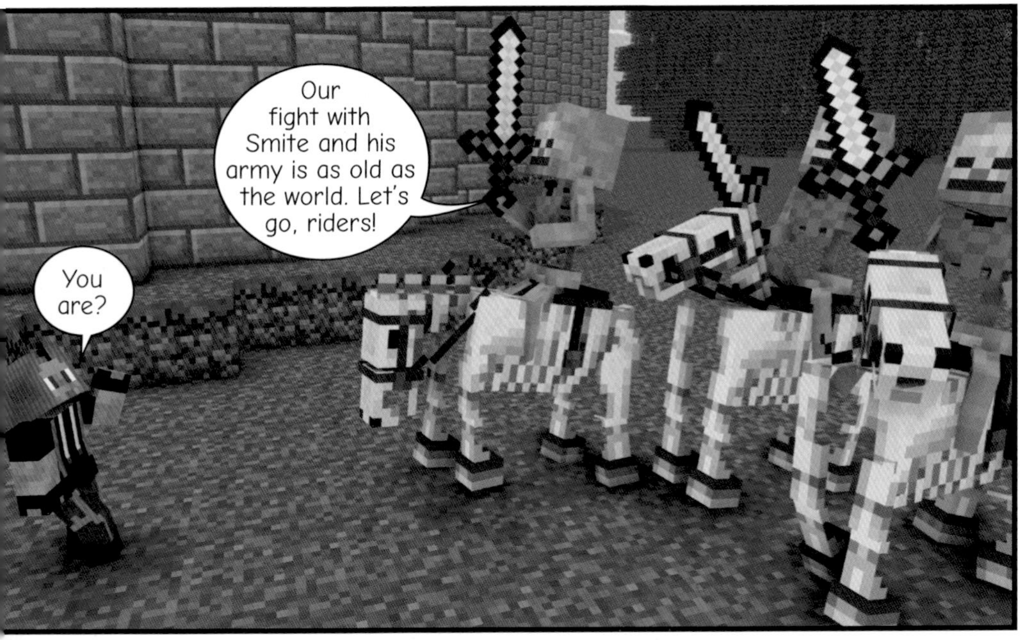
You are?
Our fight with Smite and his army is as old as the world. Let's go, riders!

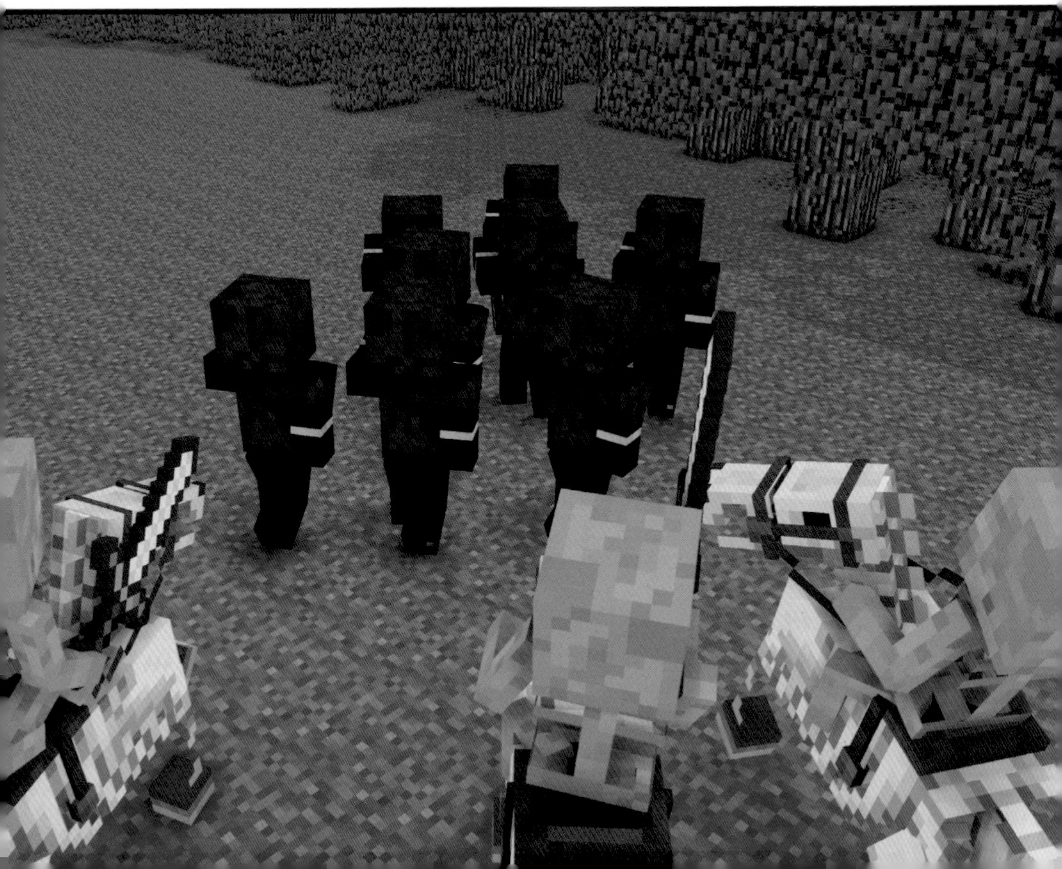

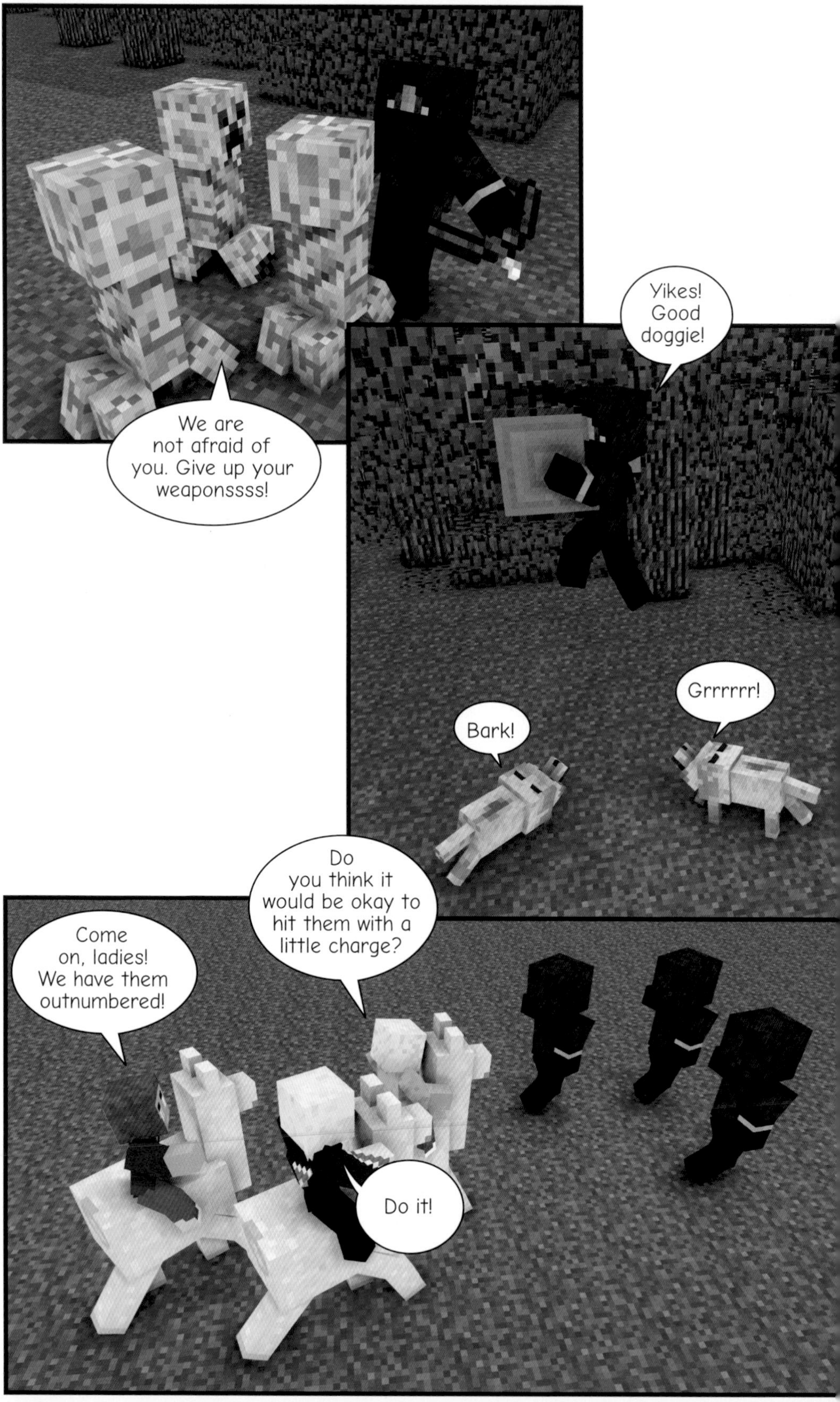
We are not afraid of you. Give up your weaponssss!
Yikes! Good doggie!
Bark!
Grrrrrr!
Come on, ladies! We have them outnumbered!
Do you think it would be okay to hit them with a little charge?
Do it!

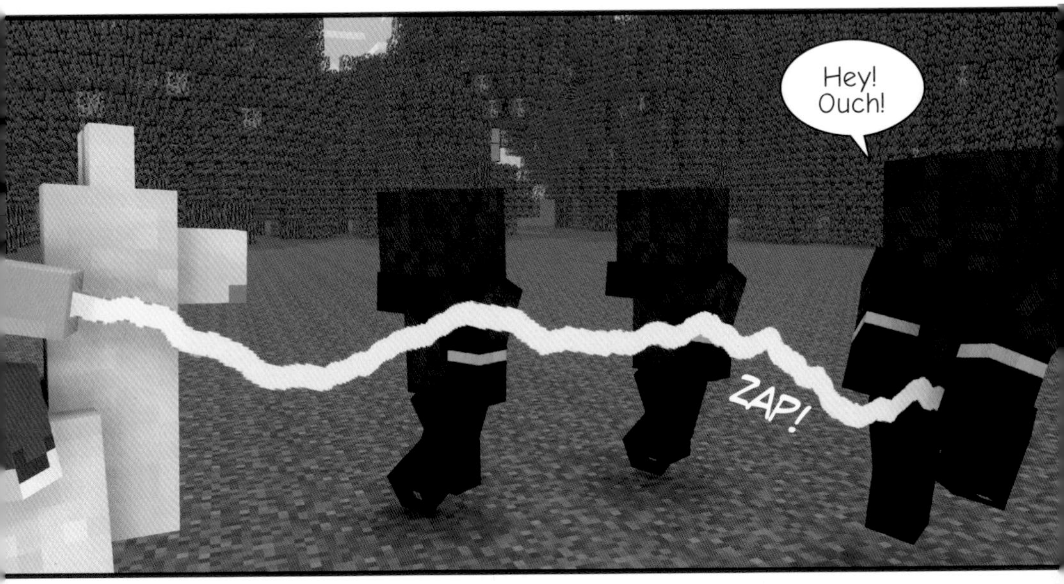
Hey!
Ouch!
ZAP!

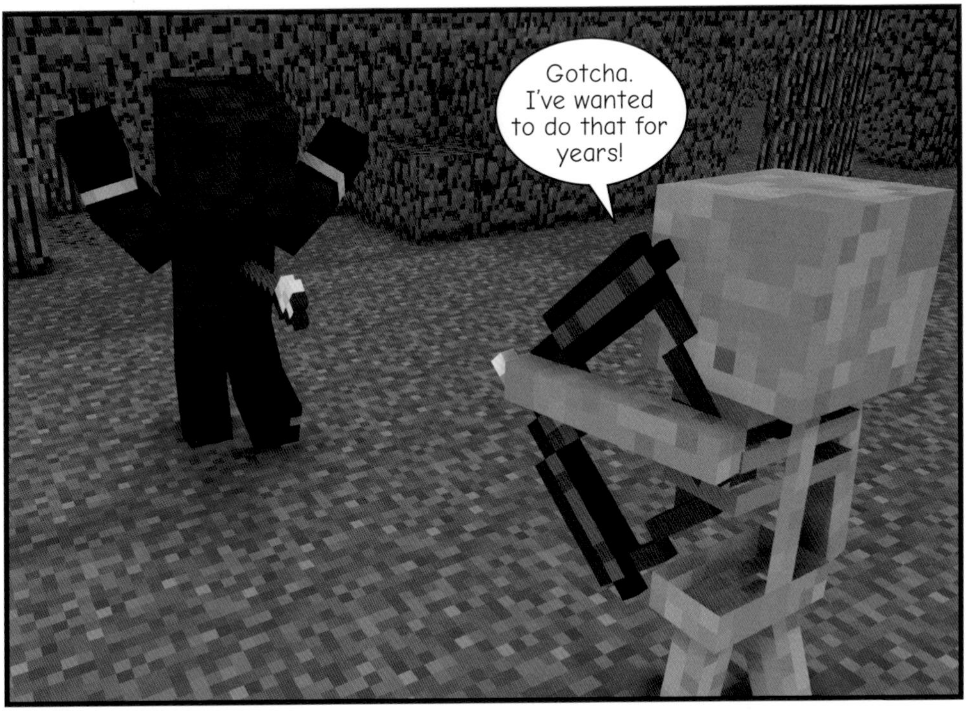
Gotcha. I've wanted to do that for years!

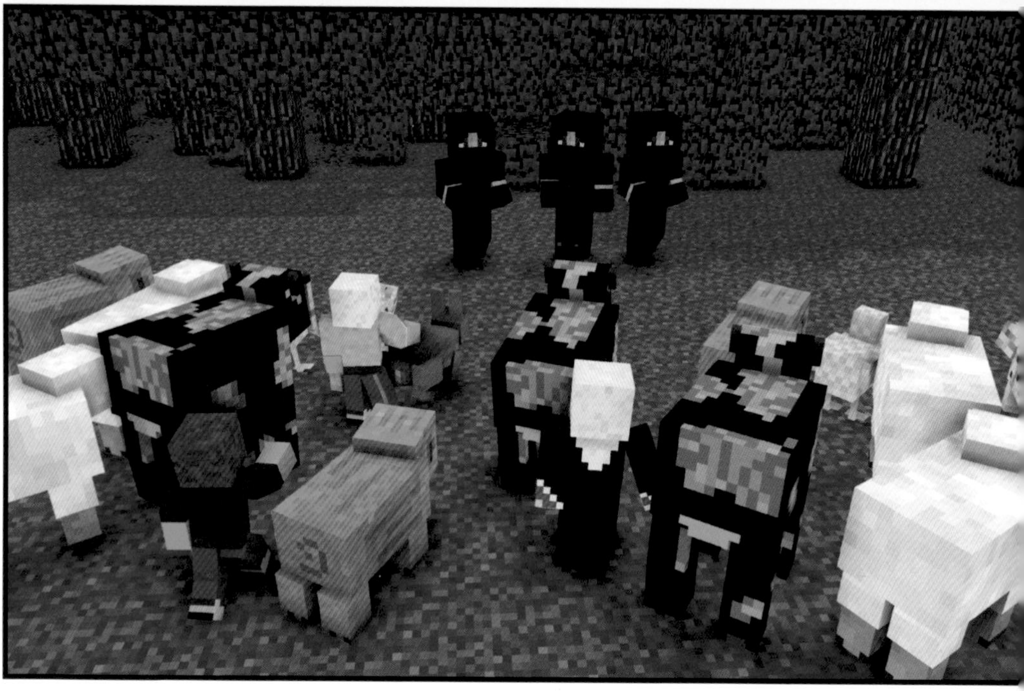

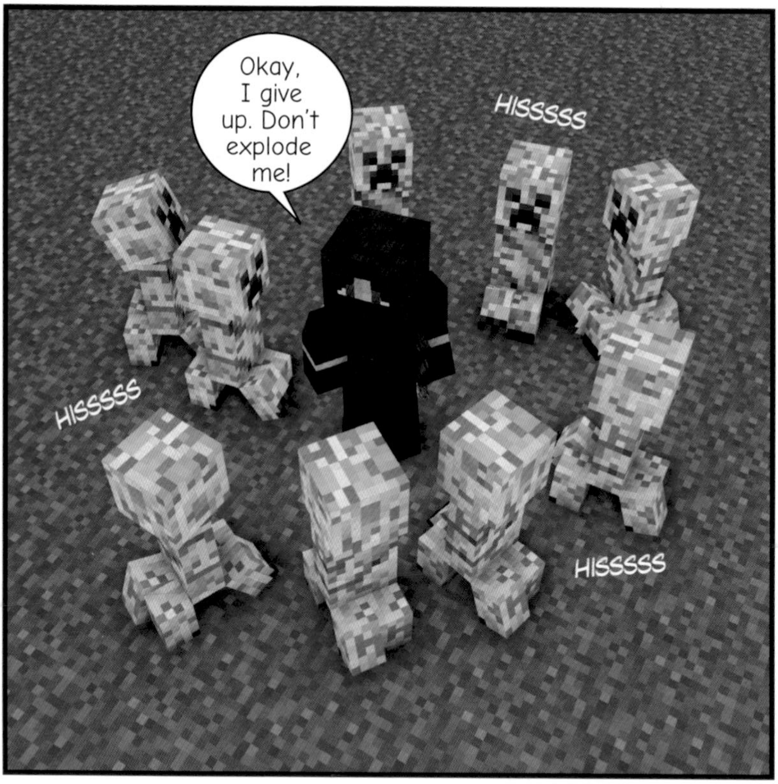
Okay, I give up. Don't explode me!
HISSSSS
HISSSSS
HISSSSS

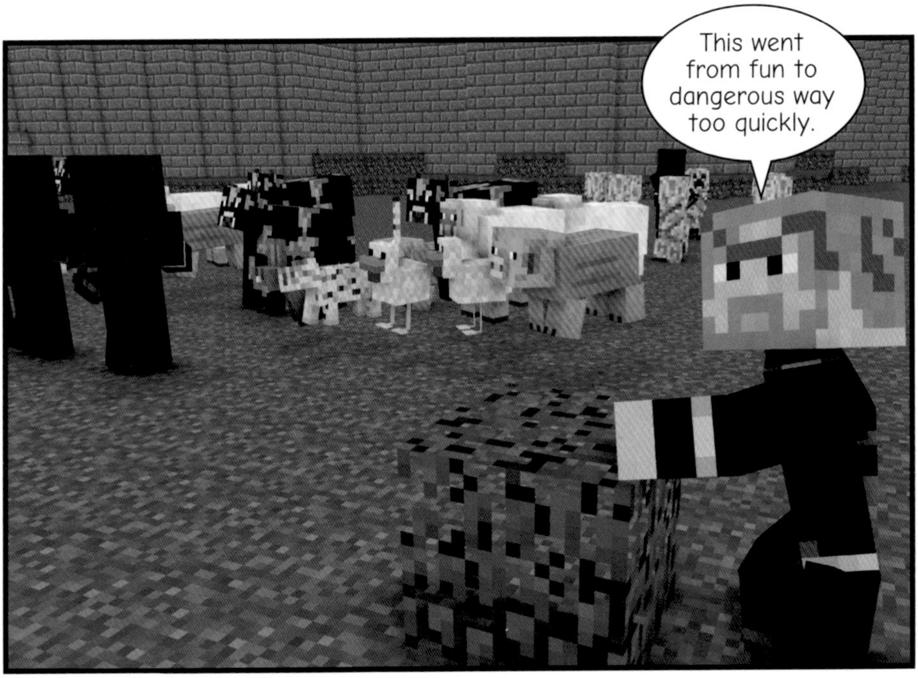
This went from fun to dangerous way too quickly.

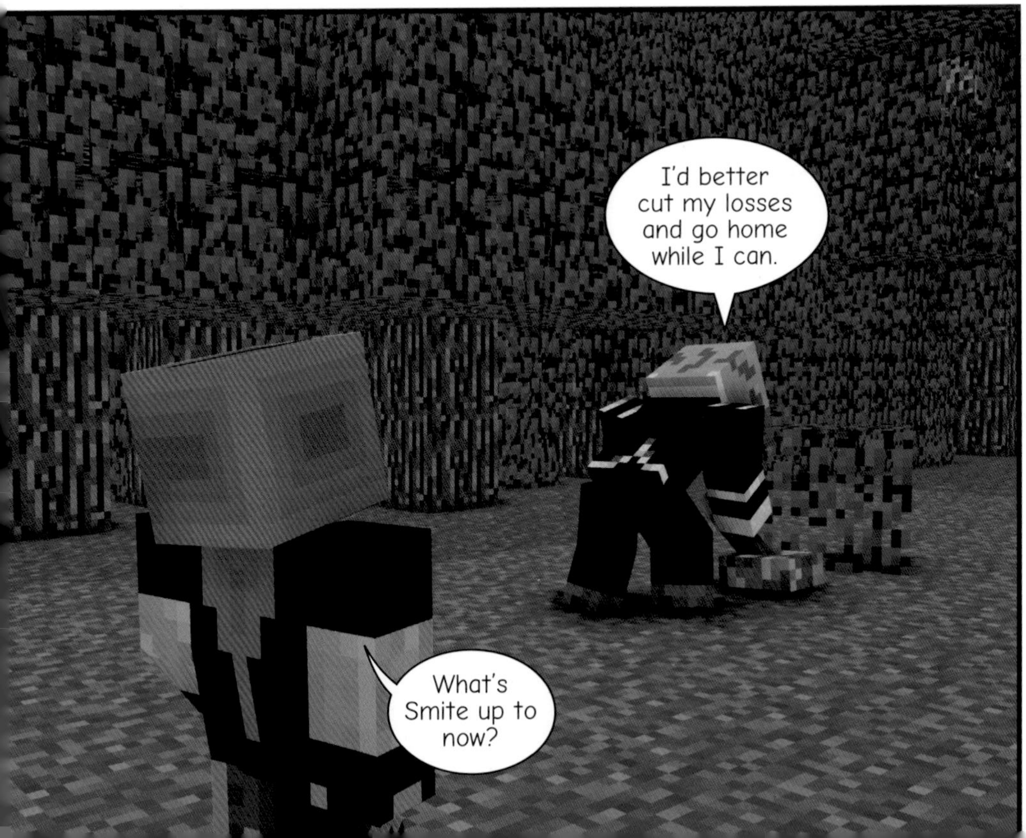
I'd better cut my losses and go home while I can.
What's Smite up to now?

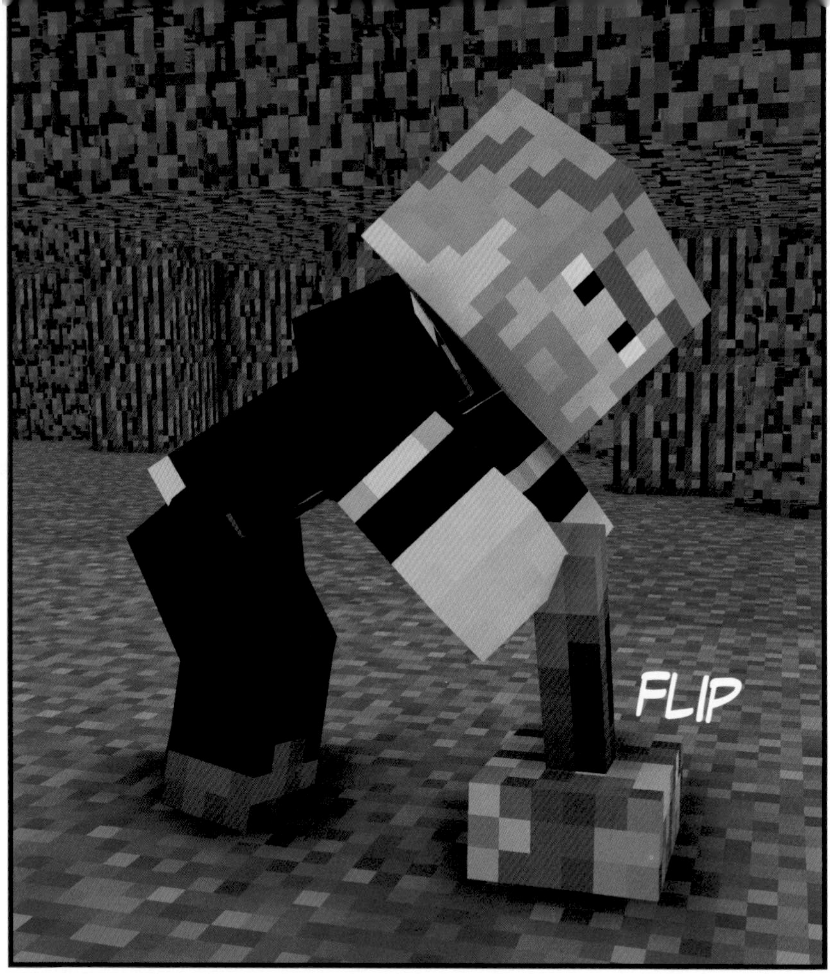
FLIP

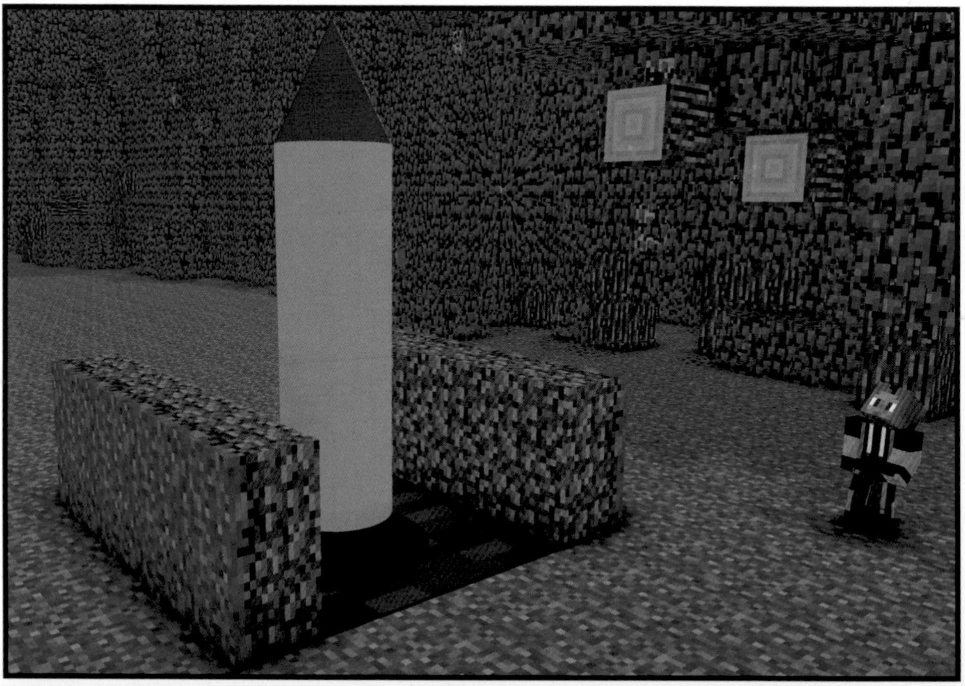

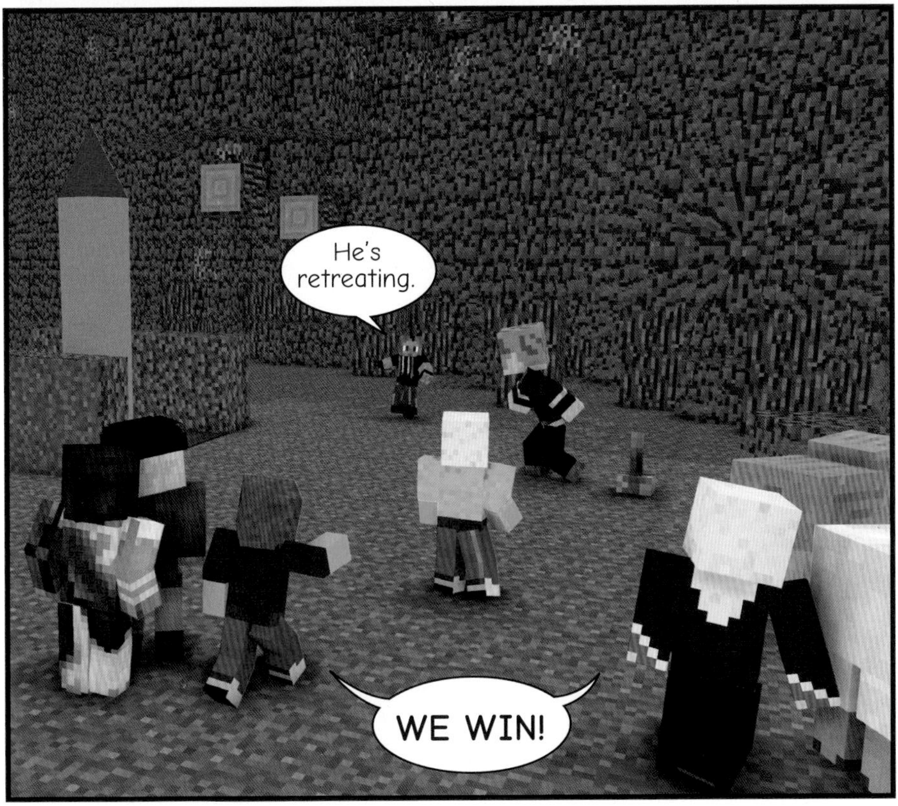
He's retreating.
WE WIN!

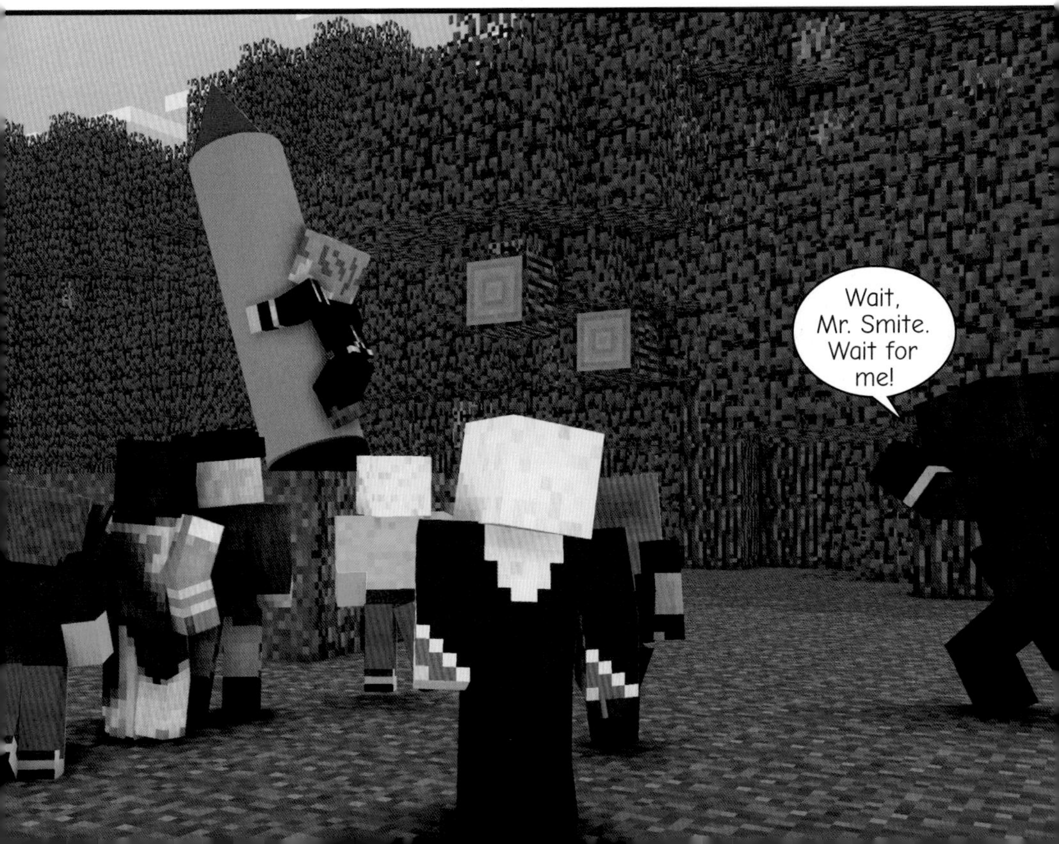
Wait, Mr. Smite. Wait for me!

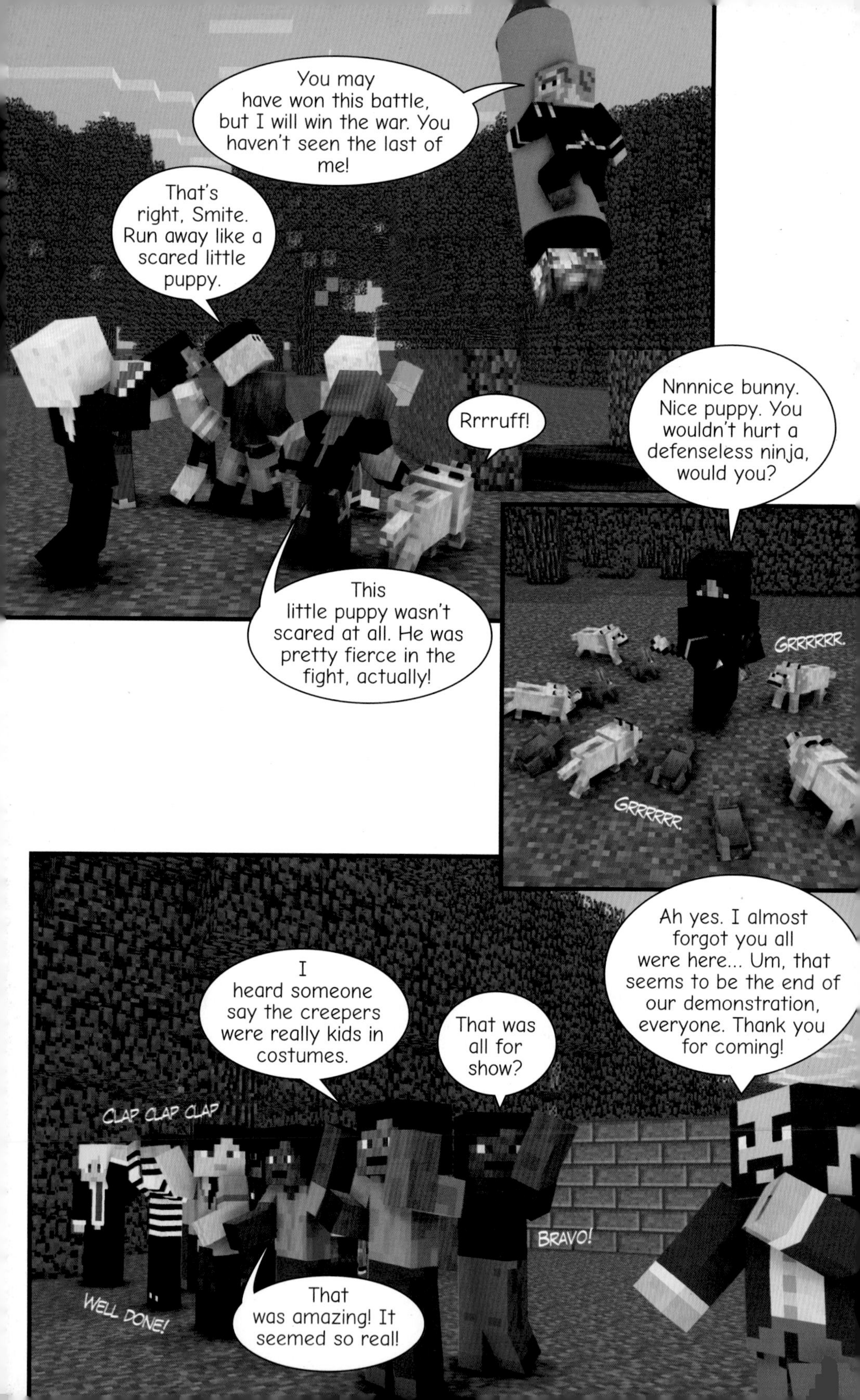
You may have won this battle, but I will win the war. You haven't seen the last of me!
That's right, Smite. Run away like a scared little puppy.
Rrrruff!
This little puppy wasn't scared at all. He was pretty fierce in the fight, actually!
Nnnnice bunny. Nice puppy. You wouldn't hurt a defenseless ninja, would you?
GRRRRRR.
GRRRRRR.
Ah yes. I almost forgot you all were here... Um, that seems to be the end of our demonstration, everyone. Thank you for coming!
I heard someone say the creepers were really kids in costumes.
That was all for show?
CLAP CLAP CLAP
BRAVO!
WELL DONE!
That was amazing! It seemed so real!

CHAPTER 11

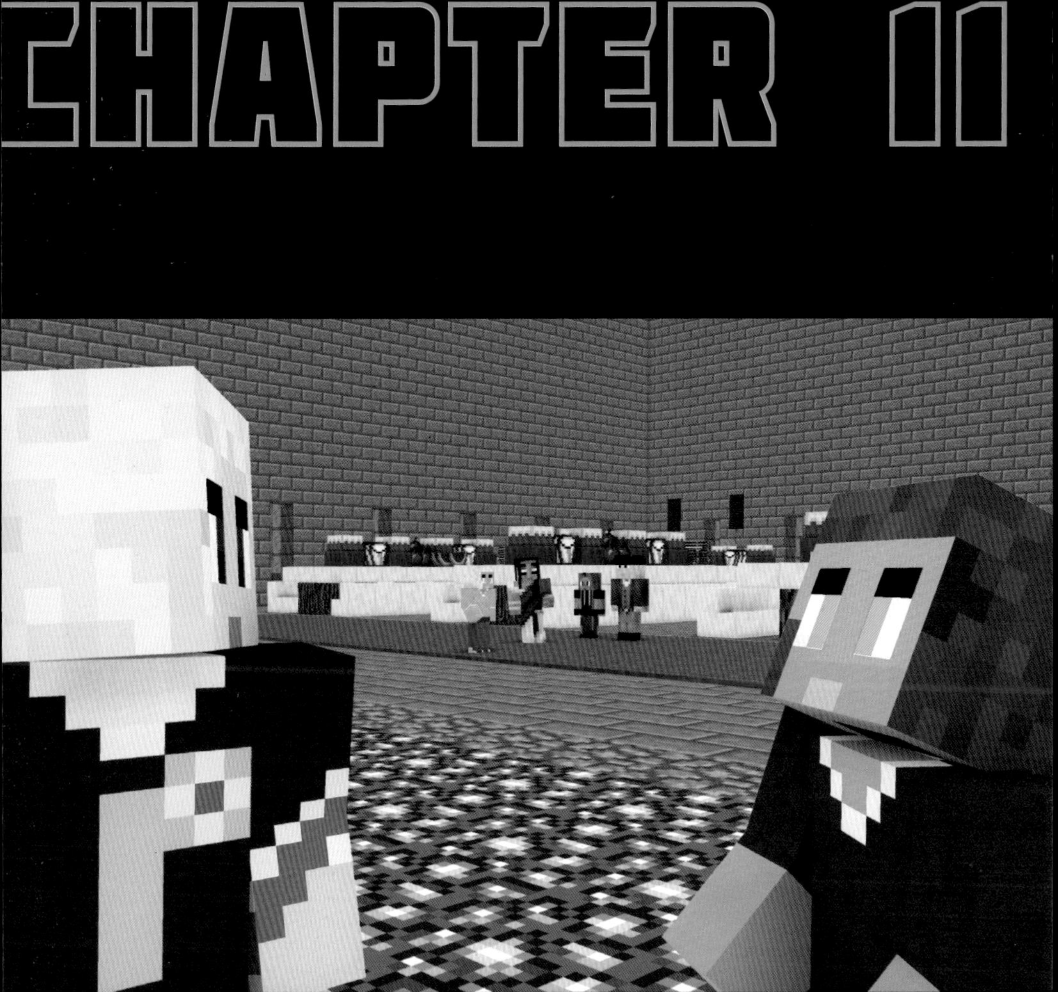

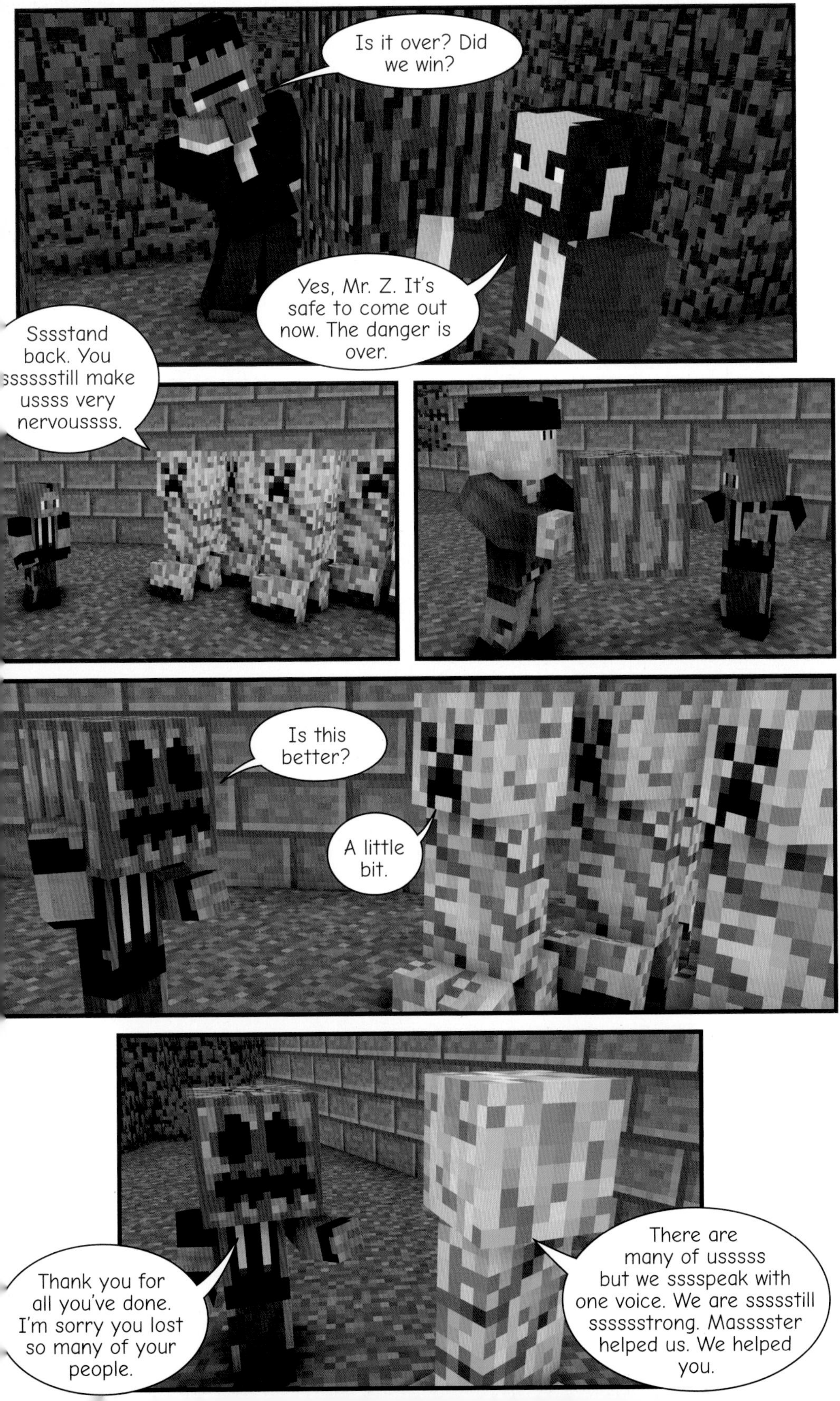
Is it over? Did we win?
Yes, Mr. Z. It's safe to come out now. The danger is over.
Sssstand back. You sssssstill make ussss very nervousssss.
Is this better?
A little bit.
Thank you for all you've done. I'm sorry you lost so many of your people.
There are many of usssss but we sssspeak with one voice. We are ssssstill sssssstrong. Massssster helped us. We helped you.

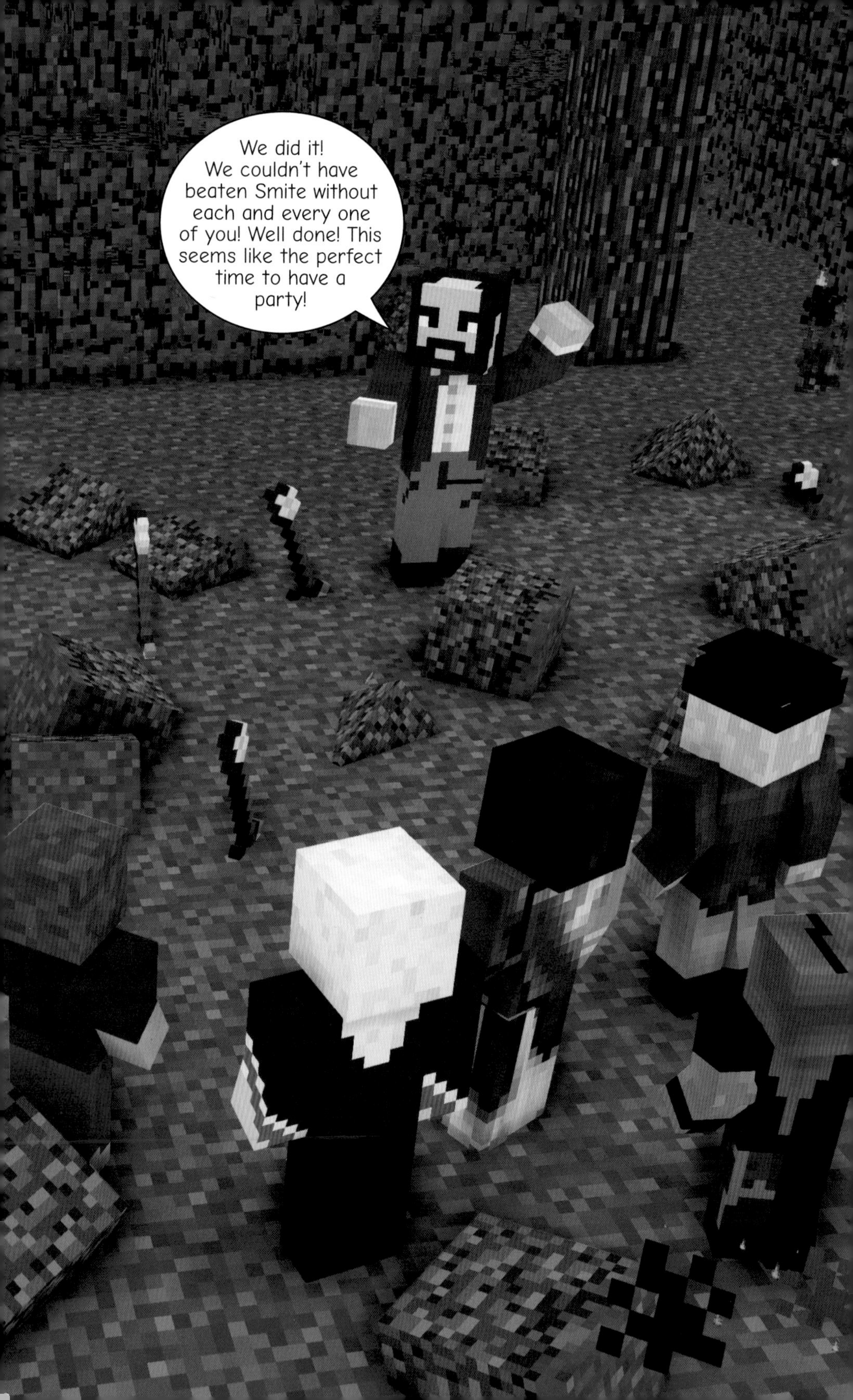
We did it! We couldn't have beaten Smite without each and every one of you! Well done! This seems like the perfect time to have a party!

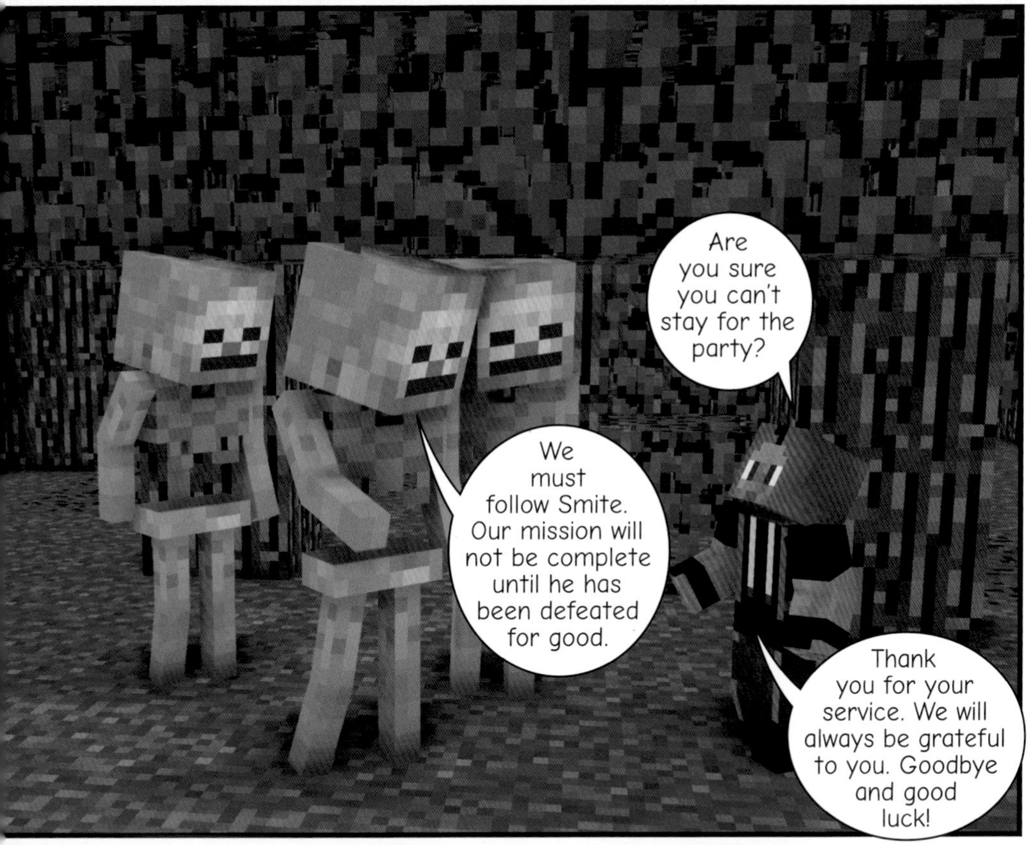
Are you sure you can't stay for the party?
We must follow Smite. Our mission will not be complete until he has been defeated for good.
Thank you for your service. We will always be grateful to you. Goodbye and good luck!

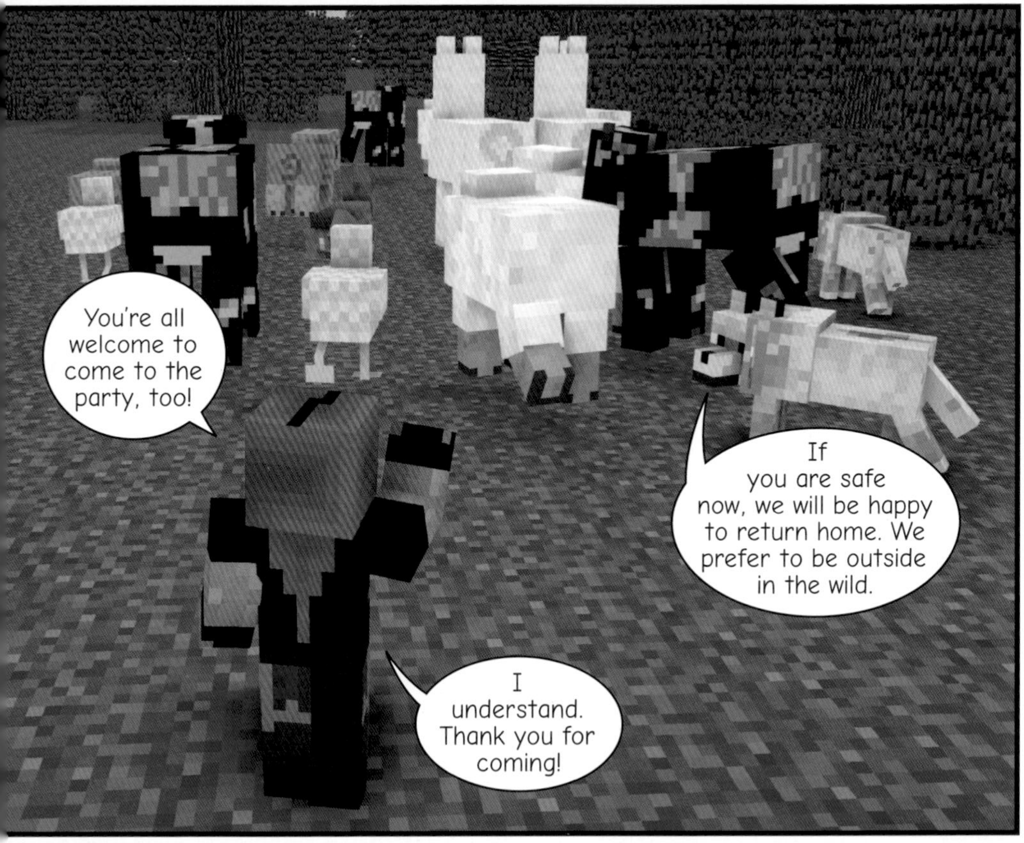
You're all welcome to come to the party, too!
If you are safe now, we will be happy to return home. We prefer to be outside in the wild.
I understand. Thank you for coming!

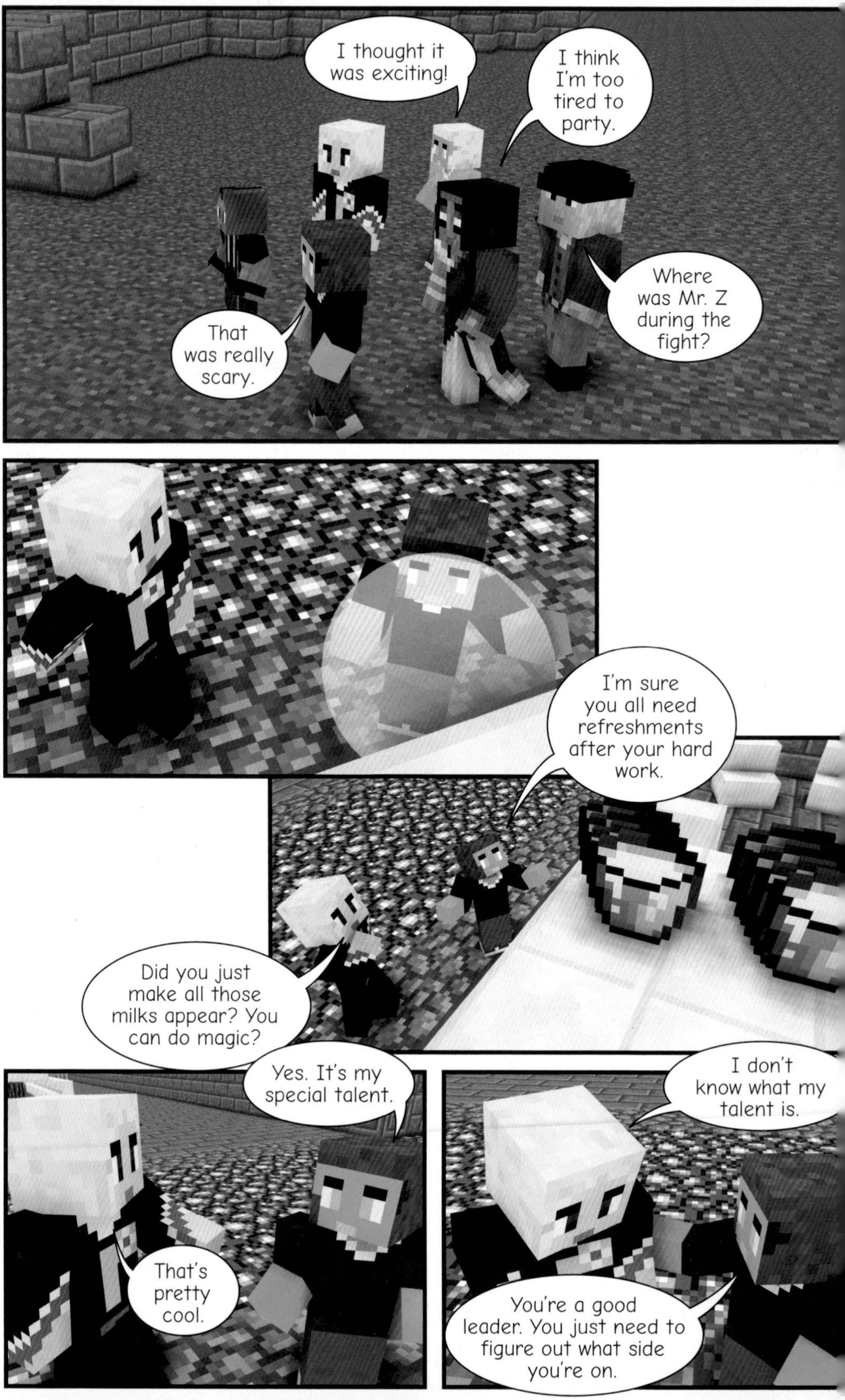
I thought it was exciting!
I think I'm too tired to party.
That was really scary.
Where was Mr. Z during the fight?
I'm sure you all need refreshments after your hard work.
Did you just make all those milks appear? You can do magic?
Yes. It's my special talent.
That's pretty cool.
I don't know what my talent is.
You're a good leader. You just need to figure out what side you're on.

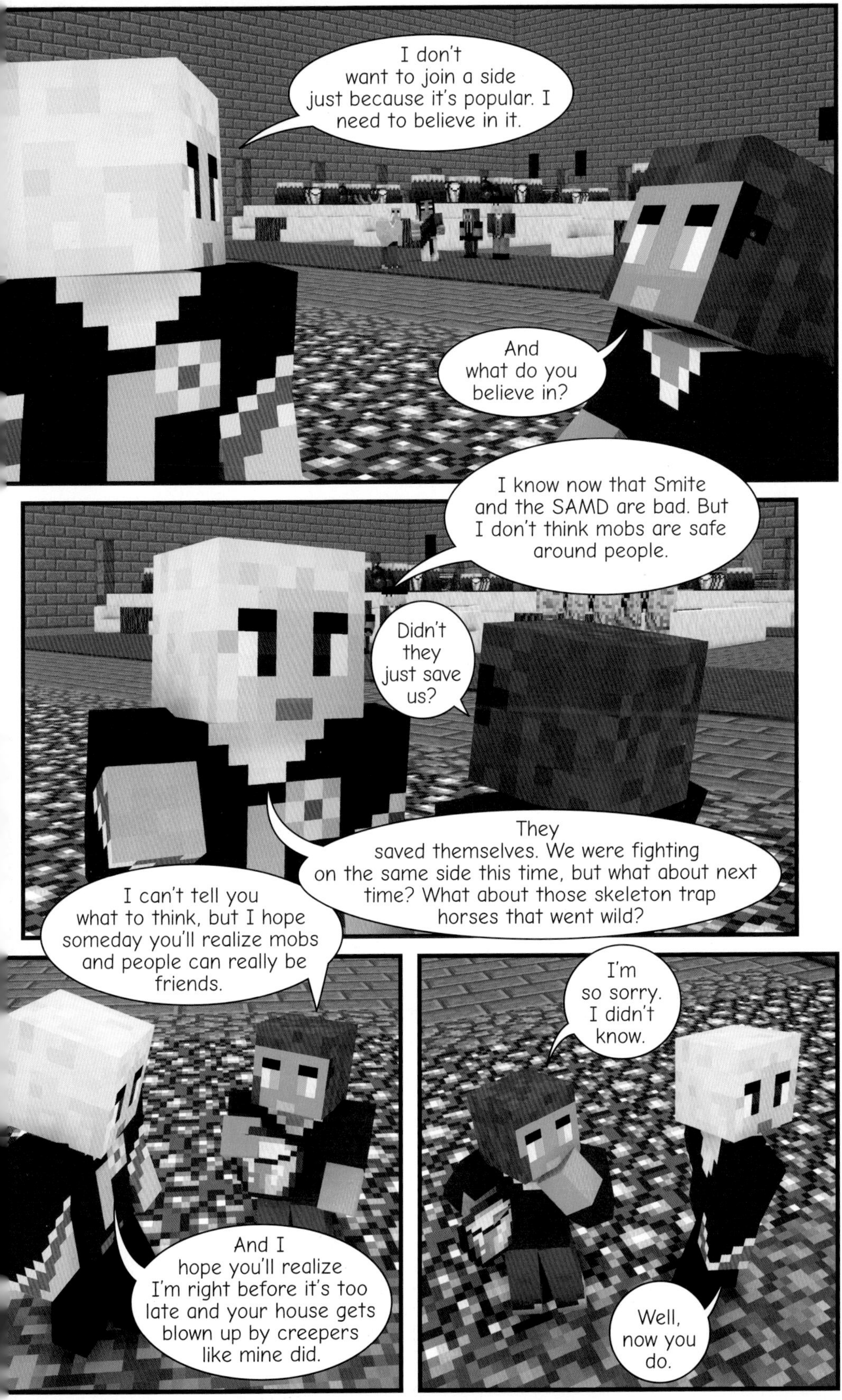
I don't want to join a side just because it's popular. I need to believe in it.
And what do you believe in?
I know now that Smite and the SAMD are bad. But I don't think mobs are safe around people.
Didn't they just save us?
They saved themselves. We were fighting on the same side this time, but what about next time? What about those skeleton trap horses that went wild?
I can't tell you what to think, but I hope someday you'll realize mobs and people can really be friends.
And I hope you'll realize I'm right before it's too late and your house gets blown up by creepers like mine did.
I'm so sorry. I didn't know.
Well, now you do.

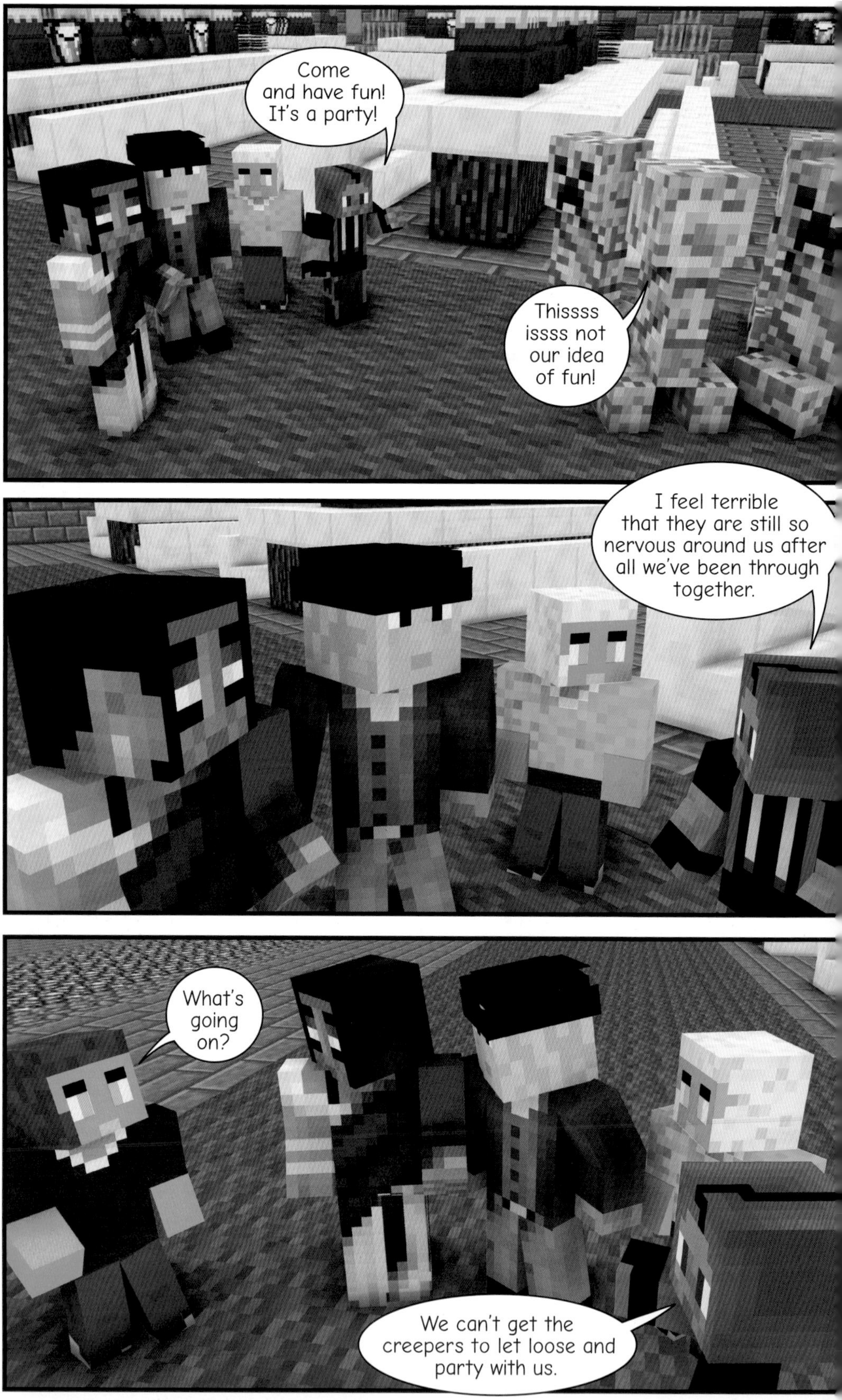
Come and have fun! It's a party!
Thissss issss not our idea of fun!
I feel terrible that they are still so nervous around us after all we've been through together.
What's going on?
We can't get the creepers to let loose and party with us.

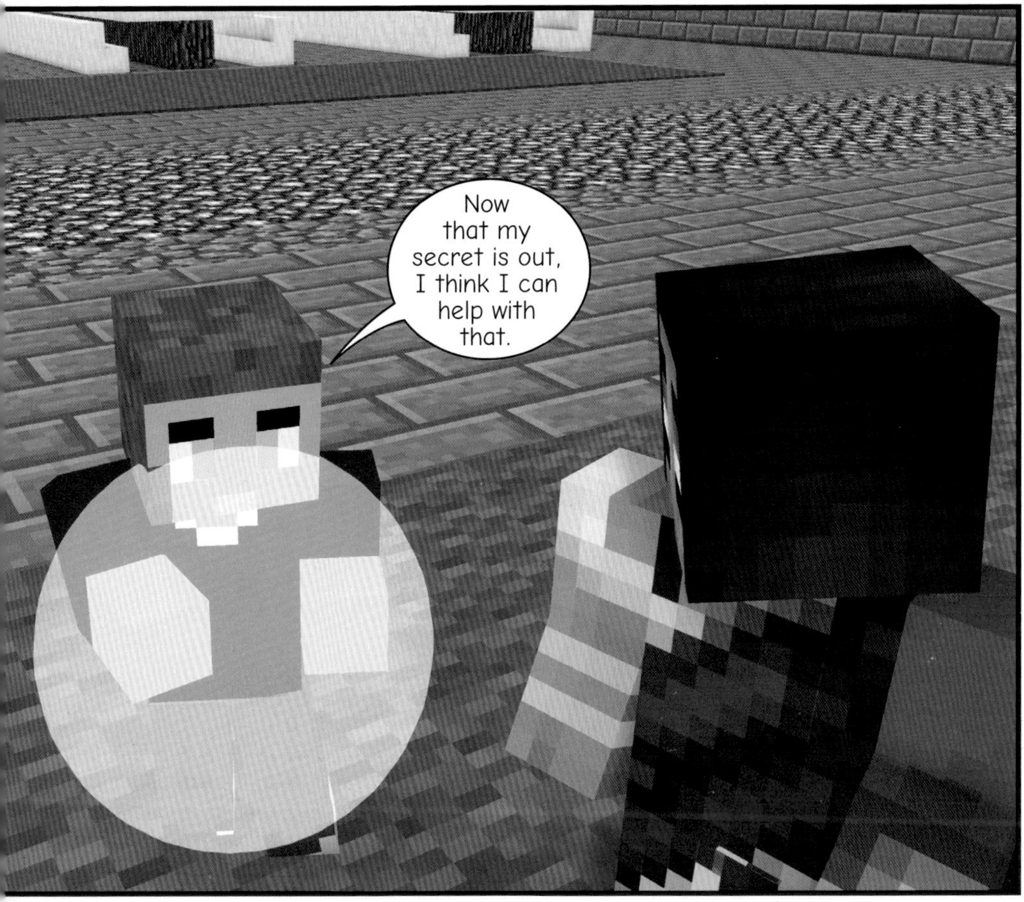
Now that my secret is out, I think I can help with that.

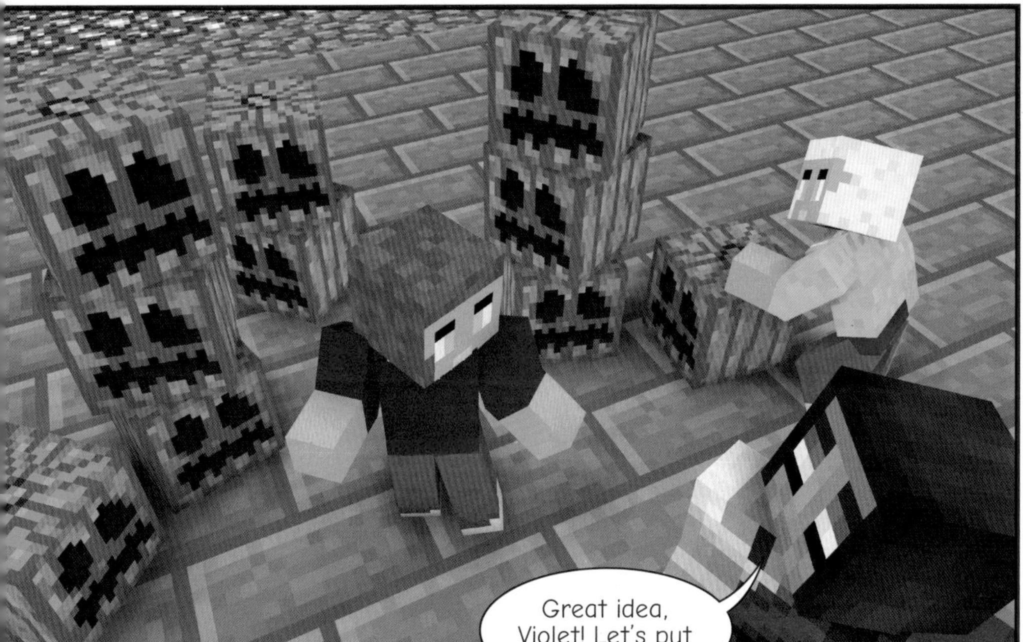
Great idea, Violet! Let's put these on!

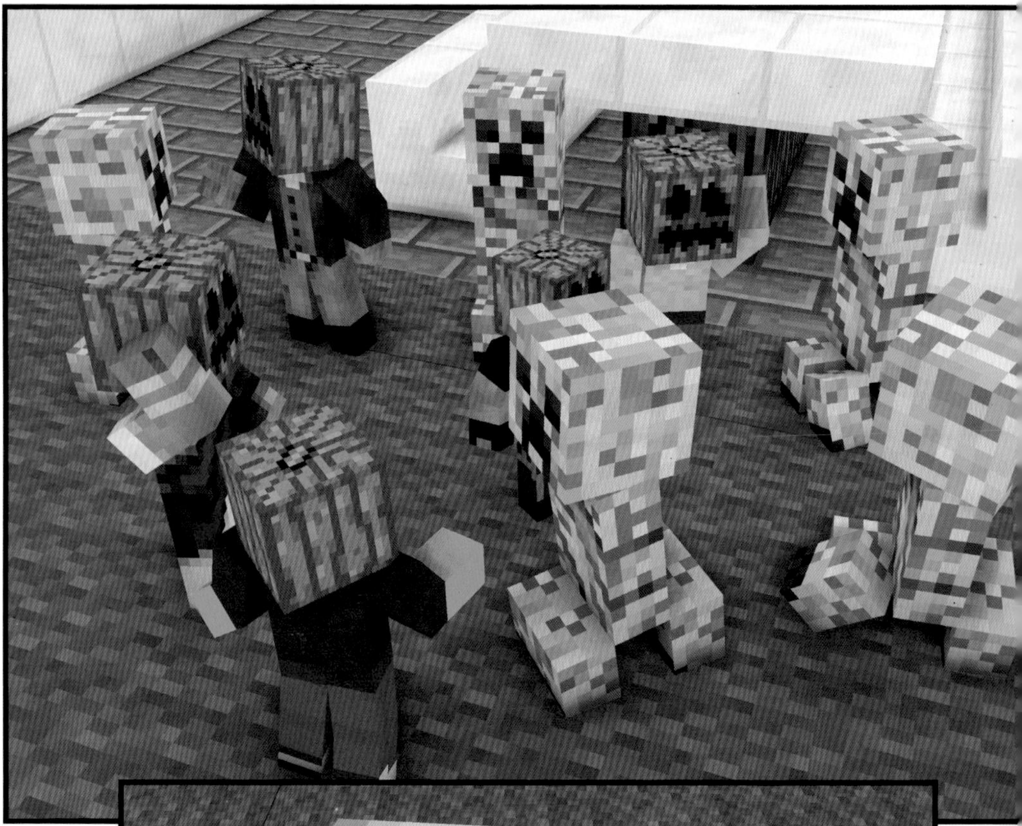

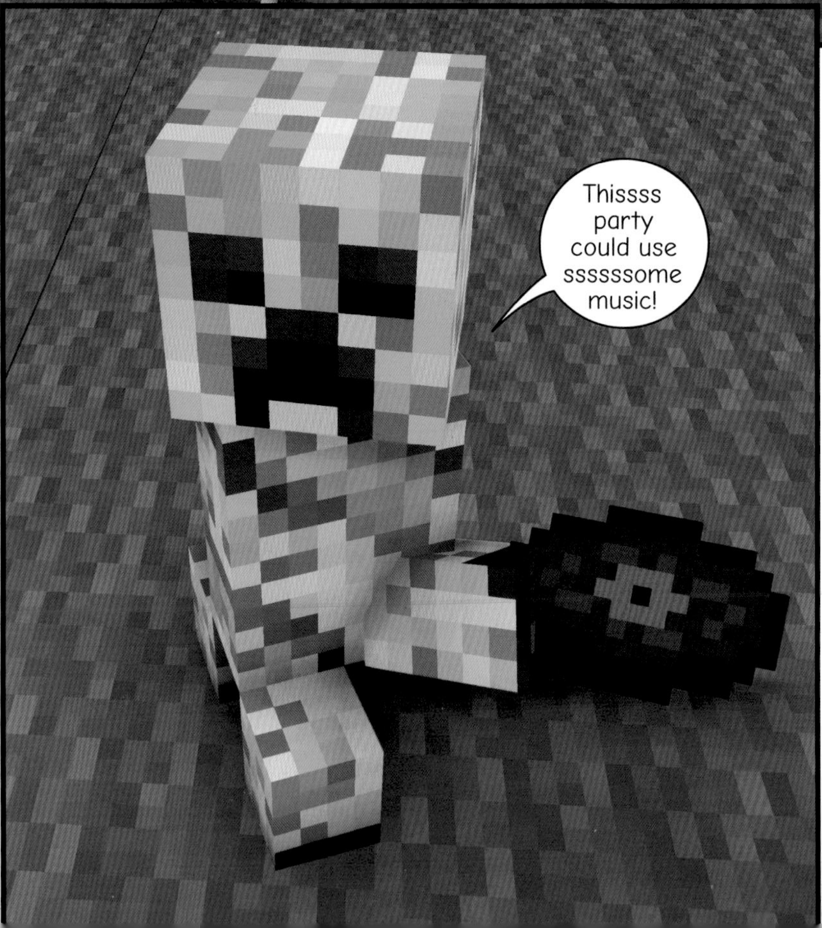
Thissss party could use sssssome music!

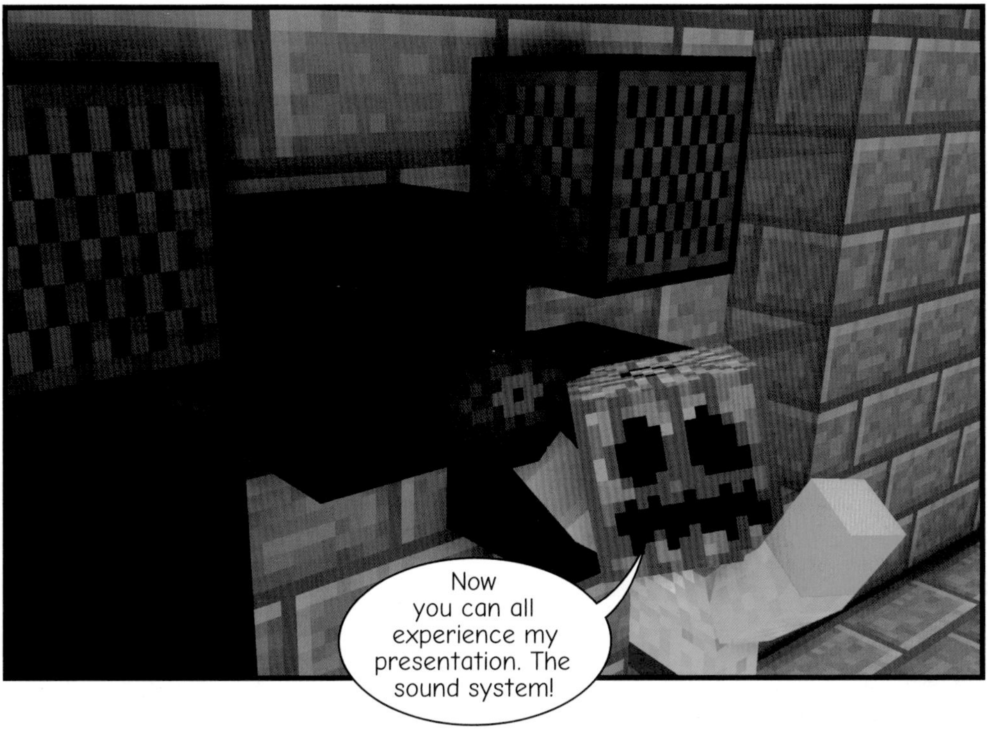
Now you can all experience my presentation. The sound system!

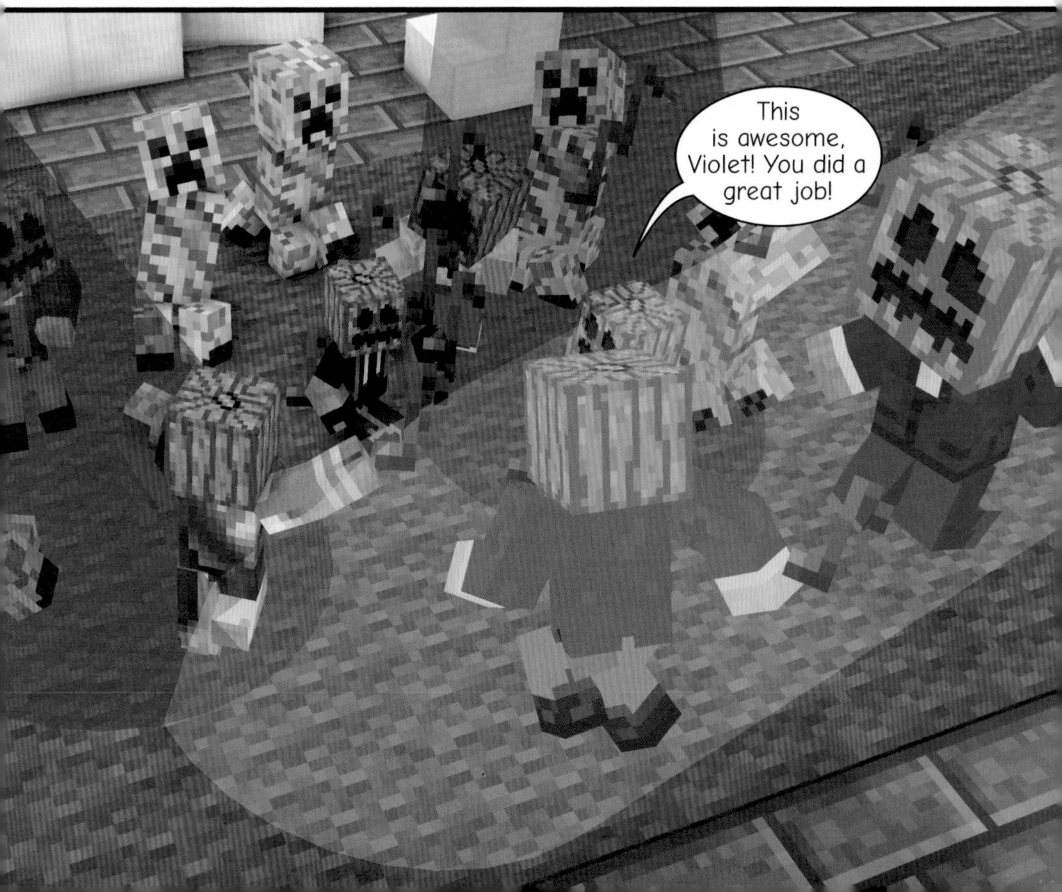
This is awesome, Violet! You did a great job!

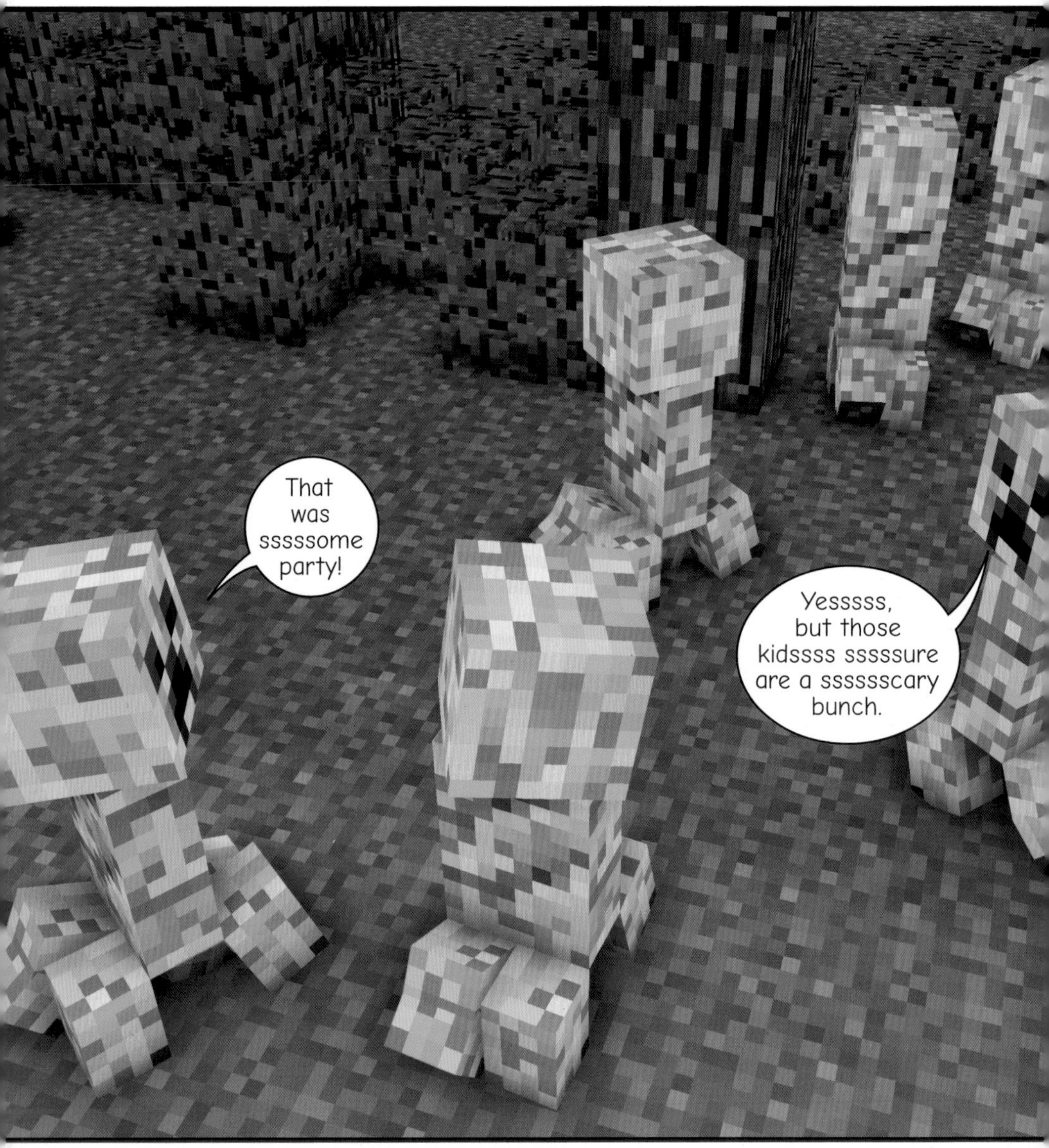
That was sssssome party!
Yesssss, but those kidssss sssssure are a sssssscary bunch.

CHAPTER 12

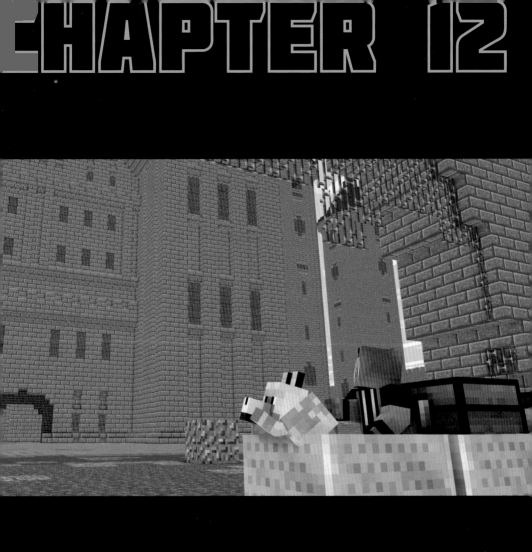

HOMECOMING

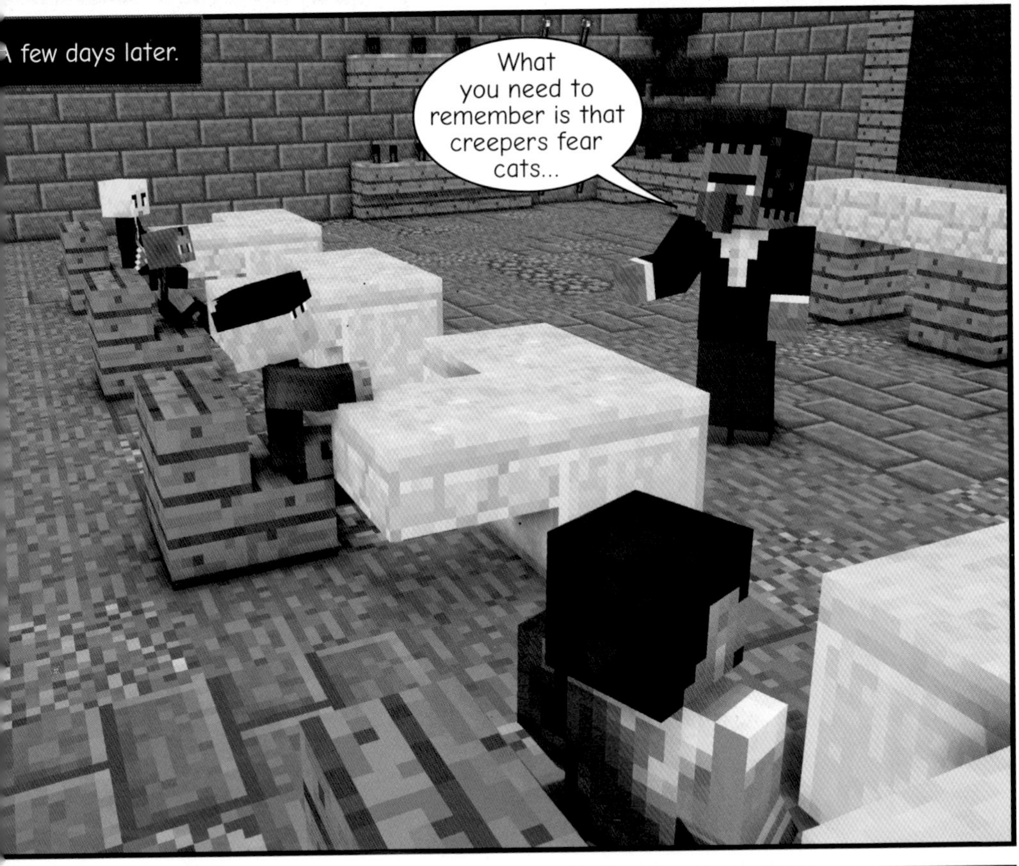
A few days later.
What you need to remember is that creepers fear cats...

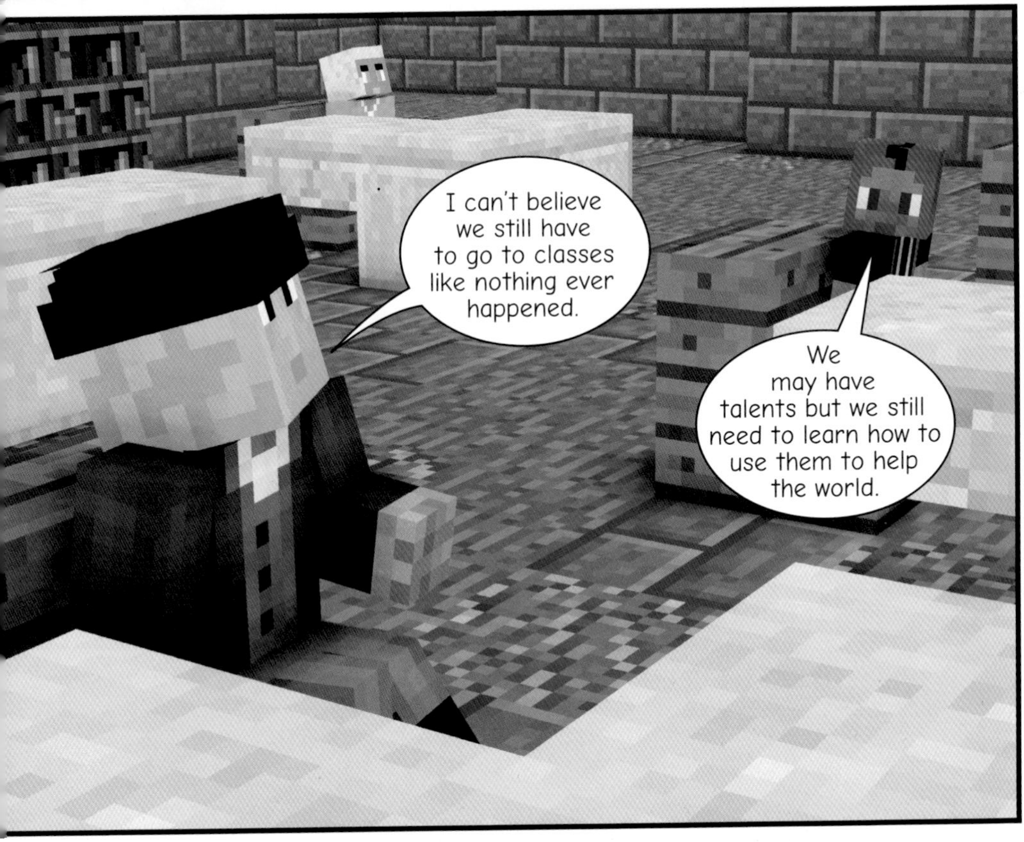
I can't believe we still have to go to classes like nothing ever happened.
We may have talents but we still need to learn how to use them to help the world.

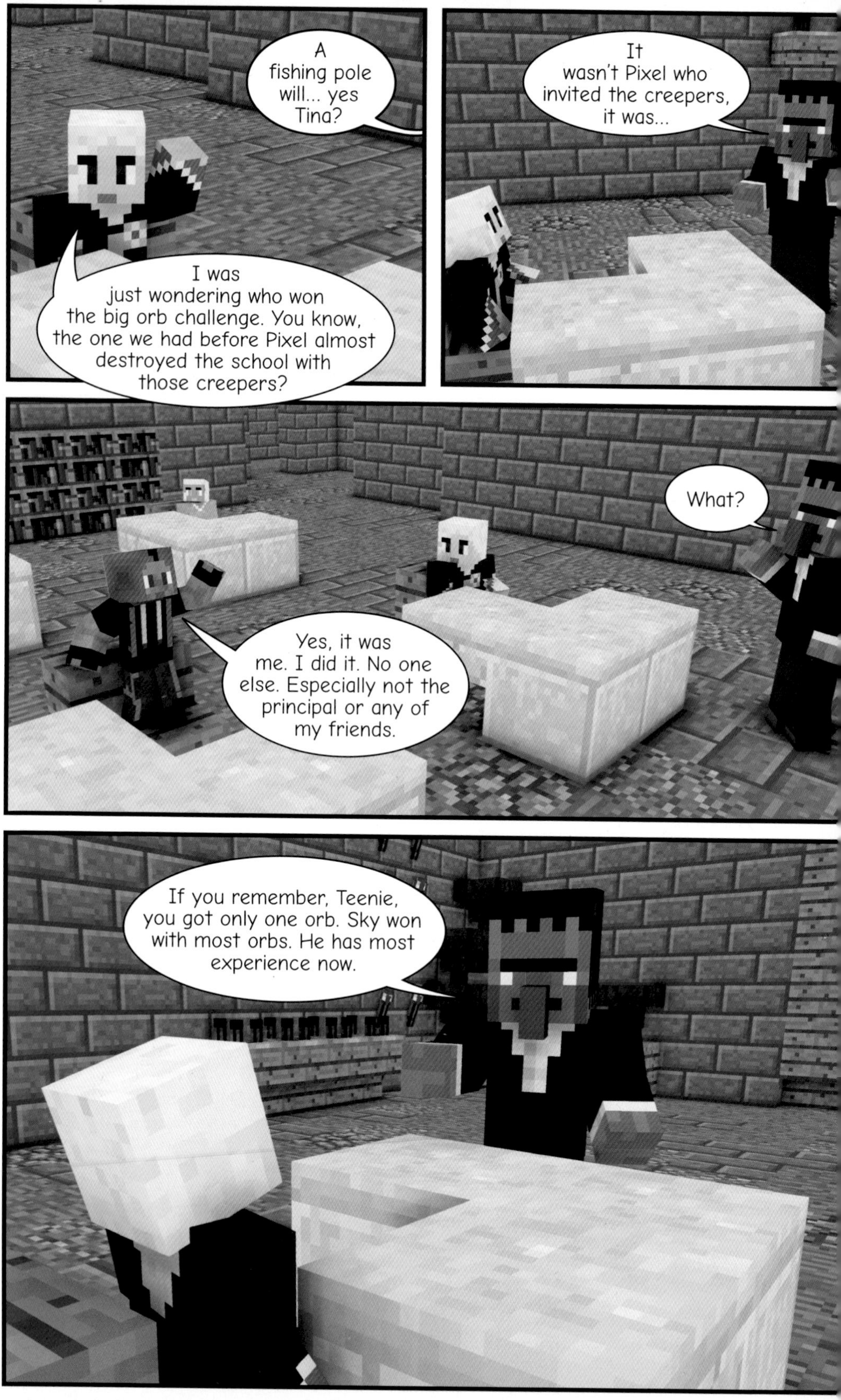
A fishing pole will... yes Tina?
I was just wondering who won the big orb challenge. You know, the one we had before Pixel almost destroyed the school with those creepers?
It wasn't Pixel who invited the creepers, it was...
What?
Yes, it was me. I did it. No one else. Especially not the principal or any of my friends.
If you remember, Teenie, you got only one orb. Sky won with most orbs. He has most experience now.

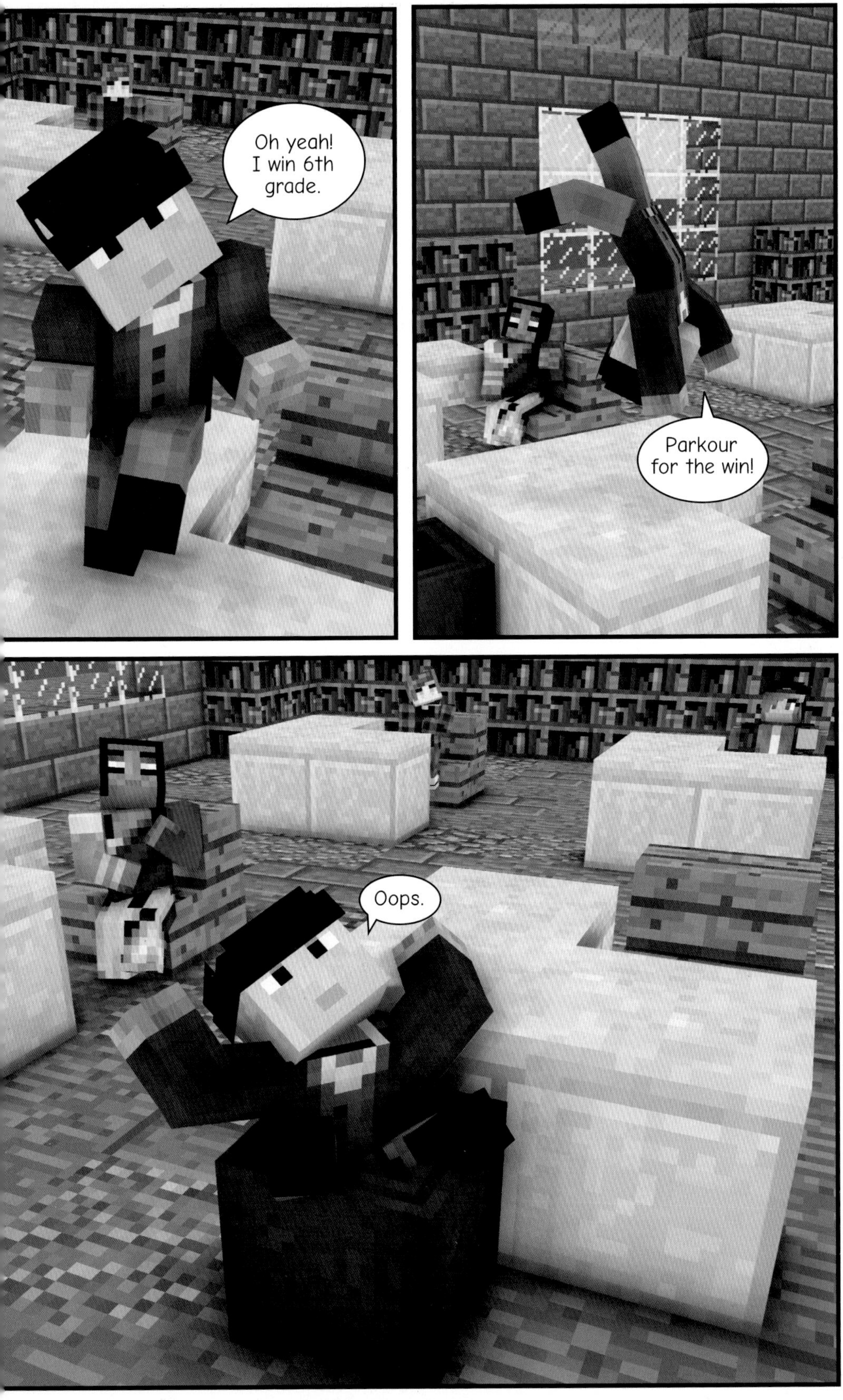
Oh yeah! I win 6th grade.
Parkour for the win!
Oops.

I am glad the rest of the school year went well. We didn't have any more surprise guests.
I kind of miss having the creepers in the basement, though. They are great party guests!

Are you sure it will be okay with your parents to bring Sprinkles home with you for the summer?
We live on a farm. There are plenty of animals for her to meet and play with. A puppy as sweet as Sprinkles is always welcome to join us.

Moo moo moo moo?
I'm sorry, Elliana. You can't come home with me. But I'll see you in the fall!

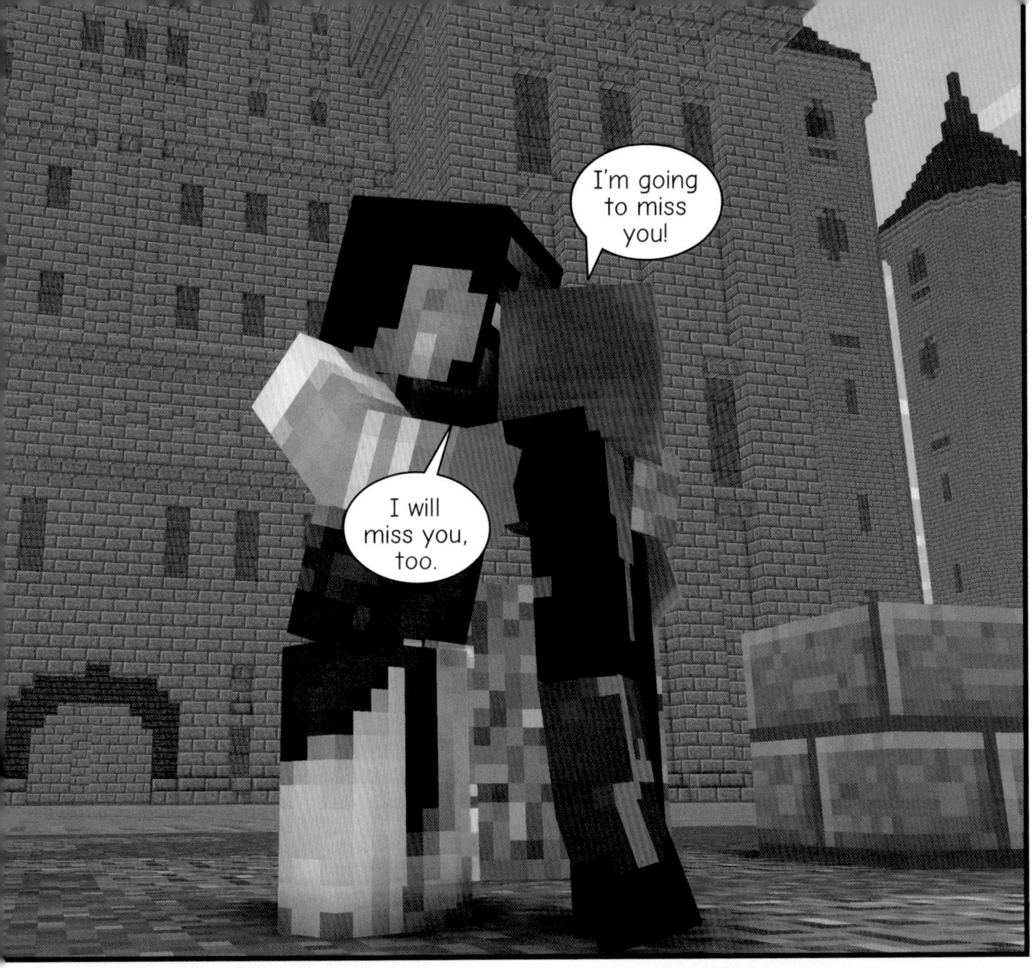
I'm going to miss you!
I will miss you, too.

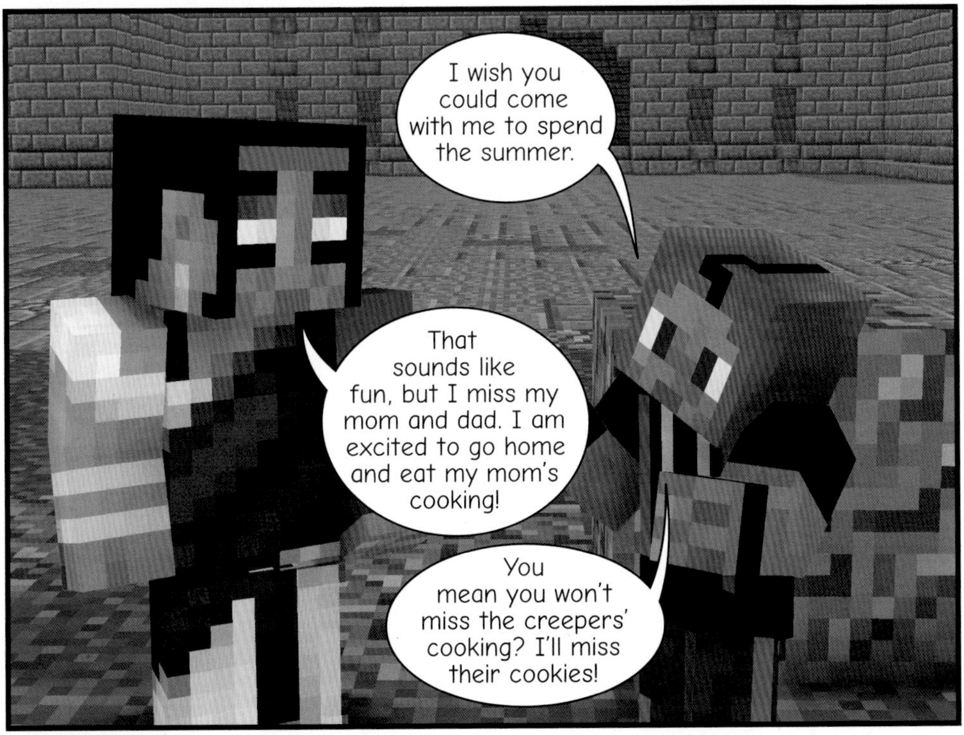
I wish you could come with me to spend the summer.
That sounds like fun, but I miss my mom and dad. I am excited to go home and eat my mom's cooking!
You mean you won't miss the creepers' cooking? I'll miss their cookies!

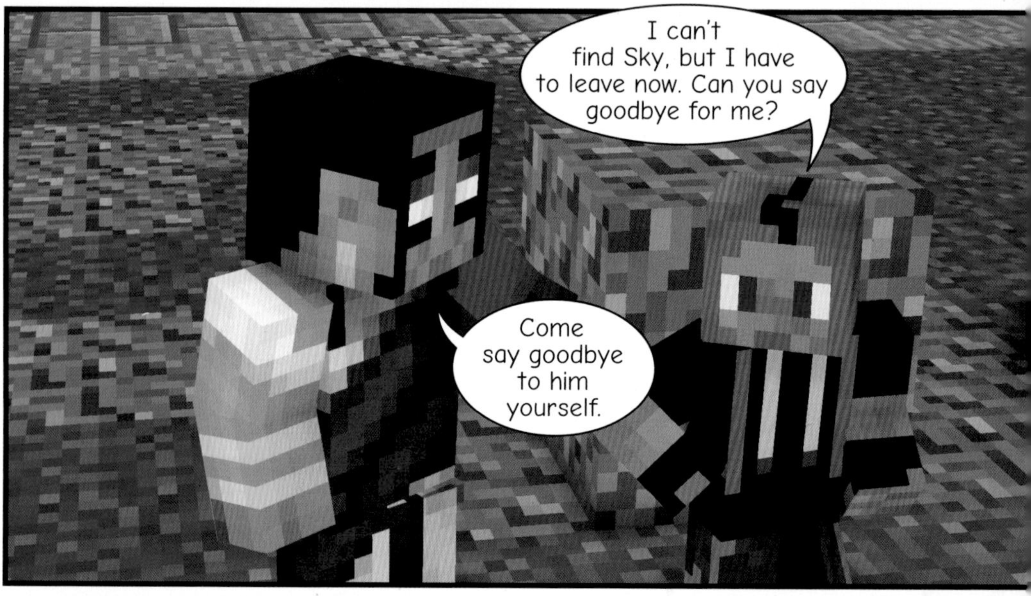
I can't find Sky, but I have to leave now. Can you say goodbye for me?
Come say goodbye to him yourself.

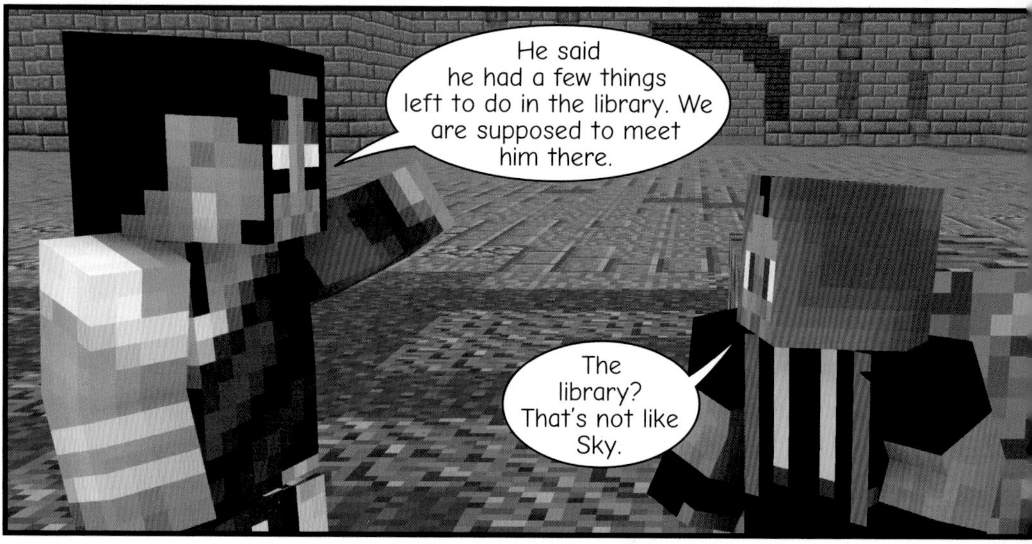
He said he had a few things left to do in the library. We are supposed to meet him there.
The library? That's not like Sky.

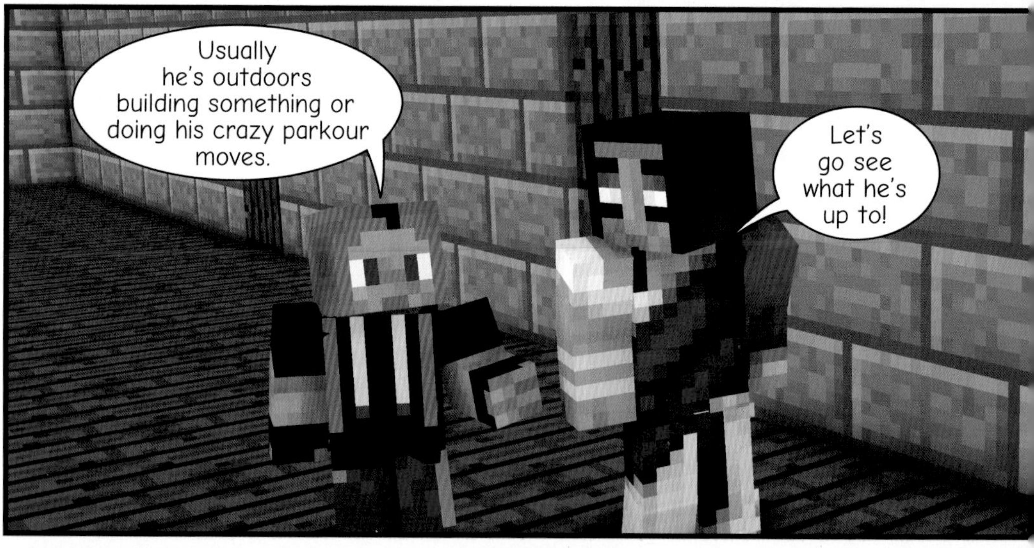
Usually he's outdoors building something or doing his crazy parkour moves.
Let's go see what he's up to!

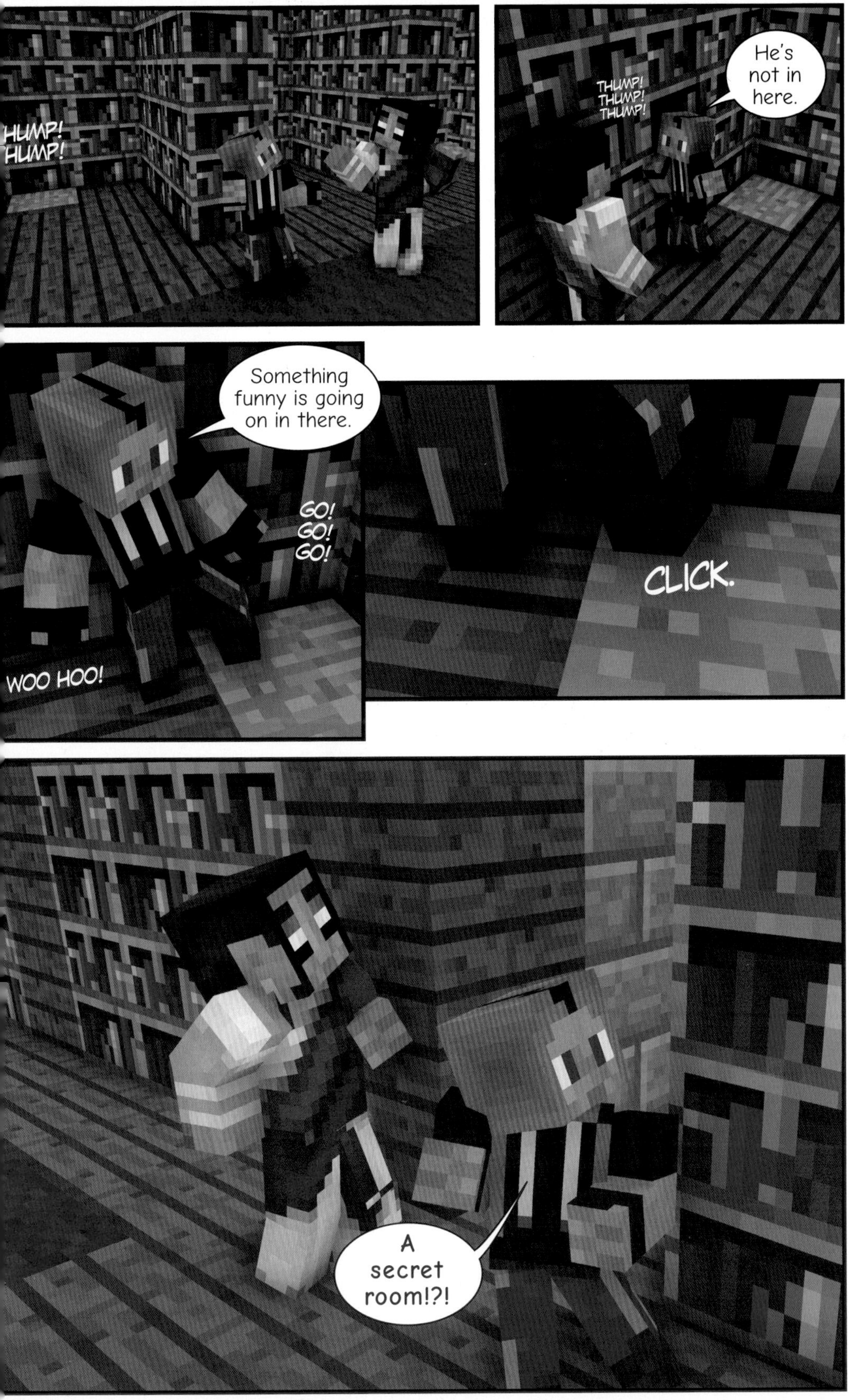
HUMP!
HUMP!
THUMP!
THUMP!
THUMP!
He's not in here.
Something funny is going on in there.
GO! GO! GO!
WOO HOO!
CLICK.
A secret room!?!

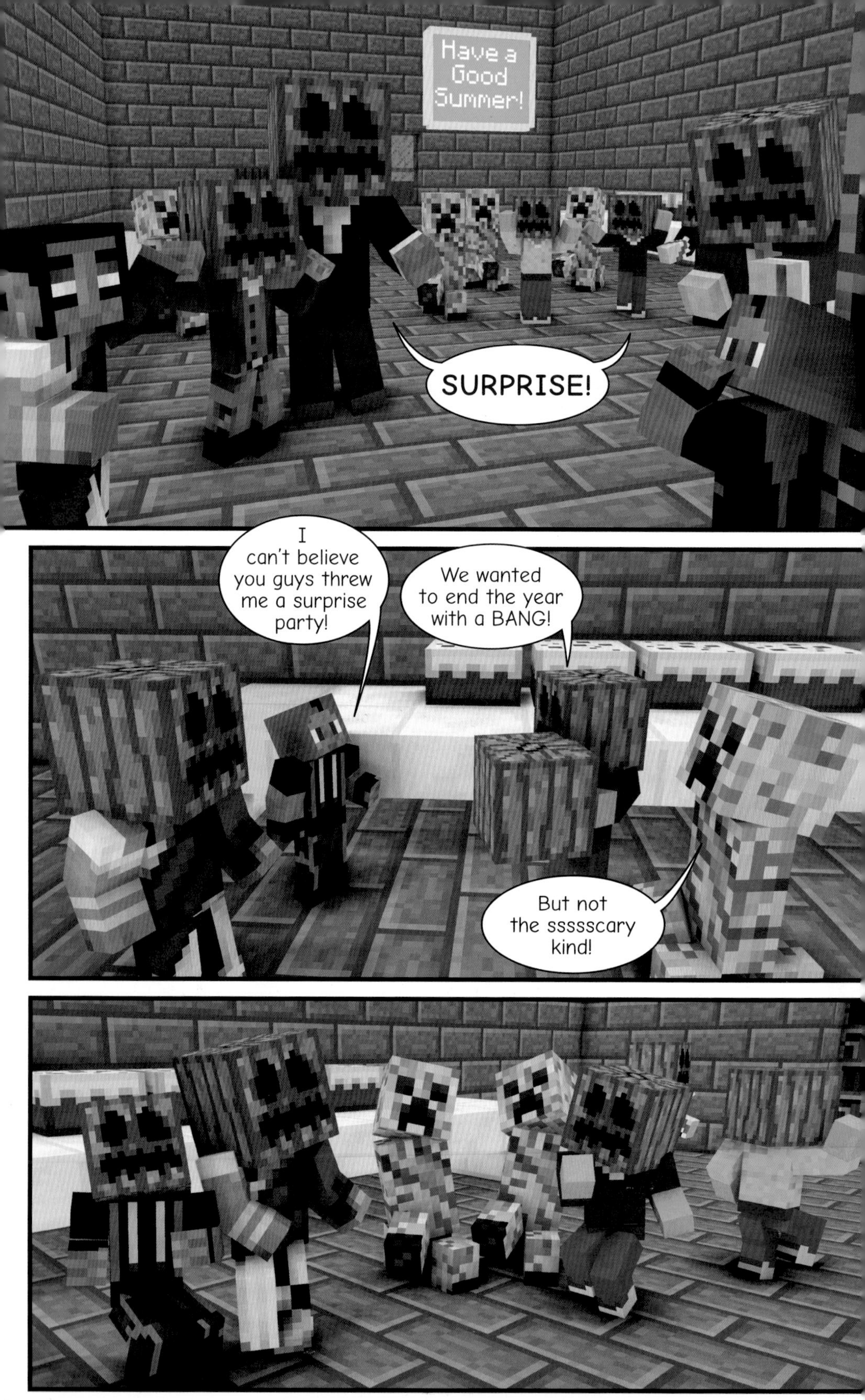
Have a Good Summer!
SURPRISE!
I can't believe you guys threw me a surprise party!
We wanted to end the year with a BANG!
But not the sssssscary kind!

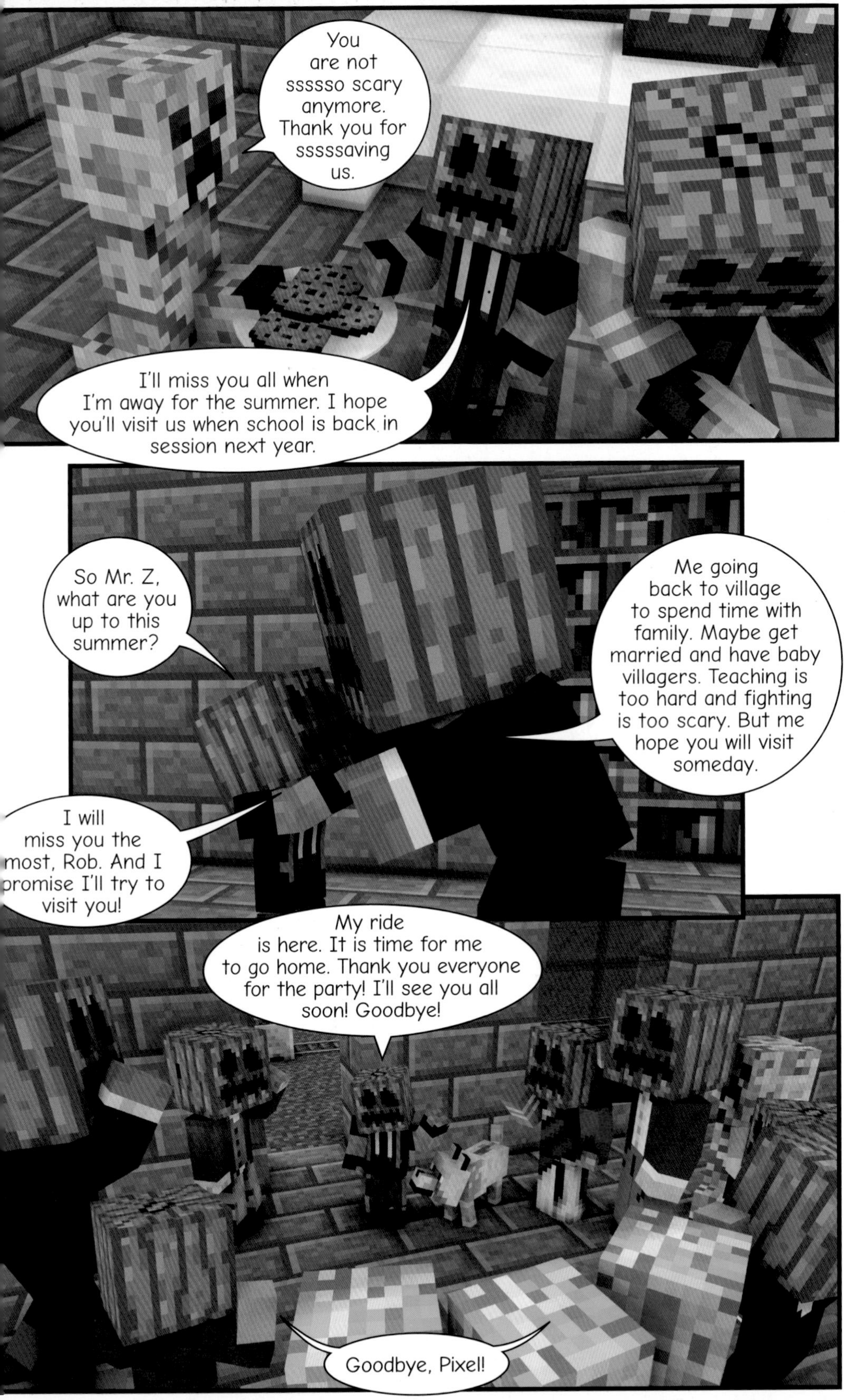
You are not ssssso scary anymore. Thank you for sssssaving us.
I'll miss you all when I'm away for the summer. I hope you'll visit us when school is back in session next year.
So Mr. Z, what are you up to this summer?
Me going back to village to spend time with family. Maybe get married and have baby villagers. Teaching is too hard and fighting is too scary. But me hope you will visit someday.
I will miss you the most, Rob. And I promise I'll try to visit you!
My ride is here. It is time for me to go home. Thank you everyone for the party! I'll see you all soon! Goodbye!
Goodbye, Pixel!

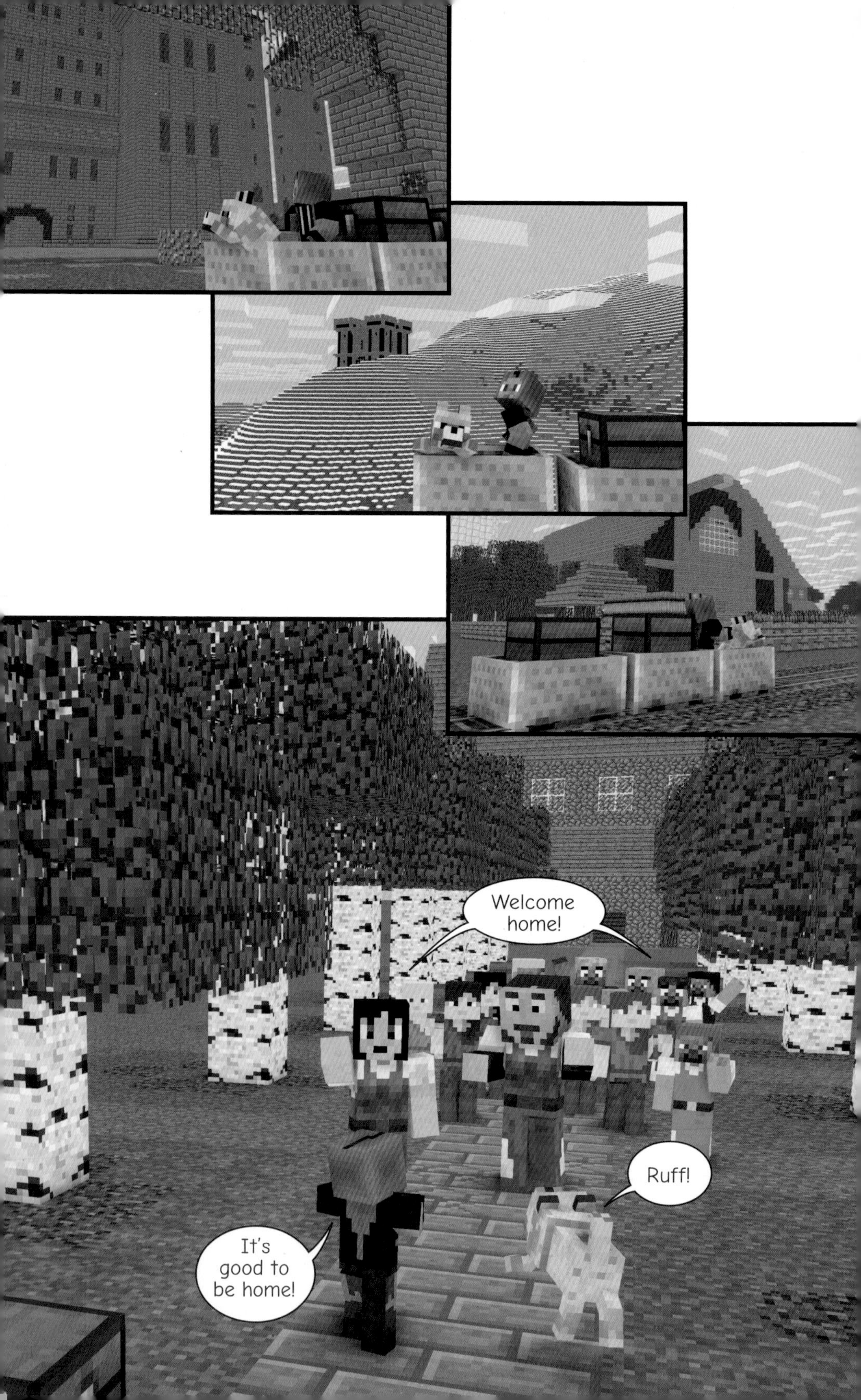
Welcome home!
Ruff!
It's good to be home!